TWILIGHT of KERBEROS

The CRUCIBLE of the DRAGON GOD

MIKE WILD

Abaddon
Books

WWW.ABADDONBOOKS.COM

In memory of
JOE HALLIWELL

2001-2009

His game over far too soon

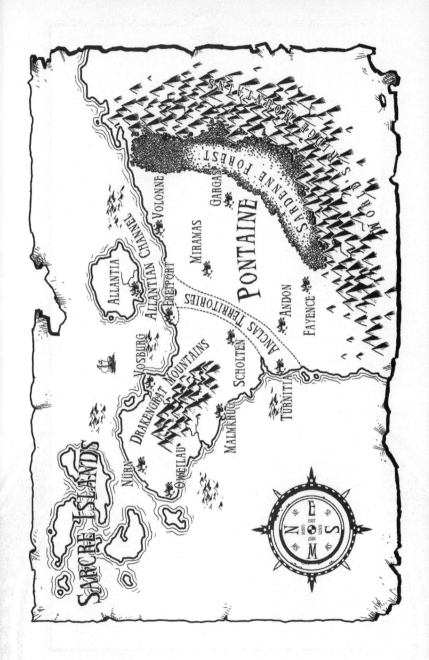

CHAPTER ONE

This is how Kali Hooper would have escaped the things that had slaughtered four men before the first of them could scream. The same things that were coming to slaughter him.

That huge, seemingly unscaleable rock, there, the one just ahead? That she would have scaled with ease. And that frozen vine beyond? The one ready to snap? On that she would have swung without thinking twice. The vine would have snapped at exactly the right moment, of course, and she would have soared with it over the abyss. This would not have worried her, though, because that ledge further on and down – yes really, *that one*, way over there – she would have flailed towards, rolling like some circus tumbler to soften her impact as she came in to land. And she would not have stopped there – oh no, though she might be grunting now – kicking up scree as she ran on and threw herself towards that crumbling ledge, and then the one beyond that, flipping, twisting and spinning, stretching all ways to grab the next small lump of salvation that would save her from a plummeting, broken death.

She would have made it, too, though rocks might have fallen in her wake – knowing her, perhaps there might even have been an accidental avalanche that would have destroyed half the mountainside – but, as usual, she would make it because she had to *succeed*. There, dangling from that last ledge, she would take a moment to catch her breath before her *piece de resistance*, a full body flip that would take her up and over until she could climb the rockface to safety. Her flight would have been done then and, from her refuge on the clifftop, she would have turned, bitten the cork from a bottle of flummox and downed the beer. And then, with a smile and a burp, she would have spat the cork at her pursuers. If she were feeling particularly mischievous, she might even have shown them her –

No. He did not want to think about that particular part of her anatomy. It seemed, now, somehow... disrespectful. Because this is how Kali Hooper *would* have escaped the things, had Kali Hooper not been dead.

That's right, he thought. Dead. Gone. Twelve hands under. The desperately running, blonde-maned archer had struggled to accept it but had come to realise that it had to be true – *had to be* given the facts. Hooper had been missing for weeks now and in that time there had been no sightings, news or contact other than that over which she'd likely had no control – the return to the *Flagons*, alone, of a half-starved and agitated Horse, and the discovery, washed-up as jetsam on a Nürnian beach, of her equipment belt attached to a blood-stained piece of her dark silk body suit. Where she had met her end he could not – *might never –* know, because she had left the tavern with a frown, telling no one what her destination was. But what he *did* know was that under no circumstances would she have missed the rendezvous she was meant to keep with him eight days before, at the base of the Drakengrat Mountains. He knew that because he knew *she* knew how important to him this expedition was. No, without doubt Hooper was gone, and whether she had met her end in the Razor Ruins of Rarg or the Blood Bogs of Bibblebobble or whatever other malignantly named hellshole had peaked her interest this time, it seemed the secret history of the peninsula she had worked so hard to unearth had, ultimately, buried her instead.

The painful truth was that he missed her like hells but it was what he, Killiam Slowhand, did that mattered now, and frankly, as far his imagined escape for Kali went... well, there wasn't a chance in the hells.

There'd be no impossible leaps up the rockface, no suicidal swings on snapping vines and no fairground acrobatics to leave his pursuers stymied. Because he wasn't Hooper. No, he was just her sometime lover, sometime sidekick and – oh, by the way, mere mortal. If he didn't spot a way out of this that was within his capabilities he wouldn't even be that. All he could do was run for his life. Oblivious to all but the pounding of his feet beneath him and the mountain winds that whistled around him, all he could do was keep moving and hope that something provided him with a means of escape.

The k'nid, he reflected as he ran, spinning occasionally to fire a volley of arrows in their direction, hoping to slow the blurry, crackling things down. Named by a Malmkrug baron after the local term for bogeyman, they had begun to appear near the town about the time of Slowhand's arrival there. Already a number of its inhabitants had fallen victim to them, lost to their sheer speed. They were not only fast, they were deadly and seemingly impervious to harm – and they seemed to be growing in number. People in Malmkrug had already shored up their homes in defence against them and their attacks on the town were as sudden and inexplicable as their origin was unknown.

Or, at least, had been until now.

For as he had ascended higher and higher into the mountains and seen the trails of more of the unnatural creatures – though most, thankfully, from afar – Slowhand knew something those below did not. That the k'nid, whatever the hells they were, seemed to be coming from somewhere around *here.*

It was typical. Pure Slowhand luck. To have fetched up in the apparent spawning ground of a plague of the deadliest things the peninsula had ever seen – and he had no one but himself to blame.

Over the past few months he'd put out a number of fresh feelers regarding his sister, and while the vast majority of them had returned nothing, the one that had led him here had shown promise. He had learned from a trader in Malmkrug that some two months before, a party of adventurers had purchased sufficient supplies for a prolonged ascent into the Drakengrat range. Despite the fact they seemed to have gone to considerable length to disguise themselves, their attitude, bearing and general demeanour very quickly gave them away as Final Faith. There was nothing, apart from the obvious, wrong with them being Faith, but the fact that they'd felt the need to disguise themselves meant they had to be up to something clandestine. That in itself was worthy of investigation. What was more worthy of investigation, however, was that the trader had said the party was led by a woman – a woman whose description he had found achingly familiar.

Jenna.

Slowhand still felt a burning rod of anger inside him every time he thought of what those bastards had done to his sister – recruiting and forcefully indoctrinating her into the Faith – and the thought that she was involved in something they found necessary to disguise their involvement with, made him as concerned for her safety as he was angered by her involvement in it. Unfortunately, that anger had had more than enough time to cool, the lead that had seemed so promising a week ago turning out to be as much of a wild frool chase as so many had before. Because if Jenna was up here, then she had discovered some chameleon spell that had transformed her into just one more of the endless snow covered rocks. No, there had been no Jenna, not even a *sign* of Jenna, and her presence had been supplanted by the k'nid, and all he could do now was cut his losses and run.

Slowhand's chest felt leaden now, and his breath was hot and rasping; symptoms not only of the altitude but of a speed and distance covered that he had not attempted since what his army passing out class, impressed and more than a little jealous, had dubbed the 'Night of a Hundred Wives.' And *that* had been quite some years ago. He was maintaining his lead on the k'nid, though, if only because one of his volleys of arrows had caused a rockfall on the narrow mountain path along which he fled. The rockfall hadn't harmed the k'nid, or even slowed them down, but it had forced them to take a detour, which was good enough for now. As he continued onward and upward, struggling more and more, he was even starting to think that he might lose them. But that was when he ran out of ground.

Slowhand came to a skidding, skittering stop, gasping with exhaustion and frustration, watching in disbelief as stones pushed by his sliding soles tumbled away only a few inches in front of him over a precipice. What made his predicament a hundred times worse was that not only had the terrain come to an end ahead of him but, unnoticed until now, to his left and right as well. In fact, there was little more than a half foot of rock on either side of him before –

Slowhand's focus zoomed in and out at the same time, and there was a vertiginous rush in his ears.

Oh boy.

Battered by wind, the archer turned slowly and carefully in a circle, taking in his precarious situation.

He was standing at the tip of a very long, very narrow outcrop of rock that, by all rights, should have collapsed under its own weight. Instead, it thrust itself defiantly and dizzyingly out into the night sky, seemingly ignoring gravity. In profile he guessed it would look like some part constructed bridge, stretching halfway across the deep chasm over which it jutted. But where a bridge might have had supports to stabilise itself, here there was nothing beneath it. Nothing at all. For a very, very, *very* long way down.

As Slowhand looked down at a river that height had reduced to the width of a hair, he realised his perch was impossible. A thing that *should* fall but didn't. And that realisation brought another – where exactly he was.

My Gods, this is Thunderlungs' Cry.

He recalled Kali telling him how she had travelled here once with Horse – the original Horse, that was – to experience the legend that had been a favourite girlhood tale.

Two tribes, split by this vast chasm in the mountains, had met only once when freak weather had driven them both into the valley far below. That meeting had led to romance between two individuals but war between the tribes themselves. When each tribe had returned to their own side, the two lovers were prohibited from ever meeting again by their elders, and all paths to the valley were barred to them. The man, who became known as Thunderlungs, managed, however, to despatch a message to his lover, Mawnee, using a carrier bird, telling her that if their ancestors favoured their bonding, they would provide a bridge across which the two of them could be reunited.

He had come one Kerberos-lit night, and there she had stood, far across the chasm. He had cried out to the souls who scudded across Kerberos's surface, asking the aid of those who had gone before to unite the pair once more. This they had done, by growing a half bridge of rock from the side of his chasm, and another from that of Mawnee's side, and the two had begun to cross towards each other's outstretched arms. The ancestors had warned, however, that if their love faltered, even for a moment, then the bridge would be no more.

Thunderlungs' love was strong but *something* that night made Mawnee falter. To her lover's horror the bridge beneath her crumbled away, and she fell to her death.

It was said that Thunderlungs roared his heartbreak into the night – a roar that some said those who had lost loved ones could still hear – until he had frozen solid where he stood. Whereupon his ancestors had laid him down and made him part of the bridge itself, so that his shadow might touch, once a day, the place where his love had fallen.

It was a sad story, Slowhand reflected, and one that might have brought tears to his eyes if they hadn't already been streaming from this farking wind. And it was not as sad as his own would be if he didn't get off this rock right now. Because there had been that sudden, strange crackling behind him once more – as if he were listening to a tavern fire – and he had spun to see the k'nid had caught up with him, reaching the start of the Cry in a clammering rush but there coming to a dead stop, as if assessing what lay before them.

Now that they were at a stop, it was the first chance Slowhand had had to properly study the creatures.

A little over the length of a stretching man when they unfurled for the kill – a manoeuvre he had seen on four occasions and fervently wished that he had not – he saw now that they seemed to be neither animal, vegetable or mineral. They looked like a tangle of roots of glistening black wood that writhed about each other, as if suffering the death throes of the tree from which they had come. Except that they had come from no tree – the way his arrows had bounced from them proving that whatever it was they were made of, it was not wood. As tough as their bodies were, however, it did not prevent them being infinitely flexible. While they seemed to favour pursuit of their prey while in the form of a rough, gnarled, rolling sphere, chance glances had revealed that form shifting constantly between tumbleweed and what appeared to be a running shnarl and, on occasion when obstacles needed to be negotiated, even the briefly airborne form of some predatory bird. But of all their incarnations, it was the one that had slaughtered his companions that Slowhand could not shake from his mind.

He recalled his horror as he'd tried to fend off the k'nid who had closed rapidly on his guide and helpers, because while he'd expected them to be simply crushed beneath the rolling forms or smashed from the rocks to fall below, that wasn't what had happened at all. Instead the creatures had unfurled to reveal a red and fleshy interior and simply swallowed their victims before returning to a tangled sphere form. And no more than two or three seconds later each man had been deposited back outside the sphere, but all they were now were piles of stripped and steaming bones.

And now it was his turn. Unless some miracle occurred.

Slowhand looked around in desperation for a way out, but there was nothing. Thunderlungs Cry simply projected too far from the rest of the rocks to provide any escape route. As the front rank of the k'nid began to crackle towards him, he was beginning to think the most merciful way out would be to jump, when he glanced something approaching from the north. Something in the sky.

What was that? A cloud? A bird? No, too small to be a cloud. Too big to be a bird. Unless it was a small cloud, of course. Or a big bird. Yes, a very big bird.

Then it slowly sank in what it actually was he *was* looking at.

It was a thing of inflated cloth like a giant balloon, with a thing of wood, like a gondola, slung beneath it. On the deck of that gondola he could just make out the tiny shapes of people. He realised then that he was looking at some kind of... *airship*.

A *flying* machine.

"Hey!" Slowhand shouted, desperately waving his hands above his head. "*Hey!*"

If the people on board heard him, however, they chose to ignore his cries, as the airship continued on its route without any reaction at all. He shouted again, but once more with no effect. The airship was closer now and he could see the people aboard, busied in the tasks he presumed were needed to keep the craft aloft.

If Slowhand couldn't bring the airship to him, then he would have to go to the airship.

Forcing his wonderment aside, the archer calculated its height and trajectory relative to the Cry, and while on the one hand the news was good – it would pass *beneath* the Cry – on the other it was bad. Too *far* beneath.

Slowhand double-taked on the k'nid and the airship. If he jumped from this height he would likely bounce right off the balloon and plummet to his death, so that height needed to be reduced. As far as he could see there was only one way to do that. He would need a rope. A rope he didn't have.

He sighed in resignation. It was as unbelievable as it was inevitable.

To make the ladder he needed, his clothes would have to come off. And to make the ladder long enough, that meant *all* of them. It was certainly the most unusual place he had had to resort to such action, and it was almost a pity he didn't have an audience but then, in the dire circumstances in which he found himself, there would be little if any time to show off his assets.

Okay, he thought as he pulled off and tore into strips his tunic, pants and shorts, and the mountain wind whistled around his lower regions, *his reduced assets.*

Standing there in just his boots, feeling disturbingly exposed considering the proximity of the k'nid, he quickly tied the clothing together and then, in turn, looped it around and secured it to the lip of the Cry. That done, he took a firm grip of the cloth and slipped slowly over the edge, where he dangled for a second before lowering himself down hand over hand as the flying machine drew closer.

A thought suddenly struck him.

I'm stark naked in a pair of thigh length leather boots, with a bow slung on my back, a thousand feet up in the air, and whoever's on that ship is in for a big surprise.

It was actually a bit kinky and he made a mental note to investigate the business possibilities of such goings on, on his return. Perhaps he could earn a few extra golds doing this for hen parties, birthdays and the like.

If he returned that was.

Because if he was going to do this it was now or never.

Slowhand hung there, his thighs clenched tightly around the stretched remains of his pants, revolving slightly as the flying machine nosed onward, manoeuvring itself at last beneath him. There was still a hundred and fifty feet or so between him and it, but for a second before it came directly under him and his view was obscured by the bag that seemed to keep it aloft, he could make out in more detail the deck of the gondola that was slung beneath it. There at least eight people continued to busy themselves with piloting the craft, a couple of them agitated, pointing and shouting roughly in his direction. But what they said, was lost in the shrieking of the wind. Slowhand tried waving once more, one-handed, keeping a firm grip on his makeshift rope, but his potential saviours were clearly too involved with their duties to notice him.

Who the hells were these people?

Timing his drop to a split second, so that he would impact

directly in the centre of the flying machine's airbag, he let go.

He manoeuvred himself as the wind whistled by him, turning so that he would impact on his back, glancing downward to ensure his target remained dead centre of his fall.

Slowhand suddenly found himself impacting so hard on the flying machine's airbag that the wind was knocked out of him. He lay there for a second, squirming and cringing in pain – not quite as soft as he'd expected considering this thing was light enough to fly.

The realisation came once more that he was lying on some unknown machine that flew like a bird or floated like a cloud but clearly wasn't either, and a sudden desire to feel something firmer than cloth beneath him possessed him.

The main centre of activity was towards the front of the airship, however, and until he knew who he was dealing with he thought it wise to descend from the airbag at the opposite end of the craft.

He turned onto his front and crawled towards the rear, using the thick ropes that reinforced the airbag to pull himself along. Slowhand was about to flip downwards when he pulled suddenly back with a "*Whoa!*"

The reason for this was what had so far been hidden from his view *behind* the vast balloon. A great, orange orb that pulsed there with an energy unknown to him, but which made his scalp itch, his eyes bulge and his skin throb. Whatever it was, it seemed to be powering the craft, but he wanted nowhere near it.

Instead, Slowhand manoeuvred himself to where he could drop to a quiet part of the deck and, using the ropes to restrain his descent, slipped downwards until he could grab the lowest rope and flip himself over to land feet first on the deck below. His impact was quiet enough but he still dropped into a gentle squat, as if his additional weight might prove too much for the airship and force it out of the sky. He stayed that way for a few moments, gazing left and right at the still level skyline, then experimented further by thumping the deck with his fist, harder and harder with each swing. Satisfied that the machine was still aloft, he rose to a standing position and jumped on the spot, once – tentatively – then again, and then, in a state of merry disbelief, over and over again. The deck remained solid beneath him.

There was only one thing left that he had to do to prove to himself that what was happening was happening. Slowhand ran to the side of the deck and peered over its railing, down towards the floor of the valley, far below. If he could have reached, he would have swung a hand below the hull, checking for invisible supports or struts. But he realised that was even more implausible than what he was seeing and, at last, came to accept that he was indeed up in the air with nothing underneath him.

No doubt about it. He was *flying*.

Well, okay, the machine beneath him was flying.

"I see your clothes still fall off at every opportunity. For the Lord of All's sake, throw him a cloak someone."

Slowhand turned around.

The crew had made their way from the nose to where he stood and were gathered in a semi circle, regarding him. Whatever individuals he had expected to be manning this strange craft, he had to admit he hadn't expected it to be *them*. He looked at the cloak emblazoned with a crossed circle without saying a word. It wasn't the fact that they were Final Faith that disconcerted him but rather who appeared to be leading them.

Tall, lithe and possessed of the same windswept mane of blonde hair as himself, she hadn't changed much in the six years since he had last seen her.

"Hello, sis."

"Brother."

Slowhand swallowed. It wasn't the unexpected encounter that made him do so, but the way Jenna had said that single word. For a moment he had forgotten that while his sister may not have altered physically, the Faith had long since indoctrinated her into their ways. She was not the person he had known, and that 'brother' had been delivered almost as if she were conversing not with her own flesh and blood but simply a fellow member of her damned religion.

"Jenna," he said. "*Jenna*..."

"As touching as this reunion is," a figure behind Jenna said, "we have a problem requiring your attention."

Jenna looked at him and the figure threw back his hood. Slowhand felt an involuntary snarl curl his upper lip. He was staring at a man he had not seen since his incarceration in the Final Faith's dungeons beneath Scholten Cathedral. Querilous Fitch. That he was here, with Jenna, made his blood boil – because this was the man who played with people's minds.

"Was it you?" Slowhand demanded. "Was it you who took my sister away?"

"I hardly think now is the time –"

"We're talking!" Slowhand growled.

"You will be *dying* if you do not heed my words," Fitch said matter-of-factly, and looked up.

Slowhand followed his gaze, as did Jenna.

The airship was now passing out from under the shadow of Thunderlung's Cry, but the outcrop of rock was barely visible for the number of dark shapes that were dropping from it towards them. The archer felt his heart lurch. Seemingly with scant regard for their own survival, the k'nid were flinging themselves at the airship, many of them plummeting past into the abyss, but others falling on the balloon, whilst their brethren clawed for purchase on the hull of the gondola.

"Dammit!" Jenna declared. "Persistent little bastards, aren't they?" She span to the crew. "All hands – prepare to repel boarders. Mister Ransom, Mister Leech, take us hard to port, full power. This'll be a rough ride, people, but trust me we'll shake our visitors off."

"Shake them off?" Slowhand said. "You must have weapons. Use them!"

"What good did *your* weapon do, brother?" Jenna snapped back at him, striking Suresight dismissively with the back of her hand. "Tell me that!"

Slowhand couldn't deny how useless his bow had proven, and looked desperately at the k'nid, biting his lip. "Is there something I can do?"

"Yes. Stay out of the way."

With that, Jenna moved off to position herself just behind the two men manning the airship's twin wheels, barking orders from where she stood, omitting only Querilous Fitch whose duty seemed to consist wholly of standing stock still and glowering at the archer. Slowhand ignored him, unable to help but be impressed with the way this crew handled their strange vessel.

Since the debacle of the Clockwork King, he had come to regard the Final Faith not only as dangerous but as dangerously irresponsible. Blundering buffoons whose interference in the peninsula's past could bring it close to doomsday. But here it was different and he was sure that was due in no small part to the tactical skills of his sister. She handled her crew with ease and they repaid her with utmost loyalty. Slowhand felt a momentary surge of pride, recognising that she had obviously come a long way since the last time he had seen her, even if her development had taken place under the auspices of the Faith.

The only thing that gave him cause for concern now was what the hells she was doing – especially as the airship was heading straight for the rock face.

"Urm, Jenna…"

"Steady as she goes," Jenna ordered, seemingly unphased. "Steady… steady… and… turn *now*!"

Both of the men manning the wheels reacted instantly, spinning hard to the left. Slowhand felt the deck tip beneath him as the gondola swung beneath the canopy. It swung so far, in fact, that as the dirigible went into its turn, the side of the hull and the airbag scraped against the face of the rock. The air was filled with a wrenching that sounded as if the gates of the hells themselves were opening.

Jenna's manoeuvre had been executed perfectly but there had to variables – the prevailing wind, air pockets – in an airship such as this, and what had been executed perfectly in theory did not necessarily turn out so in practice. It wasn't her fault, then, that the hull sounded to him like it was in danger of tearing itself apart. Despite being told to stay out of the way, Slowhand couldn't help but feel like the protective brother and raced to the guard rail, unslinging Suresight as he went and then using the bow to push off from the rockface. Slowhand staggered back, yelping, as he was punched in the face and then spun away from his position. He glared into the angered face of Jenna.

"What in the almighty hells do you think you're farking doing? You're tearing this ship apart!"

"Am I, brother?" Jenna shouted again. "Look! Look!"

Slowhand did, and suddenly realised his mistake.

The ship's impacting with the rocks hadn't, it seemed, been a miscalculation on his sister's part, but a carefully calculated strategy to remove their troublesome visitors. As he watched, those k'nid that were working their way towards them were scraped away from the dirigible's bag as they were caught between its surface and the rock. The screeching things tumbling away into oblivion. However, it only removed those k'nid that clung to that section of the hull. Slowhand was opening his mouth to point this out when he realised, once again, that Jenna was way ahead of him.

"Swing her round! One eighty degrees full rudder!"

The deck lurched beneath Slowhand as the order was instantly acted upon, and he was forced to cling to a handrail to prevent himself stumbling. Jenna, however, strode the tipping deck with ease, clearly practiced with her 'airlegs' and still barking orders as she went. Slowhand watched as she executed a series of manoeuvres that made him swell with pride, making the airship do things it was clearly not designed for. Despite the fact that the airship collided with the rocks around it on a number of occasions – and the faces of its crew were clearly concerned about the battering it was taking – they nevertheless continued to obey without question, until the last of the k'nid had been ripped away. Only then did Jenna sigh with relief.

"Resume course. Steady as she goes."

Slowhand was about to move towards her and congratulate her on the flying display when Fitch strode towards her instead, whispering something in her ear.

"Dammit," Jenna said. "How bad?"

"The orb has purged energy." Fitch said. "We need to replenish it, enter Waystation One, or we will not reach Gransk."

"We can't afford to lose the time, but I suppose there's no choice. All right, prepare to take her in."

The orb, Slowhand thought.

Presumably the pulsating orb that seemed to drive the airship, but the waystation, what was that? And what and where the hells was Gransk?

"Problem?" he said, moving forward.

"Nothing that can't be rectified."

"Where, in this... Waystation One?"

"That's right, in Waystation One."

Slowhand was getting a little tired of being left out of the loop, even if, strictly speaking, he had no place in it. "What are you doing here above the clouds, sis?"

"Where did this ship come from? What the hells is going on?"

"All hands," Jenna said. "Prepare to bring us around."

"Yes, Captain Freel."

Now Slowhand said nothing. Instead he simply stared at his sister instead.

That she had effectively ignored him – *was* ignoring him – after all this time spoke volumes for the depth of indoctrination the Faith had instilled in her, but that wasn't what disturbed him the most. What was with the Captain *Freel* bit? That wasn't her name. What was going on? He perhaps couldn't blame her for adopting another name but what he didn't understand was why Freel? It wasn't an assumed name like his own. So, unless she had become really boring in the intervening years, did that mean she had the name Freel for a reason? Had she been adopted? Gods, had she married? Whatever the reason it hinted at a history he knew nothing about, and considering that she was his twin sister, that simply wasn't right.

One thing was clear, however. The two of them were not going to be playing catch-up right now.

"Three degrees right rudder. Orb to half power. Ready a pulse on my mark."

"Aye, Ma'am."

"Half degree correction and... mark! Steady as she goes, Mister Ransom. Prepare to take us in."

Responding to Jenna's commands the Final Faith crew – with the exception of Fitch who simply stood with his arms folded, staring at him, which Slowhand most definitely didn't like.

"This... *civilian* should not be seeing this." Querilous Fitch snapped.

"What would you have me do, threadweaver. Throw him overboard? He's my *brother*, dammit."

"No. *I* am your brother now."

That was it as far as Slowhand was concerned. He was about to go for Fitch when something took his mind entirely off his intent. Because Jenna's commands had turned the airship back towards Thunderlungs Cry – or rather back and *beneath* it – and what he saw there he was immediately convinced was what had made Thunderlungs' lover falter and fall all of those many centuries ago.

Beneath the Cry was a huge cave mouth that was not a cave mouth at all – at least not a purely natural one. It appeared to have been bored out of the rock and led deep inside it. All along its sides – leading inward in two neat rows – were lines of great, glowing tubes set inside rune-inscribed arches. Tubes which pulsed in sequence as if designed to guide an airship in. And that, it seemed, was exactly what they did, because the airship passed between them and was swallowed by the huge cavern mouth.

My Gods, Slowhand thought, gaping upward. *This is Old Race – the biggest Old Race thing I've ever seen. Pits of Kerberos, Hooper would have given everything to see this.*

He only hoped that whatever Old Race ruin – for it would have been nothing else – had claimed her life at last was as awe-inspiring as this one, because then at least his lover would have died happy.

If not, well, knowing Hooper, right now she'd be spinning in her grave.

CHAPTER TWO

"*Aaaaaaaaaaaaarrrrrrrrrgggggggggghhhhhhhhh!*"

The cry of fury, of pain and of sheer frustration, that boomed from beneath the ground was sudden and startling, shattering the desolate quiet of the dusty canyon and causing the strange black birds that nested there in twisted trees to take to the air with a chorus of haunting caws. The cry reverberated out of the canyon and across the landscape beyond. But there was no one out there to hear it – no one for leagues – and after a while, as its echo died down, the birds returned to their trees. There, they did not snatch up the dropped carrion on which they had been feasting but, instead, regarded each other with furled wings, cowed heads and darting, beady eyes. Troubled by this latest disturbance to their long abandoned, isolated piece of the world, their gaze turned along the canyon, past the rusted, age-warped rails of metal and the overturned, skeletal frames of the carts which once had rode them, and towards the dark and forbidding mouth at the canyon's end. And they wondered what it was they had done to offend the angry-spirit-who-had-come-to-live-beneath-them this time.

Ever since the spirit had arrived on its strange, armoured steed and gone into that dark mouth – there first announcing its displeasure with a deep rumble, an unknown curse and a great cloud of dust that had erupted from it by sunset that day – they had struggled to understand its subsequent outbursts, no doubt intended for them, but each time they had neared their answer another outburst had come and they had fled to the skies in panic once more. So it was now – as they felt the seed of an answer within them – the words of the angry-spirit-who-had-come-to-live-beneath-them came once more:

"Owww! Rollocks! Count to ten. One-two... no, soddit... You farking hoooor!"

Far below, through a labyrinthine series of tunnels and diggings, through galleries and chambers that had never seen the light of day, and past tools and carts like those above, Kali Hooper grunted with pain as she pulled the lengths of cloth she held in each fist as taut as she could. The binding around the splints on her leg pulled tight, pressing the splintered bone in her shin tightly but agonisingly together. Causing her to bite down hard on the gutting knife she had clenched between her teeth. Her groan echoed dully, joining the still audible reverberations of her earlier cry and reminding the solitary, bedraggled figure sitting pained, sweating and slumped in a small antechamber again and again of the mess she'd gotten herself into.

No, not exactly her, she reflected, but a certain completely mad little bastard whom Killiam Slowhand, in her stead, had long since despatched to the hells. Damn the man, she thought. Even dead Konstantin Munch continued to cause her pain.

The fact was, her current predicament *was* all the fault of Katherine Makennon's one-time right hand man. It might have been months since her final battle with him at the dwarven outpost of Martak, and the dwarf-blooded resurgent might even now be floating decomposed in the still and murky waters of its collapsed ruins, but that didn't stop his misconceived plan to resurrect dwarven glory from endangering her life yet again.

Indirectly, at least. She should have known nothing good would come of it when one of Makennon's agents had contacted her with a set of papers which he explained the Anointed Lord wished to gift her in return for helping her with that affair. She should have said 'no thanks' there and then, but the fact was she hadn't been able to resist, had she? Oh no, because the papers turned out to be directions and maps to stores that Munch had established across the peninsula, and there was always a chance that there was going to be something more than a little interesting in there.

There hadn't been, as it turned out – the weapons and tools that Munch had collected to equip his fantasised army were as warped and useless as his masterplan – but in growing desperation to unearth at least *one* artefact, she had decided to give it one last stab, to follow one last set of directions. That stab and those directions had brought her here.

She really had no idea how long ago that had been, now, and she had all but forgotten that, ultimately, the trip had proven useless again, but that wasn't the problem. No, the problem this time was that it had turned out that it wasn't so much *what* Munch had stored away but *where* he had stored it away.

That this hellshole had been a mine at some point in its history – though mining what, she didn't know – was clear, but equally clearly the mine had become exhausted at some point and become... something else.

Maybe it was why Munch had chosen the place. Because, apart from its total remoteness, it was, as she had so painfully learned, a deathtrap. Not just neglected and unsafe and falling apart but a bloody *deathtrap*. The thought had even crossed her mind that Makennon had included the map to its location because she *knew* that and thought it a convenient way to be rid of her. Maybe she was being paranoid but she'd interfered once in the Final Faith's grandiose plans – even if in doing so she had saved the world – and with future plans likely in the offing maybe the Anointed Lord considered her too much of a loose cannon to be allowed to live. Not that she had any wish to get involved with that lot again.

Kali slumped against the rock wall and made a brubbing sound with her lips. The fact was, it had become increasingly unlikely that she'd be getting involved with *any* lot again if she didn't get out of here soon, not since she'd accidentally flicked that lever by stumbling over it in the dark.

One small mistake, that's all it was – an amateurs blunder – but that lever had been the key to this whole damned mess. It had transformed the mine's galleries in a loud and seemingly endless rattle of ancient chains and cranking of antique gears from the harmless tunnels they had been, into a deadly labyrinth constructed with one purpose in mind. To kill, as horribly and painfully as it could.

A testing ground was what it turned out to be. An ancient arena for dwarven rites of passage, designed to test their mettle to the full. She knew this because, whilst her own mettle was being tested by a selection of swinging blades and giant axes, she had come across a torn and blood-browned journal she could only presume had been written by a dwarf whose own rite of passage had come to a sudden end. As she had translated it, it told the whole sorry story of Be'Trak'tak, roughly translated as 'the beginning or end.'

Originating, she'd guessed, in the middle period of dwarven history – when their engineering skills were first beginning to evolve from the simple to the complex – it was to this place that the dwarven young were despatched at a certain age, sealed within the complex to face a series of elaborately designed traps and challenges whose survival would prove them to be warriors, or kill them in the process.

Gods, she'd wondered, *what the hells was it with those dwarves? Why couldn't they just go out on the twattle when they came of age like everyone else?*

Not that the dwarven traps would have proven *too* much of a challenge for her – not under any normal circumstances, anyway. The trouble was, it was the unimaginable length of time since any of them had stirred into life, because in that intervening age most of the materials from which the traps had been constructed had become rotten, making them dangerously unpredictable and unstable. It was the very reason why she was slumped here binding her broken leg right now.

She had successfully negotiated her way through all but the last of a series of swinging hammer traps – itself just one more of an endless series of swinging, slicing or rolling *something* traps – when the beam that carried the final deadly bludgeon had splintered away as it swung, flinging the hammer where it was not meant to be *when* it was not meant to be. Kali remembered the agony as, halfway through a perfectly timed somersault manoeuvre, the hammer had sheared from its mounting and crushed her leg against the wall of the mine. Gods, that had hurt – and it had also proven to her that she was not quite as impervious to harm as events of the previous months had begun to lead her to believe. It was a salutary lesson and one she was not likely to forget so long as this farking splint remained on her leg.

Kali shivered, not so much from cold, but a combination of exhaustion, slight fever and a hunger that came from subsisting only on the edible, though thoroughly revolting, fungus that grew on the mine walls. Of course, the state of her dark silk bodysuit didn't help. Having improved on the original thieves guild design by having it retailored to incorporate pockets for artefacts – it now hung in virtual tatters about her, having fallen victim not only to her need for cloth to tie her splint but to the various traps she'd found lying in wait. That wasn't the worst of it, though. The gaping patch of flesh around her hip was a constant reminder that somewhere along the way she had also lost her equipment belt, torn from her body and flung into some deep, dark and, by the sound of it, watery pit by an intricate whirlwind of jagged blades that someone, once upon a time, must have thought: *Whirling* and *jagged, eh? Oh, go for it, that's a good one."*

She had lost Horse, too. She could certainly no longer sense him above, waiting patiently for her return as she expected he'd done for at least the first few days of her entrapment. No, Horse had become her faithful companion as much as the old Horse had been, but even he must have come to realise that Kali

Hooper was not going to be returning to him anytime soon. She wondered where he had gone. Back to the Drakengrats where he had originally been captured? Or was he running free across the plains, the wind whistling through his horns? No, more likely he was galloping after some poor pack of worgles, terrorising them with his tongue.

Kali sniffed. Dammit, she missed him and she was getting maudlin. Hells, it really was time to get out of here, to beat these farking traps once and for all.

Kali heaved herself up against the chamber wall, thrusting a hand forward for balance as her bad leg took her weight, then hobbled out into the main tunnel, turning left and down rather than right and up. She knew that on the surface that seemed to make little sense but she also knew that there *was* no up – not since the landslide on the first day – and so she was going to gamble her survival on another possibility. Even the dwarves, with all their sadistic tendencies, surely couldn't expect any of their kind who had been 'warrior' enough to survive their traps to then *renegotiate* them on the way out. So it seemed logical that there had to be another way out, deeper into the mine.

There was only one problem with that. What was in the way.

Kali could hear it even from here. That rhythmic thumping, pounding and hissing that heralded the presence of the final trap. She had returned to it day after day for at least the last week, studying its timings and its intricacies and its foibles but making no attempt to pass. The reason for that was simple – this was the 'big one' and she was only going to get one chance at beating it.

There it was again, she thought, entering the cavern that opened out from the mine tunnel, a complex arrangement of giant hammers and blades, arranged vertically and horizontally, that completely lined the bridge crossing the chasm in the centre. It was no simple chasm, either. The rock walls flanking it had been carved into the shapes of giant dwarven faces whose roaring mouths randomly belched great fiery clouds of breath, hot enough to have singed the wood in the trap mechanisms over the years into hard, carbonised masses.

Kali couldn't help but admire the workmanship. The first time she'd had laid eyes on the construction she'd imagined it had once been named 'The Bridge of Doom', 'Chasm of Chaos' or 'Gauntlet of the Gods.' But she hadn't liked the sound of any of those – so instead she'd called it 'Dave.'

Like the earlier traps, Dave would once have been negotiable with relative ease, but the rot of years had left some of its components askew, others working faster or slower than they should, still others partly broken loose from their matching components and set into motion by the movement of the mechanisms around them. As if that were not bad enough, the bridge itself looked as rotten as hells, likely to collapse under foot anywhere and anytime. The whole thing was as unpredictable as hells. One wrong move and she was over the side. One small miscalculation and she would be crushed to death or sliced to pieces. There was absolutely no room for error.

Kali narrowed her eyes and took a deep breath, studying for a final time the patterns of movement in the trap. She flexed her bad leg and pinwheeled her arms, loosening up her muscles. And then she swallowed. And then she ran.

Kali roared as her feet slammed onto the first few slats of the bridge, bouncing forward immediately as she felt the aged wood creak and give beneath her weight. As she bounced, the first of the trap's death-dealing devices came at her.

Kali eyed the trajectory of the whirling blade as it span towards her and then actually ran towards it, flipping herself above and over the blade at the point metal and flesh would have met. The forward flip had to be timed slightly later than she would have liked – and she felt a sharp sting as the blade's edge sliced her thigh – but the delay was necessary for her to be able to meet the next of the bridge's dangers.

Righting herself, Kali landed on the upperside of a hammer that had just slammed down in her path and then balanced precariously on it as it began to rise. She did not let it take her all the way, instead she used its height to leap diagonally across the bridge so that she grabbed and clung onto a hammer rising on its other side. This, too, she rode until the very last second, allowing another blade to pass beneath her and then punching herself away from her perch as the hammer clicked in its mooring and slammed down.

She was between blades and hammers now but she didn't have a moment to rest. The instant she landed one of the dwarven heads belched fire towards where she was crouched. Kali didn't hesitate, snatching up a blade that had broken from its mechanism, she shored herself behind it, using it as a shield so that the fire was deflected past her on both sides. Then, the instant the fire died down, she used the now glowing blade as a wheel, rolling with it and behind it beneath the next hammer on the right side of the bridge.

The hammer came down hard, buckling the circular blade and straining the mechanism, but Kali had already dumped the metal and used the temporary jam to crawl swiftly beneath the area where the hammer would otherwise have impacted. This, in turn, enabled her to roll beneath the next circular blade before coming upright and flipping herself forward once more as its companion followed through a moment later.

Kali was moving fast and she was almost through to the end of the bridge now. She could barely contain the surge of elated adrenalin that accompanied that knowledge, because there she saw some kind of wooden elevator, as she knew she would, and all she had to do now was...

Wood splintered suddenly beneath Kali's feet and she fell forwards, cursing. The curse had barely left her lips before there was a sudden, heavy whoosh from her left hand side and the last of the mechanisms – a great hammer that swung across the bridge – came straight at her. She tried to throw herself out of its way, back into the space between hammer and blades, and would have made it safely, apart from the one small variable she had forgotten to factor into her equations. Making her leg thicker by as little as an inch, her splint made contact with one of the whirling blades she had already negotiated. Its teeth bit into the wood and cloth strip, ripping at it and tearing it away.

Kali felt her whole body vibrate bone-jarringly and then, as the teeth of the blade spat the splint out, found herself being flipped dizzyingly through the air back towards the hammer. There was no time to reorientate herself and, in the second she tried, the swinging bludgeon slammed directly into her front, knocking her, stunned and winded, cleanly off the bridge.

It could have been worse, she supposed, she could have lost the leg, but that was actually quite academic right now because she wasn't getting out of here. The place had become her tomb after all.

She looked down at the stalagmites and boulders that were now rushing towards her, estimated she had only a few seconds before she hit, and closed her eyes.

She slammed into the cavern floor. But it didn't hurt half as much as she'd imagined it might.

What? she thought.

Instead of the hard rock Kali thudded onto – and through – a layering of planks, that once upon a time must have been set there to prevent unwary miners stumbling into a dropshaft. They were so rotten she passed through without harm. Another layer was almost immediately beneath them, and then another, level after level of shoring. As Kali plummeted through, her momentum slowed slightly each time.

Kathuck, kathuck, kathuck.

It seemed to go on forever, and Kali was beginning to think she might die of suffocation as opposed to anything else when, at last, she slammed through the last of the layers and crashed, flat on her back, onto a small hillock of rotten wood on some deep, deep tunnel floor.

She lay there for a second.

"Ow," she said.

And then she flipped herself upright, ready for whatever trap was going to be thrown at her next.

But there was none. Kali knew instantly that this place was different to Be'Trak'Tak. It looked different, felt different and even smelled different. And that could mean only one thing. The whole area she'd travelled through to reach Munch's mine had been riddled with other such excavations, and this had to be one of them. She'd broken through into another mine. And what was more, there was light ahead.

Wasting no time, Kali dusted herself down and began to move towards it, trying all the time to suppress the presumption that what was she looking at was an exit. After so long it was just too much to ask for, surely? And it was. Following the light to its source, Kali came upon against a solid rock wall.

No, wait, not solid. There was *something* there.

Kali's disappointment upon discovering that the light source was not an exit was mitigated slightly by the fact that it seemed to be no kind of natural light, and she found herself intrigued. Also she saw that it was not one light source but two, only seeming to be a whole because they were embedded in the rock close together. No, not embedded, she realised as she examined them further. The lights seemed to be attached to something *else* embedded in the rock, something bigger that a roof collapse had buried at some time in the past and that had remained undisturbed since. The question was, how long had it remained undisturbed? Kali studied the collapse with a professional eye, noting the visible fossilisation, the settlement of the larger pieces of debris, and the compactness of the scree around them, which was absolutely solid. A very long time, then, she concluded. The only problem now being that, if that were true, how in all the hells could the lights – whatever they were – still be glowing?

She used her gutting knife to work away at the scree surrounding them, eventually revealing two small, orange orbs that seemed to throb beneath her touch, prompting a dull headache as they did. Suddenly, she realised what they had to be. Unless she'd missed her guess, they were some kind of power source for the thing to which they were attached.

Kali slapped the area she had revealed around the orbs tentatively, and then a little bit harder, and then harder still until her palms hurt. No doubt about it. Metal, and solid – apparently armoured or, at least, reinforced. But what on Twilight was it? She took a few steps back so that she could see the thing more fully and, with a pulse of excitement, realised that that the metal object was mounted on some kind of rotating tracks as if it might ride on them – *move* on them, in fact.

Kali continued her excavation anew, pulling now at larger stones and rocks that were embedded in the scree and then rolling each down over their predecessors until the pile was too big to accommodate more. But that didn't matter because she had managed to reveal enough of the machine for her purpose, and what she had revealed made her step back with a gasp.

She was standing in the space between the rock and what, it seemed, had been travelling *through* the rock, although what mechanism it employed to do this she could not see as she had not yet unearthed its front end. It was clearly a vehicle, however, as evidenced by the fact that there was a hatch in its side – and the hatch was covered in dwarven runics. Kali ran her palm over it in some wonderment, realising that while it was far from the first dwarven artefact she had discovered, it could very well be the first from the age that had produced it.

Through her own studies she had accredited three distinct periods of development to the Old Races – both elven and dwarven – during which they had progressed from opposing factions, utilising either magic or technology to build their individual civilisations, through periods of conflict where they had waged war using magic *against* technology, to the final age where, reconciled, both Old Races joined forces to expand each civilisation through *magical technology*. By this time both were so advanced that they would have been perceived almost as gods, and they could have been glorious and supreme if something hadn't happened. Whatever it was that had been powerful enough to wipe out these two great civilisations – to effectively *eradicate* them from the surface of Twilight – was perhaps the greatest of all mysteries but one that Kali intended one day to solve. The point was, that the vehicle she was studying appeared to come from the end of that last age, because what else could those orbs be but magical technology?

Becoming more excited by the second, Kali moved to the edge of the hatch, feeling around it until she had traced a round cornered, rectangular shape. It was sealed tightly but, being a hatch, there clearly had to be a way to open it. Perhaps that little niche there, marked with the rectangular symbol?

Kali felt inside and her hand wrapped around what felt like a small handle, which she gripped and pushed. Nothing happened, so she pulled instead. And then she staggered back as a giant, bronchial floprat with halitosis exhaled heavily in her face.

That, at least, was what it felt and smelled like. But there was no floprat, only the rank atmosphere coming from inside.

Kali watched the hatch release itself from its seal, punching away from the main body of the vehicle with a second exhalation and there waiting for a moment before, with a kind of wheeze, it slid slowly to the side. Kali understood now what she had just activated. The hatch was similar to the rune surrounded doors she had discovered in the Spiral of Kos, vacuum sealed by a method she did not understand to protect whatever lay behind them. But, where beyond those doors had lain ancient laboratories, behind this one lay only darkness.

No, she thought, not quite darkness. What appeared to be some kind of small, cramped cabin lay within, illuminated very dully by the same strange glow that had brought her to this part of the cave. As her eyes adjusted to the dark, she noticed that the glow seemed to be emanating from a number of places within, each of them small – panels, perhaps, with levers. Some kind of control cabin then? But controlled by what?

Oh, she thought suddenly, *my Gods.*

The panels were not so bright as they might have been, not because they were actually dim, but because something was blocking their glow. There was a *figure* within, just sitting there, staring straight ahead. Kali swallowed, knowing that if it moved she would very likely have a dicky fit.

But it didn't, of course. How could it? Who knew how long this machine had been stranded here, within the rock. Anything within it could not have hoped to survive. Hells, what a lonely, lonely death it must have been. But what nagged at Kali more than that morbid thought was, why had no one come to help? She wondered for a second whether it was possible that the inhabitant of the machine had died here because there *was* no one to come to help – that perhaps he had died here at the time the Old Races had gone away? And if that was the case then it begged the obvious question. *What* was she looking at?

Swallowing again, Kali leaned in and the figure emerged from the shadows before her eyes. Squat but, by the size of the ribbed uniform enclosing its now shrunken frame, once well-muscled and powerful. It remained utterly still. Dry, eyeless sockets stared straight ahead, gnarled hands gripping levers on the panel before it that had not moved since before the land was young. Though the body was completely mummified there was no doubt at all what it was she was looking at.

A dwarf.

Kali realised she had been holding her breath, and she let it out now in an exhalation that almost turned into a laugh. This was incredible! Something she had always hoped, but never thought, she would find!

The discovery was a momentous one and Kali took the appropriate length of time and appropriate reverence to appreciate it. After all, after Gods knew how long stuck in this hellshole a few more minutes would make no difference at all. But then, with a deep sigh, she moved forward, grabbed the desiccated corpse by its shoulder and turfed it out of the cabin onto the mine floor. The dwarf's remains crumbled under her touch – clothing and all – and while the arms and torso hit the rock, they left the legs behind, half sitting on the seat. Kali heaved them off with a grimace and dropped them onto the collapsed torso – and only then realised she hadn't a clue where the head had gone. She scanned the cabin, peering into its shadowed recesses, and then spotted the missing appendage lying in the far corner, out of her reach. The head was looking right at her, its empty eye sockets baleful and reproachful, but Kali ignored them – what else could she do? – because her friend had been sitting in the driving seat of something that was still *working*. She slipped into the empty seat, thinking: *Sorry, my friend, but I have a lot more need of this thing than you do.*

Whatever this thing was.

Kali peered down at the panels and the levers and realised that she didn't have a clue how to use them even if she knew what it was they did. So what followed, she thought, was going to be interesting, to say the least. She did, though, have one starting point – a button marked with the same rectangular symbol she had seen on the outside of the machine. Humming softly to herself, she pressed it. With the same judder and sliding motion that it had opened with, the hatch closed and sealed itself.

Kali felt as if she were trapped inside a metal coffin.

But she just knew this thing was her way out of here. So, it was time to see what it could do.

CHAPTER THREE

Dolorosa considered she had better things to do than chase a herb up and down the hillside. The preparations for Kali Hooper's memorial evening – a drink-till-you-drop session which all the *Flagon*'s regulars considered the most appropriate way to remember her – had taken the best part of two days. The last of them, a surprise stew for the evening – which was, of course, no surprise to the regulars, though none of them had told Dolorosa that – was all but done. But the hunt for one of its more vital ingredients was proving to be difficult. Said task had occupied her for the past half hour and, in that time, something of a murderous glint had appeared in her twitching right eye.

"I will 'avva you, you leetle red bastardo!" she threatened, her arm swooping down to grab the skittering bunch of macalorum.

But once again the leafy herb evaded her clutches, bouncing and flapping away down the hill towards the *Flagons* and causing the tall, thin woman to lose balance on the slope and flip heel over head, her skirt flapping after her and enveloping her like a tent.

"Bastardo!" she hissed again, from beneath the cloth.

A group of drinkers outside the tavern stared open-mouthed at an exposed pair of skull and crossbones bloomers and – possibly as a release of tension at the bad new they had all received – there was much pointing and loud and raucous bursts of laughter. Dolorosa's head popped out of the bundle of cloth and she flipped her skirt back over her dignity and squinted at them, *hard*. It was a squint that some said could kill – some even said it *had* killed – and the laughter stopped. Dead.

Dolorosa straightened, then squinted down at the tavern again. The drinkers had disappeared inside but she could still see their faces pressed up against the tavern's windows and she strained to listen for the merest titter from them. But there was none and they seemed only to be checking that she wasn't striding down the hill after them.

Lucky fora them, she thought, *because if they hadda tittered, I would havva to keel them horribly and withouta mercy.*

After *she had keeled the bastardo.*

Dolorosa span as she saw that the macalorum had taker advantage of her unexpected halt to turn around and bounce back up the hill, chittering as it passed her. Once again she made a grab for it, and once again missed. What had made this essential ingredient of her surprise stew quite so skittish she wasn't sure – it was normally such a docile little herb – and she wondered whether it had anything to do with the reports of strange creature sightings to the west. These things nicknamed the k'nid. Certainly macalorum wasn't the only thing around here that was uneasy at the moment, as most of the smaller wildlife in Tarn seemed to be that, or worse. Whatever the cause, the macalorum's determination to avoid becoming an ingredient only made her all the more determined to catch it.

Dolorosa bent and slid her fingers into the rim of her right boot, then rolled up her sleeves and began to stomp after the herb.

The stiletto she had extracted from her footwear gleamed viciously and the woman grinned evilly and tossed it in her palm, weighing it up, before flipping it so that she held it by the end of the blade. All she had to do now was time her moment right. And there it was, she thought, where the herb was about to hop over that small ridge into the trees beyond. The macalorum tensed it roots and Dolorosa threw.

Victory issa mine! she thought, and began to scramble up the hill towards the impaled and struggling herb.

She was almost upon it when she found herself staggering backwards. The sky above her tipped dizzily, as if she were going into a swoon.

Greata Gods of the Seas, I havva overdone myself, she thought. *My 'usband, in moments of passion, hassa warned me ovva this.*

There was only one problem with that theory, she realised – she didn't feel remotely dizzy or weak. Why, then, did she continue to fall backwards, landing on her behind with a thud and a puff of dry soil?

Anda wotta wassa happening to the hill?

To her confused eyes it seemed to be getting bigger.

Pah! Eet ees impossible.

Impossib –

"Greata Grandma of the Gods!"

Above her, no more than a yard from her upturned feet, the grass that covered the hill was breaking apart, spilling roiling piles of soil onto the otherwise green landscape, like a pan that had begun to bubble over. Dolorosa scrambled back, thinking that perhaps she was being visited by a rarely seen undermuncher, but it soon became clear that it was bigger even than that. The roiling soil was spreading ever outward now, so much so that her feet and the bottom of her legs had begun to rise with it, tipping her further backwards so that she had to steady herself on the palms of her hands. The old woman watched, mesmerised, as the mound turned into a small hillock, and then one not so small, and her eyebrows raised as something suddenly poked its nose through the surface. Something big.

Dolorosa rapidly muttered a small number of hail glorias, and then far more curses, as she was once more tipped heels over head, her skirt enveloping her again, though this time perhaps mercifully as it shielded her gaze from whatever monster was emerging from the depths. She rolled down the hill in darkness, aware as she went that whatever was emerging from the ground was rumbling loudly and that it stank of the depths and something old. Totally unnecessarily, considering she was under her skirt, she closed her eyes and waited for whatever fate was going to befall her.

Suddenly the rumbling stopped.

The unknown beast hissed loudly.

And then... nothing happened.

A second passed. Two. Three. And then, with a gulp of apprehension, Dolorosa flung her skirt off her head, squinting ahead. There, silhouetted by the evening sun, something shadowed and bulky obscured the hillside. Something with a number of projections on its front, like cannon, that seemed to distort the air in front of them. As she stared the beast disgorged something from its side. No, not something, Dolorosa realised – a figure. A strangely familiar figure, as it turned out, witha what appeared to be a bum sticking out ovva its pants.

The figure looked around, taking in its surroundings.

"Pits of Kerberos," Kali Hooper said, "it worked."

She leapt down from the cabin of the machine she had nicknamed The Mole and limped past the prone and gaping old woman, pausing only to point back and declare with girlish enthusiasm; "Dolorosa, you have *GOT* to get yourself one of those."

"Bossa lady?" Dolorosa said. And then again: "Boss?"

She picked herself up and, with a backward glance at the strange machine, raced after Kali as she hobbled purposefully towards the *Flagons*, circling her as she walked and squinting with some concern, but mainly suspicion, at the bedraggled, dirt covered figure. Once she had truly established its identity, she poked it in the chest with a bony finger.

"You are notta dead?"

"Nope. But I am thirsty. *Very.*"

"Beer eet issa notta good when you arra dehydrated."

Kali snorted. "Yeah, right."

They reached the doors to the *Flagons* and Kali flung them open, frowning in puzzlement at the fact the bar was adorned with a great strip of bunting inscribed, in Dolorosa's strangled peninsulan, with the words: 'Kali Hooper – Resta Inna Peas.'

Rather unnecessarily, Dolorosa declared to all within that "the boss lady issa back", but before the expressions of joy had even had time to settle on the regulars' faces, Kali was already seated at the bar, pointing silently, but self-explanatorily, at the cask *thwack*. Much to his wife's apparent disapproval Aldrededor was already pouring a tankard, and then another, and then – because he knew the occasion would demand it – another still. Kali downed them all in rapid succession, wiped her mouth with her forearm, sighed and burped long and hard.

"That," she gasped, "I needed. Hi, guys," she added, waving at the regulars and smiling as they welcomed her back.

"'Allo, Kaleeee!"

"Good to see yer, halfpint..."

"So – you are not dead," Aldrededor declared, taking the last empty tankard and placing another frothing one in her hand. "It is very good to see you home, Kali Hooper."

"Likewise, Aldrededor." Kali slapped the empty on the bar. "What made you think I was dead?"

Aldrededor shrugged. "The fact that you have been missing for six weeks. That there has been no news at all and, of course, this –" The one-time pirate pointed at Kali's battered and torn equipment belt, hung in pride of place behind the bar. "It washed up on a beach near Nürn. Luckily, Mister Larson was there on his holiday and managed to retrieve it. Thank you, Mister Larson."

"Six weeks?" Kali repeated. She nodded to Ronin as she reclaimed her belt. "That place really threw me out of whack. So have I missed anything?"

"Oh, the usual," Aldrededor said casually. "Red was arrested three or four times, Miss Scrubb has been nibbling the Dreamweed again and –" Rather surprisingly, Aldrededor stopped and suddenly busied himself wiping glasses.

"Aldrededor?" Kali prompted, but the swarthy Sarcrean only shrugged and devoted all his attention to erasing a tiny spot on one of the tankards, one that was seemingly *never* going to disappear no matter how hard he tried.

Suspicious now, Kali span on her barstool to face the gathered regulars, but where a moment before it had been all "Here's to Kali!" and "We should have known you'd be fine!" there was now a totally uncharacteristic silence.

Kali stared at Pete Two Ties on whom she could usually depend, but his head had descended into what was obviously a particularly challenging cryptosquare. She stared at Fester Grimlock and Jurgen Pike, who in turn stared at their quagmire board despite the fact their game was clearly over. Then she stared at Ronin Larson, the ironweaver, and Hetty Scrubb, the herbalist, who were staring hard at their feet or out of the window, the former humming something tremulous and the latter giggling uncontrollably. Of Dolorosa herself, there was at first no sign, then Kali caught sight of her peering warily from behind the bravado barrel at the far end of the bar. The bravado barrel was a game of nerve with a single arm-hole in its front and there were a number of... interesting creatures provided by Red hidden inside it, but having someone hide *behind* it was a first.

Something was definitely up.

"Dolorosa?" Kali said, cautiously.

"What?" Dolorosa objected loudly, throwing her hands in the air. "You thinka that iffa there is something you will notta like it hassa to be Dolorosa's fault?"

That clinched it.

"*Dolorosa?*" she said again, emphasising her question. "What will I 'notta like'?"

Dolorosa squinted at her, saying nothing, but from the corner of her eye Kali saw Red Deadnettle pointing towards the rear of the tavern, mouthing something that looked like 'band.' Kali turned and stared up the few ramshackle steps that led up to her Captain's Table and saw that what had traditionally been her domain, had been filled with a number of strange musical instruments, including a road-worn, sweeping, stringed affair that looked almost elven – what she thought was called a theralin. Frowning, she mounted the steps and saw that the Captain's

Chest – storehouse of her papers and sanctum sanctorum of the peninsula's history – had also been buried beneath a spread of tattered music sheets for such appropriately forgotten classics as 'Boom Bang-a Thud', 'What A Wonderful Pie' and 'Yes, She's Heavy, She's My Mother.'

"What," she asked Dolorosa, "is this?"

The thin woman threw up her hands in protest but, nonetheless, looked guilty. "Wotta you theenk eet is? Eet is, eet is –"

Her words were lost as one of the thick timber beams, supporting the rooms above, suddenly curved downward with a stressed and prolonged groan that drowned out every other sound in the bar. Kali looked upward, blinking dust from her eyes. The next beam along bowed down, as did the floorboards in between, and then the next, and then the one after that. It was almost surreal, as if the whole infrastructure of the tavern had suddenly turned to rubber.

Then the top step of the stairs sounded as if it were splintering.

"Oh Gods," Pete Two-Ties said. "They're waking up."

Kali double-taked. "What? Who? Pete – *who's* waking up?"

"Them," Pete pointed.

Kali span. Whatever it was she expected to see, the last of it would have been a small mountain range, but that was exactly what appeared at the bottom of the stairs. A small mountain range squeezing itself into the bar and made up entirely of flesh. One of the mountains spoke. "Coo-ee, boys," it said, with a wink.

Oh Gods, Kali thought. *No, it couldn't be. Not here.*

"The Hells' Bellies," she mouthed with dread. Her ordeals of the last few weeks notwithstanding she turned as white as a sheet.

The eyes in the peaks of the talking mountain lit up. "Our fame has spread! This young lady, she has heard of us!"

Kali was tempted to point out that the entire peninsula had 'heard' of them and that their fame wasn't the only thing that had spread. But she held her tongue and, instead, glowered at Dolorosa.

"Explain," she demanded, darkly.

"What issa there to explain?" Dolorosa said in a slightly high pitch, clearly going on the defensive. "We thoughta you dead and so we thoughta we woulda make a few changes..."

Kali caught Aldrededor waving from behind his wife, desperate to catch her attention. He was shaking his head vigorously and pointing at Dolorosa.

"Changes?" Kali asked, flatly.

"Entertainment!" Dolorosa declared. "Cabaret! Culture! And so I contracted the most popular dancing troupe in the two provinces!"

Kali felt her heart seize. "Contracted? For how long?"

"They havva performed for three nights," Dolorosa said, "and they havva forty one left."

Kali did a quick calculation. "You've contracted them for a *month*?"

Pete Two-Ties head thudded down onto his table in defeat and shook back and forth slowly.

"The whole of Cantar?" Kali said in disbelief. She signalled to Aldrededor to pour another thwack, which she grabbed and downed in one. "No, no, no, no, NO, NO, NO! Cancel it, Dolorosa, *now*."

A small moon suddenly orbited in front of Kali's face. Except that it wasn't a moon but another face. It took a second to fold itself into a jowly frown. "Cancel... contract?" it said, and Kali wished that Merrit Moon was there so that the Hells' Belly and the Thrutt side of his personality could communicate on equal terms.

She swallowed and used her words slowly. "Yes. Cancel. Contract."

"Pff," the moon said, throwing up its arms. Hairs the length of mools tails sprang forth from dim and horrible pits. "How can *you*, wisp of a thing, demand she cancel contract?"

"Because *I* own the place."

The Hells' Belly guffawed and Kali was blasted with the odours of stale and cheap wine, cigars, and the assorted yellow remains of potato crunchies still providing their money's worth where they were stuck between huge, horse-like teeth. "Missus

Dolorosa, she owns the place. She told us this is so."

Kali turned to Dolorosa, but the door to the *Flagon's* courtyard was already slamming shut behind her.

"Look," she said, wearily. "I'll pay you twice your contracted fee to cancel the remaining performances."

The moon loomed again. A hand snapped a garter on a thigh the thickness of a tree trunk and Kali turned away before she was involuntarily mesmerised by what happened to the flesh around it as a result. "Our fee is nothing compared to the tips we receive from our... *gentlemen.*"

Across the room, Red Deadnettle and Ronin Larson coughed in embarrassment. Kali stared at them and sighed.

"Fine. I'll give you *three times* your fee. How's that?"

The offer was clearly tempting but a frown still crossed the Hells' Belly's face. It thrust itself at Kali interrogatively. "If we leave now, how will you guarantee our safety?"

"Your safety?"

"These are dangerous times, strip of a thing. What if we are attacked on the road?"

Kali pictured bruised and screaming grabcoins flying through the air. "Are you serious? Who in their right minds would take on you lo –?"

She stopped as a hand suddenly rested on her shoulder and Aldrededor whispered in her ear.

"I do not think she is talking about grabcoins, Kali Hooper. I believe she refers to the k'nid."

"The k'nid?"

"Those things that have flooded our land and will soon be everywhere. The... *Wait, you do not know?*"

"There wasn't much news where I've been." Kali frowned. "Tell me."

Aldrededor told her of the reports of strange creatures coming from the west, of the deaths and invasions of towns, and Kali absorbed the information, worried but simply nodding. Again, she sighed. "All right... ladies. For now you can stay. But under one condition. While I'm around I do not, repeat *do not*, want any danc –"

Her words fell on deaf ears. The Hells' Bellies were already skipping, if that was the word, to the makeshift stage, clapping their hands in glee, and Red and Ronin turned their stools toward them appreciatively. As if from nowhere, a number of small, thin and sallow looking men – their husbands? – appeared and took up the instruments that lay on the stage, stroking, blowing or strumming them respectively to produce a discordant wail that would have repelled a Vossian army. Then, without any tuning up, any rehearsal, it just... began.

Thudding.

Kali grabbed her tankard of thwack before it wobbled off the bar and looked around as others did the same. She stared up at the ceiling as streams of dust began to fall in columns. She gazed at the windows, expecting them to crack at any moment. She bit her lip. There was nothing she could do here. But there was something she could deal with outside. And her name was Dolorosa.

Kali slammed the main door to the *Flagons* behind her and stood with her back to it for a second, sighing in relief. Then she jumped away as the entire tavern shook. She moved across the relative silence of the courtyard and then frowned darkly as she spotted Dolorosa pottering about near the stables. Kali moved up behind her slowly and quietly, saw that the old woman was hastily wrapping what looked to be a new tavern sign in folds of cloth. It appeared that the *Here There Be Flagons* had been in the process of being renamed – as *The Olde Crow's Nest.*

Should be the Old Crone's Nest, Kali thought. *By the Gods, I go away for a few weeks and when I get back my pub's been boarded by pirates.*

She was about to prod Dolorosa in the back, give her the fright she deserved, when her attention was distracted by a noise from the main stable. A low rumble, in fact. A strangely familiar sounding low rumble.

Horse? Kali thought.

Horse!

Kali slammed open the stable doors, making Dolorosa jump, and there he was, a living, breathing armoured tank desultorily poking his snout into a pile of hay. His big green eyes looked up as she entered and, as Kali said "Horse" once more, his head rose and a serpentine tongue curled out and slobbered itself with abandon all over her face. Kali moved forward and slapped his neck.

You came back, she thought. *You didn't return to the Drakengrats, after all. Hells, it's good to see you, boygirl.*

There was, however, something wrong. As pleased as Kali was to be reunited with her mount, Horse's whole demeanour seemed off kilter, eyes duller than usual, chitin plating less polished, and his general presence – usually quite comment worthy – less, well, *imposing*. Kali patted the bamfcat, murmuring a soothing *hey, hey...*

"Eet ees the worgles," Dolorosa explained from behind her. "They havva all gone away."

"Worgles?"

The small furballs were Horse's favourite snack – almost his staple diet, in fact – and were usually to be found in abundance all over the peninsula. It had taken Kali some time to get used to Horse's habit of scooping the poor little creatures up with his serpentine tongue, but used to it she had got, and the fact that they were apparently not around was even more unsettling than Horse's carnivorousness *before* their disappearance.

"Worgles, poongs, bladderrips, all of the small creatures they hide a fromma the k'nid. But the worgles, especially, seem to fear them greatly. It ees almost as eef –"

"These k'nid? Where do they come from? What do they look like?"

Dolorosa shrugged. "Where they come from, no one knows. Whatta they looka like is difficult to say. I have hearda many reports. All I know is thatta they are deadly. Butta you need notta worry, Dolorosa doubts they will find their way here to the *Cro* – erm, to the *Flagons*."

Kali frowned. "It doesn't strike you that the worgles and the rest have gone into hiding because the k'nid might be somewhere near?"

"*Fff.* No, the *Flagons* is special, isolated. Dolorosa feel it inna her plumbing – they will *notta* come here."

Kali grimaced and forced a certain image from her mind. But the grimace froze as, in the vitreous of Horse's eyes, she caught a glint of something low and dark behind her, moving into the *Flagon*'s courtyard. "Think again," she said.

Working its way around a bush into the courtyard was an almost indescribable shape. It reminded Kali of the brackan she had encountered in the Sardenne Forest, but of many other things also. Somehow that made it seem many times worse. Moving slowly, and crackling strangely, like an open fire, it began to work its way around the edges of the courtyard, probing in a way that made Kali think it was some kind of scout. And where there was a scout, there would be the main party not far behind.

"I take it," Kali said with some distaste, "that's a k'nid."

She moved slowly out of the stable, shutting and bolting it behind her. Then she peered along Badland's Brook where, in the darkness, she could just make out what appeared to be a blanket of deeper darkness on the ground, extending back to the horizon. The blanket undulated and rippled slightly.

"Walk slowly back to the *Flagons*," she instructed Dolorosa. "Make no sudden moves."

The old woman nodded and did as bade, walking sideways so as not to lose sight of what lay outside the tavern's grounds.

They had only made it halfway across the courtyard before the scout k'nid reared and its friends tumbled forward, as if they were leaves swept into the courtyard on a breeze. Before either of them knew what was happening one leapt straight for Dolorosa, and the old woman screamed.

Kali stared, shocked and unable to believe what had just happened. One second beside her, the next not, Dolorosa was gone, as if she had never been.

That bloody *woman*, she thought, watching the door to the *Flagons* once more slamming behind her. *Hidden athletic depths or not, she and I are going to have to have serious words. But not now. Because, right now, there are more pressing things to deal with. Namely, thanks to a certain someone, that I'm now the only target.*

As the k'nid rushed at her in a sudden, swarming sea, Kali did the only thing she could to get out of their path. With a grunt of pain from her bad leg, she leapt upwards to grab the guttering of the stable roof, using this to flip herself up and over so that she ended up crouched on the lip of the roof itself, watching as the k'nid impacted with the stable wall.

As they recovered from the impact, it was a good position for her to study the creatures. She certainly couldn't disagree that they were ugly little bastards, flooding the courtyard like a colony of insects that had been disturbed from beneath some rock. But whatever rock that had been, she had certainly never come across one like it. These things struck every fibre of her being as *unnatural.*

They did not, however, seem to be quite the destructive force Aldrededor's reports had suggested. They were certainly making no moves to destroy the *Flagons.*

Now, why exactly was that? she wondered.

It took her a second to realise that the k'nid seemed to be reacting to the vibrations from inside the tavern – actually shying back each time a thud occurred. Was it possible, she thought, that these things had worked their way across the peninsula, attacking all in their path, only to be stopped here, by a dance troupe?

Kali chided herself, almost laughed. No, that was plain daft. In fact, it was the stupidest thing she'd ever –

The *Flagons* suddenly fell silent, doubtless in response to Dolorosa informing everyone that the k'nid had come to eat their face, and sure enough each lit window was suddenly eclipsed by a number of shapes peering into the night. What mattered more, though, was that as soon as the thudding stopped the k'nid had become more agitated and their attention had turned to the tavern – and consequently the people inside.

There was a sudden rush against the side of the tavern and Kali cringed as she heard masonry and wood splintering before the assault.

Dammit.

She had to warn those inside, but there was no way she could get back to the door. Instead, she raced along the stable roof, leaping from there onto the *Flagon*'s outhouse, and from there onto the roof of the tavern proper. She clambered up its slates, slipping back twice as some broke from their fixings beneath her and then, at last, reached the apex. There, she found herself doing something and saying something – especially to its intended recipients – that she would never, ever, in a thousand lifetimes, have imagined she would.

"*Dance!*" she shouted into the *Flagon*'s chimneypot. "*Dance, or die!*"

There was a few second's silence and then a puzzled and weak reply came back

"Wotta you say? Who issa speaking, please?"

Kali couldn't believe it. "Dolorosa, it's me."

"Who issa me?"

"Kali!"

"Kali? Why arra you uppa the chimaney?"

"I'm not *uppa the chimaney*, woman! Dammit, Dolorosa, just listen..."

Kali explained what was happening – what she *thought* was happening, at least – and how it was imperative not only that the regulars stay inside the tavern but also that the Hells' Bellies keep on dancing. She explained also that she wouldn't be joining them for her memorial evening or any evening in the foreseeable future. As she did she tried as best she could to hide the excitement in her voice. For her one glimpse of the k'nid had sparked in her a familiar and – considering the alternative – quite welcome feeling: the thrill of the hunt. No, these things weren't natural and to her that shouted Old Races from the veritable treetops. So, she was off on her travels again, and she knew already what her first port of call was going to be, a certain market town and a certain half-ogur who just might have some theories as to what they dealing with.

All she had to do was get there. But was Horse up to it? After all, he'd had better days.

She should have known better than to even question the fact as, at that moment, as if sensing her impending departure,

Horse's growl was clearly audible from his stable. Then the door buckled slightly on its hinges as he gave it a gentle nudge with his snout.

Kali worked her way back down the rooftops until she was above his stable and then, keeping her eye on the k'nid, stretched down to unbolt the door.

As Horse trotted slowly out, his armour flaring slightly at the creatures, Kali reversed the manoeuvre that had got her on the rooftops in the first place, flipping herself down onto Horse's back. Then she eased Horse out of the courtyard, keeping him at a walk as they passed through the ranks of k'nid, which growled softly as they passed. Horse, in turn, growled at them and Kali could feel every inch of his body tense, ready to activate his armour fully at the merest sign of movement from the predators. The vibrations from the *Flagons*, however, still seemed to be rendering them passive. Passing without harm into the open countryside beyond, Kali spurred Horse first into a trot and then the beginnings of a gallop. There were likely more k'nid out here, she thought, and away from the *Flagons* their behaviour might be a different story, so she suspected it was going to be an interesting journey to Gargas.

As she and Horse traversed the first couple of leagues she turned back in the direction of the *Flagons* and the peninsula beyond, thinking of where she would be if she hadn't become trapped in Munch's mine. Because the thought of meeting Merrit Moon had made her think of another meeting she should have had, a certain rendezvous in Malmkrug.

Killiam Slowhand was out there, somewhere in the overrun west, searching for his sister, and wherever he was she hoped he was all right, and that he'd had the sense to keep his head – and the rest of him – down.

CHAPTER FOUR

Despite the glowering and threatening presence of Querilous Fitch lurking behind him, Killiam Slowhand could not take his eyes of what was in front of him. He leaned forward against the rails of the airship, like the excited child he had been on the deck of a far different kind of ship, a lifetime ago. Then, the *Merry B* had entered the bustling harbour of Freiport after his father had been posted from Allantia to the mainland, and to leave that island with the promise of a new life full of adventure on the much larger peninsula – even if then he'd had no idea just *how* much – had filled him with awe and a sense of wonder that he could barely contain. That wonder had returned now and Slowhand gazed upward, his mouth open, unable to believe what he saw.

The parallel with Freiport was more than the sense of wonder, however, because the sights he saw here were in many ways similar to those of that long distant shipping port. Moving slowly into a vast, and only partly natural cavern, hundreds of feet inside solid rock, the airship on which he was being carried aloft was entering its own harbour.

"Amazing, isn't it?" Jenna said, joining him at the rail.

She spent a few seconds leaning in silence by his side, watching as the airship passed gantries and loading cranes and other such devices that projected from rock walls and then, staring ahead, towards a strange cradle-looking dock towards which the airship was heading. "Before we came, no ship had docked here in thousands upon thousands of years. No one even knew it was here."

Hardly surprising, Slowhand thought. Human ignorance of such places was common – how many people had heard of Martak, for one? – but he had to admit there was something different about the place they were entering now. Its location, its position, its *isolation* suggested to him that it hadn't merely become lost like its contemporaries but had always been designed to be lost. In other words, hidden away from the world, even when that world was capable of constructing such a wonder. But, if that was the case, whatever clandestine purpose it had served was long past. Apart from one isolated area that he could see above him, the harbour was neglected, derelict, ill-maintained. Rusted and warped metal beams framed and criss-crossed the cavern like malformed ribs, twisted and time warped gears lay idle in unused machines, and crates sitting in loading bays rotted away along with their contents. Most telling of all, however, was that there were three more airships like this one – or, at least, once upon a time, there had been – and Slowhand simultaneously frowned and gaped as he stared up at the bedraggled remains of what had once been equally wondrous machines. Their canopies were rotted away now and hanging in strips from metal skeletons which would never take to the skies again. Identifying symbols that hung half obscured upon the rotted cloth left the archer in no doubt as to what he was looking at.

This was the remains of an elven skyfleet.

"You were thinking of Freiport, weren't you?" Jenna said. "The day we arrived?"

Slowhand stared at her, his surroundings momentarily forgotten. "You remember?"

"Of course I remember, Killiam. The Faith would have gained nothing destroying that part of me they valued in the first place."

"Your strategic skills?" Slowhand remembered the position she had held with the Freiport military. "They – or was it just Fitch – destroyed something, though, eh? Your free will? Your choice to leave?"

Jenna stared at him, strangely hesitant for the first time since their reunion. "Perhaps there were other reasons..."

"What?" Slowhand said, grabbing her arm and, as he did, part of her robe fell away to reveal a red choker around her neck inscribed with Final Faith runics. It was a wedding band.

"Outside, your man called you Captain Freel," Slowhand said. "Captain *Freel*. My Gods, you married one of them didn't you?"

Jenna pulled her arm away, straightened her robe. "Sorry you weren't invited to the wedding, brother. The ceremony was in Scholten Cathedral. The Anointed Lord herself officiated."

"And how voluntary was *that*, Jenna? Who is he, your husband? Is he here?"

"Lord of All, you never change, do you? No, Killiam, he isn't here. He's on special assignment, just like me."

Just like you, Slowhand thought. And just like Konstantin Munch had been before the shit had hit the fan. "Do you ever think," he said, "that the Final Faith has its fingers in too many pies?"

Again, Jenna hesitated. "They... I..."

"What?" Slowhand demanded. But before Jenna could elaborate, the airship jarred suddenly and he realised that it had just entered the cradle they had been heading towards and that the cradle was, in fact, an elevator. Clamping them into position it then began to rise. Jenna pulled her arm away, suddenly all business once more.

"Mister Ransom, prepare to couple the orb feed. Mister Blane, disengage the canopy locks. Port and starboard rudders down and neutral, people. Let's get this done and get ourselves out of here!"

Despite the sudden burst of activity around him, Slowhand wasn't going to let Jenna's comment go, and he followed his sister as she went about her business, adjusting various dials and levers as the elevator reached its destination and began to turn on its own axis, positioning the airship's strange, pulsating orb before a huge panel. The crewman called Ransom began to link umbilical looking pipes up to it, and while he and the others were professionally adept at what they did – clearly familiar with the airship's workings – a number of things were now becoming clear to Slowhand.

"This isn't your ship, is it, sis? It's Old Race, scavenged from the remains of their technology and put together piecemeal. And this isn't your final destination, either, is it?" As Jenna helped crew position a gantry so that they could reach a rock platform filled with more modern machines and crates, which the crew then proceeded to load, he persisted. "All this equipment? What are you up to, Jenna? Where are you going?"

Jenna span to face him. "Going, brother? We aren't *going* anywhere. In fact, we're running away from somewhere – as fast as we can."

"Somewhere or something?" Slowhand said with sudden realisation. "On the ship, what you said when those things came. You knew what the k'nid were, didn't you?"

"The k'nid?"

"Yes, the k'nid. The things that attacked your ship."

"Oh, so they've been given a name."

"Is it those things you're running from? What the hells are they? Where do they come from?"

Jenna stared at him defiantly, as if she were not going to answer, but then, as he held her eyes, she seemed to relent slightly. "There has been... a mistake," she said slowly, swallowing. "We need to rearm, reinforce, return to rectify what we have –"

"That is *enough*," Querilous Fitch interrupted, grabbing Jenna by the wrist and spinning her around. "This civilian cannot be allowed to know the business of the Final –"

"Hey!" Slowhand shouted, moving forward. "Get your hands

off this civilian's sister or you're gonna find out just how *un*civil he can -"

Fitch's gaze snapped to him and, for a second, Slowhand swore he could see the blood vessels in his eyes dart and writhe like a nest of snakes.

"Or what?" he said disdainfully, and the archer suddenly found himself airborne, though this time with no dirigible beneath him.

The dismissive snap of the arm with which Fitch had accompanied his words had, seemingly without any effort on his part at all, flung him upwards and backwards with such force that he found himself hurtling through the harbour towards the energy panel from which the dirigible crystal fed. He impacted so hard that the wind was knocked completely out of him.

"My Gods, Jenna," he gasped weakly. "What has the Faith done this time?"

Jenna stared but no answer came and suddenly, seemingly instinctively, his left hand shot out to grab a small node on the panel, gripping it tightly so that he dangled there. This, Slowhand found strange, because there was no way – instinctively or otherwise – that he would grab such a device having seen the kind of power it channelled. Sure enough, his whole arm buzzed with a strange energy that spread through his bones to his ribs, but however much he wanted to he found he couldn't let go. In fact, he suddenly realised, his *other* arm was reaching for the opposite node.

Slowhand felt a bolt of panic. He stared down at Fitch and saw the mage grinning coldly up at him. Damn it, it was the threadweaver who had made his arm lash out. And now he was forcing him to raise the other.

Querilous Fitch was in his head.

Below, Jenna snapped her gaze from Fitch to her brother and then back again, for a moment uncertain what was happening – but then it dawned on her. If his right hand connected with the other strut he would complete the circuit, and if that happened his whole body would be channelling the energy of the panel. Slowhand didn't want to know what would happen to him if it did. But the fact was, in his current position, there was nothing he could do to stop it.

His hand rising jerkingly, face twisted and sweating profusely, fighting against Fitch's will, he looked desperately at Jenna. His sister was clearly uncomfortable with what was happening, but it seemed her conditioning was preventing her from doing anything about it.

Fight it, sis, Slowhand thought. *Help me.*

And as if she had heard his plea, her gaze snapped to him once more, her brow furrowing deeply.

Decide who and what's important to you, the archer urged. *Make your choice.*

Suddenly Jenna was struggling with Fitch, trying to turn him away from Slowhand, to break his hold. But despite his frame, the threadweaver seemed to be as strong in body as he was in mind, and would not be turned. As the struggle continued, so did Slowhand's, his grip no more than inches away from the second node now. Groaning, he tried to fight against Fitch, but whatever part of his mind the threadweaver was manipulating it was inaccessible to him. Slowhand craned his neck to watch as his right arm rose ever upward and then suddenly spasmed in shock as it made contact and completed the circuit. The effect was agonising and the archer screamed and bucked, held as the current locked all of his muscles, seemingly gluing him to the panel. But as his body danced, he nevertheless managed to form one word in a guttural tone.

"*Jennnnnaaaa...*"

Below, Jenna continued to struggle with Fitch but then, as if he had tired of a dog snapping at his ankles, he snapped his hand to the side and Jenna was thrown away from him to slam heavily into a pile of crates. Some of the crew turned, shocked that their Captain had been treated in such a way, but it was clear that none of them would do anything about it – dare challenge the threadweaver – and they continued to work. For her part, Jenna stared daggers at her so-called lieutenant, wiping a spot of blood from the side of her mouth. But for the moment she was evidently too weak to pick herself up and retaliate. *If* she even dared take Fitch on.

Slowhand realised that if he were going to live he had to get out of this himself. Thankfully, as Fitch had used some of his energy to throw Jenna aside he had felt a fleeting and slight reduction in the threadweaver's hold. Enough for him to be able to pull his right hand away from the contact panel. If he could work on that...

Slowhand moaned with effort, not only of trying to pull his hand away but also trying to make his intent as little obvious as possible. If Fitch spotted what he was doing, he had no doubt that his hand would be struck back to the panel in a second – and then he would be a dead man.

Slowly, though, it began to work and with a sudden jerk of his limb he realised it was free of the connection, though the panel behind him continued to throb with the charge it had built up. Slowhand took advantage of this, making his body buck as if it were still part of the circuit, but secretly concentrating on the effort involved in freeing his right leg. It, too, broke free, though for a second the archer held it in place, making Fitch think he was as much constrained as he had always been.

"Hey, Fitch," he gasped. "Shouldn't I be dead by now?"

The threadweaver's eyebrow rose in surprise that his victim was able to speak, let alone breathe. Suddenly Slowhand felt a resurgence of the power, Fitch forcing him further onto the panel and, teeth gritted, he fought against the push with all of his will.

"Threadweaver. I'm starting to think you couldn't weave your way out of a papyrus bag."

Below him Fitch growled.

"Querilous Fitch," Slowhand taunted further. "You think maybe that should be Querilous Oh-There's-A-Hitch?"

That did it. As Slowhand had hoped, Fitch was the kind of man who, despite his power, couldn't resist venting his anger in a more physical form. The threadweaver lurched towards him with a snarl.

As he did, his mental hold on Slowhand relaxed and, feeling his body untense against the panel, the archer made his move.

He dropped to the floor and, as he impacted, threw himself into a forward roll, hands snatching behind his back for Suresight and an arrow from his quarrel. He came upright, the bow readied. Slowhand could have killed Fitch there and then but, without knowing exactly why, he didn't. Instead he fired off, in quick succession, four arrows aimed at Fitch's arms and legs. Flitch tried to deflect them, but he had no chance. The threadweaver was suddenly picked up and carried off his feet by their speed and power, thudding into the packing crate behind him. Fitch roared with anger, trying to pull away from the arrows that held him, but they were so solidly embedded in the wood through the folds of his cloak that he was trapped.

Slowhand took a deep and satisfied breath and walked towards Fitch, pausing only to offer a hand to help the still prone Jenna up. She snatched it without thanks – without even a smile, of relief or otherwise – and rounded on the pinioned threadweaver, pointing at the control panel where Slowhand had been trapped. It buzzed now with a release of energy that, despite Slowhand not knowing what it should sound like, didn't seem quite right.

"You're action was irresponsible and stupid," she shouted. "Have you any idea of the amount of *power* contained in those things?" She pointed at Slowhand. "Inserting *him* into the circuit has destabilised the entire system and –"

Jenna broke off, ducking, as the upper left corner of the panel exploded.

"I think she's trying to say you broke it," Slowhand pointed out. He studied the panel as another section detonated, lighting up everyone's faces. "If you ask me, I reckon this whole place is going to go up."

"You fool!" Jenna yelled at the threadweaver.

Fitch actually looked chastised. "He shouldn't have done what he did. Shouldn't have been able –"

"He's my *brother*. He's a –"

She's going to say it, Slowhand thought. The name. And when she did, then the world would know the truth. But at the same time he considered this, the panel behind him detonated once more and the conversation abruptly ceased. Because, this time the explosion set off a chain reaction that spread to more panels next to it, and then more after that, and suddenly one entire side of the waystation was aflame.

"Yep, I was right," Slowhand said, smugly.

"Fark," Jenna shouted, and she began to move among her people, shouting orders. "Get everyone back on board, now! You, do as I say! And you! Leave everything not already loaded! Mister Ransom, loose the umbilicals and prepare for immediate departure!"

"Ma'am, we haven't finished refuel –"

"It will have to *do*, Mister Quinn! If we don't get out of here now, we're not leaving. By the Lord of All, I'll *glide* this thing into Gransk if I have to!"

Gransk, Slowhand thought. There was that name again. Where the hells was it? *What* was it? As troubling as the question was, though, something troubled him even more, and that was his sister's attitude to him since he had escaped from certain death. There had been no smiles, no hugs, no anything, and he was beginning to think that the only reason Jenna had fought with Fitch was because she knew how dangerous his unauthorised actions were – that the fact that her own brother had been the spanner in the works didn't really matter to her at all. The realisation left him with a heaviness in his heart that was worse than he'd felt at the loss of Kali Hooper, but it was a heaviness that he could not afford to indulge in right now.

He looked around him, ducking as the explosions from the Old Race mechanisms increased, sending plumes of fire into the paths of the airship crew. Most were on board now, only himself, Jenna and Ransom still uncoupling the ship not on the safety of the deck. And, of course, Fitch. The threadweaver was still struggling against the arrows holding him, and Slowhand was pleased to see an expression of panicked horror had overtaken the usual arrogance that filled that face. His temptation to leave the bastard exactly where he was almost overwhelming but –

Slowhand sighed, swiftly pulled the arrows from Fitch's robes and then bundled him towards the gantry. The last thing he expected – but *should* have expected – was that at the last minute Fitch would plant his palm on his chest and send him hurtling backwards into a pile of crates. Dazed, he watched as Jenna and the last crewmembers boarded, and the airship was already pulling away by the time he rose and ran after it. The archer tried to make the jump from dock to airship but stopped himself at the last moment by grabbing onto a rail. The gap between them was just too great.

"Jenna," he shouted as the airship receded further beyond his reach. "I have to know – *is there anything of you left?*

His sister stared back, the wind whipping at her face, and Slowhand wasn't sure whether it was that or something else that made her eyes tear up.

Then she dug into a pocket, took out a small object and threw it across the widening gap towards him. Slowhand flung out a hand and then stared down at what he'd caught – a bracelet – before looking back up to question what it was. But, in the brief moment he had looked down, the airship had begun to turn away, as had his sister, perhaps not voluntarily, towards Querilous Fitch. Slowhand roared as the threadweaver approached her and then placed his palms on her skull and the hopes that he had harboured until that moment – that even now he might be able to turn Jenna away from the Final Faith – were finally dashed as his sister quivered beneath Fitch's touch.

Watching the airship descend to the harbour's entrance tunnel, Slowhand could not remember when he had last – if ever – felt so lonely. But there was no time to dwell upon the feeling as another fierce explosion from behind almost blew him off the gantry.

The archer looked around, searching for something – *anything* – that could help him get off this rock. But the only viable method of transport had already left and all that remained was the bones of its sisterships. Then it suddenly occurred to him that if Jenna and the Final Filth could build their flying machine piecemeal, then anything the Filth could do, he could do too.

Slowhand worked quickly but precisely, skewering bolts of cloth from the rotted dirigibles with arrows from Suresight, before pulling them down and framing them around struts of lightweight metal. He tied the pieces of cloth into place with catgut from his quiver, pulling each piece taut until, when he flicked them, they thrummed like drums above the two triangular sections he had created. Finally he linked the two sections together, creating a makeshift hinge by tying the metal struts to the flexible frame of Suresight itself, swung a strap beneath the two, and then stood back to admire his handiwork.

Looking like a pair of artificial wings, what he had created would not emulate a bird but he could *hang* beneath it and it would *glide*. He hoped that was all he would need. There was no time to test its airworthiness, however, as the explosions around him had now become so frequent that they were one solid, roiling mass of ever expanding combustion. The only thing that he could do now was fly.

Slowhand slung the device on his back, tightened the strap, and ran, the precipice that loomed before him doing nothing to discourage him – because if he stayed he was dead anyway. Suddenly, he was in the air and plummeting, and with desperate shifts of his weight from his left and to his right, he managed to manoeuvre the contraption between the numerous metal struts and beams that filled the cavern, dropping past and through them until the floor of the cavern was in sight.

Here, Slowhand arced his body upward, feeling the strain not only on his muscles but on the contraption itself. However, as it groaned in unison with him, his flight path gradually changed from the near vertical to the horizontal. He banked to the left, into the harbour's exit tunnel, its striplights blinking by him, and he could feel the wind from the outside on his face. But with a quite literal sinking feeling, he realised that the air currents within the tunnel were not enough to keep him aloft. Thankfully, the explosions in the harbour above obliged him at that very moment, blasting a wave of heated air and flame down into the tunnel buffeting him forward as effectively as if he had been swatted away by some giant, invisible hand. Slowhand yelled with surprise and with exhilaration and, as the sky darkened around him, realised he had exited the tunnel and was above the Drakengrats once more.

He was just beginning to think he was safe when the entire underside of Thunderlungs' Cry began to blow apart in a series of thunderous and buffeting explosions. There was an ominous cracking from above, too, and as the air about him began, suddenly, to fill with falling stones, rocks and even boulders, he realised that Thunderlungs' Cry itself was coming down. Slowhand cursed and frantically began to manoeuvre the glider through the deadly rain, avoiding pieces of the collapsing bridge by inches and aware that even a single impact could slap him from the sky. Whether through some innate piloting skill or sheer luck, he emerged unscathed, and was about to whoop in triumph when a growing shadow on the distant ground made him instinctively look up.

Ohhh, fark! he thought.

Because Thunderlungs Cry had saved the best for last, it seemed, and – seemingly in slow motion – an entire middle section of the bridge was plummeting towards him.

Slowhand never thought he'd be grateful for more explosions, but for the final, momentous detonation from the rockface, he most assuredly was.

He suddenly found himself being punched across the sky. The shockwave from the final detonation had caught the glider and punched it into a spin away from the rock face and, to Slowhand's misfortune, higher rather than lower into the mountains. As he sailed dizzyingly above the immense chasm he realised that while he had been punched higher, this did not necessarily mean that he was going to *remain* high as the shockwave had severely damaged what little integrity his invention had possessed in the first place. Swallowing uneasily, the archer craned his neck to inspect how bad things were, and his worst fears were confirmed. His jerry-rigged frame was bent and warped, and where he had lashed catgut to hold it together, it was now either snapping away from the metal or uncoiling from it with a sound like multiple cracking whips. He estimated he had perhaps a minute before the whole thing came apart.

There was nothing, absolutely nothing, he could do to keep the glider aloft, and there was nowhere he could bring it in to a forced landing. He was going down.

Slowhand found his attitude becoming unexpectedly philosophical. Maybe Hooper and he were going to meet up again, after all, and he could imagine the conversation already.

"Hooper."

"Slowhand."

"How's things?"

"Ohhh, you know... dead. You?"

"Dead."

"Mmmm."

"Mmmm."

"*So...*"

"*So...*"

Killiam Slowhand smiled, but it was a smile that faded as it formed. Because one of the last things he saw from his aerial vantage point were the k'nid, spilling towards the peninsula.

Then, abruptly, there was no more time and the glider impacted with the ground.

There was a rapid and utterly disorientating series of cracks, thuds and crunches, accompanied by the sound of a whistling wind and breaking struts and bones. Then the world turned sideways, lengthways, diagonal, upside down and, ultimately, dark.

The body of the archer lay face down amongst the wreckage in the remote peaks, twisted and spasming, and he reflected that if there had been a small chance that he might ever be found, that chance was dashed as flurries of snow blew in around him, then over him, covering him in a thick, white shroud that, come night, would freeze about him completely.

His hand moved slowly, shakily towards a pocket, searching for the bracelet Jenna had given him, hoping for comfort in its company. But his fingers felt nothing, the piece of jewellery that had seemed so important to his sister had been lost in his frantic attempts to flee the harbour. The archer sighed lengthily, though knew the sound was only partly disappointment and that, in truth, the strength to care was deserting him.

His eyelids fluttered closed and, as white flakes began to settle on them, he did not blink them away. His face unmoving now, more flakes settled layer by layer until, at last, his features were indistinguishable from the snow.

High in the Drakengrats, nature had built Killiam Slowhand his grave.

CHAPTER FIVE

The Drakengrat Mountains flared for a moment with a light so intense that it whited out the eyepiece through which Merrit Moon watched the event occur. The old man turned quickly away, rubbed his eye, and then frowned deeply. The ancient elven telescope – a rune inscribed, hand-lathed and polished thing of great beauty – was infinitely more powerful than any such device humans could have made. However, even though, at full magnification, its lenses permitted him to gaze across what amounted to a third of the peninsula, it should not have made what he had just seen seem *quite* so intense or immediate. That could mean only one thing. The explosion in the Drakengrats had been incredibly powerful and, consequently, the catalysts or combustants involved, like the telescope itself, had to have been infinitely more powerful than anything his own race could have manufactured.

The conclusion was inescapable. Something Old Race was up there – *had been* up there – but what?

Moon bent back to the eyepiece but any details on the far distant mountains were now obscured by a strange, mushroom-shaped cloud and he'd see nothing for a while. Besides, the sun was coming up, and it was time to open the shop. He was about to turn away when a slight nudge to the telescope shifted its focus down to the plains of Pontaine and something there caught his eye.

What is that?

It looked like some strange black cloud moving over the landscape, or at least would have done had it not been at ground level. And it appeared to be heading towards Gargas. There was something else, too. Something familiar. In the middle of it. A bulky black thing with something on it, moving at speed, as if trying to outrace the cloud. Moon adjusted the magnification on the telescope but, by the time he had done, the object and the cloud had become obscured by what few hills existed in that part of the province.

This was surely a day for mysteries.

Moon sighed, covered telescope with a cloth, and made his way over to the spiral staircase that wound down through two floors to ground level. The old man grunted as he began to negotiate the creaking risers, the wooden stairs having always been a tight squeeze but having become something of a tortuous ordeal since his unfortunate 'accident' in the World's Ridge Mountains. Though in the months since the events of the Clockwork King he had managed to concoct a number of potions and medicines that kept Thrutt's ogur form in relative check, his physical mass and bone structure remained twice what it had been. This left him with a physiognomy that had a tendency to make babies cry and small dogs bark. He had to force himself to be philosophical about this, however, as he had learned on a number of unfortunate occasions that what seemed to trigger the Thrutt transformation was a rise in his blood pressure. A condition flagged by a tendency for his nose and ears to turn a bright red, his eyes to bulge and his mood to become very, very angry. It was embarrassing, yes, but he supposed it could have been worse, even if he wasn't sure exactly how.

Calm, he told himself as he squeezed between the stairway's walls, dislodging pictures and ornaments as he went, cursing the resultant clattering. *Calm.*

The old man emerged into the shop, found it dark and, yawning, moved to the two windows and door to flip their blinds. Azure dawn light flooded *Wonders of the World* and, through a criss-cross of dusty motes, he took a quick inventory of stock, working out which lines he would need to replenish from the cellar. Goblin death rattles, for sure, always popular with the babies. Shnarl fur dice and the stick-on elf ears, too – the only non-authentic line he carried. And there had been quite the run on troll testicles of late, but then it *was* spring and they were always popular at this time of year.

The cellar, however, could wait. Despite the required restocking, things had been pretty quiet around Gargas of late, and there would likely be no customers for a while. It was a state of affairs Moon attributed to the rumours of new predators on the peninsula. He didn't know how much truth there was in the rumours – certainly there had been no sightings of the creatures this far east – but once these things got started, that was that, people simply weren't prepared for the unusual. Peering out through the glass of the door, however, everything looked normal to Moon. The market was gearing up and the flummox was starting to bubble on the Greenwood's nearby stall. When it was ready he might even be tempted by a glass, maybe dunk some redbread to kick start the day, slurping the juices from his chin. Since he had become part ogur his appetites had changed, though thankfully not so far as getting the munchies for the heads of the babies who squawked interminably when they saw him. The temptation, though, had been there.

Moon flipped the open sign and suddenly a figure loomed in his face, leering in at him through the glass. A customer, already? And a fop from one of the cities or larger towns by the look of him, even if he seemed slightly on the down-at-heels side. City dwellers were the worst kind of customer, because even though everything in his store was genuine they never believed it so, for the simple reason that they had never encountered it – as closeted as they were in their own, small and so-called 'civilised' world. Moon sighed then opened the door, and even before he could say good morning, it started. Except this time it wasn't about the provenance of his stock.

"By the Lord of All! The butcher across the way was right"

"Excuse me?"

The fop jabbed him in the chest, and Moon got a whiff of a pungent underarm. "This ogur thing – great idea and I have to say you have it almost bang on. The perfect way to advertise your shop. Harmon Ding, by the way, consultant to the retail trade. Consultancy's quite the big thing in the cities, you know."

Oh, it would be, Moon thought.

The Old Races constructed unimaginable wonders but now that man was the dominant race, it concentrated its efforts trying to find a better way to sell sprabbage. But what was the man on about regarding 'this ogur thing'?

"Something I can help you with, Mister Ding?"

Ding gave a cursory glance around the shop, clearly uninterested in its wares. "Maybe, maybe. All in good time. The important thing is you. Like I said, *almost* bang on." He shook his head and sucked in a breath. "This ogur thing," he added slowly, *"not quite right."*

Moon stared at him, nonplussed. "Not quite right?"

Ding stared back, in a way that suggested he was dealing with someone with the *brains* of an ogur. "The costume! The mask!" He narrowed his eyes, leaned in and then whispered conspiratorially. "Between you and me, looks a bit fake."

"Fake?"

Ding nodded. "Fake, yes. It's like you're half man, half ogur. Look, I know ogurs – I've seen pictures of them in storybooks – and while we both know they're not real, if you're going for the effect, you've at least got to go all the way."

"Oh, ogurs are quite real, Mister Ding. Trust me, I know."

"Yes, yes, of course, of course. What else could you say with this," he waved his hand dismissively, *"novelty* shop being your going concern?"

Novelty shop? Moon felt a rumble beginning in his throat and the lobes of his ears warmed slightly. "Let me rephrase my question, Mister Ding. Is there anything you would like to *BUY*?"

"Buy, Mister Moon?" Ding looked almost aggrieved. "No, no, not buy. I'm here to *sell*. My services. For a period of one month. For a one off fee of fifty full silver."

"Why on Twilight would I pay you fifty full silver?"

Ding stared at him, swallowed slightly, and then suddenly snapped an upright finger into the air, as if to demonstrate a point. Unbidden, he began to prance around the shop, pointing things out and occasionally gazing at the ceiling as if he were somehow receiving divine messages from the old man's bedroom.

"Because I'm seeing *special ogur days* to bring the punters in. I'm seeing spit-roasts and I'm seeing chase-the-child competitions. I'm seeing captive princesses, donkeys, face scribing and pig's bladders on strings. But most of all, I'm seeing you – yes you! – in a brand, spanking new costume designed by me. Huge, flappy ears. Big teeth. Green." He paused, finally, then pointed directly at him. "*You*, Mister Moon, will make a fortune!"

There was a moment's silence, then –

"I'm not paying you fifty full silver for anything."

"Forty, then!"

"No."

"Thirty?"

"*Nothing* at all."

Ding gazed at him, open-mouthed. "You're making a big mistake."

"I don't think so. For one thing, you're clearly not a full tenth. For another, I'm not *wearing* a costume or mask." His voice deepened. "*Of any kind.*"

"And you're saying *I'm* not a full tenth?"

"Twilight is an unusual place, Mister Ding."

Ding laughed. "Oh, here we go! You mean the Old Races and their ancient technology? The Pale Lord? The Clockwork King? And these new things – the k'nid?" Ding curled his fingers at Moon and made nibbling sounds with his teeth. "Just *stories*, my friend – tales to be told around the fire during Long Night and that's all. *Not real.*"

"Oh, you'd be surprised."

Ding smirked. "Trust *me*, Mister Moon. There is nothing in this world that could persuade me otherw..."

Ding trailed off, his mouth hanging open as, right in front of him, there was a crackle of energy, a whoosh of charged air and a yelling, half-naked woman appeared out of nowhere, right in the middle of the shop.

The woman was riding a roaring horse. Except it wasn't a horse, not really, but a huge, armoured, horned thing that looked like a Vossian siege machine. And *clinging* to the Horse – apparently trying to eat it and its rider – were a number of thrashing, clawing, slashing things that Ding found... indescribable. He would have blinked and rubbed his eyes, had he not been busy flinging himself out of the way, because the horse had arrived moving, and was *still* moving.

Taking in its surroundings with insane looking, rolling green eyes, it whinnied and tried to come to a halt but failed miserably, demolishing two of the shop's display stands and heading inexorably for the building's rear wall. Ding continued to watch transfixed as the beast's rider spotted where it was heading, shouted something like "oh, farking hells," and promptly threw herself from her saddle. The woman landed on her feet on a display counter, wincing slightly, and span immediately to face three of the things that detached themselves from her mount to fling themselves after her. As they did, she unsheathed a vicious looking gutting knife and slashed it in an arc across the air before her, sending the creatures scrabbling back with yellow goo spurting from their flanks. The horse-thing, meanwhile, skidded itself into a half-turn as it approached the wall and hit it side on. The things still clinging to it were crushed with a sickening crunch, spraying yellow goo upwards in a fountain of gore.

Ding swallowed hard as dust streamed from stressed, supporting beams and the shop began to creak ominously.

The woman threw herself into the air and across the room, taking the time to wave at the old man as she passed. He, in turn, waved back but Ding could see that he was clearly not as pleased to see her as she was he. As the old man regarded the wreck of a room before him, Ding could have sworn that his nose and ears throbbed a bright red, and that he appeared to *grow* slightly. This did not, however, stop him coming to the aid of the woman when she needed it. As she was now engaged in a losing hand-to-hand battle with the remaining creatures, the old man opened a cupboard beneath his sales counter and, with a yell, threw her a glove.

Oh, very useful, Harmon Ding thought.

But then his ears flapped as she slipped the glove on and blasted one of her assailants over each of his shoulders with an pulse of energy that drew crackling red circles in the air. Ding watched the two creatures crash screeching through the windows of the shop and then turned back, white-faced now, just in time to see the third creature lunge for the old man. The odd thing was, though, he didn't seem to be the old man anymore, and as the creature reached him something big and green and roaring that stood in his place simply tore it apart.

Nice costume, Ding thought, and fainted.

Or at least tried to. For as he began to collapse something shot from the horse-thing's mouth and wrapped itself about his neck, holding him up.

Oh, he thought, *it's a tongue. An impossibly long, slimy tongue.*

Instead of fainting, Ding decided, instead, to scream. As the girlish wail erupted from him, the tongue released him and Harmon Ding ran. Ran as fast as his legs could carry him, out of the shop and away. The last words he heard as he headed for the gates of Gargas were: "Fark, what a day. Who was that by the way?"

"That? Oh, don't worry about him. He wasn't real."

Far behind Ding, the old man sighed, not with relief but in an attempt to calm himself down and, as Kali and Horse looked on, his ogur physique began to dwindle until he had returned once more to his half ogur form. Done, he looked around the remains of his shop and then stared at Horse and Kali. His eyebrow rose.

"You could have knocked, young lady."

"Mmm, sorry about that. These things attacked *en route*,

tearing up Horse pretty badly, so we had no choice but to jump here. Should have been outside, of course, but obviously he's not quite himself and overshot." She looked guilty. "A tad."

"A *tad?*"

Merrit Moon walked slowly forward, feet crunching on broken vials and crushed souvenirs, shaking his head. Despite his obvious dismay about the state of his shop, however, his brow furrowed in concern as he approached Horse. Gently, he ran a palm over the wounds on his armoured flanks – wounds that bled slowly and made the huge beast wince beneath his touch.

"His armour should be stronger than this," Moon observed. "There's a discolouration in it that doesn't look right."

"I know. I think it's something to do with his diet – or lack of it."

"His diet?"

"Worgles. Won't eat anything else. But they've disappeared since these bastards came out of nowhere."

"Really?" Moon said, intrigued. He looked at the tumbleweed like bodies that littered the shop floor. "I take it, by the by, that these are the infamous k'nid?" Kali looked at him and he added: "Oh, yes, I've heard the rumours. I may even have *seen* them, earlier, out on the plains."

"Yep, that's where they hit us."

"Ah, that was you," Moon said absently. He turned back to Horse. "Well, let's see if we can get some of this fixed up." He collected some balms and a cloth from around the devastated shop began to gently rub them into Horse's armour.

"Hey," Kali said. "I'm injured too."

"What? Oh, yes. Yes, yes, of course you are."

Kali threw up her hands but smiled. The fact was, since escaping the mine, which she now realised must have been inhibiting them somehow, her recuperative powers had worked wonders on her leg and, while not perfect, it would do. Horse was the patient now, and it was nice to see the old man tending to him so carefully. Because, despite her elation at finding he still lived on the Dragonwing Cliffs above Martak, there was one thing she'd dreaded, and that was informing the old man that his own beloved horse – the original Horse – had perished during the course of that adventure.

Constant companions, until the day she'd inherited him from the retiring artefact hunter, she'd never known a relationship between man and beast be so close and knew the news would be shattering to him – hells, it had been shattering enough to her. It was during the telling of it, however, that Horse Two had begin to gently nudge the old man's shoulder, and that not only seemed to alleviate the impact of the news but also create the same kind of burgeoning bond that she herself had felt with Horse's more.... unusual replacement. Over the intervening months, either with Merrit visiting Horse's grave above the *Flagons*, or they him, here in Gargas, that bond had grown until she had begun to think once more that the old man cared more about Horse than he did about her. Or maybe it was just because he was part of *her* that he cared. That theory made her feel a little better, anyway.

"Old man?" She kicked the remains of one of the k'nid, exposing its soft underbelly – red, turning now to grey. "What are these things?"

Moon regarded them as he continued to soothe Horse.

"First impressions? Hostile. Wrong."

"Hells, old man, I could have told you that."

"No, what I mean is, they don't belong. They're not a part of the order of things."

Kali kicked the k'nid again. "At least they don't seem as indestructible as the rumours make out."

"Ah," Moon sighed. "I wouldn't chance too many arms on that particular theory. These *specimens* were transported here with Horse, remember. Forcefully separated from their pack. I believe that together they might be far more formidable opponents. Certainly the number of reported deaths reflects that."

"What? So you're saying they're some kind of group entity?" Kali fought for a comparison. "Like fussball fans?"

"You never did like that game, did you?" Moon mumbled. He patted Horse, finished with his ministrations, and moved over to the k'nid, examining it. Suddenly he pulled his finger back with a hiss and flicked a clear liquid from it, which made a small patch of floor warp and burn.

"What is that? Acid?"

"No, some kind of *destabilising* agent," Moon mused.

He had used many, many substances in his alchemical experiments but this was a new one on him. He studied the k'nid more closely and frowned.

"This isn't right," he said. He took a small vial from his pocket and sprinkled its contents over the corpse. Nothing happened for a few seconds but then the dead creature began to wrinkle and twist, shrink in on itself, until it became utterly unrecognisable.

"Now that *was* acid, right?"

Moon shook his head. "It's the same potion I use to limit the influence of the ogur upon myself – to hold the change in check, as it were. Except, of course, that I just gave the k'nid far more than is safe to use on myself."

"So, what? You're saying this k'nid was *changed* like you were? That your potion reversed the changes, made it what it was before?"

"Exactly."

Kali pulled a face. "But look at it, old man – it's just a mess. It isn't *anything*."

"That's what worries me." Moon stood and sighed. "I saw something happen in the Drakengrats this morning. A great explosion."

"Well, don't look at me. I was nowhere near it."

"For once," Moon said, smiling. "The point is, Kali, the k'nid are swarming from the west, are they not?"

"Moving down in a fan shape from what I've seen. Freiport, Volonne, Miramas, now here. Merrit, do you think there's a link? That this explosion somehow *created* the k'nid?"

Moon shook his head. "Reports of their appearance precede that. But there may be still be a link. Something *else* up there."

"Any idea what?"

Moon hesitated. "There's a legend of an Old Race site I came across during research into my own condition. It spoke of a place in the clouds where the Old Races played at being gods. A fearful, unapproachable place. They called it the Crucible."

"A place in the clouds? You think that means the Drakengrats?"

"It seems a likely contender."

"And this 'crucible'? You think that's where the k'nid came from?"

Moon sighed. "Kali, if I'm right I think they might have been *born* there."

Kali took a deep breath. "Then, old man, I guess I'm going to the Drakengrats."

"And I'm coming with –"

The old man stopped as there was a distant sound of tolling. "That's the town's sentry alarm. The guards have spotted something on the plains."

"K'nid. They must be spreading faster than I thought."

"There's one way to find out. Come with me."

Kali trailed the old man up the spiral staircase, avoiding falling pictures and ornaments as she climbed, until the pair reached the attic. Moon uncovered the telescope, adjusted its warp lenses, and then tipped it down so that it was aimed towards the town's walls. He peered into the eyepiece.

"Not k'nid," he said. "Not yet."

"Then what?"

"Take a look."

The old man stood aside and Kali took a look, focusing on the main gate of the town through which a great many soldiers were marching. Their grey canvas and lace epauletted livery marked them out as Pontaine militia, forces financed by the local land barons as a kind of home guard, and guarding the home was clearly what they seemed to be doing – quite zealously.

Ranks of them were organising the civilians near the gate into small groups, keeping them in place with what seemed the unnecessary threat of their weapons. Unless the militia had suddenly decided to become a dictatorial force, there had to be a reason for their uncharacteristic behaviour. Kali tipped the telescope upward slightly, focusing first not far beyond the town walls, and then further out, at the almost featureless agricultural plains that surrounded Gargas. She could see them stretching away for leagues, or at least *would* have been able to were it not for the dark fog that covered them like a shroud.

Except it wasn't a fog, she knew. It was the same pack of k'nid she and Horse had become caught up in. If pack was the word to describe the hundreds and hundreds – if not thousands – of them she could see. It was almost as if, *en route*, the strange creatures had been *replicating* themselves. She muttered something with four letters under her breath.

"K'nid?" Moon said.

"Oh, yeah. They're here."

The old man urged her aside and peered into the scope. "By all the gods, they *are* fast."

"Here within the hour, I reckon."

"Then it's time that we were on the move."

He walked to a chest in the corner of the attic, opened it and extracted an equipment belt similar to her own, a few unidentifiable odds and ends which he stuffed into his pockets and then a pink, woollen cloak he slung about his shoulders. Kali couldn't help but smile. The old man had been wearing that cloak the day they'd first met and she hadn't seen it since the day he'd retired – and it *still* stank of Horse. This was beginning to feel a little like old times. As Moon began to descend the stairs she too dug into the chest, extracting a new bodysuit she'd asked him to keep there for emergencies, and quickly slipped it on.

"What about your shop?" she asked as she followed Moon down. "You know it'll be at the mercy of those bastards."

"I doubt a thousand k'nid could make much more of a mess of it than you did, young lady."

Kali reddened. "For all the Gods' sake, when will you stop treating me like a bloody chil –"

She quietened. There was a soldier at the bottom of the stairs. Another behind him. And another behind him.

"Come with us," the one at the front said.

"Excuse me?" Merrit Moon responded.

The soldier's face darkened. "You are ordered to come with us. *Now*."

"The shop," Moon said warningly, "is *closed*."

Kali looked at him, coughed gently and pointed out the front door of the shop which hung buckled and ajar, then a part of the wall which had started to collapse during their battle with the k'nid.

"Actually," she pointed out, "I think you could say you were still open."

"Funny. You know they aren't here to buy things, Kali. They're here to interfere, as their kind always do."

Kali patted Moon's arm. Much as she shared the old man's healthy disrespect for authority of any kind, there were things going on that they both had to take into consideration – not least the clearly scared and trigger-happy militia. Besides, Moon's temper had become noticeably more *fiery* since the Thrutt incident and, for obvious reasons, she needed to keep him calm.

She approached the soldier and, despite already knowing what was approaching, asked: "Why are you here?"

The soldier was blunt and to the point, although a slight bobbing in his throat revealed his nervousness. "Gargas is now under martial law. A curfew has been imposed and any transgressors will be summarily executed. The population is to be evacuated to Andon."

"Andon?" Moon said. "That's ridiculous... madness! The journey will take days!"

"We go with them, old man," Kali said, to his utmost surprise. "We go with them. No arguments."

"Young lady?"

Kali patted his arm again, this time squeezing it softly but reassuringly too. Because watching the militia enter through the town gate she had noticed something that he had not. But now was not the time to share it with him.

"Trust me," she said after a second. "We go with them, and we do everything these nice gentlemen say."

CHAPTER SIX

"Young lady," Merrit Moon said, with evident disappointment, "I am very, *very* surprised. It is most unlike you to capitulate so readily."

Kali smiled. "Oh, I'm not capitulating, old man. You know I never do. I'm just looking after our interests. Ours and everyone else's."

"And how is that exactly?" The old man stared ahead at the snaking line of people, hundreds of them, six abreast, being marched across the plains, then back at an equal number in similar formation behind them. He snarled at the soldiers who marched alongside, effectively herding the people of Gargas like cattle, as they had been doing for hours. "As I believe I pointed out, this is madness."

"Old man, I think they're genuinely trying to help," Kali said placatingly. "If only to guarantee the land barons next year's taxes. It's just that they've never experienced a situation like this before."

"As you say. But what the hells are we doing *with* them?"

"For one thing, there's no way we could have reached the Drakengrats directly – you saw the k'nid swarm yourself. For another, it *does* take us closer to the mountains, albeit with a slight detour to the south west. But lastly," she added with a prod, "it's your best chance to get across the plains with your scowl intact."

Moon harumphed and stared into the distance. For the moment the horizon was clear but, having seen the speed of the k'nid with his own eyes, he knew that situation could change at any second.

"Horse could have had us to the mountains in three jumps," he said.

"Maybe, if Horse were up to par," Kali patted her mount as he plodded alongside, still weak but recovering from his injuries. Green eyes rolled. "Besides, whether Andon has the best defences in the region or not, I'm a little dubious about the logic of corralling all these people in one place. I want to make sure they're all right."

Merrit Moon sighed and shook his head, but Kali could tell she'd been forgiven. "You want to make sure they're all right. An admirable sentiment, but I don't really see what you can do to help and, I repeat, this is madness. Do you honestly think we can avoid the k'nid for the three or four days it will take us to reach Andon?"

"I don't think it's going to take three or four days. Look ahead."

Maybe a tenth of a league further on, a dust storm was beginning to brew on the plain, vast spirals of flotsam thickening moment by moment. "Oh, wonderful. We'll be blinded too."

"I don't mean the storm. I mean what's *causing* it. The people at the front. *Look*."

It was then that Moon noticed the gestures being made by a group of six individuals leading the march. Garbed in thick, plain cloaks but with hints of far more colourful robes beneath, they appeared hardly to move under their covering – except for a subtle but complex flexing of their hands.

"Are they what I think they are?"

"Yep. League of Prestidigitation and Prestige. Saw them with the soldiers at the gate. And they're *weaving*. In fact, they're brewing up the storm."

"But why on Twilight would they do that?"

"Perhaps to disguise what's inside it." She nodded forward, into the storm itself. There was a distinct glow visible inside, a swirl of energy that Moon recognised instantly.

"My Gods, they're creating a warp portal. They're going to *teleport* these people to Andon."

"Without them even realising it," Kali said with a twinkle in her eye. "It wouldn't do to let the general public know just *how* much magic was around them, now, would it?"

"These people aren't stupid, they'll realise."

"They're scared, tired, hungry and facing the unknown. When they arrive in Andon, they won't even care enough to ask."

"You knew what you were doing all along, didn't you?"

"Oh, aye."

Kali, Moon and Horse continued forward and soon entered the storm. Cloaks or hands raised against their faces to protect themselves from the swirling dust, no one other than Kali and her companions realised what was happening. Even when the teleportation magic took hold of their bodies, causing a slight tingle of the flesh, a barely noticeable buzzing in the bones, as they suddenly left one place to arrive in another. Or at least they *thought* no one else had noticed. Because as the marching refugees emerged from the other side of the dust storm, finding themselves amidst the skeletons and ruined machines of war that littered the outskirts of Andon it was, ironically, Harmon Ding who noticed something amiss.

Towards the front of the line, the small twitchy man sniffed the air and bobbed his head from side to side, his brow furrowing in confusion and consternation and his fingers rising as if to question the soldiers and the mages at the forefront of the march. Thankfully, they ignored him for the most part, but then Ding's continuing and questioning gaze looked back down the line, spotted Kali, Moon and Horse in its ranks, and his face whitened.

He grabbed one of the soldiers and pointed in their direction.

"This we can do without," Kali sighed. "Excuse me."

She began to work her way down the line, and the closer she came to Harmon Ding the clearer his entreaties to the soldier became.

"Don't let them into your city! They're not *normal.* This crazy woman has, well, a *thing,* and her friend, the old man, he isn't an old man at all, he's some kind of *monster.* A big, green monster. They're in league with those other things, I tell you. Armoured horses and big green monsters and crazy women and... and gloves that fire circles in the air."

"Excuse me officer," Kali said in an approximation of a backwoods accent. She could tell from his expression that the soldier had already decided he was dealing with someone less than a full tenth, so that made her task a lot easier. "Is cousin Ding botherin' you?"

"He seems to think your grandfather is a big, green monster, ma'am."

Grandfather, Kali thought with a smile. *Oh, the old man was going to love that.*

"Pssshh," she said, dismissively. Kali extracted a bottle of thwack she had palmed from the Greenwoods on her way down the line and shook it at the soldier, feigning clumsiness as the cap she had deliberately loosened came off and the noxious brew splashed all over Harmon Ding. "Sorry, cousin," she said. "But at least you can't stink of it any more than you already do."

"But – but I haven't touched a drop!" Ding protested. "Not a dro –"

Kali looked at the soldier and shook her head sadly. "Denial," she said, and rammed the neck into Ding's mouth, whacking him subtly in the stomach as she did so he couldn't help but gulp the thwack down. "There, there. You know it makes you feel better."

The bottle extracted, Ding sucked in a gulping breath. "Armoured horsh," he said, dribbling thwack while his eyes rolled. "Big, green monshter, gloves that – that..."

"I'm sure you have enough to deal with, so I'll take him off your hands," Kali said to the soldier. "I'll look after him, now."

"Thank you, ma'am."

"No problem."

Kali took Ding by the arm and force-marched his protesting form back towards Moon. As they neared Horse she took a quick look around to make sure no one was watching and then suddenly elbowed Ding in the face, knocking him cold. She slung the body over Horse and then fell back into step with Merrit Moon.

"Nice work," the old man commented.

"Shucks, it were nothin'... *grandpa*."

The old man turned to protest, but then thought better of it as the exodus neared the walls of Andon itself.

They were formidable – and it was immediately clear why the barons had chosen to evacuate the populace here – because in addition to the normal ranks of catapults, trebuchets and giant crossbows that lined their tops, additional defensive weapons had been added to their number. Some, by the look of them, magical in their design. If – make that *when* – they came, the k'nid would certainly have a battle on their hands.

The soldiers at the front of the line called out and, with a massive rumble, the gates began to open. Gradually, the line filed beneath the stone arch, until it was the turn for Kali, Horse and the old man to enter.

It was then that the first of the problems Kali had envisaged hit them. Inside the city walls, refugees not only from the northern towns but, by their local dress, Fayence to the south-east, milled about in an ever thickening crowd, threatening to block the main thoroughfare. Nor did they just mill. Many were crying in fear of what they had been told might come; others beseeched the soldiers for help they could not give; still others protested volubly about the situation they had been forced into. It was, in short, chaos, and the soldiers looked as confused as they did.

Kali approached one of the city guards, asked what was to happen next.

"To be honest, Miss, it's kind of every man for himself. All accommodation is already taken, and the situation isn't helped by the fact that many have already barricaded themselves in their homes, threatening to put a quarrel through the heart of anybody who approaches. Frankly, the barons have made something of a mess of all this. All I can offer you is stabling for your, er, horse. We're stabling all the beasts in the bunkers in the city walls, should be safe enough there."

"Can't these people use those bunkers?"

"They could Miss, but try persuading them. If you knew things straight from the hells were heading for the city, would you hide in the first place that might be breached?"

The soldier had a point. For that very reason, she wasn't happy leaving Horse there either. But there was no other choice and he would, when it came down to it, be safer there than out in the open. Kali slipped Harmon Ding's unconscious form from her mount and patted Horse on the neck, before handing the soldier his reins.

"Could you see to him for me? I need to find some shelter for our peop –"

Kali's words were drowned out by a sudden series of urgent cries from the city walls and a flurry of activity above as soldiers took up positions. There were mages amongst them too, standing tensed and slightly hunched, their faces dour, fists balling and beginning to flare or crackle with energy waiting to be unleashed. Within seconds there was barely an inch of space left on the walls as Andon's defenders readied themselves.

"They're coming! Seal the gates!"

My Gods, so soon?

Kali raced up the steps to the walls, needing to know what the city was facing. Pushing her way between soldiers she stared out over the Killing Ground – or at least, what she could see of it.

The advancing swarm of k'nid completely obscured the abandoned battlefield as they tumbled, rolled and scuttled rapidly towards Andon's walls. As the k'nid came, Andon's defenders responded with devastating force, unleashing a rain of missiles and magical bolts that should have created an impassable wall of death but which, after the initial volleys ended, appeared to be having very little effect on the k'nid at all. It seemed, in fact, that for every k'nid that was pounded by the defensive assault, another two appeared. As prepared as it was, Andon looked as though it was about to be overwhelmed. Sure enough, only seconds later, the first wave of k'nid reached the walls, scaled them and rushed straight into the ranks of the now panicking mages and soldiers.

As men and women fell flailing and screaming, their cries muting as they were enveloped, spasming, within the k'nid, Kali knew that Andon's walls were already lost and the city itself would soon follow.

There was nothing she could to help these people now but she had to help her own – and quickly.

Kali raced back down the steps and quickly enlisted Moon and the Greenwoods to help marshal the people through the tortuous maze of twisting and jinking streets that led to the Andon Heart. For though the city guard had informed her that all accommodation was taken, she knew of one particular hotel that did not normally open for business that might be able to provide them with sanctuary. *If* they could get there in time. Because, with most of its residents barricaded behind their doors, the city was strangely quiet, making the sound of the continuing k'nid assault ever louder.

Screams were actually coming from the side streets around them now and, among them, they could hear officers barking desperate orders to their men and the crackle of magical discharges as mages made one last, desperate stand. The k'nid assault was, it seemed, relentless. As the walls around them turned rainbow-coloured with flashes of weapon fire and energy bolts, all Kali could say to her charges was: "Run!"

This they did without hesitation, and Kali led them to the Andon Heart, and there towards the alleyway that led behind two deserted market stalls to the entrance to the *Underlook*.

As Kali neared the mouth of the alley, a crossbow quarrel thudded into the wood right beside her, stopping her in her tracks. She stared at it, and then up at the window from which it had been fired, and then at the other windows which lined the alley. Like the first, they were occupied by the figures of a man or woman aiming a weapon in their direction.

What the hells? she thought. *This was hardly time for Pim and his guild to be playing their secret headquarters games.*

"These people need shelter!" she shouted. "Tell Jengo Pim they're with Kali Hooper!"

The only answer was another crossbow quarrel embedding itself firmly in a wall next to her head.

Dammit.

"Kali Hooper!" she shouted again, but her voice was lost in the clamour that was taking over the city.

"Forget it," Merrit Moon observed. "The place is a veritable fortress."

"Yeah?" Kali said. She studied the alley anew, weighing it up. The last time she had been here – immediately after the 'death' of the old man and before her trip to Martak – she had been escorted along its deadly length, but at that time she had still been learning of her new abilities and what had seemed impossible then now seemed less impossible.

"Stay here, old man," she said, and before Merrit Moon could respond, she was gone.

The first of the window sentries didn't even see her coming, Kali already having worked out her trajectory so that she could leap off some piles of rubbish to the alley's side and springboard herself off the wall above to its opposite number. There, her momentum allowing her for a second to actually run along the vertical surface, she flung herself forward, grabbed a drainpipe and slung herself around for a leap back across the alley. Somersaulting in mid air, she hit the first wall again with her feet, kicked off and propelled herself backwards towards the window that now lay opposite, jack-knifing herself as she went so that her legs wrapped themselves around the neck of the sentry positioned there in a scissor grip. Thus anchored, Kali allowed herself to flop loosely, hanging upside down from the window with her back to the wall. As she did, she jerked her legs so that the sentry was flipped forward and out. She opened her legs and he screamed as he plummeted to the ground, hitting with a dull thud.

Five or six crossbow quarrels slammed into the wall where Kali hung, but she was already gone, dropping down to the ground and pinwheeling on her hands across the alley's width.

Back on her feet once more she leapt straight upwards, directly beneath the second window, grabbed and twisted the front of the crossbow that was wielded there, then quickly pulled the trigger so that its quarrel impaled itself in the shoulder of its bearer.

Only seconds had passed since she had begun to run the gauntlet, but it was long enough for those sentries who remained to realise that she would now be coming for them. Shouts and cries of alarm bounced back and forth across the alleyway.

Kali went inside now, pulling herself through the window she had just vacated, knocking the groaning sentry cold then running through the room beyond, along the corridor, and into the adjacent room. She didn't slow her pace, however, indeed she accelerated, then launched herself straight through the room's window. Straight as an arrow, she flew across the width of the alley, waving a casual 'hi' to the stunned occupant of the window opposite, before slamming into him and winding him so severely that he sat down with an *oomf.*

The *oomf* became a groan as Kali wasted no time knocking him cold.

Here she changed her tactics, grabbed the sentry's crossbow and threw herself to the side of the window she had just entered. Then, with two perfectly calculated shots a second apart, fired a quarrel through the forearms of the next two sentries she could see from her position. Both cried out in agony and their weapons fell from their hands to clatter and break on the alley floor. Now, only one sentry remained, but she would be the most difficult to take out, and Kali quickly studied her surroundings, looking for a way to finish the job.

Old building, she thought. *Unused, neglected, probably riddled with woodworm and dry rot. Fine, that was the way to go.*

Without hesitation, she leapt upwards, straight into and through the ceiling of the room, spitting dust and splinters as she broke through plaster and slats. Heaving herself up into the roof space she ran a palm over the underside of the roof itself, found a weak spot and then punched through the tiles. Half a second later she was on the roof, racing along its sloping surface towards the end of the alley and the last sentry post in her way. Calculating when the window would be beneath her, she lay down on the roof surface and let herself slide down it headfirst, dropping off the edge of the roof and plummeting straight down. There was a gasp of surprise as she hit and grabbed the outstretched arms and crossbow of the last sentry, and then a cry of alarm as she realised Kali wasn't intending to let go. Weighed down by her mass, the woman was pulled from the window in to Kali's embrace. The two tumbled towards the ground, Kali wrapping herself around the Grey Brigade member to protect her, and then they hit the ground in a cloud of dust, the woman exhaling loudly as much from shock as the impact. Kali pulled her up. The two of them were standing directly in front of the main entrance to the *Underlook*.

The woman stared at Kali, gasping in disbelief.

"The door," Kali said. "Get it open. *Now*."

"It will do you no good."

"I got this far, didn't I?"

The woman shrugged and rapped on the door, a code that had changed from the one Kali remembered. As it opened, two men appeared on the threshold and Kali despatched them swiftly with punches to the nose. Moving inside, she worked her through the corridors of the old hotel until she came to its ballroom – the centre of operations and throne room of Jengo Pim.

As expected, Pim sat on his makeshift throne, and regarded her coldly as she entered.

"Pim, what is this?" Kali said.

"Kali Hooper," the thieves guild leader replied slowly. "So, which of my people dies horribly this time?"

Kali was somewhat thrown by the tone of her reception. Pim had understood the death of his man during her incursion into the Three Towers had been unavoidable and no fault of her own.

"I don't understand."

"Tom Daly!" Pim snapped. "You do remember how you got him turned to stone?"

Oh yes, Kali thought, *I remember. But I also remember that his name was Kris Jayhinch – and that was not something Pim himself was likely to forget.*

Something was wrong here. And now that she knew that, she was suddenly aware of the tension in the room – the beads of sweat on Jengo Pim's face and, more importantly, those on the faces of the men who surrounded him. She studied the man right behind Pim – a man she did not know – and saw how his arm was tensed, as if holding something to Pim's back. A knife, it had to be. It wasn't Pim who had closed his doors to the refugees, it was these others. Pim had become the victim of a cowards' coup and, by the looks of things, quite recently

"As you can see," Pim explained, "you are not welcome here. Leave now or... my men will fire."

Kali could see that well enough and, for a moment, she said nothing, biting her lip as she tried to work out a way out of this. The number of crossbows that were trained on them made it impossible to pull off any sudden manoeuvres. Deprived of that possibility she could only try to talk her way out. But that, in itself, seemed a likely unsuccessful path.

"Perhaps," a voice said, "I might be of some assistance?"

Kali turned and saw that Merrit Moon and the others had worked their way into the *Underlook*. But it was not Moon who had spoken. A figure pushed his way through the clamouring crowd and threw back his hood, and Kali found herself staring at a silver haired, bearded figure whose presence made him seem to loom tall over the others.

"You," she said.

The man inclined his head slightly. "Poul Sonpear at your service."

"Who's he?" Merrit Moon whispered in Kali's ear.

"Archivist for the League of Prestidigitation and Prestige, particularly the forbidden bit. Oh, and part time Final Faith spy." She glanced at Jengo Pim and then back to Sonpear. "Well, this is turning into quite the reunion."

"Odd, isn't it, how certain *pivotal* figures always seem to turn up in the right place at the right time." Sonpear smiled, but it was a smile that seemed aimed only at Kali. "One might almost say it was *preordained*."

Kali eyes narrowed. Was Sonpear alluding to something? Something, perhaps, to do with her own origins and place in the scheme of things, much as a certain fish thing had alluded in Martak some time back? If he was – in the presence of all these people – if he *knew* something, now was not the time to talk about it.

"What are you doing here, Sonpear? Shouldn't you be closeted with your buddies in the Three Towers?"

"I should, but clearly I am not." He shrugged. "A small distraction. A liaison in the Skeleton Quays, where I found myself detained. By the time I returned to the towers, they had already been sealed."

Kali smiled. Detained in the quays, eh? She knew just the place and wondered how business was down the *Bound to Please*. So, despite the fact Sonpear had already proven he was literally capable of wiping the wall with her, he was quite human after all. And now he was stuck here as much as they were. Or, then again, perhaps she was jumping to conclusions.

"I have made myself known to you because I believe I can help with our mutual predicament." Sonpear said.

"How's that, then?"

Sonpear said nothing and simply moved his right hand in a motion like he was turning some invisible dial, and the man with his knife in Pim's back – as well as two others within stabbing distance – rose from the floor of the ballroom making choking sounds and clutching their necks, their feet kicking beneath them for a purchase they could not find. Kali had seen such magical 'persuasion' techniques before but not to the extent Sonpear seemed to be taking them. She swallowed as the eyes of the infiltrators began to bulge, then turned away as Sonpear suddenly flicked his wrist and their heads snapped around a hundred and eighty degrees. Three dead weights fell to the floor with a thud.

"You didn't have to do that."

"Didn't I?"

"He's right, Miss Hooper," Jengo Pim interjected, gesturing for the bodies to be removed. "We are nothing without our code. These men needed to be taught that there should be honour among our kind."

"I think it's a little late for them to learn anything."

"I wasn't referring to the dead," Pim responded. He nodded to the others in the room and, as Kali looked, saw the change of attitude in them. The sense of insecurity that had pervaded the *Underlook* since she'd first arrived was gone now, replaced by a renewed and total allegiance to the true and proper leader of the Grey Brigade.

"I would suggest," Sonpear said to the other crossbow wielders around the room, "that you put those down. Now is a time to work together, not against one another."

Pim's men capitulated, and Pim himself rose from his throne with a relieved sigh.

"Right," he said. "Miss Hooper, get your people inside. Ferret, see to their wounded. Rathbone, once everyone's safely gathered in seal those bloody doors. I believe we have ourselves a siege situation."

The men went about their duties and it was only seconds later that the outside walls of the hotel reverberated with a series of impacts from outside, sifting dust from cracks in the ceiling of the ballroom. Many of the people from Gargas looked around in fear and hugged each other.

"They wasted no time," Kali said coolly. "Pim, are you sure this place is fully sealed?"

"Tight as an ogur's underpants," Pim said, glancing at Moon when his comment elicited a strange growl. "The question is, how long will the walls *themselves* hold."

Kali nodded. "The place is old but it's better than nothing. Still, we can't stay here for ever." She turned to Merrit Moon. "Old man, have you got any i –"

A sudden boom from outside, much louder than before, shook the hotel to its foundations, and Kali stopped speaking. Another such boom caused her to look around in alarm.

"What the hells?" she said.

"I believe that my people may be attempting to provide a solution," Poul Sonpear said.

"What the fark are they doing – bombing us?"

"In a manner of speaking."

Kali span to face Jengo Pim. "Is there any way to see?"

Pim nodded. "Upstairs, on the top floor, in the old turret room. Follow me."

Kali and Sonpear raced after Pim up flight after flight until they came to a small, circular chamber which Kali noticed, with some amusement, Pim appeared to have turned into a shrine to the Hells' Bellies, the walls plastered with handbills and memorabilia. What was evidently his *sanctum sanctorum* was otherwise featureless apart from a panoramic circle of shuttered windows. Pim moved to open one but Sonpear redirected him to another. "No, there. The view will be... better."

Puzzled, Pim did as he was told and flung the shutters wide, then stepped back as the full scale of what was occurring struck him. Kali pushed in beside him.

"My Gods!"

The eastern quarter of Andon spread out beneath her and there wasn't a street or an alleyway, a square or a cul-de-sac of it that wasn't overrun by the k'nid. Smoke, screams and chaos were the order of the day, and it seemed there was no escape from it anywhere. As Kali looked down in horror she saw at least ten people who had not managed to make cover stalked and taken by the k'nid, their skeletons left discarded on the scarred streets. It was not, however, the events that were occurring below her that made Kali gasp, but rather *above*. Because it seemed that ,in reaction to the invasion of their city, the Three Towers were going on the offensive.

Kali had been inside that complex and had heard it thrum with its strange power, had known it to be magical, but it was not until this moment that she realised just *how* magical it actually was. The three towers, that were the headquarters of the League of Prestidigitation and Prestige, were *moving*, each of them twining like immense snakes, the bridges that connected them having seemingly retracted – or perhaps simply disappeared – to enable this new and unexpected freedom. But it wasn't just the fact that they were moving that stunned Kali, it was what they were doing as they moved – and what they were doing were blitzing Andon. From the top of each of the looming, swaying structures, huge, orange balls of energy were being fired down into the streets, each so powerful that, as it departed its tower with a *thwoom,* Kali felt the floorboards of the hotel beneath her vibrate. The vibration was nothing, though, compared to the shaking that followed as the spheres impacted, not only at ground level but occasionally on rooftops as they targeted the k'nid wherever they were. Explosion after explosion lit the battle torn streets. Not only k'nid but buildings and people were blasted apart, flailing and spinning through the air.

"What the hells are they *doing*?" Kali demanded of Sonpear.

"It's the League's self protection protocol. The towers are defending themselves as best they can."

"You arrogant – this isn't the way, you bastard! Your people are destroying their own to protect themselves. You have to stop this!"

"There is nothing I can do. The Towers are sealed."

"Well, think of something, dammit! They're tearing Andon apart!"

Sonpear hesitated, clearly torn between his League responsibility and the damage that it was causing. For a second he just listened to the sound of the fireballs and to the battering the exterior of the hotel was taking from the k'nid.

"There might be weapons," he said finally, "that may prove more effective in an offensive than those you currently possess. There will, however, be some hazards involved in obtaining them."

"Pal, they can't be any more hazardous than opening that front door or waiting here while it gets blown off," Jengo Pim interjected. "What do you have in mind?"

Sonpear sighed, as if what he were about to announce he should not even be considering. He was about to speak when there was a sudden warning cry from Kali and he stared toward the Three Towers. Or rather, at the space *between* themselves and the Three Towers. Because one of the towers had turned towards them and, thrumming deeply as it came, growing larger every second, one of the fireballs was on direct collision course with the *Underlook.*

There was no time to run, nowhere to hide and absolutely nothing they could do. Heart pounding, the last thing Kali saw was Sonpear rushing at her, pushing Pim into the fireball's path. And then the fireball struck and the top of the Underlook was gone in a blazing inferno, just like that.

CHAPTER SEVEN

One thing made Kali question whether she was in the afterlife and that was that Jengo Pim seemed to be sharing eternity with her. When their times came she granted they might be near neighbours in whatever level of the hells she was despatched to – close enough to pop round for a cup of sulphur, perhaps – but, hey, she hadn't led the life of crime he had. She guessed, she had one or two redeeming features he hadn't, hadn't she?

She stared at Pim, picking himself up off the ground. He was staring at her in the same way she was staring at him – which was to say completely bemused - and it looked very much like he was thinking the same thing as she was, too. There was no way on Twilight the two of them couldn't be dead.

Both of them then turned to take in their surrounding. Or rather lack of them.

Wherever they were, it certainly *looked* like the afterlife. At least if one subscribed to the idea of it being some almost featureless limbo; dark, unoccupied and silent. The kind of place where one might wander until the Gods had counted up your good beads and bad beads on their divine abacus, or whatever the hells it was they did. It certainly *felt* like the afterlife, at least in the sense that her arrival here had left her rather numb. The one thing it didn't do was *smell* like the afterlife. But, to be honest, that was more likely to be Jengo Pim.

No wait, Kali thought, *and sniffed her underarm. Okay, it had been something of an energetic twenty four hours.*

"What," Pim said slowly, "just happened?"

Kali remembered the *Underlook*'s turret room; a series of fleeting images that included the fireball, Sonpear shouting a warning cry, and then him staring her in the face, shoving her back into Pim, *hard*. The shock she had felt in that moment – that Sonpear was saving his own skin – didn't tally with the look she saw on his face. It no longer struck her as homicidal but somehow desperate, as if the mage were doing the only thing he could in the circumstances.

"I think he pushed us..." Kali said, vaguely.

"Oh, the bastard pushed us all right. Right into an early grave."

"Do you *feel* dead?"

Pim looked himself up and down, patted his arms and legs and chest, frowned slightly when he noticed one of his sleeves was smoking gently. He patted it down. "Well, no, but..."

"Like I said, I think he pushed us out of the way. *Magically*, I mean. I think we're somewhere else."

Pim took a moment to absorb what Kali said. "Somewhere else? This looks like nowhere."

"That's exactly where I think it is. Nowhere. I think this is Domdruggle's Expanse."

"Who's what?"

"Domdruggle. His expanse. It's *another place* – an echo of our own, existing on a different plane. At least that's how the story goes. It's very old, supposed to be something of a myth."

Pim shrugged. "Something of a boring myth, if you ask me."

"No, we're just becoming acclimatised to it." She stared out into the dark. "Look, Pim. *Look.*"

The thieves' guild leader followed Kali's gaze, where shapes were indeed forming out of the nothingness, but instead of displaying an expression of wonderment, he frowned.

"You said it was an echo of our plane of existence. But if we're still where we were, it looks nothing like it."

"No, it doesn't, does it?" Kali said, smiling. She continued to gaze into the darkness, making out rolling fields, and vast fortresses and soaring towers in the distance. Things other than clouds or birds scudded across the sky.

Great, winged things. "That's because we're looking at the distant past."

"Are you telling me we've travelled through time?"

Kali shook her head. "Nope, we're exactly *when* we were. This is what Andon looked like when Domdruggle conjured the echo. Of course there was no Andon then, only the cities of the elves and the dwarves..."

She trailed off, her wonderment at what she was seeing coupled with the promise of what she could explore out there leaving her speechless. She almost left Pim and walked off into the ghostly landscape.

"So this is the time of the Old Races?" Pim asked.

"The memory of it. I wonder what day it was, what season, what year? *When* in their calendar was this?" She gazed up at the stars to see how different from her own time they were, but instead of seeing the stars saw something else, and gasped.

Kerberos loomed above, twice, three times the size it should have been. So immense its sphere was almost enveloping the planet, creating an eerie fogginess to the light. And that light was not the azure light they were used to but a deep, blood red.

"My Gods!"

"That doesn't look right," Pim observed, bleakly. "It's like it's *swallowing* Twilight."

Kali nodded. "I think this might be the End Time."

"End Time?"

"The time when the elves and the dwarves died. When the Old Races disappeared."

"What? You're saying that Kerberos *killed* them?"

Kali shook her head, not sure what to think. When she spoke, it was almost in a whisper. "I don't know. But by the looks of things I'd be willing to guess it had *something* to do with it."

"Perhaps one day soon, you should find out what, Kali Hooper," a voice said.

"What? *What?*"

"What?" Pim echoed. It seemed that he had heard nothing.

Kali rubbed the side of her skull, feeling a strange irritation, almost a scratching within.

"Awe inspiring, isn't it?" the voice said again, and this time it sounded more familiar. "Some say the whole expanse exists on the head of a pin."

"Sonpear?" Kali said.

"Sonpear?" Pim repeated.

"My apologies for your abrupt departure. In the circumstances, I am afraid I acted instinctively, my magic reflecting what was on my mind."

"Hey, don't worry about it," Kali said.

"You're talking to Sonpear?" Pim chipped in again.

"Yes!" Kali snapped. And then more slowly: "Although I'm not sure how."

"'Sending' and 'receiving' is my trade, Miss Hooper. Or had you forgotten?"

Kali hadn't. Sonpear's abilities as a telescrying spy had helped lead the Final Faith to the Clockwork King. She just hadn't realised his talents were quite so powerful.

"It isn't exactly telepathy," Sonpear went on, and Kali could almost *hear* a smile in his voice. "But I challenge any thaumaturgist to explain to me the difference."

"So you're a man of many talents. Does one of them include a way of getting us back from where you've sent us?"

"Do you not prefer to remain where it is safe? Do you not yearn to explore your new environment?"

Oh, Kali yearned to explore, all right – very much. But she also knew that now was not the time to do so. As it happened, Pim vocalised the question she was about to ask.

"How bad is the *Underlook*? How are our people?" he shouted into the air, turning as he did as if that might help Sonpear hear him better.

"There are no casualties. The fireball destroyed the hotel tower in quite dramatic fashion but the resulting damage was, thankfully, localised."

"I asked you a question! Answer me, dammit!"

"Um, I think only I can hear him," Kali pointed out.

Pim faltered. "Oh, right. Well, then, what did he say?"

"The fireball blew the roof off but, otherwise, everyone's all right."

"The turret's gone?" Pim said and, clearly thinking of his collection, his face darkened. "When this is over, I am going to sue the wands off those bastards in the League."

"*When* this is over. And somehow I don't think it will be unless we stop it."

"I'd welcome any suggestions as to what we can do," Pim said.

"Wait," Kali said, and then addressed Sonpear. "Earlier you said 'what was on your mind'? We were talking about weapons, Sonpear, so why should that make you think of this place? Are the weapons here?"

Sonpear sighed. "Among countless other artefacts. The Expanse was considered by the Guild to be a safe depository for such items, yes."

Kali remembered her visit to the Three Towers forbidden archive, where she had summoned virtual projections of its treasures, mere *representations* of the real things. But this was where the real deal was. This was where the artefacts actually *were*.

"Tell me where. They could help."

Sonpear paused. "I remain reluctant to do that. Such weapons, were they to find their way into the wrong hands, could easily tip the balance of power on the peninsula."

Kali slammed her hands on her hips and shouted at the sky, without feeling even vaguely foolish. "Sonpear, listen to me. In case you hadn't noticed the balance of power has already been tipped. In favour of the k'nid. *They* don't belong on the peninsula any more than these weapons do. Give us the means to fight them!"

"Proceed west," Sonpear instructed. "But I warn you again, Miss Hooper – there may be hazards involved."

"What kind of hazards?"

Sonpear hesitated again. "I pray that you do not find out." He sighed. "I need to cease our communication for now. The effort is exhausting."

"Okay. But, Sonpear, don't go far."

"Fear not. I shall return to you as soon as I am able, Miss Hooper."

Kali and Pim moved cautiously through the ghostly darkness, in a direction that, if they were on their own plane, would be taking them towards the Andon Heart. It was somewhat disorientating, the knowledge of what they were passing through back home jarring with the sights around them, the towers and spires in the distance, the topology of this unknown time. Amidst it all, however, there soon came visible something that was strangely familiar – and strangely disturbing.

Ahead, soaring above them were three thick and writhing pillars of energy, powerful not only in appearance but in the discomforting buzz they produced in Kali and Pim's bones. As she and the thieves guild leader moved closer, Kali saw that they were more than just pillars and seemed to be filled with the ghost-like hints of a floor level here, a doorway there, a staircase between them.

"This looks like –" Pim began.

"It is."

The almost impossible structure that was the headquarters of the League of Prestidigitation and Prestige had always generated speculation among the people of Andon as to how *exactly* it had been built and remained standing – with sorceries, surely, but now Kali and Pim knew the truth. The Three Towers had its foundations here in Domdruggle's Expanse, magically rooted in another plane of existence. In other words, it was unique. The only thing on Twilight that spanned two worlds.

As revelatory as that was, what grabbed Kali's attention more was that this translucent echo of the Three Towers wasn't empty, filled not with the mages who thronged there in its physical reality but a variety of objects that glowed more brightly than the structure itself. Kali knew immediately what she was looking at. The Forbidden Archive. It was one hells of a warehouse.

"Come on," she said to Pim.

The pair of them approached the towers slowly, Kali's head craning upward, Pim's turning from side to side, still taking in the Expanse and clearly not at ease with it.

"It's lonely here," he said. "Eerie. Soulless. Why do you suppose whatsisname – Domdruggle? – did this, conjured the Expanse? I mean, what possible purpose could it have?"

"Before seeing it, I'd have said your guess was as good as mine. But now we know *when* it was created – the End Time – maybe it was meant to be some kind of bolthole. Somewhere to hide. And don't ask me from what, because I haven't a clue."

"Bolthole? What, for the entire population of the peninsula? *All* the elves and the dwarves?"

"Why not? It's as big as our world."

"Yes, but..." Pim trailed off. "There's *nobody* here."

"I know, and that's what worries me."

"I don't follow."

Kali thought about the body of the dwarf she'd found in The Mole, that lonely metal coffin buried far deeper than any grave or resting place should be, and wondered again how it was that no one had come to help him.

"*If* Domdruggle conjured the Expanse as some kind of sanctuary from whatever wiped out the Old Races, they obviously never had time to come here. That suggests to me that they were gone, just like that."

"Pits of Kerberos, that fast?"

"Maybe."

"Fark."

"A question for another time, though eh? Right now we have our own problems, the main one being what the hells we're looking for."

"Allow me to assist you with that, Miss Hooper," Poul Sonpear interjected. "I would suggest the artefacts you seek will be found on the third level."

"Suggest as much as you like, Sonpear, but I've a better idea. Why don't *I* choose what'll be most effective against the k'nid?"

"You are there and have that prerogative, of course. I would question, however, how you would endeavour to transport from this place a dwarven sonic cannon, say, or a –"

"Okay, fine, point taken. So what are we looking for?"

"Portable armaments, light but powerful. In this case, discharge weapons. The elves called them crackstaffs."

"Crackstaffs?"

"You will recognise them when you see them."

"Right, fine. Third level it is, then." Kali moved forward then hesitated. "Sonpear, the stairs in this place – they are negotiable?"

"This Three Towers possesses residual corporeal mass, yes. But the experience of negotiating it may be a little disorientating."

Sonpear wasn't kidding, Kali soon discovered. The disorientation hit she and Pim as soon as they entered the structure, mainly because all of their senses persisted in telling them that they hadn't entered anywhere at all, misled by the translucency – and, in some areas, almost complete transparency – of the sorcerous manifestation. Kali couldn't describe it any other way than as weird – like walking through a hall of mirrors where the mirrors cast no reflection at all. Nevertheless, she and Pim managed to navigate their way to the central staircase and, treading warily on its insubstantial risers, made their way up to the third level.

Kali's heart thudded, though not from the climb. Laid out before her were any number of objects that she had summoned in the Three Towers' virtual forbidden archive many months ago. Though here, of course, they were real. They could be touched. Examined. *Explored.* And she longed to do all three. For a moment she felt that it wasn't fair that she was stuck with having to risk her life exploring all manner of lethal ruins when the League of Prestidigitation and Prestige had such a collection – perhaps years worth of adventuring! – here for the asking. But then she reminded herself of the lesson Merrit Moon had taught her long ago. Twilight simply wasn't ready for certain things, and that to unleash these objects on the world might well bring about catastrophe. Even so, who were the League to make such judgements? And could they even be trusted to be the guardians of such potentially devastating might? To be honest, she was actually a little surprised that they hadn't rolled out these big guns during the last war, because they would have been pretty much guaranteed to put Vos in its place.

"Here," Pim said, interrupting her train of thought. "These look pretty staff-like to me."

Kali moved to where Pim stood examining four racks of what appeared, at first glance, to be simple lengths of metal. But closer inspection revealed them to be inscribed with complex runics and tiny studs that had to be part of a magetech device. The metal tubes seemed to be of different ages and all had been preserved in varying states of wear and tear. This suggested to Kali that they had been collected from various locations, rather than a single source. Perhaps some of them – the more dented and bashed ones – even from some long ago won or lost battlefield. But if they had been used in battle, she wondered who the combatants might have been, because from the look of them they came from the third age of dwarven and elven development, when the two races should have been at peace. She sighed at the fact that it was just one more puzzle to ponder over.

What mattered now was that they worked and, to that end, Kali hefted one of the tubes from a rack and was surprised to find herself thrown of balance because the object was so light. It was strange because the staff *felt* heavy – cold, hard, unyielding – and yet it was perfectly balanced and weighed so little that she could spin it in the palm of her hand. One possible reason for that, she discovered, was that it was hollow. Thinking that Sonpear had sold them a dud, she first shook it and then peered down its length, moving it around until she had Pim framed in a small circle. It took the thieves guild leader a second to spot what she was doing but, when he did, he waved and frowned.

"Do you mind?" he said, stepping out of the way. "That thing could go off."

"Don't see how. Unless there's a rack of blowdarts around here somewhere."

"Even so..."

"But," Kali mused to herself, "I suppose it has to be called a crackstaff for a reason."

It was, as Kali discovered that very second.

What *exactly* she had touched on the length of metal she had no idea but, whatever it was, it appeared to have been the 'on' switch. Kali suddenly found herself blown backwards as a bolt of blue energy fired from the crackstaff with a recoil like a kick from a giant mool. Winded and dazed, Kali slid to the floor and watched the powerful bolt of energy that had been discharged still fizzling away around the edges of a jagged hole in the far wall. Instead of a pained expression crossing her face Kali began, slowly, to grin.

"Wuhh-ow."

"Hells," Jengo Pim said softly, echoing the sentiment. "How the hells did it –?"

Kali flipped herself up onto her feet.

"No idea," she said, moving over to the racks and sweeping up as many of the crackstaffs as she could carry, before thrusting them at Pim. "Maybe these tubes channel magical threads or maybe they somehow *concentrate* them but one thing's for sure – they work. Pim, we've got something with which we can even up the fight a little bit."

"I'm not so sure we have – *yet*." Pim said slowly.

"What are you talking about? Pim, we don't have much time so grab some more if you can!"

"Miss Hooper, I think we have company."

"What?" Kali said.

For the first time she noticed the thieves guild leader was staring past her, back towards the stairway they had used to get here, and followed his gaze. Several things were climbing – no, *sweeping* – up the stairs towards them. Spectral, ghostly shapes that Kali couldn't quite pin down enough to identify but knew immediately she didn't like.

"Oh, fark. I guess there is no such thing as a free lunch."

"I warned you this might prove hazardous," Poul Sonpear's voice commented. "I am afraid your careless use of the crackstaff has disturbed them."

"Them? Them, who? All right, Sonpear, so these are your hazards but what in all the hells *are* those things?"

"We call them residuals. They have become attracted to your vital energy."

"I'm flattered." The figures had reached the top of the stairs now and she could see them in a little more detail. "Wait a minute. Are they what I think they are?"

"They *were* what you think they are."

"How can that be?"

"It is believed that when Domdruggle created his expanse there were sacrifices that had to be made. An area effect at the point of conjuration that ended the lives of Domdruggle and they who assisted with the ritual, condemning them to a half-life here in the Expanse. They volunteered for it, Miss Hooper, elves *and* dwarves, but now I doubt that they even remember who or what they were. They know only what it *felt* like to be and hunger for that feeling, still."

"Hunger. Okay, I'm not sure I like the sound of that. So, they're attracted to us *why* exactly?"

"To extract the life force from your bodies. Make your souls part of the Expanse."

"Gotcha. Sonpear, why didn't you tell me about these things before?"

"There was a chance you would not encounter them, and so I did not wish to worry you."

"Next time, Sonpear. Give me *all* the facts." Kali grabbed another crackstaff from the rack, then shoved the thieves guild leader. "Out of the way, Pim."

Bracing herself this time, she aimed and pressed the same stud she thought she had previously used, gratified to find she'd made the right choice.

A crackling lance of blue energy shot impacted in the centre of the approaching residuals. But instead of blowing them apart, as she had hoped, the lance passed through them harmlessly, doing no more damage than a hand might wafting at some fog. It did something, though, because the spectral figures suddenly quickened their approach, coming right at her with a renewed determination.

"Shit."

Suddenly they were close enough for Kali to see them in full detail. She could make out wasted bodies and haunted faces with gaping mouths and what she thought might be weapons. With flowing beards or streak-like, angular heads, they looked as if someone had drawn them on the landscape and then had a hasty rethink, half rubbing them out with repeated swipes of an eraser.

Kali staggered backwards as one of them screeched like a banshee and slammed into her. Then, with a cry of alarm, she scissored back to avoid the wisps of a blade whooshing by where her stomach had been. The passing blade left behind tracers, like tiny furls of mist.

Somewhat aggrieved by the development, Kali threw a punch in retaliation but, as had the energy lance, her fist went straight through. Next to her, Pim suffered the same experience.

Now *that* was a little unfair. They could touch them but not the other way round? In the circumstances there was only one thing they could do. Dodging another rush, Kali pulled off her belt and made a makeshift strap for her back before grabbing an armful of crackstaffs and snapping her gaze at Pim, instructing him to do the same.

"Run," she then said to the thieves guild leader.

"Where? There are more of them on the stairs!"

Kali thought fast. "The hole I made. Out through there."

"This is the third level!"

"You got a problem with that?"

"Yes!"

"Pim, trust me – just do as I do."

Pim swallowed. "Go."

The residuals hot on their trail, the pair of them raced for the breach in the Three Towers wall and hurled themselves through. It was the first time that Kali had been grateful for what she considered the somewhat disturbing design of the Three Towers. Because, as she expected, the two plummeted out not into empty air but onto the tapering, semi-organic slope that, at their base, was a more gentle incline than further above. *More* gentle but they weren't out of the frying pan yet. The pair landed on the taper on their behinds, bouncing slightly and scrabbling for purchase to slow their descent before riding it down towards ground level, then tumbling into a heap at its base. Behind and above them, the residuals – probably about fifteen of them now – poured through the breach. Untroubled by such considerations as gravity, they began to sweep down towards them.

Kali quickly picked herself up. "Move!"

"I hate to repeat myself, but where exactly?"

"Away from here!" Kali shouted, already on the move. She tilted her head to the sky. "Sonpear!"

"You are doing the right thing, Miss Hooper. Avoid physical contact of any kind."

"I *know* that, dammit! Can you just get us the hells out of here?"

"I am endeavouring to prepare a return portal. Continue in your current direction and please be patient."

"Patient!" Kali repeated breathlessly as she glanced behind her.

The residuals had formed themselves into one amorphous mass that was pursuing them with even greater speed. What was worse, they seemed no longer content simply to chase. From within the mass they were hurling or firing the weapons they wielded and, disturbingly, they shot ahead of the mass in whip-like tendrils before snapping back to their owners to be launched at them again and again, narrowly missing each time.

"What the hells are those things?" Pim shouted. "Remember I'm only getting half this conversation."

"Er, can we go into that some other time?" Kali requested in a slightly higher pitch than normal.

She ducked as a hail of elven arrows pierced the air where her head had been a moment before, petering out into wisps ahead of her before, again, snapping back. Pim's question had raised one of her own. Namely why it was that Domdruggle's assistants – *if* she was right about the time he had conjured the Expanse – possessed such archaic weaponry. She could only put it down to some kind of race memory manifestation of their forms. It didn't really matter, though, did it? What *did* matter was that they were deadly and were not going to miss for much longer.

Kali muttered something as she continued to run, still seeing no escape route ahead of her.

"What?" Pim asked, breathlessly.

"Oh, just reflecting on something Sonpear said."

"What?"

"Just that this is a farking big pin."

"The portal is forming now, Miss Hooper," Sonpear advised. "Please try to stay alive a few moments longer."

"Oh, right," Kali responded. She could now see something materialising a couple of hundred yards ahead of her – like a small storm cloud. "Actually, I was going to stop, turn and blow them a kiss."

"There is no need for sarcasm."

"Well, for pits sake!" Despite her words, Kali *did* turn, if only to glance over her shoulder to gauge the gain the residuals had made, and promptly wished that she hadn't. Because something *else* was materialising behind them, looming over them – something spectral and massive that, in the brief moment she saw it, she could have sworn was a giant face.

"Pim, I don't want to worry you but –"

"Now what?" the thieves guild leader said.

He, too, snatched a glance over his shoulder and promptly turned white. For what Kali had seen was indeed a giant face; gaunt, sunken and haunted. It regarded them hungrily with huge shadowed eye sockets and an oval of a mouth that was slowly widening into an all-encompassing maw.

It swooped down towards them, clearly intent on sweeping them into that maw. And it roared deafeningly as it came.

"What the hells!" Pim shouted.

"Domdruggle, I think."

"Ah. Run faster?"

"Run faster."

The pair of them put on a final, desperate burst of speed and closed the gap between themselves and the now partly formed portal. Kali thought that she could see the interior of the *Underlook* through it and, despite its current circumstances, nothing had ever seemed so welcoming. The only question now was, would they make it? Because behind them Domdruggle had accelerated beyond the amorphous mass of his assistants and the maw that had been his mouth seemed, like some dislocated jaw, to be stretching unnaturally forward, ready to scoop the pair of them inside. Kali could no longer hear Pim's shouts of alarm as the Expanse seemed now to consist only of a looming darkness and a deafening roar. For a second her own scream of protest at her faltering body was completely lost as the maw drew alongside, and then around, her running form.

Her last thoughts as the Expanse faded were: *Jump now, Pim, now! Sonpear, this had better farking work.*

Suddenly, she could hear herself screaming, and then she was crashing into something hard. The realisation that she was back in the *Underlook* was interrupted as she felt something collide with her equally hard. She and Pim found themselves in a tangle on the floor, being stared at by a number of the Grey Brigade and Gargassians whose mouths were agape. She was vaguely aware that, across the room, Sonpear was gesticulating madly, managing to just close the portal as a grey and fog-like snout burst through with the haunting echo of the roar that had been deafening her only moments before. Then, it was gone.

Kali coughed. "Okay, that was interesting."

"You have a knack for understatement," Pim said, dusting himself down. The thieves guild leader wasted no time in getting back to the business of their own reality, frowning as he listened to the k'nid battering still at the outside of the hotel.

"How's the situation?" he asked one of his lieutenants.

"The walls won't last very much longer. Reckon maybe ten minutes or so before they're breached."

Pim sighed. "Then it's time we took the fight to them." He dumped the bundle of crackstaffs on a table. "These are weapons.

Anyone who feels they're up to it, take one. We'll show you how they work in a moment." Pim's men hesitated. "Well? What are you waiting for?"

"There's another problem," Sonpear announced, stepping forward. "The fireballs, the k'nid, they did something to your friend. He went crazy when the turret room exploded, *changed*. And he went outside, as if looking for revenge. The old man's out there in the middle of the bastards. He's missing."

CHAPTER EIGHT

Kali had no idea how long she and Pim had been in the Expanse, but it had been long enough for Andon to turn into a full-fledged warzone.

The city was all but obscured by smoke and dust, filled with the sound of explosions and agonised screams. Her plan to take the fight to the k'nid began as soon as she, Pim and the other volunteers flung open the doors of the *Underlook* and began blasting their way out of the alleyway. Bolts of blue crackled into the narrow space, filling it with so much magical energy that it was at first difficult to tell whether the crackstaffs were effective against the k'nid. But the gratifying crunch of their blasted and twitching chitinous bodies beneath their feet, as they continued to advance towards the Andon Heart, soon told them what they wished to know. Their fight had just got a little more even.

Kali and the others burst into the marketplace and fanned out, beams lancing out to take down the k'nid who had made it their business to consume the market stalls. Their targeting was not random, each shot chosen quickly but carefully, and Kali found herself impressed by the marksmanship of Pim and his men. K'nid after k'nid were blasted, screeching, scuttling and dismembered. She supposed the dexterity of hands trained to slip a wallet from a pocket, without a hint it had ever been there, had other uses, too.

She wished only that the same were true of the Three Towers. The spires continued to blast away above them and this close to the structure, in its very shadow in fact, she could feel the raw power. A power that made her limbs feel weak and her brain tight. Such power did not, however, stop those k'nid who had chosen the towers as their target from flinging themselves at its sides. As she watched they joined an earlier assault wave, working away at the tallow-like walls to find a way to the mages inside. Kali debated giving the mages a helping hand by blasting the k'nid away, but only for a second. As far as she was concerned the League could stand or fall by its own devices, as they had so callously left the people outside to stand or fall by theirs.

The marketplace cleared, Kali and the others moved on into the streets where they split up to cover the warren of small streets and alleyways individually.

As she worked her way along one such street, Kali could hear the discharge of crackstaffs echoing all around her, and she smiled slightly at the damage that was obviously being meted out. Firing as she moved, her attention was nevertheless split between the next target and the location of Merrit Moon. She thought she caught sight of the old man – in his ogur form – once, but only as a possible presence amidst a small hill of swarming k'nid who were being batted and tossed aside. The chaos of the streets, however, prevented her from reaching him before he had moved on, leaving a path of destruction in his wake. Soon after, their paths almost crossed once more – but this time the old man's presence was announced only by a prolonged and savage roar of fury that was carried to her from beyond the rooftops, a street or maybe three away. By this time, however, Kali was beginning to realise that she had other, more relevant concerns.

The fact was, the sound of discharging crackstaffs that had been so prevalent not so long before was lessening somewhat. What was worse, she was beginning to hear cries of alarm and screams that she somehow knew came from Pim's people.

It did not take her long to work out why. The alarm bells from the city walls were ringing again and, glimpsed in streets all around her, Kali saw more k'nid were entering the fray, flocking to their unnatural brethren and bringing reinforcements into the battle that seemed inexhaustible. She and Pim and his people had made a difference in the defence of the city, but the fact was there were just too many of the creatures and more were coming all the time.

"We have to pull back!" Kali shouted to one of Pim's men as he stumbled out an alleyway nearby, his crackstaff firing into the shadows.

The thief looked at her, his face desperate, and Kali staggered back as she realised half of it was a bloody mess, all but gone.

"They just keep coming," he gasped. "There's no stoppi –"

As he spoke, two k'nid sprang from the alley and enveloped him. In the time it took his face to crumple in horror he was no more than a pile of steaming bones on the ground. Kali could do nothing but fire off a couple of bolts in retaliation and then, as more k'nid poured from alleyways and began to pursue her, she turned and ran. All she could do was try to carry the message to Pim and the others herself now.

Spinning occasionally to fire her crackstaff at the pursuing k'nid, Kali raced along the street, weaving from side to side as the fireballs from the Three Towers continued to pummel down, obliterating buildings all around her and forcing her to duck or roll as great chunks and shards of stone exploded across her path.

Damn the League, she thought.

They actually seemed – probably in increasing desperation – to be intensifying their bombardment and if their self preservation protocol continued like this, they'd be responsible for as many Andonian deaths as the k'nid themselves.

And she'd be one of them if she didn't get into some kind of cover soon.

Kali dodged into a side alley but there found herself tripping over her own feet, her route blocked by a man busied with another pack of k'nid streaming in from its other end. He was holding his ground well but, whoever he was, he wasn't one of Pim's men and he wasn't using a crackstaff to defend himself. In fact, he wasn't using any kind of weapon at all, except himself.

Bursts of fire, ice and magical energy roared and cracked from his fingertips, wielded against his attackers to devastating effect. She'd seen shadowmages at work before – mainly using their magics against *her* – but never one who handled the threads with such absolute confidence, dexterity and power. Tall and becloaked – with a handsome, if weather beaten, face visible beneath the hood – he wove complex patterns with his hands that seemed less the result of years of dedicated training than a natural, instinctive affinity with the craft.

"Nice handiwork," Kali said, running to his position. K'nid followed her in, thrashing at her heels. Too many of them.

"You, too," the man said. "Saw you earlier – some of the moves you pulled off. *Look out!*"

Kali span, firing burst after burst at the k'nid and found herself pressed back to back with the stranger. She could feel him lurch with each magical bolt that he unleashed and they balanced each other as she expended the power of her crackstaff.

"Yes, well, I seem to have a peculiar knack for what I do," she shouted over her shoulder.

"Me, too."

"The name's Kali Hooper."

"Lucius Kane."

"Pleased to meet you, Lucius. But unless we break this up and get the hells out of this pitsing bottleneck, we're stuffed."

"Not quite the language I'd use to describe our present predicament, but wholeheartedly agreed. Ideas, Miss Hooper?"

Kali glanced upward, at the walls tightly confining the alleyway. High and sheer, they seemed to be the only buildings in Andon that hadn't been buttressed with balconies, makeshift extensions or dropbogs of some kind. As such they would be near impossible to scale. She knew she could make it up with a few well-timed moves but the question was what good would that do her new comrade-in-arms?

"The only way out seems to be up. But..."

"Up it is, then. Shall we?"

"Shall we wha –?"

Before Kali could finish, she felt Kane's back detach from her own, and then caught a glimpse of a flitting and dwindling shadow above. There might have been nothing for the man to cling on to but he apparently didn't *need* anything, rapidly flinging himself up some invisible ladder in the wall that only he could see. As far as Kali knew, there was no 'invisible ladder' spell in the grimoire or whatever it was these people used. So what the hells was he doing – using the *threads* themselves as rungs? Gods, yes, it seemed that was exactly what he was doing, using the threads as *physical* things, manipulating the world itself to his own ends. She had never seen any – *any* – shadowmage do that before.

He was looking back down at her and *grinning*.

Bastard!

Despite their predicament, he was clearly throwing down a challenge and, with a roar of determination, she kicked off after him, booting two k'nid out of the way. She used the subsequent scramble of the pack's bodies as a launching pad to throw herself up against one wall and then another, each time higher and higher, repeating the process until she had caught up with Kane.

Kali flipped herself over the edge of the roof.

"Not very gentlemanly," she gasped, "leaving a helpless girl alone like that."

"You're no helpless girl, and you know it."

"That's as maybe but –" Kali stopped suddenly, and it was her turn to shout a warning. "Kane!"

Somehow, one of the k'nid had managed to follow them to the roof, and was leaping for the shadowmage as she shouted. Spotting it, Kane's arm shot out and, for a moment, Kali thought he was about to unleash another elemental bolt, but that wasn't what he was doing at all. Instead, he punched the k'nid solidly as it came, but instead of knocking it back, his fist disappeared *inside* its chitinous shell so that the creature was caught, dangling, thrashing and impaled, on the end of his arm. Impossible enough that the man had somehow penetrated its natural armour, Kali thought, but what he did next actually made her stagger back. His mouth twisting into a grimace, his eyes widening and staring at the creature directly, Kane seemed somehow to suck the very life from it. The k'nid crumpled and decomposed in seconds, leaving behind a brittle and lifeless husk.

The shadowmage shrugged the remains off and crushed them beneath his boot. Clearly, what he had just done had been *nothing* to him.

Kali stared.

"Who *are* you?"

Silhouetted by the fiery oranges of the ongoing bombardment from the Three Towers, Kane stared back. And when the shadowmage spoke, somehow Kali knew his words were as much about her as they were about himself. What was more, she saw reflected in his eyes the same inner torment that she had felt ever since the day she had begun to realise that she was... different.

"That," he said, "remains to be seen."

With those words, Kane turned and manoeuvred himself over the other side of the roof. Their brief liaison had been, it appeared, just that.

"Wait!" Kali said. "What plans do you have now?"

Kane inclined his head towards the Three Towers. "I have business at the League of Prestidigitation and Prestige. Suggestions that might help the current crisis. And you?"

"Like you. Try to stop these bastards. But first I have to find the old man."

"Old man?"

"A friend. He went missing during the assault."

"And what is this friend's name?"

"Merrit Moon. Bad haircut, beard, pink horse blanket. Or, actually, he could still be big, green and roaring. It's, um, a long story. Have you seen him?"

"No. But I might be able to help you find him."

"Be glad of any help."

"Call it a professional courtesy."

"You're on. How about I take the west gate and you the –?"

"Not *physically*. Have you anything that belongs to the old man?"

"No, I –" Kali began, then thought again. "Wait." She dug in her equipment belt, pulling something out from its very bottom and shoving it in Kane's hand. The shadowmage regarded the mouldy, half eaten pie with an unfathomable expression.

"He baked it for me," Kali said. "About four years ago."

Kane smiled slightly and, without elaborating, moved his arm out above the rooftops in a gesture that looked half salute and half as if he were sowing seeds, and Kali swore that some kind of fine, shimmering dust took to the air. Kane waited for a few seconds while this dust settled and then pointed in the direction of the city walls, where a faint glow could now be seen rising from street level like a beacon. "There. Your friend is there."

"How in the hells did you –"

But Kane was gone.

"There one minute, gone the next," Kali shrugged, and smiled. "Lot like myself, really."

Wasting no time, Kali took a few steps back from the roof edge and then ran, leaping the gap between the building and its neighbour, reckoning that the safest and quickest way to reach Moon's beacon was by rooftop, avoiding the battleground below. Thankfully, her progress towards the city walls was taking her away from the epicentre of the k'nid invasion, the creatures – with the help of the towers' fireballs – having already devastated this part of Andon and moved on. Thus it was that when she finally dropped back down to street level, she found herself in an area of relative calm in the shadow of the city wall itself. There a few scattered guards and civilian survivors had set up a makeshift field hospital that, so far, had gone unnoticed by the k'nid. Still, they were close and while those who tended tried to help those they could, or comfort the maimed and dying where they couldn't, they were forced to stifle their moans or sobs with their hands as they worked.

The old man wasn't among them, but he was nearby. Kali found him in the doorway of the bunker where she had left Horse, talking to the beast. But her relief at the discovery that the two of them were still alive was lessened somewhat by the appearance of the old man.

Kali bit her lip as she approached, taking in the fact that he was all but slumped in position. The shallow breathing and raised and pulsing veins on his arms, coupled with his bloodshot eyes, were testimony to the fact that he had only recently recovered from a full Thrutt transformation.

But, by the look of things, Thrutt had sated himself before he had burned out. The bloodied and cracked remains of various k'nid covered the old man's clothes, along with a considerable amount of blood from the old man himself.

"We are losing this battle, young lady," Moon breathed, wearily.

"I know, old man." She only hoped that those she had despatched back to the *Underlook* were not facing their last stand. "I know."

"It is good to see, however, that you have not become one of its victims."

Kali smiled. "Not for the want of their trying. The k'nid *and* the pitsing League."

Moon sighed. "I don't think the latter will be a problem any longer. Observe, young lady."

Kali turned and, as she did, noticed two things – that all of those who were able in the makeshift hospital were turning to look the same way, and that the incessant thrumming and pounding of the fireballs from the League had ceased. And with good reason.

As the people around her stared, muttering curses, words of disbelief or even prayers to their Gods, she saw that the Three Towers had given up on its offensive. Its soaring and majestic towers were doing something she had never seen them do before, or even *knew* they could do. They were *twining* around each other, apparently for protection, looking for all the world like the tails of whipped curs.

And, even from this distance, Kali could see swarms of k'nid skittering up their heights, scrabbling for a way in.

"If the Three Towers has fallen, Andon has fallen," Merrit Moon said, matter-of-factly. He eased himself up with a groan, to stand by his protégé. "It's up to us, now, young lady. We must reach the Drakengrats and stop these things at their source, find a means to destroy them. And we must *hurry*."

"You think more of the k'nid are coming?"

"Oh, that I don't doubt – but more coming is not the only problem. I saw it when I fought them, when *Thrutt* fought them. When the k'nid have consumed a certain amount, they *duplicate* themselves. Their numbers are doubling at a regular rate, Kali, and eventually there will be so many that their presence will be absolute."

"I saw it happening. When they first stormed the walls."

"That isn't all. They consume *everything* and their presence must already be changing the land, making it unsuitable for crops, for livestock, for *any* kind of habitation. Why they're doing this I don't know, but soon they will cover the peninsula like a living shroud and the damage will be irreversible."

"Gods, Merrit... how long?"

"A week."

"*Five days*?"

"Five days. No more."

Kali's face set with determination. "Then I'd better get a move on."

"*I*?"

"Old man, you're in no state to –"

"Pardon me, Miss," one of the guards interjected. He looked exhausted. "A moment ago, your grandfather mentioned travel to the Drakengrats?"

Despite the circumstances, Merrit Moon coughed and said something under his breath. Kali patted him.

"He did." Kali said, warily.

"Then I'm sorry, but our scouts report the Vos military have closed the border at the Anclas Territories. Apparently, their population centres have taken considerable damage and their people are crowding the old war shelters, and they refuse to compound their crisis by allowing anyone from Pontaine through. All refugees are being detained at the border."

"They're leaving us to our own fate," Moon said. "Sealing us in with the k'nid."

"The bastards. It isn't even *their* land." Kali said.

She considered their options. The fact was, she could probably make it through Vos's defensive lines but it would be a tricky business. One wrong move and, in the current state of trigger-happiness Vossian retribution might encompass execution of the refugees. She couldn't and wouldn't risk that. But, still, she had to reach the Drakengrats. There had to be a way.

She suddenly realised that there was. And that it might even expedite matters.

"Would you excuse us, please?" she said to the guard, and then turned to Moon. "Old man, I need you to take Horse and get to the *Flagons*, take a message to Aldrededor for me."

"I'm *coming* with you."

"*No*, you're not. You and Horse are both out of this fight but can still help by doing what I ask. I reckon Horse has one more jump in him so use it to get to the *Flagons*. It, er, might be a little noisy but, trust me, you'll be safe there."

Moon looked puzzled, and his eyes narrowed. "What are you planning, young lady?"

Kali told him.

"What? O-ho, no, young lady, no." The old man stared at her. "Impossible! It would take specialist equipment, mapping, planning, *weeks* of preparation. Your own research has shown what a potentially deadly maze they might be, unstable and likely collapsed at multiple points, to say nothing of the fact that you have no idea *what's down there*." He shook his head, adamant. "No, young lady, be realistic. You'll never make it through."

"Since when have I been realistic, old man?" She stared at him and smiled. "Besides, as far as specialist equipment goes, I think I have just the thing."

CHAPTER NINE

The Lost Canals of Turnitia.

Kali had been planning to explore them for as long as she could remember. They were, however, a massive undertaking. Some references she had unearthed about them suggested that they went on for hundreds of leagues and, until now, somewhere between the planning and the exploration of them, something had always managed to get in the way. Last year, there had been the matter of the Red Queen, for instance, and only a few months before she'd been considering their allure when she had been distracted by the small affair of the Clockwork King. Her current circumstances were perhaps not the ideal ones in which to finally fulfil her ambition, but Kali was quietly relieved that fate had pushed her in this direction and she had to admit that she was more than a little excited by the prospect ahead of her.

The journey from Andon had taken her a day and a half, moving slowly and cautiously through the stonewood forests of southern Pontaine, on a horse hired from the city wall stables, which she had dismounted and slapped back home when she had neared the Anclas Territories. She had used the cover of the forests not only to avoid the k'nid, but also to avoid the gaze of the surveillance scopes with which the Vossian army had equipped their forts.

Dividing the peninsula – and thus Vos and Pontaine – like a great thick belt, the Anclas Territories stretched from Freiport in the north to Turnitia in the south, and had once been neutral farmland. After the Great War between Vos and Pontaine, however, the former had wasted no time in establishing a number of forts on the land whose official reason for existence – the protection of the Vos Empire – had always struck Kali as somewhat ironic considering that it was they who had invaded Pontaine in the first place. Whatever the politics of it, Pontaine, battered by the war, had been in no position to dispute the placements. While they remained little more than observation posts, the number of additional forts, garrisons and service structures that had grown alongside and between them over the intervening years, had transformed Vos's presence in the area from a broken series of scattered bases to a virtual wall, over which they held complete autonomy and control. They hadn't exercised its strategic power until now, allowing relatively free trade and passage between the neighbouring states, like Pontaine, having no wish to precipitate another conflict, but in doing so it had become abundantly clear how insidious its growth had been to the area. Simply put, when they had closed the borders they had had the capability to do it literally. There was no way through.

Lucky, then, that Kali hadn't wanted to go through. All she'd had to do was make sure they didn't see what it was that was going *under* it. And the two bound and gagged and struggling guards at her feet were testimony to the fact that she had succeeded.

Kali stood, now, on one of the more remote guard towers towards the southern end of the Territories, staring through the surveillance scope with which the guards had unwillingly provided her. The looks on their faces as she had suddenly appeared before them, forty feet up in the air, had been priceless.

While they weren't to know that she had, in fact, been dangling from a strip of shadow wire at the time, their surprise had lasted long enough for her to be able to slam their heads together, disabling them before they could sound the alarm. The action had been necessary because, out of all the towers in the Anclas line, it was this one that overlooked her destination. Or, to be more accurate, the *entrance* to her destination; one of the huge roundels to which she had given the name *dropshaft*.

That was the thing about the Lost Canals of Turnitia – they were not lost in the sense that no one had been able to find them. They were only lost in the sense that they had been long abandoned. *Long, long* abandoned by Kali's reckoning. Because, as far as she could make out, the inscriptions on the dropshafts were neither elven nor dwarven and seemed to her old enough to predate both. What exactly the implications of that were, she had no more clue than she had to what purpose the dropshafts served. In all the time she had been planning an expedition to the canals, she had located three of the dropshafts, one south east of Scholten, one west, near Malmkrug, and the third here, near the coastal city of Turnitia. That Turnitia had been honoured with giving its name to the canals was not, though, in reference to this particular dropshaft but rather that – unique among the canal network – this part of the coast had once had an entrance to the canals leading in from the *sea*.

Kali trained the surveillance scope to the north east, and it was from that direction, from the *Flagons*, that she expected her companion to come. Anytime now.

Sure enough, as she watched a small, though bulky and unnatural, shape appeared on the horizon and began moving towards her, weaving erratically in a way that suggested its driver was not quite used to the controls. As she had instructed in her note, the headlights of the machine had been dimmed upon approaching the Anclas Territories.

It was time to go, to make her rendezvous. But first she had to make sure that two sets of eyes did not lay sight on something they shouldn't. It was Merrit Moon's old edict, told to her long ago in the *Warty Witch*. Certain discoveries from the world's past had to be kept to themselves, for *everyone*'s peace of mind. So, to ensure the guards neither saw nor heard the approaching dwarven artefact, Kali smiled sweetly and apologized. Then she bent down and punched both guards hard on the nose, knocking them cold before leaping onto the shadow wire and lowering herself to the ground.

Now came the hard part.

Kali had left the actual opening of the dropshaft until the last minute because she had not wanted any Vossian patrol stumbling across it in the dark, ruining not only her privilege of being the first person to access the network in an unimaginable time, but also any chance of a successful stealth operation into the bargain. She reckoned she had perhaps fifteen minutes before The Mole reached her and in that time, she would put into practice what she had been researching ever since she had first learned of the canals' existence.

One of the more unusual aspects of the dropshafts was that they were sealed with a metal door containing one of the most complex locking mechanisms Kali had ever seen. It was designed, if an attempt to open it was made incorrectly, to jam the chambers in place permanently, preventing anyone ever accessing it again. One thing was certain – whoever had built these things had gone to extreme measures to ensure no unauthorised person could access them, accidentally or otherwise.

Just what the hells were they going to such lengths to conceal?

Reaching the dropshaft, Kali worked slowly and carefully, following the diagram in her head that she had worked out over long nights at her table by the Captain's Chest. First, she disengaged the perimeter safeguards, then locked down the punchbolts in a predetermined order and, finally, released the chambers one by one, until the entire centre of the dropshaft door rotated counter-clockwise. She moved to the right of the metal plate, repeating the procedure – though, when it came to the punchbolts, in a different order – until, again, the centre of the door rotated, this time clockwise.

Kali sighed with relief. There was only one thing left to do.

Directly in the centre of the door, a circle of ten metal projections rose from the otherwise flat surface. These, she knew, had to be depressed in exactly the right order, otherwise the entire process would cancel itself out. There was only one problem – according to the ancient records she had found, the order was different for each of the dropshafts, and there was absolutely no indication of which order applied to which dropshaft. She had a one in three chance of success, so it was lucky, then, that she liked a gamble.

Tongue sticking out of her mouth, she crouched on her haunches and tried to put herself in the mind of whoever had last – if ever – operated the projections. Then, swallowing, she plumped for the third from the left, depressing it with a strenuous groan, until it was almost flush with the surface of the plate. There, with a metallic boom, it locked into place. Bingo – but that was the easy one, because two of the sequences started with that projection. The sixth from the left, then, or the eighth, the antepenultimate one? The eighth. She was sure it was going to be the eighth, and after that it would be plain sailing.

Be sure. Be very sure.

Kali depressed the eighth projection. There was another metallic boom. She cast a quick glance around all the perimeter chambers and they all seemed to be remaining in place. *Yes!* she thought.

Boom. Boom, boom, boom.

The locks were cancelling.

Shi –

All kinds of things went through Kali's mind, not least how stupid she had been. With her one-in-three chance of success, she had been presuming that the three sequences related to the three dropshafts she knew of, but if the sequence she was using was *wrong* that meant there was another one out there somewhere. This made the network potentially even bigger than she thought! The thrill she felt at the prospect was, however, rather comprehensively subsumed in the fierce rush of adrenalin produced by the realisation that she had only seconds to stop her work being in vain.

With a grunt of exertion she flung herself across the dropshaft plate, whipping a small metal bar from her equipment belt and jamming it between the chamber bolts before they could slam shut. The collision of metal on metal vibrated the whole plate and almost took Kali's hand off, but at least it had prevented the reverse sequence going any further. But it was not the only one. Kali back-flipped, grabbing another metal cylinder from her belt and jammed it into the second chamber feed before sighing in relief. That should have been that but Kali's interfering with the delicate balance of the locks and chambers had clearly knocked the whole mechanism out of kilter. She looked around in disbelief as chambers and punchbolts began to engage and disengage themselves in no particular order and with ever increasing speed.

Dammit. There had *to be an order to it somewhere.*

As she leapt around blocking or freeing those bolts that *looked* as if they should go this way or that, Kali tried to visualise the underworkings of the dropshaft plate. Rapid calculation after rapid calculation followed, Kali flinging herself here and there like something possessed, and she was beginning to think that she'd be doing this until she dropped dead of exhaustion when there was a sudden heavy clank from beneath her.

The plate had just released itself.

It began to rise.

There was only one problem. If Kali were to keep it open she had to remain in the position she was in, a kind of crooked spreadeagle with the sole of her left foot jamming one punchbolt, the calf of her right leg another, one hand pushing upward to block yet another, and a painfully positioned elbow blocking the last. She looked as if she were posing for some strange art class.

The plate had risen fully now, and Kali with it, and while she could not see what was beneath it, she *could* smell it. A dank, briny mouldiness that was redolent of the rot of ages. It made her want to gag. She didn't, though, because her mind was taken off the desire by a prolonged and bass rumble that originated somewhere from within wherever the opened plate led.

Or at least she thought that was where it came from. It was difficult to tell because The Mole was nearing her now, the sound of its engines drowning out everything around it. And all Kali could do was wait until it fully arrived. She was glad that she had incapacitated the guards in the watchtower because this, frankly, was embarrassing.

The Mole manoeuvred into position beside her and, after a second, there was the hiss of its opening hatch. A tall, wiry, moustachioed and ear-ringed figure eased itself out of the hatch, took in Kali's predicament with an amused glance, and then stroked his moustache.

"I see you are enjoying yourself," Aldrededor observed.

"Not... quite... the... words... I'd... have... chosen," Kali gasped as she strained to keep the punchbolts in place. "Do you think, maybe, you could give me a hand here?"

Aldrededor applauded softly.

"*Aldrededor!*"

The ex-pirate smiled again, sighed, and began to look around for suitable pieces of rock or detritus with which he could jam the spaces Kali's appendages currently occupied.

"Is it any wonder," he commented as he worked, "that we at the Flagons worry about you all the time? Why is it that you get yourself into these ridiculous situations?"

"I have a knack for it."

"Clearly. Tell me – just what would you have done had we not come along?"

"*I don't know,*" Kali said through clenched teeth. It took a second for what Aldrededor had said to penetrate. "Hang on. What do you mean, 'we'?"

"There," Aldrededor said, fitting the last block into place. "I believe you can climb down now."

"Thanks. *Ahhh. Ooohh.* Aldrededor, what do you mean, 'we'?" She repeated before becoming distracted as what appeared to be a thick cloud of brown fog roiled from The Mole's cabin.

A second later, it happened again, and Kali moved to the door, coughing as she was engulfed in a cloud of cloying reekingness.

Oh no, she thought, and stepped back as something tall and thin *articulated* itself, in the manner of a brackan, from the inside of the cabin and stood, cheroot in mouth, arms folded.

"Dolorosa?"

"Of coursa Dolorosa! Who you expecta, thatta red-headed tart, the Annoying Lord?"

"Anointed," Kali corrected, absently. "Dolorosa, what in the hells are you doing here?"

"Our land is plagued by man-eating *theengs* and you think I woulda let my 'usband make thisa journey alone?"

Kali stared at the aforementioned and Aldrededor shrugged, picking at a tooth.

"Who's looking after my pitsing pub?"

"Do notta worry. Horse issa behind the bar."

"*Horse!?*"

"Hah! I havva her! Eet ees a leetle joke. No, thatta reprobate Deadnettle, he looka after the place. Notta that there are any customers. Nothing, and I mean *nothing*, comes near while the fat women dance."

"The Bellies are still dancing?"

"They havva leetle choice."

"True," Kali reflected. She paused for a second, looked at the two of them, and shook her head fondly. "Look, I appreciate you bringing The Mole, but I have to go now."

"Offa to save the world."

"Again," Kali sighed.

She patted them both on the shoulder and moved to the dwarven machine. She settled into the pilot's position but found her legs bent up against the control panel, as they had been when she had first found The Mole. Again, she tried to push the seat back but this time it would not go, blocked by some object. Kali leant around and found that Dolorosa was not the only unexpected extra to arrive with the dwarven machine. Something was jammed behind the seat. A small, wicker basket. Kali flipped the lid and stared inside. There were a number of bottles of flummox and two small mountains of slices of bread, layered in pairs, with filling between them. Kali prodded the uppermost layer of bread tentatively then pulled back with a grimace as a thick, brown substance slowly oozed from beneath it.

"What," Kali asked cautiously, "is this?"

Dolorosa looked surprised. "It issa beer anda butties for our trippa into the mountains."

The beer Kali didn't have a problem with, but it was these 'butty' things, and what was still oozing insidiously from inside them, that had disturbed her. She picked one of the creations up and it flopped under its own weight, plopping a lump of brown stuff onto her lap.

"Surprise stew butties?"

"Ovva course!" Dolorosa looked affronted. "Wassa the matter, eh? You havva gone offa my signatura *dish* while you havva been away?"

"No, no," Kali said quickly, having no wish to incur the old woman's wrath, especially by mentioning you couldn't *have* a signature dish if it was the only dish you ever made. The fact was, while she had nothing against surprise stew as such, she'd rather have eaten her own knees than the mess that was being presented to her now. That wasn't really the point though, was it? "Dolorosa. This isn't a picnic."

The woman stared at her, squinting her eyes, then turned to her husband and threw her hands in the air. "Pah! Now she thinks I amma some kind offa buffoon! A madda olda lady whose marbles havva rolled away, eh?"

Aldrededor curled his moustache and smiled, saying nothing, and Dolorosa span back to face Kali.

"Ovva course I know this issa no piccaneek! Eet ees going to be *very dangerous.* Alla the more reason to keepa uppa our strength, yes?"

Dolorosa seemed to entering full flow, so it was going to be useless to argue. "Well, yes, I suppose so, but –" Kali began and then faltered. Dolorosa had just said what she'd thought she'd said, hadn't she? *Our* strength. Yep, she'd definitely said *our,* as in 'we.'

"*Ohhoohhhooooo no.* If you think you're coming with me, you've got another think coming. This isn't a day trip into the country, old woman, it's the *Drakengrat Mountains* we're talking about."

"I thought itta wassa the Lost Canalsa of Turnitia first?"

"Those, too! And you can guarantee that they became *lost* for a reason. There's *always* a reason with these places. Deathtraps, monsters, insatiable, grasping *hairy* things that lurk in the dark..."

"I havva shared my bedaroom with Aldrededor for forty-five years, this issa *nurthing.*"

Aldrededor blew her a kiss.

"What?" Kali said, looking at him. "Oh no, uugh, I don't want to know. The point is, it's what I do – and I do it *alone.* You could die down there."

"Anda we coulda die uppa here. Or havva you forgotten the k'nid?" She leaned in towards Kali and added: "Havva you forgotten that when you take thissa *machine*, we woulda havva to *walk* home to the *Flagons*? Howwa long do you thinka we'd survive outta there, hah?"

"What?"

Dammit!

In all the chaos of the past few days she *had* forgotten that. Her own trip here from Andon had been perilous to say the least, and she couldn't reasonably expect Dolorosa and Aldrededor to make a journey ten times that length. And neither could she leave them here, where Vossian patrols might find and detain them, or worse. Maybe they could camp just inside the entrance to the Lost Canals, she pondered briefly. But then remembered the deep roar she thought she had heard when she had first breached its gates. It might have been nothing – an acoustic trick of the waiting labyrinth – but then again...

Dammit!

"All right, all right! But the two of you do *everything* I say, understand? You keep quiet when I tell you and you keep your heads down when I tell you and –"

Aldrededor interrupted her. "Young lady. My wife and I have survived the Mirror Maelstrom of Meenos and the Seven Sirens of the Sarcrean Sea, we have stood fast in the path of ripper gales and laughed in the face of the Chadassa themselves –"

"Like a this – *hahahahaaaar!*" Dolorosa interjected.

"– we have sailed the acid surf, we have swum the shadowed waters, and we have rode the boiling waves of the north."

"Enough!" Kali said. She had to admit she sometimes forgot that these two had... *history* and, being reminded of it by them, she felt vaguely chastised. She couldn't help but worry nonetheless. Neither of them were any longer in their prime and, when it came down to it, they were family. She made no apologies for trying to keep them safe.

But what choice did she have?

"Aldrededor... Dolorosa?"

"Yes, Kali Hooper?"

"What say we get this show on the road?"

The pair released a satisfied sigh. "Yes, Kali Hooper."

Kali gunned the engines of The Mole as Dolorosa and Aldrededor clambered into the seats behind her, checking they were settled before she flicked the lever that closed the hatch. The loud and sibilant hiss as it sealed made what they were about to do seem all the more immediate. But Kali wasn't sure what was worse – the unknown region they were about to negotiate or the sudden overwhelming odour of garlic and piratical aftershave that pervaded The Mole's cabin. *This* was going to be a long journey.

Having become quite used to the dwarven machine's controls by now, Kali pushed forward the lever that set it into gear, and then another that turned it on its tracks until its nose pointed towards the open hatch. Then, without further hesitation, she urged the machine forward, swallowing slightly as its front dipped onto the slope that lay beneath the opening. Outside the small observation portholes, the ambient light turned from the azureness of above to a strange and somewhat eerie rippling green.

"So theesa canals, they are what?" Dolorosa queried. "Some kind ovva sewer?"

"Not a sewer," Kali said. "But, to be honest, I haven't a clue what they actually are. All I know is where they go. At least, *part* of where they go."

"Whicha beggas the question. If you avva thees 'Mole', why is it you didda not drill into them somewhere else, inna stead of using thees hatch? Somawhere less dangerous?"

That, Kali could answer, and did. The fact was, she had made one exploratory dig at the location of one of the canal's branches over a year before, but had hit a layer of *something* that had been as impenetrable as the dropshaft plates she had later discovered. Whatever the material was, it defied damage from all the tools in her possession and then some. She seriously doubted that even the dwarven drill bits would make much inroads without taking damage. No, the dropshafts were the only realistic way in – and now that she was actually *using* one of them she hoped that she might find some answers as to what the material was. Because if she knew that, it might give her more of a clue as to who it was had built the bloody canals in the first place. Speaking of which, The Mole was coming to the end of the access tunnel.

"Lady and gentleman," Kali said as she flicked on The Mole's headlights. "The Lost Canals of Turnitia."

Both Aldrededor and Dolorosa leaned forward to peer through the portholes, and gasped. Kali almost did the same. Only the fact that her brain was working overtime to process what she was seeing preventing her from doing so.

Because with the affair of the dwarven testing ground and then the entrance passage to this network, she was beginning to think that she'd had enough of tunnels to last her half a lifetime, but the fact was tunnels were not what she had got. Instead, ahead of The Mole, she found herself staring at an arched thoroughfare that was as large and as grandiose as the inside of a cathedral. What was even more awe inspiring was that this passage was only one of the canals. Beyond further dark arches, to their left and right, as far as they could see, were many more of them, routing away to Gods knew where beneath the surface of the peninsula.

"By all of the Gods," Aldrededor breathed. "I never thought I would see this place."

"You know it?"

"From tales told on the high seas."

"Itta reminds me ovva the crystal caverns beyond Sarcre,"

Dolorosa whispered. "You remember, Dreddy? Where a we founda Davyjonz Locket?"

"I remember, darling," Aldrededor said, his eyes twinkling. "Ah – it is good to smell the sea again."

The sea? Kali thought, and then realised that what Aldrededor said was true.

That briny odour she had smelled above was stronger here, detectable even through the filters that were bringing air into the cabin. The fact that they were a good number of leagues from the sea, then, could mean only one thing. The canals down here were *seawater* canals, pumped throughout the network by who-knew-what kind of mechanisms.

"It's nice to be somewhere where there's a little peace and quiet," Kali commented.

Aldrededor's eyebrows rose.

"Wait – you do not know?"

"Know what?"

"These canals. The tales on the high seas tell of something that lives down here." He stroked his moustache. "As my beloved wife might say, something *beeeg.*"

CHAPTER TEN

If there was something *beeg* living in the Lost Canals of Turnitia there was, after half a day's travel through them, no sign of it. But then there was more than enough canal left for it to hide in. Or, if you were a glass-half-empty type, more than enough for it to leap *out of*. *If* it leapt, Kali mused. After all, it might crawl. Or slither. Or hop. Whatever it might do, Kali tended towards the glass half-empty principal, and so had been guiding The Mole through the canals cautiously and in low gear, its headlights dipped and sweeping slowly across broad banks and shadowed arches.

Despite Merrit Moon's warnings of tunnel collapse, they had come across few obstacles so far, and those they had, had been little more than piles of rubble which The Mole's sonic cannons made short work of. Having already made the decision not to stop until they were through the canals, Kali could only experience what they had to offer by peering through the Mole's forward viewing slat, and this she did, squinting, to occasionally purse her lips, occasionally raise her eyebrows and also, occasionally, frown. It was the way the canals made her feel. It was strange but, regardless of how many ancient sites she had visited, this place felt different. Though she couldn't quite put her finger on why. It was as if she had taken a step *too* far into the past and, for some reason, she felt like an *intruder* here. The feeling was not, though, one that would prevent her from intruding *again* – it actually quite intrigued her – and this she was determined to do, when she had the time.

Speaking of time, she had estimated that at their current rate of progress it would take The Mole about two days to navigate the canals beneath the Anclas Territories. Not as quick as other methods that might have gotten her to the Drakengrats but the only one she had.

When her unwanted passengers had joined her she'd imagined the journey was going to be interminable but Aldrededor had, in fact, turned out to be amusing company, sharing more of his tales from the high seas. As pleasant company as he was, however, the same had not turned out to be the case with Dolorosa.

Crammed behind them in the cabin, not only was her habit of smoking cragweed cheroots sending the air scrubbers into overdrive, but it had not taken long for her to start complaining that she was suffering badly from the bone-ache. This was only one of, what turned out to be, a series of complaints. Interruptions that included frequent prods in the back accompanied by suggestions of which way to turn, whether to slow down or speed up and, on occasion, louder cries of "stupid-woman-watcha-out-forra-that-bump ahead." There had also been repeated questions along the lines of "Are we there yet?" Last but not least, she had emitted an ear-piercing shriek when she had discovered there was a dried dwarf's head beneath her seat. This then promptly, and unexpectedly, ended up on Kali's lap, causing screeches from both she and Aldrededor and reducing everyone to a nervous wreck. Admittedly, Kali had forgotten about the head, and she might have given Dolorosa that one were it not for what happened next.

Dolorosa leaned forward and whispered something in Aldrededor's ear, but it was just loud enough for her to hear.

"You want *what*?"

"She wishes to answer the call of nature," Aldrededor whispered diplomatically. "To powder her wart. To enhance the realm of the gods of the sea..."

"I *know* what she means, Aldrededor! But hells, woman – can't it wait?"

"Eet issa the shock of this *theeng*, eet has sent my plumbing into spasm," Dolorosa objected, pointing at the dwarf's head and shaking her own. "No, I can notta hold it any longer. I warna you, Kali Hooper."

"Fark, haven't you got a *bottle* or something?" Kali said with exasperation.

"I cannotta – and willa notta – tinkle while you listen!"

It wasn't a thought that appealed much to Kali, either, and the fact was she doubted *she* could last two days. "All right, all right!" she said, sighing heavily. She squinted through the observation slat, looking for a suitable parking space and then, with a grinding of levers, brought The Mole to a stop. The hatch hissed open. "Go. But don't go far and make it quick."

"Actually, I too might..." Aldrededor said hesitantly, then smiled and shrugged.

"Pirates!" Kali cursed as the two squeezed by her. She sat there for a second, looking out of the hatch, and then thought *what the hells, let's have a look*. It was a good excuse for her to stretch her legs, anyway.

Trying to ignore the conspicuous head of Dolorosa behind a pile of debris and a whistling and flexing Aldrededor against the wall in the opposite direction, Kali stepped out onto the bank of the canal and took her first good look around since they had entered the network. She tried not to breathe in too deeply because, frankly, whether they were in an ancient wonder or not, the Lost Canals of Turnitia stank to the high clouds, worse even than a sludgestrider's socks. The reason for that was possibly as a result of its collapsed sections or simply because it had been long unmaintained. But whatever the cause, the whole system of canals had stagnated. Not only did thick moss – glistening and pungent – cover the walls of the tunnels like a thick skin, but the canals themselves seemed not to be filled with seawater but dark green vegetation. The entire surface looked thick enough to walk on. Despite all that, though – and something *beeg* or not – the arches that led off into tunnels in the distance pulled at Kali but, again, she knew that now was not the time. She looked towards Aldrededor and Dolorosa, willing them to hurry up, but while the former was already nearing her with a sigh and declaration of how much better for that he felt, the latter had not moved from behind her pile of debris. In fact, she seemed to be waving at her to join her with quite some desperation.

Gods, Kali thought. *What now?*

"I amma stuck," Dolorosa confessed as she neared. "My feet, they havva become caught in the weeds."

Kali took a step forward and then stopped. "Are you decent?" she said warily.

Dolorosa gave her one of her killer looks. "I amma stuck, notta the senile old bat, Kali Hooper."

"Sorry. Okay then, let's see what I can do."

Kali clambered over the debris and saw that the thin woman was indeed entangled in a mesh of aquatic weed, but nothing that couldn't be handled. She pulled her gutting knife from its sheath and began to cut at it with sawing strokes. The growth was larger than it looked, part of a mass that had climbed the wall of the tunnel itself. It took quite some effort and a number of tugs from both of them to free it. Unfortunately, when at last it did come free, it did so unexpectedly quickly. Kali found herself suddenly flying backwards towards the canal, plunging through the algae covered surface. She emerged safe, however, and gagging and choking, swam to the side and waded back out, her hand outstretched to Dolorosa for help.

"You arra the mess once more," Dolorosa declared as she heaved her up. "We cannota take-a you anywhere."

"Hey!" Kali objected, loudly. "It was *you* that –"

Kali stopped in mid-sentence and then, as Dolorosa started to protest, hushed her with a wave of the hand.

Without another word, Kali began to walk forward, gazing up, and Dolorosa gazed where she gazed, and gasped.

Because the mass of weed that they had pulled away had had a knock on effect on the weed that covered the tunnel wall, and part of that now lay exposed for the first time in no one knew how long.

And it was covered in symbols. Great, golden symbols from some iconography that Kali had never seen before. She pulled away more of the growth and the symbols seemed to go on for as far as the wall did.

"Gods of the Sea," Aldrededor breathed, joining them.

"What arra those? Do they belong to one of your olda races, like those, what issa it they arra called - dwelfs?"

"*Elfs*, Dolorosa. I mean *elves*. There were two races, elves and dwarves, tall and thin and short and bulky, not difficult to tell apart. But these don't belong to either of them."

"So, you arra saying there is a *third* race?"

"No... maybe... I don't know. It's just that..."

Kali trailed off, running her fingers over one of the symbols, generating a strange keening vibration as she touched the metal. This she ignored, more concerned that she was tracing a *familiar* pattern, even though she hadn't seen the symbols before now. One of the shapes was a dead ringer for the creature she had encountered in the murky waters beneath Martak – the strange, water-breathing life form that had known all about her.

"Boss lady?" Dolorosa said, prodding her.

"Hush, woman!" Kali snapped.

She wouldn't normally have been so short with her but her mind had suddenly gone into overdrive. *Fish symbols here?* she was thinking. But if that was the case that probably meant that fish people had built these canals. But why in the hells would fish people want a set of tunnels that stretched *everywhere* under the peninsula? What purpose would they have served? What did the fish people *want* here?

"Boss lady?"

"I thought I said –" Kali began, spinning on her, and then stopped.

Because she suddenly realised that Dolorosa hadn't been trying to interrupt her, she'd been trying to alert her. Something was coming. Something big.

Not that they could see anything, yet. It only manifested itself in the form of a distant roar. The surface of the canal had begun to undulate, like a tide coming in their direction, as if something massive had stirred it.

"Both of you get inside The Mole. *Now!*"

Dolorosa stood her ground. "I may have letta you down at the *Flagons* but do notta worry," she said, slipping her stiletto from her boot. "Whatever thees theeng is, I will – *heeeeeeeee!*"

The tall, thin woman made a sound like an expiring goose then promptly fainted, fortunately straight into her husband's waiting arms, who then swept her up and did as Kali had instructed. Kali herself remained where she stood for a second longer, just enough time to take in what had prompted Dolorosa's abrupt departure from consciousness.

What she saw was not the creature itself but the creature announcing its presence with its shadow as it emerged from a side channel far up the branch. A shadow that, despite the distance, filled the arched thoroughfare completely, looming like a fast approaching night.

Make that Long Night, Kali thought. Because the shadow went on and on and on.

There was another deafening roar and the tunnel began to pound and shake, as if the unseen creature were slamming itself against the sides of the canal in fury. And then, fleetingly, she *did* see it, emerging from the water, to flash at incredible speed up and *around* the roof of the tunnel, negotiating a full three hundred and sixty degrees before it reached the other side and slipped beneath the surface again. Not all of it disappeared at once, though and, briefly, its long shadow flitted here, there and everywhere, impossible to keep track of, before then it, too, disappeared. Kali suddenly found herself awash with the canal's sluggish water all the way up to her chest.

It was coming right at them under the water.

"Two-Faced Bob called it the *yhang-dor*!" Aldrededor shouted as Kali waded as quickly as she could towards The Mole. "He thought it was elvish for 'That which never ends.'"

"Actually, it just means *big bastard*!" Kali shouted back as she forced herself forward against the wash. She stared at the bobbing ridge of weed and algae moving disturbingly fast down the centre of the canal, realised she couldn't see its end, and swallowed. "Aldrededor, get The Mole moving, *now*!"

"Kali Hooper, you will not make i –"

"*I'll make it, Aldrededor! Do it!*"

Aldrededor sighed and the Mole began to move forward, slowly at first, fighting against the wash, but gradually picking up speed.

Kali stopped wading and threw herself into a crawl, head splashing left and right, spitting out small clumps of weed and algae as she swam. She was about a yard from the tail end of The Mole and she doubled her efforts to reach it with a grunt of exertion. She managed, with one stroke, to grab onto a rail on the vehicle's rear. Kali looked back and couldn't shake the feeling that the monster was going to swallow the lower half of her legs at any second.

Desperately, she twisted in the water and managed to grab a second handhold before heaving herself up onto the body of The Mole. The surface of the vehicle was slick beneath her feet and she slipped twice, each time looking back to see how much space they had – or hadn't – gained on the yhang-dor. The Mole seemed to be holding its own for the moment, but they really needed to get the vehicle out of the wash to escape its drag, because the thing seemed to become more determined with each second they eluded its clutches.

She looked up and saw that there was a rise in the bank up ahead, and hoped that Aldrededor had noticed the same thing. Thankfully, the ex-pirate proved to be as reliable as always and, a second later, The Mole veered up the bank, its tracks churning and sloughing liquid and weed as they went. Kali threw herself through the open hatch of the vehicle.

Aldrededor immediately swapped places with her, allowing Kali to take control of the levers, but not before activating the one to seal the door. Before it closed something long and serpent-like hove into view outside the hatch, overtaking The

Mole. Suddenly, all that was visible through the observation slat was what appeared to be a large reptilian mouth filled with thousands of tiny, razor sharp teeth.

Oh no, Kali thought. *One bloody great gob trying to eat me is enough for one week, thanks very much.*

Kali quickly yanked and pushed levers, a combination of moves that threw The Mole into a skidding u-turn and shook the cabin, awakening Dolorosa just as the rear end of The Mole slammed into the body of their pursuer, before racing off in the opposite direction. Except that racing wasn't quite the right word. Because even though they were once more free of the drag effect of the canal water, The Mole was a machine built for tunnelling, not for speed. Only the fact that the lengthy creature seemed to need a few seconds to literally catch up with itself bought them distance. The trouble was, that distance would be eaten up in seconds. Kali decided to use the only advantage they had and steered the Mole towards where a number of branch junctions left the main canal. She hoped to use them and subsequent branches to stymie the creature's manoeuvrability, constantly shifting position to lose it in the maze of tunnels. But to do that she'd need to know the creature's location at all times.

"Dolorosa, open the rear slat. I need you to keep an eye on that thing."

"Whatta theeng?" Dolorosa said, shakily attempting to light a cheroot.

"The bloody great *theeng* outside!"

"Eeet was real?"

"Yes, Dolorosa."

"Eeet ees following us?"

"Yes, Dolorosa."

"*Heeeeeeeeeee...*"

"Oh, crap. Aldrededor?"

"I am doing it, Kali Hooper," Aldrededor said, climbing over his seat to stub out the cheroot and flip the observation slat. "My beloved," he said by way of apology, "she had the embarrassing experience with a large slithering thing many years ago."

"I'm betting I don't want to know the details, right?"

"You are correct, Kali Hooper."

"Hokay. Where is the bastard?"

"It has just finished turning towards us. Moving now."

"Then hang on – we're going right."

Kali spun the Mole, skewing it as she tried to eke as much speed as possible from the machine.

"Where is it now?"

"Turning into the junction. It does not look pleased."

"I don't care if it's suicidal. Aldrededor?"

"Still with us and gaining, Kali Hooper."

Kali spun the Mole into another u-turn.

"Turning left again, straight on, right," she warned her shaken passengers. "Sharp left, coming up... now!"

"Kali Hooper, what is this thing?" Aldrededor asked, clinging on. "Despite the tale of Two-Faced Bob, I do not recognise it as a serpent of the sea."

Neither did Kali. She'd seen a couple of such beasts in her time and this resembled neither of them, reminding her more of some *worm* than any subaquatic behemoth. From what detail she had managed to see, the thing was certainly the shape of one, though covered, along its considerable and most *unworm* like length, with a thick coating of barbed bristles that appeared not only to give it traction on any surface to which it adhered but also propelled it along. From the amount of collisions it was shrugging off, it had to be quite hardy. She imagined that beneath the bristles there was a protective coating that was more shell than skin. Its bulk was another thing. No creature designed like this should be as big or as wide as it was. Kali was starting to suspect that the k'nid were not the only unnatural creatures she had encountered in the past few days. Its whole physical make-up and the fact that it had seemed to first be drawn to them when she had touched the symbols on the wall had actually begun to make her wonder whether the creature had not always been such as it was. Perhaps once upon a time it had been some *tool* of the tunnels' builders – a life form that kept their canals clean and navigable, perhaps – but, in the unimaginable length of time since they had become sealed and disused, it had nurtured itself on what it had once removed, mutating as it did into what they faced now. In that case, in a sense, it had every right to not look pleased, because it had lived here longer than humans had walked the peninsula. This was its home.

Kali was suddenly flung against the control panel as the Mole was impacted hard from the rear. Outside, there was a loud roar that sounded almost like one of triumph.

"*Aldrededor?*"

"Apologies, Kali Hooper. A sudden spurt of speed. It seems our friend is becoming more adept at the chase."

"Then let him chase this,"

Kali said, gritting her teeth. Suddenly she was pushing and pulling the levers as if she had used them all her life. The Mole started to buck wildly as she threw it through a number of accelerations, decelerations, sudden twists and skidding turns that the unwieldy creature could not possibly hope to keep up with, screeching at last to a halt in tunnel.

"Aldrededor?" Kali asked over the stressed rumbling of the engine.

"No sign, Kali Hooper."

"Then it looks like we're out of the... oh fark!"

Kali stared through the observation slat at a branch of the canal that was *branchless*, stretching ahead of the Mole for as far as its headlights could penetrate, which made it look like forever. And for all she knew, it might go on just that far. In other words, there would be no dodging left or right and no u-turns here. *If* the creature managed to catch up they would be totally exposed.

"Kali Hooper?" Aldrededor said again.

"What, Aldrededor? Can you see anythi –"

The creature slammed into the side of The Mole and sent it crashing from the bank into the canal, overturning it until its buoyancy righted it once more. In the cabin, Aldrededor clung on to Dolorosa, while Kali squeezed herself tight between seat and control panel. Outside the cabin, the creature roared while the rest of its lengthy form followed its head into the tunnel.

"Dammit!" Kali shouted, gunning the engine of The Mole,

riding it up onto the canal bank. "Doesn't this thing ever stop?"

Aldrededor sighed. "It is as persistent as my wife's advances and there is no way we can elude it now."

"Wanna bet?" Kali said.

She was as fired up as The Mole itself. She rammed her foot to the floor and the vehicle responded by accelerating to the speed it was designed for, even she realised that with their current limitations and circumstances they had no more chance of fleeing their now immediate pursuer than one of the Hells Bellies would have outrunning a shnarl.

"Kali!" Aldrededor said with uncharacteristic seriousness

"Aldrededor? You don't get out with me much, do you?"

"I do not."

"You don't really know how I work, do you?"

"I have a feeling I am going to find out."

"The fact is, Aldrededor," Kali said, making a slight course correction and ramming levers forward, making The Mole lurch, "I make things up as I go along."

"Kali Hooper, you are heading straight for the tunnel wall."

"Oh, yeah," Kali said, nodding determinedly.

Kali aimed the Mole at the wall and then, at the very last second, swerved. Instead of hitting the wall head on, the vehicle careened against it along its side, stripping away weed and algae until metal grated hard against the stone beneath. Rather than pulling away, Kali teased the Mole even further to the left, again and again, as if she were trying to smash through the wall. In fact, wasn't her intention at all.

Inside the cabin, a rather confused Aldrededor steadied his insensible wife while The Mole vibrated so much it seemed in danger of coming apart. Kali, however, seemed little concerned. She rammed the vehicle again and again against the wall and, as there was a series of judders and snapping and clanking sounds from its lower regions, it at last clicked with the ex-pirate what it was Kali was trying to do. She was not trying to destroy the whole vehicle, but only part of it.

Aldrededor turned to look out of the rear observation slat, directing his gaze right and groundward, and sure enough the tracks on the vehicle's left hand side were breaking apart, its connecting links buckling and separating as the bolts holding them together sheared and loosened. As he watched, the individual plates of the tracks folded, piling up against the hatch, and then the whole lot came loose, flapping away behind the Mole like a discarded belt.

The Mole dropped onto its metal wheels on its left hand side and was in danger of going into a spin. However, Kali handled it expertly and instead quickly plunged the vehicle through the canal to a rise onto the opposite bank, where she began the same process again. A minute later, the tracks on the Mole's right hand side joined their discarded opposites. Dropping fully onto both sets of wheels now, the vehicle accelerated along the canal bank, spurting a shower of sparks and leaving a rather confused looking yhang-dor in its wake.

Both Kali and Aldrededor were flung back into their seats.

"*Wahoooo!*" Kali shouted.

Behind her, Dolorosa stirred slightly. "My 'usband, what is 'appening?"

Aldrededor shrugged his arms helplessly and smiled. "Kali Hooper, she is making it up as she goes along."

The Mole continued its flight along the canal bank, three or four times its original speed now that its wheels had been freed of the constraining gears of the tracks. Kali smiled as the compass on the control panel informed her they were heading west, exactly the direction they needed to go. Her smile faded, however, as Aldrededor informed her that the yhang-dor was once more in pursuit. Now that it had a perfectly straight tunnel to traverse, it wasn't gaining on them as fast as it would had the tracks still been present, but it was still gaining.

"Okay, I've had enough of this overgrown toothbrush," Kali declared. "Aldrededor, take the levers."

The ex-pirate scrambled back over the seat. "Kali Hooper, what are you doing now?"

Kali flicked the hatch lever and grabbed the crackstaff she had stored beneath her seat, then climbed towards the opening, wind whipping at her hair.

"Just keep on in this direction, Reddy! Back in a mo ..."

"You're the boss, Kali Hooper."

Kali heaved herself out of the now opened hatch and steadied herself against the side of The Mole, its passage far from smooth now that it was running only on metal wheels. Nevertheless, she managed to lock herself into a secure position so that she was staring back along the side of The Mole, and raised the crackstaff. Some two hundred yards behind the vehicle, seemingly untroubled by the shower of sparks the Mole still trailed, the yhang-dor roared, its maw opening, displaying its countless razor teeth.

Somewhat hampered by the fact that she had to cling on for dear life with one hand, Kali steadied the crackstaff as best she could and fired, loosing a bolt of energy that ricocheted off the canal bank and into the ether, while simultaneously almost blowing her off the Mole with its recoil. She anchored herself and fired again. This time the bolt impacted with the weeds on the wall, frying them before again ricocheting back down the long, dark tunnel. Trying not to look at the tunnel floor, as it raced blurringly by immediately below her, Kali fired once more. The bolt careened off the tunnel roof and back down at forty-five degrees into the stagnant water, where the canal erupted with a sudden geyser of steam.

Dammit! she thought, this was going to be next to impossible unless she found a better position.

She looked up and, deciding, flung the crackstaff onto The Mole's roof with a grunt, then climbed up after it until she was scrambling on top of the vehicle as it swayed under her. There, lying flat and facing straight back, she lodged the crackstaff beneath her, took aim and fired. An energy bolt slammed into the canal bank directly in front of the yhang-dor, blowing shrapnel in its face.

Adjusting her aim slightly, she fired again, and then again, and the bolts scythed along the creature's side, burning a path through its layer of bristle. The creature roared and reared, momentarily slowed, but then continued coming on. Kali fired again, again and again, the energy discharges reverberating in the confines of the tunnel. The length of the yhang-dor flared with multiple hits. It launched itself up and around the tunnel walls.

Keep still, you slippery fark! Kali thought as it spiralled towards her.

But it did not stop her firing and this time all but one of her multiple shots found their target. Almost pulsating with the blue of the energy bolts now, and shedding sections of skin from where its bristles had fried away, the creature's roar had become one less of anger and more of pain. But still it came on. It was a tough bastard, without a doubt. However, Kali was certain that all it would take to finish it was a few more shots. Particularly if she could get one straight down its throat.

She was lining up just such a shot when her world suddenly span. The Mole was skidding, trying, for some reason, to come to an emergency stop. A moment later, it succeeded, and she found herself tumbling from the roof to land on the ground with an undignified *oof.*

Ahead of them, the roof of the tunnel had collapsed completely.

"I am sorry, Kali Hooper," Aldrededor said from inside the cabin. "There was nothing I could –"

Kali double-taked on the collapsed tunnel and then on the approaching yhang-dor, estimating they had perhaps thirty seconds before it caught up with them.

She leapt into the cabin, sealed the hatch behind her, and flicked the Mole's cannons on to full power. Through the forward observation slat she could see the sonic pulses staring to effect the fallen debris. A second later, she pulled back as a rain of pulverised stone and rock began to impact with the vehicle's front. But in her heart of hearts Kali knew that there was really no time, that the collapse looked far to thick to penetrate before the yhang-dor was on them. And sure enough, a second later, The Mole lurched horribly.

Suddenly all that Kali could see through the observation slat was a set of thousands of razor sharp teeth, then something horrible and squishy and, then, utter blackness.

In the darkness, Aldrededor swallowed so hard Kali could

actually hear it. "Did what I think just happened happen?"

"A-ha."

On the back seat, no doubt disturbed by the impact, Dolorosa stirred. "All is quiet. Have we stopped being chased by the *theeng?*"

"In a manner of speaking, my dearest." Aldrededor said. "Why don't you go back to sleep?"

"Bossa lady? What issa wrong?"

"Oh, I think we're in the shit," Kali said, casually. And paused. "Or will be soon, anyway."

"Kali Hooper, I must ask you not to use such language in front on my delicate flower."

"Aldrededor, it was your 'delicate flower' and her desire to *flow* that got us into this mess in the –"

Suddenly The Mole lurched again, far more violently than the first time, and all three of its passengers clung onto their seats as it began to move forward. The relative quiet of the last few moments was replaced by the noise of a series of loud crashes that, together with the *thwooming* of the still active sonic cannons, was deafening. Kali realised that, with the combination of the yhang-dor's momentum and the cannons themselves, they were actually ploughing *through* the obstacle ahead of them. Not only that, if her senses weren't betraying her, but *up*.

What was more, the cannons were clearly damaging the yhang-door from the *inside*, and by virtue of the fact that its resultant screeching was becoming louder than the cacophony caused by their passage through the roof-fall, it didn't like that at all. It began, in fact, to vibrate and spasm around them, and Kali was just beginning to wonder what would happen to the Mole when two things happened at once.

The yhang-dor smashed through the last of the blockages and promptly exploded, and the forward observation slat – after taking a moment to drain itself of clinging gore – exposed the interior of the cabin to a brilliant white light.

Either they had just ascended to Kerberos, Kali considered, or The Mole's two day journey through the Lost Canals of Turnitia had been considerably shortened by the fact that they had been forced to move a lot more quickly than anticipated. And if she was right, they were just where they wanted to be. There was only one way to find out.

Kali activated The Mole's hatch, then licked a fleck of snow from the end of her nose. Yup, that tasted right. She smiled and turned to a somewhat stunned Aldrededor and Dolorosa.

"Welcome to the Drakengrats. I think we walk from here."

CHAPTER ELEVEN

Three dots moved across the pristine white landscape. Some leagues, and a day's climb, behind them, the landscape was stained by a great splotch of yellow gore that spread away from a jagged, irregular hole in the snow. Next to that sat the skewed, abandoned remains of a broken machine from which smoke curled lazily into the pure mountain air. Ahead of the dots lay a series of jagged peaks, rising ever higher until they seemed to touch the clouds themselves. But the majesty of these seemed, for the moment, lost on those who trudged wearily through the snow.

The crunching of their boots echoed through the ether, and then the echo of their voices - and then that of a slap.

"Do notta droppa the litter!"

"It is but a crust, my darling."

"Anda who willa pick up the crust in this Gods-forsaken place, hah? No, 'usband, it issa the litter!"

"My wife, we are dreaded *pirates of the high seas* – we have done worse things."

"We *were* pirates, my 'usband! Nowwa we are the respectable proprietors of a tavern witha the great potential!"

A cough echoed alongside the voices, and a second passed.

"Nowwa we are the respectable *managers* ovva taverno witha the great potential, and we –"

"Nice butties," the owner of the cough interjected. Its tone suggested the matter should be closed.

"I amma sorry, boss lady," the first voice said again.

Kali stared at Dolorosa and Aldrededor as the two of them ate and trudged wearily alongside her, chewing on her own surprise stew butty ruminatively. That she had finally decided to eat one of Dolorosa's mushy concoctions was a reflection that the current trek had, for all of them, turned out to be more gruelling than expected. Even her normal wariness about one disturbing aspect of the ex-pirate's signature dish – that it never, *ever* cooled down – had been set aside in favour of getting something warm inside her. Because the one thing that could be said about the Drakengrats was that they were *farking cold*.

She hadn't expected to lose The Mole, of course. With The Mole this whole affair would have been one hells of a lot easier, but at least they had the furs and equipment she had instructed Aldrededor to bring with the vehicle. Trouble was, even with The Mole, they would have faced the same problem. That she didn't have the faintest idea where she, Aldrededor and Dolorosa were meant to be *going*. It was all right for the old man to send her to 'a place in the clouds' but there were a lot of clouds, and a lot of mountains beneath them – exactly which one of them had he meant?

Kali could only hope that she and the others stumbled across some kind of clue. A signpost 'To The Crucible', perhaps. Or another explosion that no one for leagues could miss. Or, best of all, another pack of k'nid swarming from the place they originated, so that they could follow their trail back whence they came.

Yes, just like those.

Exactly like those, in fact.

"Kali Hooper, something comes," Aldrededor pointed out, rather unnecessarily.

"It issa the theengs like-a leaves fromma the *Flagons*."

Kali stared up the narrow pass they had been negotiating. At its very top, the k'nid were swarming over the ridge like a dark avalanche, before tumbling down the white mountainside towards them. At the speed they were moving, she estimated they had about two minutes before the things were on them.

"Hide," Kali instructed, in a tone which left no doubt how important a manoeuvre that was going to be.

"Hide-a, she says," Dolorosa protested, throwing up her arms. "And-a how exactly are we meanta to do that?"

"My wife is correct, Kali Hooper. There is nowhere for us to go."

Her attention having been so fixed on the k'nid, Kali hadn't noticed they were in a part of the pass totally devoid of any cover and edged by sheer rock faces on either side. *She* might be able to make a leap up them to safety but the Sarcreans had no chance of doing so, and there was no way she was leaving them down here alone.

For the first time since they had started on their journey, she truly regretted allowing them to come along and, for a moment, felt a totally uncharacteristic bolt of panic. Her friends were going to die unless she did something quick.

Kali was about to unsling her crackstaff, ready to make a last stand when –

"Looka!" Dolorosa cried suddenly, and pointed up. "There!"

Kali snapped her gaze to where Dolorosa pointed and, at first, wasn't sure what she was looking at. Then she realised that *something* was caught, flapping in the wind, on a sharp piece of rock thirty feet above their heads. It looked to be, of all things, a large torn piece of white sailcloth. But that was impossible, surely. After all what kind of ship – wrecked or otherwise – would have been able to find its way here?

Impossible or not, it appeared to have galvanised Dolorosa. Eyes sparkling, she turned to Aldrededor and said: "I never though I would havva the chance to say this again, my 'usband, but we must *battena down the hatches*!"

Aldrededor's eyes also sparkled. "My wife, I love you!" He turned to Kali and pointed at the cloth. "Kali Hooper, if you would be so good as to..."

Kali didn't have a clue what they were on about. "Why?"

Dolorosa thrust her face in hers, her dark eyes narrowing. "Because, bossa lady, it ees oura turn to save youra life, forra once. *Nowwa do as I say!*"

That was good enough for Kali and she went for the cloth, reaching it in three acrobatic leaps, delivering it seconds later to the hands of Dolorosa. The ex-pirate and her husband pulled it taut and then held it about a foot above the snowy ground, whereupon Kali was ordered to lie underneath. This she did without argument and, a second later, Aldrededor and Dolorosa joined her, pulling the cloth down tightly over them all.

To an outside observer they would now look like nothing more than a small rise in the snow.

"We used to-a use the sails to secure our cargo inna the bad storm," Dolorosa whispered in what, Kali had to admit, were quite cosy confines. "Eet issa what gave-a me the idea."

"You are a genius, my wife."

"I havva my moments, yes."

"Hang on," Kali said. "All we've done is hide under a big piece of cloth. Do you really think that'll fool the k'nid?"

"Whya not? Itta fooled Short Jack Copper when thatta slimy bastardo boarded our ship. We-a waited for his men to come aboard and then sprang from beneath the sail like-a the... like-a the –"

"Springy things?" Kali offered.

"Like-a the springy things, yes! And thenna we *keelled* them all witha oura very sharpa knives! It wassa *horrible!*"

"A-ha. Dolorosa, why are you whispering?"

"So-a the k'nid do notta hear us, of course."

"Dolorosa, they're hurtling murderously down a mountainside towards us, probably causing an avalanche as they come. I doubt they'll hear –"

"Be silent now, Kali Hooper," Aldrededor interrupted. "They are upon us."

Aldrededor was right. Distracted as she had been with her surreal exchange with Dolorosa, the approach of the k'nid swarm had somewhat taken a back seat but there was no mistaking it now.

The sound of their approach was audible even over the winds blowing through the pass, and it was building second by second to a level that would soon be deafening. The sound began to approach a crescendo and Kali, Aldrededor and Dolorosa remained utterly still, in readiness.

The sensation of the k'nid passing was difficult to describe – like being massaged by a horde of heavy insects, each and every insectoid leg discernable as a fleeting touch to the very bone – and for the few seconds it took for their numbers to progress over their hiding place, Kali felt every nerve in her body scream out with a desire to leap up and flee from her frozen position. She did not, of course, because that would have meant instant death, though resisting the desire was a struggle. Next to her she could see Aldrededor and Dolorosa suffering in the same way. The only way that they could communicate was with their eyes, but the message they sent to each other was nonetheless clear.

Do not move, do not cry out.

They remained that way for what seemed to be an interminable time but was likely only seconds and then, miraculously, it was over.

Even so, Kali waited a few seconds before moving the piece of cloth off their prone forms. It was heavier than she expected, laden with a layer of snow that the k'nid swarm had caused to avalanche over them, but Kali wasn't complaining as that snow had likely offered an extra layer of protection.

The three of them stood and stared down the mountain pass, catching view of the tail end of the swarm as it moved out across the peninsula.

Kali turned her gaze upward, biting her lip. "No doubt now where they're coming from. You two okay, ready to move on?"

"We are ready, Kali Hooper."

"Wait," Dolorosa said. "There ees something..."

The thin woman moved ahead of them, bending to pick up

something glistening in the layer of fine, disturbed snow. It was some kind of band and Dolorosa bit it and turned it in her hands, shrugging, before handing it to Kali.

"What issa this theeng?"

Kali held the band up to the light. It was old, possibly of elven origin, and inscribed with a series of runics so small she couldn't make them out. It appeared to be, though, only decorative. "Some kind of bracelet, but how in the hells it ended up here is anybody's guess."

"May I see, Kali Hooper?" Aldrededor asked. "Hmm, yes. I have seen something such as this before."

"You have? Where?"

"The *Ramar'Est*. The wreck of an elven ship many believed haunted, for from within the sealed cabin of its captain, many, many centuries after he died, his voice could still be heard."

"I take it wasn't a ghost?"

"No, Kali Hooper. It was this."

The Sarcrean held out the bracelet and rubbed its side with his thumb. Kali and Dolorosa jumped back as the figure of a young woman materialised before them. Garbed in a cloak of the Final Faith, attractive and with a mane of long blonde hair, the figure was ghostly, flecked with the snow that penetrated its form, but Kali knew who it was.

"My name is Jennadayn Freel," she began. "Eleven years ago I was abducted by agents of the Final Faith under the command of Katherine Makennon's first lieutenant, Konstantin Munch. Since that day I have been stripped of my individuality, my liberty and free will, bent to the cause of the Faith through the machinations of the mindweaver Querilous Fitch. He is with me – he is *inside me* – always, and it is only in rare, stolen moments such as this that I am able to remember who and what I once was. This bracelet enables me to record my thoughts at these times. This I do under my own conditioning, so that when Fitch's influence reasserts itself I will remember nothing of the bracelet's capabilities or what I have said."

The figure flickered and faded for a second, and then reappeared in slightly different garb. It began to speak on another matter, one that seemed to have been recorded some time later, but the mountain pass in the middle of a snowstorm was no place to listen to what was said. Kali signalled Aldrededor to thumb the bracelet again, and the image disappeared,. He handed the band to her.

"Who issa that woman?" Dolorosa asked.

"Slowhand's sister."

"*The* Slowhand? The one witha the snake-like hips and the cute-a ar..."

She trailed off, whistling and kicking her heels, looking sheepishly at her husband.

Kali coughed to hide a smile. "Yes, Dolorosa, *the* Slowhand. But the question is, if this bracelet belongs to Slowhand's sister, what in the hells was Jenna doing up here?"

"Perhaps," Aldrededor said, pointing, "something to do with that."

Kali and Dolorosa turned. What neither she or her companions had noticed until now – distracted as they had been by the k'nid swarm – was that further up the pass, high on its left hand side, smoke trailed from a gaping hole in the rockface, curling lazily and looking as if it were the dying tendrils of an explosion from some days before.

How about three days before? Kali thought. Because she had little doubt that was she was looking at was the aftermath of what Merrit Moon had seen through his elven telescope back in Gargas.

She had to find out what was up there, but she was not going to do so now, as the light of day was already fading into azure twilight, bringing with it a deeper cold that would make any route up to the mysterious gap in the rocks doubly treacherous. Instead, Kali yomped with Dolorosa and Aldrededor further up the pass, to a point perhaps a tenth of a league from where the hole loomed, and there found a small cave where they were able to make camp for the night. More surprise stew butties were consumed for supper and her two companions were soon wrapped up in their furs together, sound asleep and snoring. Kali took the opportunity to examine Jenna's bracelet once more, thumbing through her recorded entries and getting to know a little more about the woman who, until a few months before, she had never known existed.

It was a tragic and troubling tale, relating the abduction, years before, that Slowhand had told her about, and Jenna's subsequent indoctrination into the ranks of the Final Faith. But, more intriguingly, there were accounts of the various tasks she had thereafter been asked to perform on their behalf. Investigations into the strategical advantages of a considerable number of Old Race discoveries, some of which Kali knew about or, indeed, had beaten them to. There were other entries, too, but they were clearly meant for her brother alone and so Kali skipped through them quickly, until she came to the last entry of all.

Recorded only a week before, it detailed Jenna's last assignment and as Kali played it through she wandered, frowning, to the cave mouth and gazed up at the smoking remains of what she now knew was the first stage to finding the Crucible.

The next day Kali rose early and whispered to the still half-asleep ex-pirates that they should wait where they were for her return.

Moving out, she ascended the pass to the point where the hole loomed above, and there her heart sank. For the pass beneath had become blocked, recently by the look of it. While she scaled the massive pile of collapsed rocks with ease, using it to begin her ascent to the hole, she knew that Aldrededor and Dolorosa would never make the climb. Upon her return, they would need to find another way past the blockage, a delay she wasn't sure that they could afford. Her concerns on that matter were, however, soon replaced, by a growing sense of familiarity about the spot in which she climbed. She realised that the only reason she hadn't recognised it earlier was because the unmistakable landmark that was missing should not be missing at all. My Gods, she thought, the rocks she was climbing were the remains of Thunderlungs' Cry. But that was impossible, surely? Because the Cry was a thing of magic and could never be destroyed.

No, that wasn't *quite* right, she corrected herself. Thunderlungs' Cry might be impervious to any *natural* threat but if the thing that had destroyed it was *itself* magical then it could tumble like anything else. Was that what had happened here? A *magical* explosion? If that was the case, it had to have been incredibly powerful, on a scale such as she had never heard of, and that told her one thing – that it was likely caused by something from the latter stages of the Old Races' evolution, from their third and final period of development, just before the End Time.

Another realisation hit her as she remembered the legend of Thunderlungs' Cry. What if it was no legend? What if what had distracted Mawnee was the hole in the rock she was climbing towards now?

Oh boy. Now *that* was exciting.

Kali climbed swiftly, moving beyond the collapsed rocks, flinging herself from outcrop to outcrop as she scaled the almost sheer face in a zig-zag fashion, then heaving herself into the lip of a tunnel. There she saw the burned and twisted remains of a metal superstructure that formed the tunnel walls and, further in, a massive gantry – some kind of elevator? – that could only have been produced by a more advanced technology. However advanced the technology that had constructed it, though, it was academic, because it was unusable now. As bent and twisted as every other piece of metal in the cavern.

But what pieces of metal they were! Even at this distance Kali could make out the burned metal skeletons of craft that were moored above her. Craft that, by their very situation, must have been capable of flight. Airships, then! She had suspected that the Old Races had been capable of as much but until now...

Kali's train of thought stopped and her nose wrinkled. As acrid as the air in the cavern entrance was, she had suddenly smelled something that had been caught upon it, as if in passing. But passing or not, it had made its mark and still lingered strongly. In a second, she had it.

It was Slowhand's aftershave.

Quiver.

Slowhand, here? How in all the hells had he gotten here?

And more to the point, where the hells was he now?

Kali moved along the cavern floor to the base of the ruined elevator and began to climb, picking her hand and footholds carefully, as the battered metal was in danger of collapse at any moment. Despite the creaks and the groans of the unstable structure, she made it without incident to the top and clambered onto the very same platform which, unbeknownst to her, Slowhand had leapt from three days before. She called the archer's name, but there was no response. Hardly surprising, she thought, for anything caught in the explosion that had taken this place out was unlikely to any longer have the capacity for speech. But if anyone had died here – and she tried not to picture Slowhand in such a conflagration – then there would surely be some remains. But there was nothing. Somehow, Slowhand must have made an escape.

For the moment Kali could only imagine what had happened here and she picked her way through the wreckage, searching for some clue to enlighten her, but anything that had been present before the explosion not made of metal had been reduced to ash. Still, what did remain offered hints to the place's original function. There were signs, for example, of great volumes of supplies, and the remains of a crane that must surely, at one time, have stowed such supplies aboard the airships. What these supplies had been for – and more importantly, where they had been *destined* – was, however, a question it appeared she would be unable to answer for the time being. Even the remains of what seemed to be some kind of refuelling device extending from the wall was so ruined that it was able to offer no clues. It did, though, help to explain one thing. For the remains glowed with the same amber energy she had seen glow in The Mole and her crackstaff. She realised that in some way it must *power* those devices and others. But what the hells was it? For future reference – and to keep things simple – she named it *amberglow*.

Kali continued her search without any other significant finds but then, bolted to the wall of what appeared to have once been some kind of office area, she found a metal panel that had been seared but left otherwise undamaged. A panel that seemed to be inscribed with some kind of map of the mountains. Amongst the diagrams depicting the mountains and their relative positions there were other symbols that showed, as far as she could work out, docking airships, which she could only assume were meant to represent places such as the one she was in now. Intrigued, Kali brushed away soot and studied the charred metal plate, tracing the symbols with her finger, jabbing the one whose relative position corresponded with her current location. Yes, it was the one lowest down in the mountains and, therefore, the first of four similar such locations inscribed on the plate. She *was* looking at a map whose purpose appeared to be as an aid to guide airships from one location to the next. The question was, what kind of destination required the amount of traffic that these waystations had clearly handled? What kind of destination needed this amount of raw materials and equipment on what had to have been a fairly constant basis? More – for what purpose?

Kali swallowed, looking at the one ideogram she had not yet studied in any detail. Because there, in a position that corresponded with the very heart of the Drakengrat Range, was a marker in the shape of... well, she wasn't sure what it was. But it *looked* like something half elven and half dwarven and it was big and it sure as hells wasn't natural.

Was this what Jenna had referred to in one of her log entries? Kali wondered. She took the bracelet from a pocket on the thigh of her bodysuit and thumbed it into life once more, finding and replaying some of the last entries. Jenna flickered into pseudo-life before her, and began to speak.

"Reports have reached us from the Drakengrat Mountains. An Order of the Swords of Dawn contingent has discovered something unusual that is believed to be an Old Race location worthy of further investigation. I have just received word that I am to leave for this location in the morning..."

Kali thumbed ahead.

"The location is of a scale hitherto unfound, though its purpose continues to elude even our finest investigators. I cannot shake the feeling that something *unnatural* happened here, though for the time being I can only guess at what."

Again.

"At last, a breakthrough! We cannot pretend to understand the science of it but it seems that the Old Race had developed a process of..."

And again.

"There has been a mistake. Something has gone horribly wrong with our equations and the capabilities of this place are out of control. Many of my people are already dead and, I fear, many will soon follow. We need to stop this but, to do so, we need help."

And finally.

"A number of us, including Fitch, have managed to flee the location on the airship we discovered. I intend to pilot the airship to Gransk, where our people are already aware of our problem. We shall, I hope, return to this place and end what we began. Even if it means we have to wipe this foul experiment off the face of Twilight. If we fail to do so, then the Lord of All save us."

Kali frowned, as she had the first time she had played these extracts, but now it was a frown exacerbated by what she had seen with her own eyes. The implications of it were worrying to say the least, but her greatest concern was for the fate of Slowhand himself. Dammit, if she hadn't gotten herself stuck in that *farking* deathtrap she would have been here to help him. She could only hope that the archer wasn't lying dead and frozen in some unmarked mountain grave.

Kali took a deep breath, realising that, while there was nothing she could do for Slowhand, she still had a responsibility to those who had accompanied her. If she, Aldrededor and Dolorosa were to follow the map she had found to its ultimate destination they were going to need more than Surprise Stew butties to keep them alive. There was a chance, perhaps, that, if they were packed in anything other than wood, some of the more modern supplies remaining here might be food.

Again, Kali searched. And came upon a number of charred metal boxes bearing the symbol of a crossed circle. Well, if there had been any doubt that Jenna and the Final Faith had been here, that was now dispelled. Kali broke the seal on one, stared, and laughed.

The supplies belonged to the Final Faith, all right. Who else would bring wafers and wine to the mountains?

But it was something. It didn't take Kali long to make her way back to the cave and she was actually quite looking forward to breakfasting on the alcohol, but then she stopped suddenly.

Something was wrong.

The place was too quiet.

And Aldrededor and Dolorosa were gone.

Kali entered the camp slowly, looking for any sign of her companions – or worse, what might have taken them. But there were no tracks. She moved over to the campfire, found it recently rekindled, then felt the cups the ex-pirates must have been drinking from. The liquid inside was still warm. In this temperature, that likely meant that whatever had happened here had happened in the past few minutes. But there was no sign of anything untoward.

There was, however, the slightest of sudden noises. It came from a previously unnoticed passage towards the rear of the cave and occurred at exactly the same time as Kali's sixth sense alerted her to the fact that something was wrong. She was about to unsling her crackstaff when the slight *pfft* she'd heard was followed immediately by a sting on the side of her neck.

Kali raised her hand, felt a tiny needle embedded there.

And then, her eyes glazed and, her body stiff as a board, she fell face down onto Dolorosa and Aldrededor's empty furs.

CHAPTER TWELVE

"UNKA-CHAKKA-UNKA-CHAKKA-OH-OH-OH!"
UNKA-CHAKKA-UNKA-CHAKKA-OH-OH-OH!

The chanting came from beyond the passage that led from the cave, loud and then soft, loud and then soft; never ceasing. The only visible signs of those responsible for the ominous mantra were the grotesquely misshapen shadows that loomed and rippled across the rough passage wall. Sometimes the shadows loomed so large that it seemed their owners were about to enter the cave, but then they dwindled once more, the only other activity the occasional burst of shadowboxing – perhaps jostling, perhaps some altercation – but, whatever their cause, they never lasted for long.

What did last was the gnawing and grunting that could be heard beneath the chanting.

And the smell of roasting flesh.

"UNKA-CHAKKA-UNKA-CHAKKA-OH-OH-OH!
UNKA-CHAKKA-UNKA-CHAKKA-OH-OH-OH!"

Yes, yes, all right, enough already! Kali thought. *Will you please, for just one farking minute, shut up*

She sighed heavily, and rattled the chains that bound her. She reckoned it had been about eight hours since the sting on her neck, and it was only now that the effects of whatever the tiny dart had been coated with were starting to wear off. Starting, mind, because although her paralysis had gone it had left her feeling distinctly betwattled. A condition she was not unfamiliar with but would have preferred to have enjoyed slumped in the *Flagons* rather than here, chained to a pillar and dressed in nothing but three strategically draped strips of animal hide. It was a development she had to admit had caught her a tad by surprise. Steaming pits of bloody Kerberos, it could only happen to her.

A sacrificial virgin!

Kali pouted.

Okay, then, sacrificial... offering.

Where the hells was she? Who were these people? And most of all, why was she dressed in this stupid, farking costume?

She frowned. The fact was, there were other, more serious questions. Specifically, what had happened to Aldrededor and Dolorosa? There was no doubt that the couple *had* been captured with her because she had caught glimpses of them, by her side, slung beneath the same kind of pole on which she herself had been tied and carried here. Those glimpses had been fleeting and utterly random, however, as her inability to move her eyes, let alone the rest of her body, during the enforced journey had left her with no choice but to see only what the twists, turns and ups and downs of her unexpected excursion had thrust before her frozen eyes. It hadn't helped that she had been lapsing in and out of consciousness, also.

What she *did* remember was that their captors seemed to have taken them higher into the mountains, and that the route had begun in the passage at the rear of the cave where they had sheltered. From there on in, it had become confusing – one minute exposed on the mountainside, the next travelling through rock, snatches of fur-hooded faces leering in both the light and the dark – leaving her with the impression that, far from being deserted as she had thought, the Drakengrats were riddled with a warren of caves and tunnels which were clearly inhabited. She remembered wondering whether she was in the hands of ogur, but then ogur would hardly dress her in a skimpy outfit as it would only stick in their teeth when they ate her. Besides, ogur would have downed her with club not dart, and she would have been in no position to wonder anything at all.

Also, her captors didn't smell anywhere near as bad – let's face it, nothing did. They just smelled... odd, actually.

Kali looked about the cave, gleaning what she could about her captors. Various skulls and other pieces of skeleton were hung on the walls. Animal skins were draped across the floor and littered across them were various implements and tools, bowls, cups and the like, all of which appeared to have been carved from bone. One thing was immediately clear. Everything here was designed or scaled for human use, though she had never come across a human settlement as primitive as this. What were they doing here in the Drakengrats, and why was their culture so stagnated? It was as if *nothing* had changed here since the days of Thunderlungs Cry.

She needed answers – especially if these people knew anything about the Crucible – and she wasn't going to get them bound to this farking pillar. Again, Kali rattled her chains, pulling with wrists and ankles to test for signs of weakness, but all her struggles achieved was to dislodge the strips of hide from where they had been strategically placed and, cursing, she tried to jiggle them back. As she did, the chanting from the other cave suddenly stopped, and she snapped a look at the passage. Shadows loomed again, and this time they didn't go away

"Shit" she said, and jiggled harder.

She succeeded just in time. Four figures dressed in skins entered the cave and stood in silence by the passage, just staring at her. She could barely make them out, silhouetted as they were, but they appeared to be human from what she could see. Human, if a little on the beefy side.

Kali swallowed, thinking: *One step and, I promise, you will regret it.*

The figures did not move towards her. Instead, a moment later, they stood aside to allow the entrance of a fifth figure – one who was more surreally dressed than they. It wore a loincloth, a plethora of dangling fetishes and, worst of all, a mask that covered its head and shoulders and made its upper half resemble that of an exploded chicken.

The figure approached then slapped both its palms onto its thighs. Then it suddenly squatted down, sticking its tongue out as far as it would go, which was quite some way, and waddled its head from side to side.

"*Wadaladalla!*" It shouted – or something like that. A curious sound that made even its companions look at him askance.

"Hey!" Kali shouted. "Unless w*adaladalla* means 'release the girl *right* now,' I am going to be very pitsed off!"

Everything went silent. The figure stared at her, and both hands suddenly produced ominous looking objects not unlike the goblin death rattles Merrit Moon dealt in and shook them violently in her general direction. Then it stomped gradually nearer, like some wrestler at the Scholten carnival, until it came face to face, whereupon it shook the rattles again and its tongue flicked at her nose.

There was just enough give in the chains for Kali to knee him in the groin.

"*Ohooooooo... huuuurrrr... Gods and farking pits!*" A man then.

As he staggered back cradling himself, Kali ignored the disturbed murmurs from his friends and stared at her victim hard. Something wasn't right here, she suddenly realised. For one thing, it had occurred to her that all that *unka-chaka* stuff reminded her very much of a song she'd once hated and, for another, it had only just clicked that this strange man wasn't anywhere near as hairy as his mates. Not at all, in fact. Above all else, though, there was the matter of a couple of familiar tattoos she could make out between the fetishes he wore – those and one she *wasn't* familiar with on his muscular left bicep. A declaration of love for someone called, of all things, *Endless Passion*.

Only one man would wear a tattoo like that, Kali knew.

"Slowhand?"

"*Guhhhhng...* h-hi, Hooper, how you doing?"

"How am I doing? Oh, you know, shot with a paralysing dart, kidnapped, stripped, chained to a sacrificial altar, *you?*"

The exploded chicken mask bobbed back and forth. "Oh, you know," he said, and paused to cup his lower regions once more. "*Hoooooo, hells...* fine, fine."

"Whatever you're doing wearing that farking thing, take it off! *What the hells are you doing here?*"

Slowhand slapped his palm over her mouth. "Trying to get you out of here. So will you please keep your voice *down?*"

Kali's eyes narrowed and, for a second, she debated kneeing him again. Instead, she spoke quietly. "*Whyfmychayndupwifnocloffson?*"

Slowhand withdrew his hand. "What?"

"Why am I chained up with no clothes on?"

"Oh, yes. Bit of a long story. Seems these people are having a problem with their god. Think it's angry because strangers invaded its – invaded *their* – holy ground."

"Strangers?"

"The Filth, from what I've pieced together." Slowhand said. He noticed the figures standing in the cave were regarding their lengthy and hushed conversation with some suspicion and, to appease them, did a little dance. Then, he frowned. "Led by my sister, as it happens."

Kali was already beginning to suspect that this 'holy ground' was the discovery Jenna had mentioned in her recordings – but that someone was *worshipping* it came as a surprise. Despite her current predicament, this was becoming more and more interesting.

"I know about Jenna. Aldrededor, Dolorosa and I found a bracelet."

Now it was Slowhand's turn to be surprised. "I *lost* that bracelet. She gave it to me before I fell out of the sky."

"You were on one of their airships?"

"Yes and no. Another long story." Slowhand glanced over at his companions, and shook one of his rattles for effect. "But now isn't the time."

"I'd go with that. So, exactly *how* are you getting me out of here?"

"I'm not."

"Excuse me?"

Slowhand hesitated. "Thing is, these people think a sign of their God's anger is the k'nid. That they're demons whose release into the world is a punishment which can only halted by the sacrifice of one of the strangers. They had their eyes on me when they found me but... I managed to persuade them otherwise."

"Don't tell me, you beguiled them by summoning balloon animals. Pits, Slowhand, you *still* carry balloons?"

He shrugged. "Well, they weren't *balloons* exactly, but..."

"I do not want to know!"

"Shush! Okay, forget the balloons. If you must know, I trained them in the making and use of bows, as well. They'd never seen such a weapon before and, with the scarcity of wildlife up here, believe me, they come in handy."

Kali sighed. "That explains the gnawing out there."

"Aha. Before, they sustained themselves mainly on mountain fungus and *vegetables*."

"Oh, Gods."

"I know. Anyway, Hooper, the point is, I survived. But they still needed to sacrifice *someone*."

"Aldrededor!" Kali said, concerned. "Dolorosa!"

"No, no. They're *fine*. Because I suggested you."

"*What*?"

"I figured the only way to get us all out of this was to convince them we're *not* strangers, that we're like them. And our best chance of doing that was with you..."

"What are you talking about?"

"One of the first things I noticed about these people – they call themselves the yazan, by the way – is that they're different."

"Different?"

"Look, there's no time to explain," Slowhand said, and

produced a vicious looking knife from beneath his fetishes. "Just be grateful I managed to persuade them to let me perform the sacrifice, my way."

Kali stared at Slowhand in disbelief as he placed the point of the knife on her sternum, then hissed in shock as she felt it penetrate the skin.

"Ow! Liam, what the hells do you think you're doi –"

"Don't move!"

"Don't move?! The hells I'm not going to move!"

Slowhand gripped her arm firmly and unexpectedly winked. "Trust me, Hooper, all right? The Death of A Thousand Cuts is the only way out of this."

"The Death of A Thousand Cuts!?"

"Will you please calm down."

"Slowhand, you're sticking a farking knife in my chest!"

The archer paused, leaning in and whispering in Kali's ear. "Hooper, I cannot tell you how good I felt when I saw you were still alive." He shrugged. "Do you really think I'd spoil that by slicing you open now?"

"It does seem a little odd, even for you."

"Fine, then trust me. *Please.*"

Slowhand's grip on the gutting knife tightened. And Kali felt its tip being held against her measuredly.

"Do what you have to." Kali said, staring him in the eyes.

Slowhand nodded, and then drew the tip of the knife down her sternum, scoring a shallow red line about six inches in length, and she moaned softly as it began to ooze blood. As it did, Slowhand span around to face the yazan, throwing his hands in the air to reveal the wound – what Kali fervently hoped was the first and last cut. But then the yazan stared at it and, to her discomfort, nodded. Their meaning was clear – *continue.*

"*Wadaladalla!*" the archer cried and span dramatically toward her, knife raised. Then – rather too theatrically, Kali thought, he suddenly leapt back and pointed at her wound, uttering a shocked variation on his usual cry that sounded like: "*Wululadadalula?*"

The yazan stared where he pointed, and then moved forward to crowd around her.

What? Kali thought. *What?*

Had she suddenly grown a second head in her cleavage? Had the cloth come loose from her bits? Then she looked down to where Slowhand pointed, and gasped. She guessed that she'd never really thought too much about her recuperative abilities – just wondered at their presence – and, as a result, she'd never really studied them in action, but now she realised for the first time just how *dramatic* they were. Right in front of her eyes, the shallow wound that Slowhand had inflicted was sealing itself, healing in seconds.

Not for the first time, Kali thought, *what am I?*

But her concerns about her own abnormality were immediately replaced by a more pressing. Namely, the implications of what had just happened for her current predicament. Slowhand had pulled a surprise card from up his sleeve, that was for sure, but the question was, how was he going to play it? Was he going to try to pass her off to these yazan as some kind of God? She sure as hells hoped not, because Twilight's mythology was littered with cautionary tales of why that kind of hubris was really, *really* not a good idea.

Slowly, she looked up at the faces of the yazan, and gasped again. For a second she wondered whether it was a trick of the light, but Slowhand's words seemed to suggest otherwise.

"That's why it had to be you, Hooper," he said. "Because you're *different...* like them."

Her mind reeling, Kali was only dimly aware that the yazan were backing off, gesturing to Slowhand in a way she guessed meant 'release her'. But, as momentous as what she had just seen had been, something else niggled at her as Slowhand freed her from her chains.

"Hold on just one farking minute," she said, and gestured at the pillar and chains and the hides that barely garbed her. "If you knew this was going to save me, why didn't you just slice me when I was paralyzed. Why all this pantomime?"

Slowhand coughed. "It was, erm, a tribal elder thing. Tradition. Yes, tradition."

"Really? And which ones are the tribal elders, then?"

"The elders... yes," Slowhand said, hesitantly. He moved his finger slowly round the cave and pointed at the yazan who stood near the entrance. "They would *beeeeeeeee...* that lot over there."

Kali folded her arms and tapped her foot. "I see. They don't look very *elderly* to me."

Slowhand paused. "Yes, well. They like their elders, er, young."

"It was you, wasn't it? The pillar, the chains, this *costume*. You said you wanted to do the sacrifice *your* way. Great Gods, you never miss a trick, do you? Hells, I'm surprised you didn't have me *oiled*."

"They only had yuk fat."

"You are a pervert, Killiam Slowhand."

"I know! I can't help it!"

"Well, I can't help this." Kali retorted. She booted him in the groin once more and, as the archer crumpled into a wheezing heap, turned and smiled at the yazan. "Sorry. Tradition."

The yazan accepting her as one of their own, now, Kali was permitted to leave the cave only to find herself in another, larger one. This appeared to be some gathering place for their people. Here, she found herself reunited with Aldrededor and Dolorosa who, despite their raised eyebrows at her garb, were, like the yazan themselves, comfortably seated around the fire whose glow she had seen from the pillar. She saw the reason for the shadowy altercations she had witnessed, too. The ex-pirates and the yazan were all gnawing heartily at chunks of roasted meat and, on occasion, some of the yazan tried to snatch Dolorosa's meat from her. The older woman was having none of it – as a rapidly unsheathed knife and a snarl proved – and, while Kali could appreciate her hunger after her ordeal, she found it quite *disturbing* how easily Dolorosa slipped into the tribal way of life. She smiled as the tall, thin woman winked at Slowhand as he hobbled in from the other cave, a greasy mass of dribble running down her chin.

Kali's smile faded, however, as she sat amongst the group, and it was replaced by a look of puzzlement. The yazan were different, all right. Human, yes, but sitting next to her was a man whose eyes were the colour of Long Night. Across from her, a woman whose skin was scaled as if her blood ran cold, and, next to her, another man whose skeleton, in places, grew outside his skin. She couldn't be sure but it looked as if one of them even had *gills*.

"Slowhand," she whispered as the archer, maskless now, settled beside her, "who are these people, what the hells is going on?"

"I don't know, but there are more like them, in caves all around here. Even some who are able to heal like you. Heal others, too. Believe me, I was in quite the mess when they brought me here."

Kali looked at him, concerned, but found herself staring instead at his *Endless Passion* tattoo. Was it, she wondered, anything to do with the younger female yazan who was blowing kisses at him from across the fire?

"Oh dear," she said, giving her a hard stare. "Still, you certainly seem to have *settled in*."

Slowhand harumphed, embarrassed. "Yes, that. Look, I told you, Hooper, they were thinking of offing *me*. I, er, had to *bond* with them."

"Bond with them? Right. And tell me, Killiam Slowhand, how many times, exactly, did you *bond*?"

"Hooper, it wasn't like that!" the archer protested, then reddened. "Besides, she's... different too."

"Pits, Slowhand, I leave you alone for a few weeks and suddenly you're setting up home with some tart with what, an extra orifi –? Oh, no, don't tell me, I don't want to know. I mean, it just occurred to me, even that chant of theirs – that *unka-chakka* – is the opening to that pitsing song I hate isn't it? *Isn't it*!"

"So ever since I've been in a stupor, because of that lass named Kali Hoooooper..." Slowhand sang, and smiled. "Truth is, Kal, I didn't feel much like coming down out of the mountains because what was the point? I thought you were dead."

There was something in Slowhand's tone that made Kali falter. "You're serious, aren't you?"

"Never more so."

"I thought you might be dead too."

"Well, I'm not," Slowhand grinned. "So... how you doing?"

"Oh, you know – *shit!*"

"Shit?"

"No, sorry, I..." Kali began and then trailed off.

Because, while Slowhand's *unka-chakka* had been nagging at her, something else had too. The name of the people they were with. The yazan, they called themselves. Despite her knowledge of ancient languages - elf, dwarf *and* human – she had never heard such a name before. There *was*, though, an elven word which was spelled differently but pronounced much the same. Only it wasn't a name, it was a description.

Yassan.

It meant *changed.*

She couldn't help but think of her own past, of how she had been found as a babe by Merrit Moon in that long lost and sealed Old Race site – and how different she had found herself to be in the time since. Just like the yassan. Neither she or the old man had ever found out where she had come from but could she have come from here? Was she really *like* them?

She shared her thoughts with Slowhand.

"Doubt it," Slowhand said. "There's a reason these people have never left the mountains, a reason their culture remains stagnated. Thing is, *if* they leave the mountains, they die."

"What? That's ridiculous."

"Tell the yassan that. They have funerals *before* they die – their old ones simply walking down the pass until they turn to dust. Dust, Hooper. Literally. As if abandoned by their God."

A place in the clouds where the Old Races played at being Gods. "It has to be something to do with the Crucible."

"Crucible? You mean the Crucible of the Dragon God?"

"The Crucible of the *Dragon* God?"

"That's what they call it."

"They worship a dragon God? Why in the hells would they do that when dragons have been extinct for thousands upon thousands of years, since before humans were around?"

"That is something I've been trying to work out."

"From what?"

"Their cave paintings."

"They have cave paintings?"

Slowhand smiled, as if he knew where he was going all along. He rose and offered her a hand up. "I know you love it when I talk dirty."

The archer took a flaming torch for each of them and escorted Kali through a series of caves heading upward, chatting as they walked as if simply out for a stroll.

"So, I guess the fact that you've turned up here means the world is ending again, right?"

"Pretty much."

"The k'nid?"

"The k'nid."

Slowhand nodded. "The yassan told me they've been pouring out of the mountains once every *seharn* – that's day to you. Met them myself. Lethal little bastards but I wouldn't quite have put them in the world-ending category."

Kali told him about Andon, and about the k'nid's ability to replicate.

"Hells. I shouldn't have been twiddling my thumbs up here. I could have done something to help."

"No, Slowhand, you couldn't. But you can now."

Slowhand stopped, smiled, swept back his hair. "Sidekick?"

"Sidekick."

"Gods, it's good to see you," the archer declared suddenly, and planted a smacker on her lips.

"*Iffgudderseyoodoo...*"

"What say that when we've saved the world we find a little cave somewhere, spread the furs and –"

Slowhand stopped as Kali froze in his arms then pushed him away, hard enough for him to collide with the wall. He raised his eyes as he realised where in the cave system they were, and what she must have seen behind him. The cave paintings.

The archer stood by her but Kali completely ignored him, already engrossed in what was depicted on the walls, running her fingers back and forth between the pictures as she concentrated on their meaning.

"Well?" he said. "They tell you anything?"

"Only the entire bloody history of the yassan. Gods, Slowhand, these people are descendants of Thunderlungs' and Mawnee's tribes, only they're not *true* descendants because the true blood line was interrupted. It's possible even that the original tribes died out long ago." Kali paused, and took an excited breath. "No, this relates *another* legend about how their people were *taken* – taken to a place beyond the mountains – where they were changed by the God who lived there. A Dragon God, Slowhand! It goes on – *look* – saying that, in return for their service to the dragon god, they would inherit the place beyond the mountains when the Dragon God ascended to... fark, that bit isn't clear. But the point, *the point is*, that this place beyond the mountains is described as a place in the clouds. A *place in the clouds*, Slowhand! It has to be what we're looking for. It has to be the Crucible!"

"So those jiggly lines are mountains?"

"The yassan – their Crucible – is it near?"

"Well, I don't know about the Crucible itself but the *way* to it certainly is."

"Where?"

Slowhand smiled in a way that suggested *he* now had the advantage, placed his hands on Kali shoulder's and turned her around.

"Oh!" was all that Kali could say.

Because, in her eagerness to examine the paintings, she hadn't even noticed that the part of the caves in which they stood were open on one side, a high snow-covered ledge looking out over a pass below. But it wasn't the pass that had left her lost for words. It was what lay across it.

Kali trudged onto the snowy ledge, exposed to a bitter night sky, hardly noticing the winds that buffeted her as she stared at a mountainside which, though some distance away, completely filled her field of vision. She was looking at one of the central peaks of the Drakengrats, heights almost as unscalable as those of the World's Ridge that should have had no way over them or through – except that this one did. Sort of.

The entire mountainside had been carved into the shape of an immense dragon's head, and beneath a pair of giant, brooding eyes and promontory sized snout, the dragon's roaring maw appeared to be some kind of tunnel. Appeared, that was, because the maw itself was exhaling a huge and constant, roiling mass of flame.

"They call it the Dragonfire," Slowhand said.

"Oh, we have *got* to find a way in there."

"Hooper, *finding* a way in might not be the problem. Chummy as we now are with them, I'm not sure how the yassan would react to us treading on their holy ground."

"Leave that to me," Kali said.

She turned swiftly away and retraced their steps through the caves, returning to the main gathering chamber and calling a meeting of the tribal elders – the *real* ones this time. Slowhand had to kick his heels as she conversed with them for an hour or more but, at last, she took up position on a raised part of the cave and addressed the yassan as a whole.

The archer wasn't to know how guilty she had felt manipulating the elders – telling them that she was obviously yassan but *special* yassan because she had lived beyond the mountains and survived – let alone breaking her own rules of hubris, because in the end the ploy seemed to work.

"Your elders have declared that I have been chosen!" Kali declared. "Chosen to calm the one you worship in this time of anger! Tomorrow myself and my followers depart for the Crucible of the Dragon God!"

For a moment the chamber was silent and then, increasing in volume as more and more voices joined in, echoed with a sound that despite the *followers* bit made the archer bow and preen.

"*UNKA-CHAKKA-UNKA-CHAKKA-OH-OH-OH!*
UNKA-CHAKKA-UNKA-CHAKKA-OH-OH-OH!"

CHAPTER THIRTEEN

They started out at dawn, taking most of the morning to reach the Dragonfire, the colossal scale of the cliff sculpture and its preternatural centrepiece deceptive, making the phenomenon appear much closer than it was and turning a seemingly short hike into a long, arduous trek. There were six in the party, Kali, Slowhand and four of the yassan. One to act as guide through a tortuous series of hidden mountain paths, caves and ravines, and three to tend and give offering before the enormous Godhead as other members of their tribe had done for countless years. Kali had decided she had already risked the lives of Aldrededor and Dolorosa too much to bring them along and so, to their frustration, had told them to remain behind with the tribe. They would rendezvous with them when they were done. The decision had, naturally, not gone down well, though the Sarcreans seemed somewhat mollified after she had taken them aside and suggested a way to make themselves useful.

Her overall plan was, she thought, a sound one, though with

one pitsing great hole in it – the 'when they were done' bit. The truth of the matter was, she didn't have a clue what *was* to be done, because she didn't have a clue what to expect when they got where they were going.

The party arrived at last at the base of the Dragonfire and, standing beneath it, a somewhat breathless Kali found she could not crane her neck back far enough to take it all in. That the Godhead was awe inspiring was beyond question and their proximity to it had the effect on the four yassan that she had anticipated. Their heads bowed and eyes lowered, they diligently cleared its base of detritus and arranged their offerings of mountain flowers and intricately woven fetishes in rock bowls, their manner reverent and vaguely fearful. It was clear they dared not look upon the *Dragonfire* itself, let alone climb higher and actually approach it, which was handy for she and Slowhand because they could slip away without much attention being paid to them. Kali wasn't particularly happy that she had been less than truthful with the yassan, but if on the way up the rockface she suffered any *unchosen one* like falls, it was perhaps best they didn't see.

For a while as she and Slowhand clambered up the lower parts of the vast sculpture, she began to wonder whether that might indeed be their fate, because even though the wind whistled more harshly about them with each yard they climbed, it was as nothing compared to the roaring that reached them from above – from where the Dragonfire itself roiled into the world. It did indeed sound like the exhalation of some angry God, and only the fact that every bone in her body told her that it *couldn't be* stopped her turning back to rethink her plan. Slowhand reached the level of the fire before her and pulled himself up onto a ledge before it.

"Keep back!" she shouted up. "The heat could –"

To her surprise, Slowhand merely turned in a circle before it, his arms outstretched. "What heat? Hooper, it looks like fire, it roars like fire, but it isn't fire! It's just an illus –"

His words were cut short as his rotation brought him too close and the Dragonfire, rather than burning him, blew him back across the ledge. The archer thudded to the ground with an *oof!*

Kali flipped herself onto the ledge and made sure he was all right. "Serves you right. Idiot."

"Hey, how was I to know? You told me illusions are a favourite trick of the Old Races, right? Like the dancing beds at Cannista."

"Dancing *heads*," Kali corrected. *Gods, he really did have a one track mind.* "And I probably tell you far too much."

She offered a hand to help Slowhand up, and he grabbed it – the pair yelping as a spark of residual energy from his blow-back arced between them.

"Fark," Kali said, shaking her hand

"The power of the Dragon God?" Slowhand mused as he rubbed his own tingling fingers.

"More like the power of ancient technology. Some kind of force barrier. Very old and much weaker than it probably once would have been. Otherwise, you wouldn't be standing here now."

She stared up at the Dragonfire. The area over which it roiled was massive. Large enough, she realised with growing excitement, to permit an airship to pass through it.

"You're not telling me the yassan built this thing?"

"No, only the Godhead around it. The fire thing goes part of the way to explain their choice of deity, though, don't you think?"

"I think a better question is, is there any way through?"

Kali examined the area. "Doesn't seem to be any way to shut it down so I guess anything *meant* to pass through it, like an airship, must be recognised somehow – perhaps some kind of onboard, runic key."

"Doesn't do us a lot of good, then. All out of airships *and* runic keys."

"True, but maybe we can fight the magic with magic, *force* it to recognise us."

Slowhand spread his hands, looking around. "Except we seem to be lacking a mage."

"But we do have this," Kali said, unslinging her crackstaff. "It made a hole in the Expanse's echo of the Three Towers so maybe it can do the same here."

Remembering the force with which Slowhand had been blown back, she eased the tip of the staff into the Dragonfire, intending to build its charge slowly. "Better hide," she advised, feeling the tingle of the force barrier running through her body. "Don't want this blowing all your clothes off, do we?"

"Oh, funny," Slowhand said. Kali sensed him disappear from her side, then heard, "This do?"

Kali looked at him looking at her, his face wavering on the other side of the barrier. "Yes, that's fi –" she began, then stopped when she realised what she was seeing.

"Not so much of a know all, then," Slowhand said, with a grin.

"How in the hells did you –?"

"Think about it, Hooper. If the ancestors of the yassan – who obviously didn't inherit the place because they're *out here* - and the k'nid escaped the Crucible, then they had to have a way out, right?" Slowhand looked insufferably smug and then cocked his thumb left. "Spotted it a moment ago. A small fissure just over there."

Kali looked where he indicated. "Dammit."

"Nice hairstyle," the archer commented as she retrieved the crackstaff and made her way to his side. "Vertical."

Kali patted down the stiffened stack. "Shut it."

Slowhand pretended to stagger back. "Are you *sulking*?" he asked, and glanced at the fissure. "Just because I found –?"

Kali slammed her hands on her hips. "I am *not* sulking."

"You *are*. You're *sulking*."

"Look, can we just get on with this, please?"

"Fine, fine," Slowhand capitulated, then winked. "But you'd best let me go first, eh? Just in case you miss anything."

Kali growled and elbowed him out of the way, taking the lead into the tunnel. Her initial stomp soon turned into a slower and more awed tread, however, her neck craning again as she gazed upwards, realising just what a tunnel it was. Absolutely circular and clearly cutting right the way through the mountain, it was easily the size of one of the Lost Canals of Turnitia. The perfect smoothness of it indicated it had been bored using technology similar to the dwarven Mole, except on a much more ambitious scale. Hers was not the only mouth to hang open as she and Slowhand walked its length, their way lit by the same massive glowing tubes as had lit the waystation. Their passage through the mountain took some considerable time but, as they neared its end, they began to glimpse slivers of sky ahead, obfuscated by what appeared to be a mass of thick vegetation, possibly the tops of trees. That there was such growth here was surprise enough, but exactly *where* it grew was what took the proverbial redbread.

"Hooper," Slowhand said as they finally reached the tunnel's end. "Are you seeing what I'm seeing?"

"Oh, yeah," Kali responded, breathlessly.

They had emerged half way up another cliff-face and spread out before them, here in the highest heart of the Drakengrat Mountains, was a lush jungle valley. Completely surrounded by impassable and overlooming peaks – between which appeared to roil another barrier like the one they had passed through – it was a strange and fully verdant lost world that sat amongst the clouds. And there were structures in it. Structures that were not part of the jungle but had been overgrown by it. It was difficult to make out the details of them from where they stood because much of what they saw was obscured by the jungle itself, but both Kali and Slowhand got the impression they were looking at a number of *worlds*.

"The Crucible of the Dragon God?" Slowhand hazarded.

"Why don't we go ask him?"

"That looks as if it might be easier said than done."

Slowhand was right. The structures loomed high in the jungle and so they were going to have a problem accessing them. There was another problem, too, though one that was more theoretical than practical. It was now clear to Kali that this valley – *these worlds* – were meant to be reached only by air, and as a consequence of that only by those with the *technology* for air travel, and that troubled her. That they were here, so remote, so hidden, and that the force barrier at their only entrance was designed to stop unwanted intruders, made one previously unrealised question nag at her mind. If this place *was* Old Race – and in her mind there was little doubt of that – who exactly was it that its inhabitants had been protecting themselves against? There would have been no one else around at the time who *had* the technology to reach here except more Old Race. So were the people who had built here defending against their *own*? Why? What the hells was the Crucible of the Dragon God for?

There was only one way to find out. They had to negotiate the jungle.

Kali and Slowhand began to carefully descend the rockface into the thick and overgrown mass. She had the impression that the valley – if, indeed, it was a natural valley at all – had been razed some time in its distant past. Razed to allow the construction of these worlds, but in the endless years since these structures had last been inhabited nature had reasserted herself, entwining, enwrapping and growing between the artificial interlopers to their present state. That fact was reinforced as they moved across the jungle floor where, progressing towards the centre, they began to come across various constructions attached to them – support struts and the like – which *had* to have been built in the absence of the rampant vegetation. Both of them were on constant alert for any creatures that might call this place home, but none came, and the feeling that Kali hadn't been able to shake – that they were the first to tread here in an unimaginable age – became all the more pervasive. There was, she felt, a *reason* nothing was here. There was something horribly lonely about the place, almost unbearably still and sad, as if once upon a time something momentous had happened but that its effect upon the world had, in the end, been ultimately insignificant.

She and Slowhand continued to work their way through the jungle – he pulling branches out of the way, she slashing through the tendrils with her gutting knife – and eventually reached the centre of the valley. Here they were beneath the largest of the worlds they had seen, whose size completely obscured what little sky they had previously been able to see. It was a vast sphere, supported high into the trees by a framework of girders that made it look like a giant bulbous spider suspended in a metal web. It was impressive and inviting but Kali's appreciation of it was somewhat dulled by the fact that, from her and Slowhand's position, there seemed to be no way in. None designed, anyway. But the fact that the valley had returned to the wild offered an alternative.

"We can use the vegetation to get part of the way up," Kali said. "After that, we'll have to make it up as we go along."

Slowhand craned his neck and saw the branches of trees twisting and spiralling heavensward until they were lost from sight. "One hells of a climb, Hooper."

"I'll go first."

"Oh, be my guest."

Kali gestured for Slowhand to give her a boost up and, kicking off from his entwined hands, she leapt for a branch, grabbing onto it with a grunt. She pulled herself up and walked its length, before leaping for another branch above. The thickness of the foliage was stifling and she was already beginning to lose sight of Slowhand. For a moment she wondered why he hadn't yet started following. He was probably waiting for her to get out of the way, she reasoned, so the smaller branches didn't slap him in the face. Continuing on, she worked her way higher and higher, through branch after branch, until the trunk's appendages became more pliant beneath her hands and feet. Kali used this, however, to her advantage, bouncing and springing from the lower ones to their higher counterparts, speeding her ascent to double what it had been before. At that speed, it took her no longer than five minutes to reach the uppermost part of the tree, and suddenly she found herself able to peer out across the canopy.

Unfortunately, the canopy was still not as high as the metal structure, and from here on in her makeshift ladder would no longer be natural but Old Race made.

As Kali worked her way to the outer tip of one of the highest branches, coming closer to the upper side of the sphere, she saw that it was definitely of Old Race construction. The smooth, runic covered and organic quality of its material a dead giveaway. The only problem was that said material, though close to the end of the branch, was just beyond a distance that she could leap, even though her leaps could be considerable. But the tree came to the rescue once again as Kali realised she could use two of the branches to slingshot herself across the gap.

Tricky, but possible.

Kali positioned herself back near the trunk, pulling the branches with her until they were tense, then, releasing one, used it to fling herself into the second, releasing the tension in that as she did so. The double spring effect catapulted her from the foliage of the tree and into open air, and then she slammed onto the curve of the sphere itself.

From here it became trickier. Although the sphere's incline was not acute, it was slippery, and Kali found herself scrabbling for purchase as soon as she landed, then having to flatten herself on its surface to prevent herself sliding off. Thus positioned, she began to inch her way forward and upward. But though vegetation had so far aided her ascent, now it stymied it.

Unmaintained and exposed to the elements for countless years, the upper curve of the sphere was covered in a slippery lichen and each time Kali tried to pull herself across it, she slipped back. There was no way around it and the only other access to the top of the sphere was via some kind of walkway that curved above it, but that was at least a hundred yards higher than her current position.

There was nothing else for it. She had to negotiate the lichen.

Pulling herself upward, even more slowly than before, Kali began to inch her way over the grassy coating, digging her fingertips and toes into the material for purchase. But the purchase was slight and, again and again, Kali found herself taking one step forward and two steps back. Increasingly frustrated, she found herself flinging any attempt at a negotiated passage to the wind, and instead simply clawed her way forward whichever way she could.

She had gained perhaps fifteen feet when a whole swathe of lichen became detached from the sphere, its tiny roots ripped away beneath the weight of her body. Kali tried to throw herself over it but felt one foot skid under her, and the other, and then thought, *oh-oh*.

Suddenly, she was accelerating back down the sphere, the carpet of lichen on which she lay now acting as a sled.

"*Whoooooaaaaaahhhhh!*"

She was too distracted by the likelihood of imminent death to hear the *ziiiip* of something thin and fast shooting past her. She was too distracted to notice had it been an inch to the left the shaft of wood that had made the sound might have gone right through her. But she was not too distracted to feel herself jar to a sudden stop, in the arms of something that smelled strangely familiar.

"Slowhand?"

"Hi, Hooper, falling for me?" the archer said, with a broad grin.

Even as she watched his long mane of blonde hair being buffeted by the wind, and as she felt the two of them begin to rise, she couldn't believe he'd said it.

Kali looked down. There was nothing beneath them, nothing at all. She looked up, and saw a thin wire stretching up to where it was fastened by an arrow in the underside of the walkway. And she looked at Slowhand's free hand, clutching a small and complex looking device, which seemed to be, thanks to some mechanical workings, carrying them up the wire.

"Little something I worked on during my time with the yassan."

"Really?"

"Yup. Call it a whizzline."

"A *whizzline?*"

"Yup."

Slowhand's smile of satisfaction was rapidly erased as Kali suddenly shouted in his face.

"Are you telling me that I just went through all that for nothing!"

"Hooper, now hang on –"

"Hang on, he says! Do I have a lot of farking choice!"

"Well, no, but –"

"Slowhand, you are a –"

"Hey, I saved you from a horrible death, didn't I?"

"You wanna know about horrible deaths? I'll show you..."

The exchange might have continued were it not for the fact that, at that moment, Slowhand's whizzline device reached its apex and the two of them found themselves dangling beneath the walkway, having come to a dead stop. They stared at each other as, beneath their combined weight, the line creaked above them, and then in unison yelped as the arrow holding it loosened slightly from where it was embedded.

"I think we'd better – *yaaaarrgh*!" Slowhand said.

They fell.

Kali didn't hesitate, swinging her legs up so that they wrapped Slowhand about the middle, and then flipping backwards in mid air so that her feet hooked over a small rail on the underside of the walkway. Then, with a grunt, she jacknifed herself upwards and grabbed onto the same rail, lowering her legs until Slowhand dangled between them, beneath her. The archer stared up from between her thighs.

"This," he said, "is like a dream."

"You want me to open them?"

"Er, not right now, no."

There was a moment's pause.

"Right."

A few seconds later, Kali had manoeuvred the pair of them onto the walkway and they stared at what lay in front and beneath them.

"Slowhand," Kali said, bending to place her palms on her thighs and taking a deep breath. "I think we're here."

"*Hoooo, boy.*"

As the highest point amongst the whole, strange series of structures, the walkway afforded the two of them their first proper view of the complex. Kali realised then that she hadn't been far wrong with her first impression that the valley was full of worlds.

A number of spheres of various sizes – though all massive – dotted the hidden place, some projecting ornate walkways to their neighbour, others on, or attached to, huge metal tracks or arms – one of which bore cradles and the rotted remains of more airships like those at the waystation – all sitting there amidst the overgrown trees. *Literally* complex and wondrous, Kali could see no reason why such should be its purpose but she couldn't help be reminded of something she had once seen used by the Sisters of Long Night. A mechanical contraption they told her was meant to emulate the movement of the celestial bodies on and around which they lived – something they called an orrery. That was what the Crucible reminded her of – a giant orrery, constructed for reasons she couldn't yet begin to imagine.

There, roughly speaking, was Kerberos, the largest sphere and the one beneath them, there, in its shadow, Twilight, and there, further out, its size perhaps representative of its actual distance, Twilight's sun. The only sphere Kali could not reconcile with what she knew of the heavens was one that was positioned somehow jarringly amongst the others – a sphere constructed of a darker material than its companions that looked as if had once drawn ever closer to them on a perfectly straight track through the trees. Kali frowned – in all her explorations she had never come across anything like this, and the only way she was going to discover the purpose of the spheres was to get inside them. Fortunately, there appeared to be a gap in *Kerberos* – as if once upon a time the upper half of the sphere had, for some reason, opened to the skies. Its edges now browned with great patches of rust, it seemed jammed in that position, but it was wide enough for their purposes. The only problem would be in reaching it without a repeat of her recent, almost fatal mishap.

"Remember Scholten?" Slowhand asked, winking.

He unslung Suresight and strung an arrow with a wire attached. Kali nodded. She wouldn't easily forget that stormy night and the suicide slide from the heights of the Cathedral. A slide that had come to a rude end when Katherine Makennon's guards had cut the line.

"You joining me this time?" she queried.

"Wouldn't miss it for the, er, world," Slowhand told her, nodding at the sphere.

He raised Suresight, aiming the arrow on a shallow trajectory, and then fired it through the gap. A second later he tested its tension and then attached the zipline. "Grab hold."

Kali did as instructed, wrapping her arms around Slowhand's torso and her legs around his, ignoring some ribald comment as the archer shuffled himself against her. Then he lurched and the two of them began to speed down the wire towards the shadowy gap.

As they slid through it into a dark and still interior, the metallic *zuzz* of the zipline sounded suddenly sharp, though not as sharp as would have been their cries of pain had they struck any of the odd, unidentifiable shapes that whizzed by them in the gloom. Thankfully, the interior of the sphere was vast, and none were in their way. Exactly what they were sliding into remained a mystery but, as was her habit on entering any Old Race site, Kali sniffed as she descended, trying to take in the odour of the place. There was metal and oil and the rough, sour tang of machinery. An odour she had smelled before in a site called Kachanka, one of her finds that had been some kind of dwarven factory. She never had discovered what it made. For all she knew it could have been dwarven razorblades, in which case, no wonder it had gone out of –

"End of the line!" Slowhand warned suddenly, and the two of them released their grips, dropping with a clang onto metal where they rolled to soften their impact.

Unexpectedly, they continued to roll, and – after mutual yelps of surprise – they realised they had landed on a sloping surface and were apparently sliding now towards the base of some huge bowl. When at last they came to a stop, they were up and ready to defend themselves, Slowhand panning a primed Suresight around him, Kali the same with her crackstaff. They saw nothing coming at them out of the dark, however, and reslung the weapons. Now, they listened, but the only sounds they heard were those of their own, heavy breathing and of the sphere itself – loud, eerie creaks and groans of metal shifting and settling. One such shift was so pronounced that the sphere actually shook, and the pair rocked on the soles of their feet.

"Whatever this place is," Slowhand commented, "it feels as if it's coming apart at the seams."

"It's *ancient*, Slowhand. What do you expect?"

"I've a feeling it's more than just age that's caused this."

Their eyes began slowly adjusting to the gloom and, as they did, they gasped.

Because they seemed to have landed on a walkway that curved along the base of the sphere, and off to their left and their right. The trouble was, as their slide had testified, it didn't *stop* to their left and their right. Instead it curved up the sides of the sphere and then, disorientatingly, not least because of the dizzying height involved, curved across its top, crossing the gap through which they had entered, and down again in a complete loop, coming full circle back to the spot where they stood. Nor was it the only walkway to do so. The interior of the sphere was criss-crossed with them, weaving a web-like pattern over its cathedral sized interior, as if the terms up, down, above and below had no meaning here. To be certain what she was seeing was true, Kali attempted to renegotiate the curve of the walkway but made it only so far before its incline slid her back. Craning her neck and turning on the spot, she gazed open mouthed, tracing all the walkways and wondering whether some sorcery that had enabled people to traverse these impossible ways had, once upon a time, been at play here. This remained a possibility until Slowhand noticed that the walkways were suspended a little way above the shell of the sphere, and that between the two a series of tracks, gears and gimbals hinted that they had been designed to move around its inside. A latticework sphere *within* a sphere, apparently rotatable through three hundred and sixty degrees in every direction so that any point of any walkway could rapidly shift into any position it needed to be in. It was a more prosaic explanation than sorcery, for sure, but was no less staggering for it. An incredible achievement of Old Race engineering unlike any they had ever seen. One question nagged at Kali, though. What exactly was it *for*?

Maybe part of the answer lay in what slowly became visible *between* the walkways. The vague shapes that had had whizzed by them during their descent were revealing themselves now to be tools and machines of various shapes, unknown purposes and sizes, all of which were aligned towards or – on their *own* independent tracks – capable of being aligned towards the centre of the sphere. Strange instruments like giant thrusting lances and claws, huge lenses and multiple-jointed things that looked like nothing less than upturned metallic spiders. The central focus of these tools made Kali rethink her initial impression of the place, feeling now that this was no razorblade factory but designed to build something big and she suddenly desired to see the ancient machinery in action. The huge inner sphere whirling and swirling about its task – whatever it was – and all of those various machines and tools at play, perhaps flashing and sparking with unknown energies, would have been of such complexity that it would have made the mechanics of the Clockwork King seem like those of a child's toy.

It *would* have been wondrous but, sadly, Kali doubted that it would ever work again. The interior of the sphere was almost as decayed at its exterior and, in parts, as overgrown as the jungle beyond. Swathes of lichen draped the walkways and machines, choking them, while great curtains of the stuff hung from the sides of the opening itself. Here and there plants had actually taken root amidst the machines. The sphere had gone almost to ruin, the vast mechanism that seemed the reason for its existence appearing, for all intents and purposes, dead.

Almost.

It was Slowhand who noticed it first, squinting at the heart of the sphere.

What had previously appeared to be empty space shimmered and rippled slightly, as if he were looking at some great globe of transparent liquid suspended in the air, extending out as far as the machinery around it and big enough that, if he so wished, he could almost reach out to touch it. The liquid reflected its surroundings in such a way – refracted them, in fact – that it seemed almost not to be there at all. It hung undisturbed, as if it were somehow part of an entirely different reality.

"Erm, Hooper?" the archer said. "What the hells is this?"

Kali turned her attention to where Slowhand pointed. Her heart missed a beat. What she was looking at was something she knew existed from her researches but which, before now, she hadn't encountered. It was one of the older sorceries of the elves, a thing that toyed with existence and was designed to mislead, to obfuscate – to *hide* those things, that they wished kept secret from the world. The elves had a name for it. They called it a glamour field.

"You know what it is?"

"A-ha. But the question is, what's inside?"

"Some magical portal? To the realm of the k'nid?"

Kali frowned, bit her lip. Here in this place of technology that didn't feel *right.* "Somehow... I don't think so."

"So what do we do, shut it down?"

Kali shook her head. "Even if we knew how, that wouldn't be wise until we know what we're dealing with. We need to take a good look around."

Slowhand raised his eyebrows. "That's a tad cautious for you, Hooper. What happened to 'ooh, ooh, ooh, what does this big red button do?'"

"Funny. But usually the sites I explore don't have the bloody k'nid pouring out of them."

"Point taken. Well, there's no sign of the little bastards here so... the other spheres?"

"The other spheres." Kali agreed.

The pair began to look for a way through to the next sphere but, while they found it, accessing it was easier said than done. The non-manoeuvrability of the internal walkways meant that the entrance to one of the connecting bridges – a passage near to the construction's equator – could only be reached either by Slowhand's zipline or a long and complicated climb. Rather than risk an arrow coming loose at the wrong time if the sphere shook again, they decided on the latter. The archer took the lead, deftly negotiating the various projections, and Kali followed noting, as she did, that despite their condition some of the machines still seemed to thrum slightly beneath her feet, a sign that their surroundings were not quite as dead as they had first appeared.

Something else, however, was.

Slowhand had just reached the lip of the passage and grabbed onto it, ready to heave himself up, when his hand skidded away from the surface and he fell back with a cry, only escaping a rather swift and bumpy return to his starting point when Kali grabbed him by the wrist. She held on tightly as he dangled beneath her, giving him a chance to regain his footing, helping him roll himself over the lip. Unexpectedly, he cried out again, but only because he had discovered what it was that had made his hand slip in the first place.

"*Ohhhh, hells!*"

"What is it?"

"Trust me, Hooper, you don't want to know."

"I do. It might be important."

"Oh, I've no doubt that it is. But –"

Kali quickly leapt up next to him then, with a squeal, leapt just as quickly aside.

"Warned you."

Kali grimaced. She had been standing on – more accurately, *in* – the rotting corpse of one of the Final Faith. The slimy and bubbling remains were clearly victim of a k'nid attack, brought down on this spot as it – its gender was hard to determine – had apparently tried to run. What made it so repulsive and different to other victims they had seen was that it clearly hadn't been fully absorbed. As if, for some reason, the k'nid involved had abandoned the process part way through. But, as Slowhand rather irreverently pointed out, it wasn't like them not to finish a snack.

"So what happened?" he asked.

"I don't know. Maybe it was interrupted by something."

"Interrupted?" Slowhand repeated, panning Suresight about him once more. "By what? The place is abandoned. Isn't it?"

"That's the theory."

"*Right.*"

"I know one thing, though," Kali added, nodding ahead, "and that's that we're on the right track."

Slowhand looked. "Ohhhh, hells."

"Exactly."

Kali and Slowhand moved into the passage they had found and, at its end, onto a bridge between spheres – half overgrown with trees – picking their way carefully past more of the Final Faith; ten or so, all similarly and horribly dead. As they crossed, the *Kerberos* sphere shook once more behind them, more violently than ever.

"I guess these are the ones that didn't make the airship," Slowhand commented.

Kali swallowed. "Do you think your sister abandoned them?"

Slowhand took a second to answer, the face he pictured in his mind not Jenna, then said through gritted teeth, "I'd like to think she didn't have a choice."

The pair reached the far end of the bridge and entered the sphere Kali had designated *Twilight*.

The first thing they noticed was that the difference between it and 'Kerberos' couldn't have been more marked. For one thing, this sphere was not hollow like the other, possessing a floor at the level they entered which was divided into corridors and chambers. For another, its style of interior construction was distinctly opposed to the sphere they had left. Where *Kerberos* and all its heavy machinery had struck her as being predominantly dwarven, the almost organic and membranous make-up of *Twilight* was unmistakably elven. The fact that both spheres co-existed in the same complex – together with the presence of the elven glamour field in the dwarven *Kerberos* – led Kali to only one possible conclusion: this was a joint venture of both of the Old Races. That in itself wasn't unknown in the latter years of their civilisations' existence – where their magics and technologies had combined for the good of both – but in a place such as this, in such a way and on such a scale? What had brought them together to do this?

Kali and Slowhand began, slowly and cautiously, to explore the corridors and chambers about them. Some of these, however, were not immediately accessible as their doors were either sealed with thick membranes or they appeared to have been barricaded by the Final Faith in some desperate attempt to stave off the k'nid. The latter tactic had not been overly successful, judging by the number of bodies they found littering the place. Kali found it astounding that the Faith had sent so many of their people here – top-ranking academics judging by their robes – and realised that they had obviously attached great importance to the complex's capabilities, whatever they were.

Some clues started to present themselves as they explored further, not only *in situ* but also in a number of containers the Faith academics had packed with carefully preserved anatomical and biological diagrams of ancient origin as well as information crystals of a type Kali recognised from previous sites. That these containers were found in laboratories filled with vials, test tubes, examination slabs and other kinds of scientific trappings, including complex and delicate machines beyond understanding, suggested that they were records of experiments the Old Races had conducted – perhaps that the Faith wished to replicate – but experiments into what, with what, and for what purpose? A further clue came when Slowhand somehow triggered the opening of a number of small and strange, crystalline drawers in an adjacent chamber. Kali looked and saw that, indexed with elven pictograms, were what appeared to organic tissue samples of every animal that she knew existed – and many, many that she didn't. There was the grank at the top of the food chain, to the bassoom in the middle, all the way to the humble worgle at the bottom. There were samples of insect life, too, of avian, reptilian and aquatic lifeforms, and there, in a section of their own, those of elves, dwarves and – Kali swallowed slightly – humans.

What disturbed her the most was that, in almost every case, the indexing attached to the specimens were cross-referenced to others – sometimes two or three, sometimes seven or eight, or sometimes as many as twenty other specimens in the collection.

"What *is* this?" Slowhand said.

"Disturbing," was all Kali could say in reply.

Again, she and Slowhand moved on, working their way towards the hub of *Twilight* now, passing chambers even more mystifying than those they had already investigated.

Here was a chamber whose circumference was lined with membranous booths, most of which stirred with what looked like variously coloured gases; here one whose laboratory equipment was, bafflingly, positioned on the ceiling; and here a considerably larger and perfectly circular chamber whose only content was a strangely shaped chair suspended on the end of a metal arm looking like the hour hand of some giant clock. The purpose of these devices was, for now, beyond their ken and, shrugging to each other, they ignored them, coming at last to a point where the corridor joined – *became* – a circular affair surrounding the hub itself. This was clearly a centre of activity as other corridors joined it at regular points but, like some of the earlier doors, they had all been barricaded by the Faith. Neither Slowhand or Kali were very much interested in what lay along them, however, because their attention had instead become fixed on what actually lay at the heart of *Twilight*.

"Slowhand?"

"Don't look at me. I haven't a clue."

They were staring at another sphere within the sphere, or at least half of one. For a broad hemisphere lay in front of them – one that perhaps would take a hundred men to surround with arms outstretched – but this one was transparent, made of a substance that felt like soft glass, and its interior slowly roiled with a thick green fog. From what Kali and Slowhand could see through the fog, the interior of the hemisphere did not end at floor level but went much deeper, and they realised that they were looking through some kind of observation dome into the lower half of *Twilight*. There was some kind of chamber down there, a completely organic space whose uneven floor was punctured by perhaps fifty circular holes, each the size of a farmstead's well. They appeared to contain liquid, too, but it was not water. Instead, there was a slowly bubbling, lava-like gloop the colour of the mist it produced that was slightly overflowing their edges.

"Looks like pea soup," Slowhand commented.

"Oh, I think it's *some* kind of soup, all right. Just not the kind you'd serve at dinner."

Kali studied the chamber further, noting three demi arches that arced over the wells, their tips almost meeting above their centre. An odd looking runed prism was suspended between the tips, though it looked damaged and skewed. But even so, every few seconds, it discharged spidery, slowly dancing bolts of energy into the wells themselves, as if it were in some way *vitalising* them. Kali's attention turned to the hemisphere itself, and here she noted that it was not completely transparent but instead etched all around its circumference with the same pictograms that had indexed the specimen drawers. Thousands of them, one after the other. The fact that these etchings glowed slightly suggested they were more than simple decoration. They reminded her of the 'orchestral' selection controls she had once used in the Forbidden Archive and knew instinctively that if she danced her palms over them she would be combining one species with another in whatever combination she wished. Merrit Moon had been right when, back in Gargas, he'd said that the Old Races had been playing Gods. The wells beneath them were not wells, they were *birthing pools* for whatever was created within them.

"The Crucible of the Dragon God," Kali said. "We've found it."

"So we know where the k'nid come from. Unfortunately, I don't think we've come at the best time."

"What?"

"Time's up, Hooper. They're spawning again."

Kali snapped her gaze back into the fog and thought, *dammit.*

Their exploration of the spheres had obviously taken longer than they had reckoned because something was indeed happening down there. Something they had come to prevent but were now forced to be witness to. From each of the birthing pools a small platform was rising and atop each platform, gloop dripping from it's irregular, angular flanks, was a k'nid. The dark, unnatural creatures did not move until they had fully risen from their pools but then they burst into frantic activity. Some sped up what appeared to be a circular pathway just discernable around the wall of the chamber and a second later could be heard battering at one of the Faith erected barricades, others headed out of view of the observation dome and did not return, perhaps finding some other exit from the chamber. Still others, sensing Kali and Slowhand above, launched themselves the not inconsiderable height towards the dome itself. One actually made it, thudding upside down against the transparent substance, and was followed in quick succession by another, and then another.

"Whoa!" Slowhand said, backing up. He unslung Suresight and aimed at the dome.

"I wouldn't worry too much. This stuff is probably tougher than it loo –"

The soft glass tore before her eyes, rent by the scrabbling of the k'nid. Fog billowed through – noxious and foul.

"Yeah?" Slowhand said, loosing three rapid arrows while coughing. "You wanna think that one through again?"

"Shit!" For a moment Kali considered blasting the k'nid with her crackstaff, but she had no idea how volatile the fog that accompanied them might be. There was only one alternative. "Run!"

"Where?"

"Anywhere!"

The sound of the dome tearing accompanied Kali and Slowhand's footfalls. These were soon drowned out as more of the k'nid trailed the others through the newly created exit. Kali didn't look back to count, but from the noise she reckoned at least another five of the things were in pursuit. It didn't take an arithmetical genius to work out that eight k'nid was eight too many. Nor did it take a genius to work out that if they didn't get the hells out of their way, they were dead. But where to run to? All of the laboratories they had explored so far were open and offered no protection, and the sealed doors were out, but there had to be somewhere. Finally, she noticed one of the chambers they had passed earlier – the one with the gas filled booths – and ran towards it. One of the booths appeared clear of gas and, hammering on it to test its strength, Kali punched a panel on its outside which she hoped would open it. The front of the booth slid aside.

She grabbed Slowhand and threw him into the chamber, before following him. As she squeezed up to the archer the door slid shut. A second later, the k'nid slammed into their makeshift refuge, shaking it but otherwise unable to gain entry.

Slowhand stared out at the scrabbling things, the sound of

their assault muted, his face pressed up against the side of Kali's head. "Cosy."

"Cramped is the word I'd use."

Kali shuffled round so that they were face to face, trying to avoid as much body contact with Slowhand as she could. But it wasn't easy – thigh pressed against thigh and breasts against torso – she could barely raise her arms before they were touching the smooth walls of their circular confinement.

"Closet?" Slowhand hazarded.

"There's nothing in it."

"We're in it."

"I'd noticed."

"Okay. One of those elevators then?"

"Not going anywhere."

"True." Slowhand smiled as the tips of their noses touched, and he puckered up. "Maybe it's a private *lurrrvv* chamber."

"Then maybe Endless Passion would like to join you in here." Kali said through gritted teeth.

"Hey, I already said, nothing happe –" The archer stopped, looking taken aback. "Hooper, are you *hissing* at me?"

"I *do not* hiss." But she had heard the sound herself. "I thought it was, you know... your problem."

"What problem? Hooper, I do not have a prob –"

If Kali had been able, she would have put her fingers to his lips, shushing him, but all she could do was body-bump him to keep him quiet. "I think you do now."

There was indeed a hissing but neither of them were responsible for it. For a second, Kali worried that the chamber was flooding with gas like the others, but if it was it had no colour or odour. Then, both isolated the source at the same time and looked up. There was some kind of fan above, rotating ever more swiftly, and as Kali watched it was time for Slowhand's hair to progress in an upward direction. Amusing as that was, it clearly wasn't right. Neither was the fact that she was having difficulty breathing.

"Slowhand, do you feel hot, breathless, as if you're expanding?"

"Every time I'm near you," the archer said. The fact that he wheezed and his eyes bulged, took some of the humour out of it.

"I think something's sucking the air out."

"Oh, come on! Why would someone build a room that sucked the air out? Hooper, are you making eyes at me?"

"No. The pressure's dropping, fast, and if we don't get out of here right now, we're dead."

Despite the fact the k'nid still scrabbled no more than an inch away, she was willing to take her chances outside rather than in, and thumped the booth. But the door did not reopen. She tried again. Nothing.

"Must be on some kind of timer," she said.

"What? *Ow!*"

"Ow?"

"My ears just popped!"

"Ow! Mine too. Hey, Slowhand, you know you're getting fat?"

"Hey, *you* can talk!"

Kali stared at the archer, who was indeed fatter, his face, particularly, bloating to perhaps twice its normal size. She was aware of her own doing so, too. But it wasn't just their faces – their whole bodies were starting to expand now, pressing them even more tightly together. Kali could see Slowhand's blood vessels bulging on his temples and neck even as she felt her own blood beginning to pulse painfully in her veins. *The air's gone!* she tried to say, but nothing came out – no sound at all – and across from her Slowhand's mouth moved uselessly. Kali tried to reach her equipment belt for her breathing conch, but it was too late, their expanded forms too crushed, and instead all she could do was look at Slowhand in panic, noticing how his tongue had begun to swell from his mouth, as she felt her own doing from hers.

Hooper, Slowhand mouthed, though it was difficult to make out the forming of even that one word. She didn't really need to, though, because the expression on her lover's face said everything that he wanted to say. He was confused and knew they were going to die, but he was also glad he was by her side and wanted to say goodbye.

She mouthed his name in return, so very, very sorry that she had gotten him into this mess. Furious, too. But only with herself. Gods, how could this have happened so quickly? How could she have come so far only to let it end like this. By stupidly stumbling – stupidly dragging them *both* – into something she didn't understand?

Her vision began to flare and darken until she could barely see Slowhand. Then, in that darkness, she felt her brain began to thud in time with her heartbeat, each beat clutching and agonising.

The beats got heavier and slower.

Heavier and slower.

Then her heart seemed to explode, and she no longer felt anything at all.

CHAPTER FOURTEEN

"Hooper, can you hear me? Hooper?"

The voice filled her mind, resonant and familiar. All there was in an otherwise deep and dark world. She floated there until the voice spoke again, and this time shook at the sound of it. No, something shook *her*. *Was* shaking her, again and again. The darkness began to swoop about her, blooming and flaring with light, and then her mind seemed to surge upwards, bringing a dizzying confusion, a lurching imbalance and a desperate need to steady the world. But all it did was shake some more.

"Hooper? Hooper, dammit, wake up!"

She sat upright, her eyes snapping open. There was a man in front of her, holding her tightly by the arms. Instinctively, she nutted him.

"*Ow! Dammit!* Steaming pits of... easy, Hooper, it's me."

"Slowhand? Shit, sorry."

"You okay?"

"Think so," Kali said, though from the lump on the side of

her head she'd taken one hells of a bump. She looked around, saw she was sitting on the floor of the booth. "What the hells happened?"

Slowhand pulled her to her feet. "Dunno. A noise. Don't know how to describe it – wailing, spooky, like the sound of some old elven instrument. Whatever it was, it spooked the k'nid. They left the booth alone, disappeared, and the next thing I knew, the door opened and we were falling out. That's where you got the bump."

"Someone chased away the k'nid and let us out?"

"Looks that way. And that's not all. One of the doors in the corridor – one that was sealed before – that opened, too."

Kali raised an eyebrow. "Then why are we waiting. Let's go meet our saviour."

"Hold on. Our *saviour* could be the one who built that bloody deathtrap in the first place."

"I don't think it *is* a deathtrap."

"Pitsing well feels like one to me. I mean, come on, Hooper, what else could it be?"

"Don't know. But if the other door's open, maybe it's an invitation to find out?"

She moved out and, shaking his head, Slowhand followed. The pair passed through the unsealed door and neared another that was still sealed, seemingly a dead end until, somewhat unnervingly, it opened of its own accord. The same thing happened further on, and then again, their route clearly being manipulated through areas of the complex which, judging by the undisturbed layers of dust and cobwebs, the Final Faith had not been allowed to tread. In fact, these new chambers had a lonely feel to them that suggested to Kali that no one had entered them since the time of the Old Races themselves.

At last they came to a spiral staircase winding up the wall of an otherwise featureless chamber and both paused at its base, peering through thick and foreboding strings of cobweb to darkness above. The fact that the sphere shook at that moment seemed somehow appropriate.

"I think we're there," Kali said. She brushed the web aside

and placed a tentative foot on the first riser. "Lair of the Dragon God, anyone?"

"Hooper, are you sure you –?"

Kali gave him a look and Slowhand shut up. Because he knew that look – *the* look – the one of girlish excitement she couldn't contain when she knew she was near some significant find. Sometimes he wondered why she just didn't jump up and down, clapping her hands ...

"There's something here, 'Liam. I feel it. There's *intelligence* here."

Slowhand nodded, and the pair of them took the steps slowly, one at a time, until they emerged into a spacious, yet almost featureless chamber. The one feature it *did* contain, however, was another sphere. In this case a large, membranous one filled with a liquid clearer though not dissimilar to that in the birthing wells. Stirring within it was what appeared to be some kind of plant. A fragile, multi-stranded, frond-like affair that made Kali think of some wavering growth on the ocean floor.

"It's a fish tank," Slowhand said flatly, pulling a face. "Gotta say, bit anticlimactic."

"Probably not a fish tank, Slowhand..." Kali said, patiently. She hoped not, anyway.

"Oh, *come on*. Can't you just see some little gogglefish darting in and out of that water feature ther –"

The archer quietened as Kali touched the sphere and, in response, another voice overrode his own, booming around them.

"Welcome, Kali Hooper. I have awaited your arrival for a very long time."

Kali and Slowhand stared at each other as the greeting resonated through the chamber, but while both waited in expectation of what might follow, no more words came. Kali stared around the chamber, hoping to discern the origin of the voice but, failing, fixed her attention back on the sphere. She guessed some reply to the greeting might be in order but, in the circumstances, she wasn't quite sure what she should say.

"Really?" she hazarded, after a second. "That's nice."

"That's nice?" Slowhand repeated, incredulous. The more

cautious archer was already readying Suresight to loose an arrow at anything that came at them. "You may have been around a bit but don't you find the fact that something in this graveyard knows your name just a little disturbing?"

Kali couldn't deny that she did find it disturbing. But not because she had been referred to by name – as far as she knew her name could simply have been overheard sometime during their explorations. No, what disturbed her was the fact that the voice had said she had been *awaited*. Because this reminded her once again of her conversation with the fish-thing in the ruins of Martak, and its comment then that she was *where she should be*. Ever since that encounter, she had railed against what that meant, and to be faced with a similar comment now brought back all the worries that somehow, without her knowledge or consent, her life was following a preordained path.

"Who are you?" she asked. "Where are you?"

"My being, all around you. My physical form, before you."

"You? You're –?"

"Hooper," Slowhand said worriedly, "maybe that bump did more harm than we thought. You do know you're talking to a plant?"

Kali ignored him and studied the sphere again. What she saw could easily be mistaken for a plant, that was for sure, but there was something more to it. A complexity about the hairy fronds and an energy *inside* them that suggested something more advanced, more *alive*.

"I don't think it's a plant. I mean it *looks* organic, yes it *is* organic, only not in that way."

"Not in what way?"

Kali stroked the sphere, tracing the outline of the shape within. "Strip away our flesh and our bone," she said, "our veins, organs, muscle, sinew, tendons, and what do you think you get?"

"A bloody mess?"

"I mean what's *left*, Slowhand. The very core of our being."

"Your companion shows a knowledge beyond that of her world, archer," the voice said, startling them both. "You see before you the nervous mesh central to the body of everything that lives.

The threads, if you will, within us all."

"*Right.* So, your sphere, it's some kind of grow bag?"

"Slowhand!"

"*Joke*, Hooper. Breaking the ice with the plant is all."

"It *isn't* a plant."

"*I know that*, for fark's sake. Of all the steaming pits – you really do think I'm thick, don't you?"

"No, no, of course I don't. Not at all."

Slowhand stared challengingly and found Kali couldn't hold his gaze. He shook his head in resignation and ran his own palm over the sphere. "What I don't get is, are you saying it was once one of us. Human?"

Kali looked around at the decay of ages, and smiled. "Oh, I wouldn't think human, no."

She was only just beginning to appreciate the possible nature of the being whose presence they were in, and despite the gravity of the situation that had brought them here she couldn't help but almost giggle with the thrill of it. The mummified corpse in Be'Trak'tak was the closest she ever thought she would come to meeting a member of the Old Races, but now?

"Why don't you ask him?"

"Him? How do you know it's a him?"

Kali was getting a little tired of questions when so many of her own were clamouring to be asked. "Maybe because if it was a her – maybe someone called Endless Passion - you'd already be working on some unlikely contrivance to make your pants disintegrate."

"Hey. That is below the belt."

"No, we know what's below the belt. And where it's been."

"*Hey!*"

"*Hey!*"

They stopped, remembering where they were. Kali turned towards the sphere to apologise but then stood back, gasping.

"What the hells...?" Slowhand said.

Inside the sphere, the liquid had begun to flood with clouds of grey. They were clearly more than clouds, however, as not only did their mass seem to be made up of tiny organisms but they moved with purpose, variously wrapping, obscuring and agitating the fronds of the 'plant' until they began to change, thicken and grow. What their unexpected host had described as 'the threads within us all' were beginning to take on a fuller form, one gradually becoming more recognisable as a living being.

First came a skeleton, one bit of bone at a time, the bones lengthening to join others, creating joints, limbs, ribs, a skull. Next came sinews, organs, tendons and muscle, these growths in turn becoming interlaced and overgrown with capillaries, blood vessels and arteries, which, when whole and connected, began to flow with blood the colour of sky. Over these vessels grew tissue and then flesh, a body forming before their eyes. And, lastly, came eyes, hair, features, until both Kali and Slowhand found themselves staring at a fully formed being, floating before them in the sphere.

But it was like no being either of them had seen before.

At least, not quite.

The thing was, Kali recognised elements of the creature she saw before her – the musculature of the limbs, the shape of the torso, the physiognomy of the face – but what confused her was that they seemed to come from two different anatomies. She was familiar with this creature and yet wasn't at the same time. Because while it had always been her dream to meet a living, breathing member of one of the Old Races, she had never, ever dreamt she would meet a living, breathing member of both Old Races *simultaneously*. It was hardly what she'd expected the Dragon God to be.

"You?" she said breathlessly. "You're –"

"The first of the dwelf. The last of the dwelf."

"My Gods!"

"Dwelf?" the archer said, confused.

"Work it out, Slowhand."

"Are you telling me this thing is half dwarf, half elf. A hybrid?"

"Yup."

"Glad I wasn't hiding in the wardrobe in *that* boudoir."

Kali raised her eyes. "I doubt it happened like that."

"No? You wanna tell me another way you know of making," Slowhand paused and shuddered, "little dwelfs?"

"I am not the result of physical procreation," the dwelf explained, "but of other processes."

Slowhand wasn't sure what that meant. "Are they as much fun?"

"*Slowhand!*"

"Sorry, sorry"

"You said 'other processes.'" Kali said to the dwelf. "You mean those birthing pools? Is that what this sphere is - your own birthing pool? Were you *created* here?"

"Created when your race was young."

"Looking good on it, pal," Slowhand said, then pulled a face as he visualised the frond thing the dwelf had first been. "Now, anyway."

"Actually, I doubt he's as old as we are," Kali corrected the archer. "That's right, isn't it? When we saw you grow, you were being created all over again, just like the first time, weren't you? The liquid in this sphere is the same as that in the pools but... more complex, somehow. It enables you to form and reform at will?"

"Nutrients, proteins. The essential building blocks of life. I would not have survived this long had I not been able to revert to a state of stasis among them."

"You're thousands upon thousands of years old," Kali breathed. "But at the same time, *so young.*"

"Oh, come on," Slowhand objected. "He can pop in and out of existence, just the same as he was, every time, with all his memories intact? I may be just an old soldier boy, Hooper, but –"

"Perhaps you simply do not have all of the facts, Killiam Slowhand," the dwelf said.

As he spoke, his body *faded* into a state of translucency for a second and something that looked like a length of stretched and shimmering gold could clearly be seen coiled throughout his body.

Slowhand stared. "What the hells?"

Kali could hardly believe it herself. She thought back to her meeting with Kane in Andon, the way he used the threads as *physical* things. It seemed the Old Races had too, but in a way that even Kane would likely find hard to believe. The Old Races, particularly in their last age, had been outstanding engineers, but she had never imagined – never could have imagined – that they had begun to engineer *themselves*.

"I think that's a line of thread magic," she said. "An actual magical thread interwoven with his very being."

"Yeah?" Slowhand responded, perhaps not quite grasping the enormity of what she said, or perhaps, being Slowhand, simply asking the sensible question. "Why?"

"It is a necessary part of the process," the dwelf said.

"Necessary for what? To churn out those *things* from the pools? Or maybe just try and *suffocate* anyone who pops by?"

"The atmosphere chamber," the dwelf said. "That was not I."

"Oh? Then who?"

"No one. Your entrapment was accidental, the process automatic. However, I regret the facility was left unsealed."

"Atmosphere chamber?" Slowhand asked but Kali placed a hand on his shoulder, preferring the conversation walked before it ran.

"If you were the one that freed us, thank you," she said. "And for chasing away the k'nid, however you did."

"That is what you call the spawn? Interesting. But yes. The *k'nid*, like most organisms, are susceptible to certain harmonics and vibrations which cause them discomfort, in this case forcing them to flee."

"Harmonics and vibrations you've used before. To interrupt the absorption of those bodies out there."

The dwelf was silent for a second.

"I had no interest in saving the intruders," he said. "Only in protecting this place." As he spoke, the structure shook once more, rumbled deeply. "The birthing *k'nid* have inflicted considerable damage on the complex."

"The Faith, too, by the look of what we've seen out there," Slowhand chipped in. "Why the hells didn't you use these harmonics to get rid of them, too?"

"Because I have observed your world and know their motives, the singular, dark mission of their Church. Had my presence been revealed to them it would have served no good and perhaps have led to other discoveries. Also, my influence over the complex is no longer absolute. The damage it has sustained even without the k'nid – *naturally* over the long, long years – has left areas of it dead to me."

"Like the birthing pools - the Crucible," Kali said, and the sphere rumbled again as she spoke. "The Final Faith turned it on, didn't they?" she said, remembering Jenna's recordings. "That was what she meant by their *mistake*."

"And now you can't turn it off," Slowhand said.

"The Faith disturbed the precise calibrations of minds long since dust, spawning the k'nid in numbers not intended. Worse, the prism central to the birthing process – the same prism that could *abort* the process – became misaligned beneath their meddling hands." The dwelf sighed. "You are correct, archer. I cannot stop it."

"Stop it?" Slowhand repeated. "Why in the hells did you *start* it? For gods sakes, why on Twilight would you want to create such creatures in the first place?"

The dwelf's answer sounded regretful and – considering what it seemed he, or at least his people, were responsible for – also somewhat unlikely. "To save the world."

"News for you, pal, that's her job," Slowhand said, nodding at Kali. "So what's the real story?"

Kali wasn't as hasty in responding. The dwelf's regret had sounded genuine enough for her.

"Do you have a name?" she asked.

"I was created to be a guardian," he said. "The elven word for such a role would be Tharnak."

"Tharnak it is, then. Tharnak, please, I don't understand. How would creating these *things* save the world?"

"Our world faced a threat foretold in tomes of as great an age as divides our civilisations now. A threat both from the unknown and unknown in essence. Though both elven and dwarven races knew of its coming, we knew also that it was *alien* to us. We did not know what could stop it because we could not know what its weaknesses were. And so we constructed the Crucible. Its purpose was the creation of a singular life form specific in its purpose – to combat *any* threat."

"Must have been a pretty unique threat."

"It was. As unique as the solution we devised. The creatures you call k'nid were the result of complex manipulations of Twilight's life forms – extracting from them those elements which brought them victory in the survival of the fittest. In the process we gave birth to *other* creatures, and these, too, became part of the process. Our survival was at stake and so we had to create the ultimate defence. A life form capable of surviving any environment, of winning and *transforming* that environment and becoming its dominant life form. The *only* life form."

"So overwhelming it would spread like some disease," Kali said, "consuming the enemy. Tharnak, we're not the enemy and your creations aren't saving our world, they're *destroying* it."

"Because," the dwelf said, "they were never meant to be unleashed here."

"Unleashed *here*? I don't understand."

"On this world."

"*What?*"

"The k'nid were destined for the heavens."

"Okay, pal, that's it," Slowhand cut in. "Hooper, don't waste breath on this guy. He's a short wick in a long candle."

"Slowhand, let him fin –"

"No, Hooper. Think about it. What isn't ringing true here? Apart from this *heavens* rubbish? If this project of theirs was so damned important – so vital to the future of both their races – why is it stashed away up here at the top of *our* world, hidden in a secret valley behind the Dragonfire? I'll tell you why. Because it's a farking loony bin, is why."

"My friend has a point," Kali said, biting her lip. "If elves and dwarfs were working together, in a time when there were only elves, dwarves and a handful of primitive humans who would have posed no threat, who exactly were you hiding yourselves from?"

"Many of our peoples were against what we would achieve."

"Hardly surprising," Slowhand said.

"Do you imagine that because we were races who had attained greatness, that we did not have as many fundamental divisions among us as divide the peninsula today? There were those who ignored the threat to us, those who courted, even welcomed it, and those who actively sought to prevent us stopping it, for their own reasons, insane as they may have been. We were called blasphemous, sacrilegious, and even within our own ranks there was doubt. Doubt that could only be assuaged by my creation. A living compromise between elf and dwarf factions, a believer of *both* sides."

"So the Crucible was built in secret?" Kali said. "Your rulers, governments, churches, knowing nothing about it?"

"For three years our people – those who *believed* – worked with and within them, utilising their resources and hoping, also, to recruit some to our cause. But – as is the case with your own Final Faith – the ideals and aims and beliefs of most were too intractable, entrenched to change. Had we been discovered we would have been banished, or worse. Still, our people managed to establish a chain of contacts, supplies and the means to transport them, the cooperation of sympathisers to our cause and, eventually, began to establish their presence, here, in the Drakengrat Mountains."

"The waystations," Kali said.

"Constructed, again, in secret, and as defended in their time as the Crucible itself. Not only a means to ferry our materials but designed to intercept any who might wish to stop what the Crucible hoped to achieve. Some of the airships therein were fighters."

"Fighters? It sounds like a war."

"More than just a war. A holy war. We had no wish to spill the blood of our own but we *had* to protect the complex whilst its purpose was achieved."

"A holy war?"

"As I said, the k'nid were designed with a specific purpose and that purpose was to destroy the *deity* in our heavens."

"Destroy the deity?" Slowhand echoed. He almost laughed. "Are you saying their purpose was to *kill God*?"

"Some called it God."

Kali found herself almost physically staggering. "Deity," she said. The dwelf had spoken in the singular so presumably he was not referring to the various Gods whom most on Twilight had worshipped before the coming of the Final Faith. Was he, therefore, speaking of *their* god, the one god? If that was the case, did that mean the Old Races acknowledged its existence literal ages before the Faith came into being – as an actual entity? That it might be real was something she struggled to accept. "Tharnak are you talking about the *Lord of All*?"

The dwelf almost spat his response, so vehement was it. "I am talking about the Lord of Destruction, the Lord of Nothing!"

Kali frowned. Lord of Destruction? Lord of Nothing? What the hells did those phrases mean? Were these just other terms for the Lord of All, or for something else entirely? She was about to ask when another tremor ran through the Crucible, more violent than any that had come previously, and she was forced to steady herself against the sphere as growth fluids sloshed about inside. Even Tharnak himself seemed concerned.

"Would that I could show you," the dwelf said with a sigh. "Make you understand. But there is so little time."

Tharnak's weary resignation made Kali realise that she was unlikely to get any further with this line of questioning for the moment and, while she still didn't understand the meaning of the threat, there was something becoming increasingly obvious to her – something made inherently clear by the fact that the Old Races were no more.

The threat, she thought. *Is this what happened to the Old Races? My Gods. Is this how they died?*

"Your attempt to eradicate this deity," she said, "it failed, didn't it? *Why?*"

"Hubris, arrogance, *foolishness*. At that stage in our civilisation, though we possessed the technology to do what we did, it was not enough. We needed the magic, too. But the magic, by then, had become weak, for we had destroyed those who made it whole."

"Destroyed? Destroyed who?"

"The Dra'gohn."

"The Dra'gohn? You mean *the dragons*?"

"If that is what you call them, yes."

Kali didn't have a clue why the absence of dragons should affect the magic – make it whole – but that hardly seemed the point. The Old Races were the reason they had gone away?

"How?" she asked. "Why? What happened?"

The sphere shook again and the dwelf's weariness returned, almost as if he were dying with the Crucible. "Cowardice... greed... does it really matter? They were gone – and with them, our only chance to survive."

"But this place," Kali protested, aware as she spoke of how naive the question seemed. "All of its potential – couldn't you have somehow *remade* them, brought them back?"

The dwelf actually laughed, although the sound was guttural and bitter. "How many times over these countless, lonely years do you think I have been tempted to try? To rectify *our* mistake, and to *apologise* to them, even though it would have been too late? No, it would have been an empty exercise, for that is why we failed. The magical threads that bind our creations are weak. Nothing *made* here can survive for long if it leaves the Crucible." The dwelf paused. "How could I bring the dra'gohn back knowing that when they took to the skies I would once more be responsible for their end – that they would *die?*"

"You mean like the yassan, you bastard?" Slowhand said. "How do you think they feel – out there, *changed*, unable to leave that frozen wilderness they call home? Tell me, *Tharnak*, did you really need to make them part of your *soup* or were you just playing games?"

"We took no pleasure in our experiments on them. It was our wish that, when we left, we gifted this valley to them in return. But, of course, we did not leave."

"And that's meant to make things all right?"

"'Liam, don't," Kali said. She stared at the dwelf. "If that's the case, why are the k'nid able to survive?"

"They are not. Their capability for self-replication grants them a longer life span than others but eventually they, too, will revert to nothing. They would not have reached the heavens. Beyond this valley they have, perhaps, a matter of days."

Which we don't, Kali thought. "Then, please, is there a way to stop them?"

"The prism above the birthing pools. It holds upon it the runics capable of reversing their creation, *removing* them. Combined with the magic of your Three Towers – if your men of magic channel their threads of destruction through them – the plague upon the peninsula will be ended."

"It's that simple?" Slowhand said, beginning to revise his opinion of the plant.

Easy for you to say, Kali thought. She calculated she had some hours before the next wave of k'nid were spawned but, from what she'd seen of them, that didn't necessarily make the birthing pools any less dangerous. "So this is the bit where I risk life and limb in some potentially lethal hellshole to save the world once more, right? Fine. I'll go get it."

"Then you must do so with all speed. There is little time."

"There should be hours yet."

"Until the next birthing cycle, yes. But that is not the threat you face." The dwelf's eyes closed, as if he were sensing something far away. "The Final Faith have returned. They have their own airships. And sorcerers who, even now, are attempting to break through our force barrier."

"Airships?" Slowhand said. "There was only *one* airship."

"Gransk," Kali said. "I think Jenna had a telescryer in her party, sent them the information how to build them."

"'I'll glide this thing into Gransk', Jenna said," Slowhand remembered. "Hooper, what the hells is Gransk?"

"Final Faith shipyards, on the coast between Turnitia and Malmkrug. Top secret."

"Right."

Kali turned to the dwelf. "How long do we have?"

"The force barrier weakens. They will gain access by dawn."

"When they'll blow this place to bits," Kali said.

"Sounds good to me," Slowhand said. "So why don't we get

the hells out of here right now?"

"The prism," Kali said.

"Fine. Then we get the prism and *then* get out of here."

"I cannot allow you to leave this place, Killiam Slowhand," the dwelf said, unexpectedly. "Not yet."

Slowhand raised Suresight without hesitation, an arrow pointed unwaveringly at the hybrid.

"Yeah? Difficult to see how you'd stop us with this sticking out of your forehead."

"Please. I do not intend my words to be a threat."

"Sounding pretty pitsing much like one to me."

Kali raised an arm and lowered Suresight, much to Slowhand's consternation. "'Liam, wait. Let's hear what he has to say."

"Hooper, I do *not* see the problem. Whether this guy's on our side or not, it was his people who caused this mess in the first place. You tell me – what exactly is wrong with having the Crucible destroyed right now? Isn't it what we came here for?"

"Because there's something else, isn't there, Tharnak? There has to be." She thought back to Slowhand's comment about the yassan, and about the atmosphere chambers and other strange rooms the two of them had seen. The dwelf had said that they were creating the life form but he had also said 'that and those who could deliver it to its goal.'

The dwelf nodded and, across the chamber, on a shimmering patch of air, a view of the *Kerberos* sphere appeared – in its centre the glamour field.

"We learned early in our experiments that we, the elves and the dwarves, would not survive the journey to the heavens but that humans – *changed humans* – would. We were creating four such travellers when the end came."

"What happened to them?"

"I do not know. It was necessary that I reverted to my hybernartion state to survive the end and when, finally, I awoke they, like the races which sired me, were gone and I was alone."

Slowhand saw the disappointment cloud Kali's face. He knew she needed to know *exactly* how the Old Races had died.

"In other words, you were here when it happened but you

missed it because you were *asleep*?"

"In essence, yes. But perhaps you will be able to glean some knowledge from this ..."

In the *Kerberos* sphere, the glamour field began to dissolve.

"In my solitude I became guardian not only of this place but what remained within it, hidden from view for countless years. But now my time is over, and another guardian is needed."

Kali and Slowhand stared.

"Is that what I think it is?" Slowhand gasped. "I mean, I'm not sure what I think it is... *but is it*?"

"*Oh, my Gods!*"

CHAPTER FIFTEEN

Kali knew right at that moment that everything was going to change – *fundamentally* change – and life would never be the same again. She didn't know how it would change, she didn't know when it would change, but this was the *beginning*. She knew it.

The resulting numbness she felt had barely wavered even when, in the image the dwelf had called forth, Kali could see two familiar piratical figures clambering into the *Kerberos* sphere; having presumably come to warn them of the Faith only to end up gawping at what had been revealed, as she was. Because in that same moment she had been back in the *Warty Witch* in Freiport, having her first conversation with Merrit Moon, he the twinkly eyed exponent of the world's lost past, she the wide-eyed girl. The topic had, of course, been the Old Races and the wonders they had produced. In his cataloguing of such wonders the old man had cited one whose seemingl sheer implausibility had haunted her ever since.

"Tales from the Final Age," he had said, "tell of them actually preparing to send ships to the heavens. To explore Kerberos itself."

Ships to the heavens.

In truth, she had never really believed they could exist.

But now she was looking at one.

She and Slowhand worked their way in a daze down to the *Kerberos* sphere – there reuniting with Aldrededor and Dolorosa – and now the four of them were gazing up at what was clearly the ultimate achievement of the Old Races.

Sitting on some kind of fluid, semi-organic cradle, the ship was a great flowing, sweeping creation that was unlike any mode of transport Kali had ever seen, human *or* Old Race. The main part of its hull the length of ten cattle carts and the breadth of four, it widened further where its wings curved majestically and seemingly without join from port and starboard down to the hangar floor. As Kali and the others drew closer, they saw that the wings, like the hull, were seemingly made up of, but in fact overlaid with, hundreds of small and overlapping sets of fluted funnels, like flattened panpipes. Combined, these gave the impression the ship was covered from bow to stern in rippling scale. The impression that it was some kind of living organism was further enhanced by the fact that every one of the funnels was inscribed with delicate runics resembling the porous flaws of skin. They, in turn, rested on a membranous, flexible underlayer that was soft like flesh. Kali stroked one of the wings almost reverently, realising that here was another reason why the yassan had chosen what they had as the basis for their religion. They were not misguided, their ancestors had simply been mistaken in what they had seen. Because by accident or design, the Kerberos ship looked for all the world like some stylised dragon ready to take flight.

"A thing of beauty, is she not?" Aldrededor observed with a heavy sigh.

"As beautiful as I, my 'usband?"

"Ohhhh, definitely not."

"But, er, what is it?"

Kali smiled. "I guess you could call it a... spaceship."

"A *space* ship?" Dolorosa repeated. "What kind ovva space?"

Kali pointed upwards – straight upwards – and the tall, thin woman inhaled sharply. Then her eyes narrowed and she stared with great suspicion. "You take-a the peees, yes? You havva the laugh atta Dolorosa!"

"Nope," Kali said, shaking her head. In truth, she only had half a mind on the conversation with the Sarcrean woman, still absorbing the words of the dwelf when he had revealed the ship to them.

The Final Faith will destroy our creation along with the Crucible. You must take it from this place, to a place of safety, where it, and its cargo, must remain in your care.

It's cargo, Kali had thought. Tharnak meant k'nid. This beautiful thing was laden with their ultimate weapon, he had said, sealed in a magical stasis inside its shell, lying dormant, awaiting the day when they would travel to the heavens. Only they couldn't travel to the heavens now, could they? Because without the dragons the magic that would keep them alive was not *whole*, whatever the hells that meant.

Maybe one day, Tharnak had said, the magic would return.

Kali exhaled. The fact was, she had no idea why they should save these k'nid. That, though, wasn't really the point, because what had *really* been given into their care was the ultimate artefact of the Old Races, the ship itself. As such it was invaluable – a source of information about those who had gone before that was absolutely unparalleled in its importance. Gods, even if she hadn't been asked, she would have *had* to save it herself!

The only problem now was how to get it out of here.

The ship will accept you, Tharnak had said. *The ship will choose its saviour.*

But what did that mean?

There was only one way to find out.

Kali took a step up the sloping cradle, towards the stern of the ship, pausing warily as the spine of the semi-organic hull parted before her, as if someone were slipping the covers from a wagon. Where it parted, a long, narrow, railed deck was revealed, running from stern to bow, and at the far end an organic-looking control panel glowed a dull green. Kali took a breath and stepped onto the deck, noticing now that it was translucent, another organic membrane, and beneath could be made out the still forms of dormant k'nid. It was something of an uncomfortable feeling treading over the lethal predators but, when it became obvious that they were not going to stir, Kali's confidence grew and she began to marvel at her unique surroundings. The combination of structured hull and semi-organic interior clearly marked the ship as a co-endeavour of both the Old Races and, born in crisis or not, it was a magnificent achievement.

She beckoned the others aboard and Slowhand, Aldrededor and Dolorosa stepped tentatively onto the deck, joined her at what seemed to be the controls; a collection of fleshy nodes forming a sweeping curve. But though they glowed that dull green Kali had noticed as she'd come aboard, nodes were all they appeared to be – lifeless.

"Now what?" Slowhand said.

"The ship will choose its saviour." Kali whispered, and stepped closer to the panel. The nodes made a squishing noise and pulsed at her approach, like pods about to open.

"Easy, girl," Slowhand said, pulling her back. "We have no idea what the things *are*, let alone what they'd do to you."

"Slowhand, someone has to *do this*!"

"I don't deny it. Only it isn't going to be you." As Kali opened her mouth to protest more, he placed a finger on her lips. "It's more than concern. Don't you have a prism to find?"

"Mister Slowhand is correct, Kali Hooper," Aldrededor said. He examined the still pulsing nodes and pulled his moustache, intrigued. "This, I think, is a task for Aldrededor."

"Husband?" Dolorosa queried.

"With you at my side, wife, I captained a ship of the outer seas for over forty years," the ex-pirate pointed out. "I should be the one to captain her now."

"No, Aldrededor," Kali said. "This is *my* responsibility."

"No, Kali Hooper. *Your* responsibility is finishing the job *you* have to do."

Dolorosa stuck her face into Kali's. "Or do you thinka you canna do everytheeng, heh?"

"Aldrededor –" Kali began again, but it was already too late.

The ex-pirate placed his hands onto the two central nodes and, with the same squishing sounds as earlier, his hands were absorbed *into* them. The Sarcean's eyes widened in surprise and, for a few moments, he suffered a series of small spasms that made Dolorosa slap her palm over her mouth. Her husband seemed, though, to be unharmed, managing, a few moments later, a small and slightly stoned looking smile.

"Aldrededor?" Kali enquired. "What's happening?"

The Sarcrean did not reply immediately, but only because he did not know how to answer Kali's question. Because he was seeing things which no one had seen before, the world on which they lived in a new light, and not through his own eyes but those of the ship. And what the ship *saw* were the very threads on which Twilight's various magics depended, filling the air around the craft with ribbons of colour, thick and thin, long and short, like the component parts of some as yet unmade, planet sized tapestry. But the ribbons were not still. Instead, they wove in an out and around each other like snakes, in places touching and releasing bursts of more vivid colour, in others drifting apart and fading, but all in constant motion. If the waves of the seas were coloured silk, Aldrededor thought, this is what they would look like.

One thing marred the beauty, however. Here and there amongst the ever moving patterns were black threads that hung heavily, disturbed occasionally by the other, coloured threads but themselves unmoving, apparently lifeless. And when they touched their vibrant counterparts, they seemed momentarily to leech them of colour. It was as if these threads had once been a part of the flowing sea but were no longer, remaining within it now with no purpose other than to fill the space they had left behind, yet at the same time weakening the sea as a whole.

"Dra'gohn," the pirate whispered sadly to himself.

"What?" Kali said. "What did you say?"

"I amma worried," Dolorosa said. "Aldy has notta been like this since last he smoked the weeds of the sea."

"Wait." Kali instructed. "Give him a little longer."

Still amongst the threads, Aldrededor heard Kali's words and nodded. A little longer, yes. Because the threads were starting to make sense now – at least in the way they related to the ship. Or rather, the way the ship related to them. *Used* them, in fact. Because it was the way that it *flew*.

Eddies and tides and currents of threads. The ship navigated them not with wheel and rudder but with the funnels that coated the ship, drawing in and then channelling and manipulating the threads a thousand different ways to propel it through the sky.

Aldrededor pulled his hands from the nodes with a long sigh.

"My 'usband?" Dolorosa said.

"My wife," he replied. "The ship has shown me what I need to know. It has shown me the invisible ocean of Twilight."

"Aldrededor," Kali said. "Are you telling me you can fly this thing?"

"I believe I may even be able to *sail* it." His chest puffed. "It has chosen me, Kali Hooper."

"Then what are we waiting for?" Slowhand asked. "Hooper, let's get that prism and get the hells out of here."

"Unfortunately, Killiam Slowhand, we are not yet able," Aldrededor advised. "The ship's energy has leaked away over the long years and is all but depleted. It needs to feed."

"Feed?" Slowhand repeated, with a note of distaste.

Amberglow, Kali thought.

After all, if the other Old Race magical technology – The Mole, the crackstaff, the airships – relied on it, why shouldn't this? The only question was, what would it feed *from*?

"We must depart the sphere, that is all I know." Aldrededor said. "But first we will need to free these holding mechanisms or we will go nowhere."

"Free the mechanisms, feed the ship," Slowhand recited. "Will we get that done before the Filth arrive?"

Aldrededor paused. "I do not know, archer. But the question, in any case, is academic. We cannot travel through the Dragonfire while the Faith wait on the other side."

"Am I missing something here? This is a *spaceship*, right? So why the hells don't we just fly it *over* the mountains and bypass the Faith entirely?"

"Because the ship's depletion of energy is not the only damage it has accrued over time. There is some damage to the integrity of the ship itself and it will be unable to withstand the stress of high-altitude flight. Air turbulence above the mountains, or higher, would tear us apart."

"Oh, luvverly."

"Sounds like we need to get a move on," Kali said. "Sorry I can't stay to help but try not to leave without me, eh?"

"Try not to leave without *us*," Slowhand added, and turned to Kali. "I'm going with you."

"No. You're not."

"The bossa lady is correct, bow bender, I need you here," Dolorosa said.

"*You* need me here? I thought Aldrededor was Captain? And don't call me bow bender, it sounds vaguely dirty."

"I need you here," Dolorosa said, "because while my 'usband was Capitano for forty years, I was sheep's engineer, and now the sheep's engineer needa your help freeing the mechaneesms."

Both Kali and Slowhand stared at Dolorosa. The idea that she had been 'sheep's' engineer had tempted a smile onto both of their faces, but it faded quickly when the old woman took to the job at hand with surprising skill.

"Okay, okay," Slowhand agreed, begrudgingly. "But, Hooper, you watch your back down there."

"Always," she said, and was gone.

Wasting no time, Kali retraced her route through the complex to the gallery overlooking the birthing pools, and there took a rope from her belt and tied it to the frame of the membrane the k'nid had penetrated. She eased herself through the wrent, coughing as the noxious gases from the pools thickened about her and sucked at her lungs, though this time she *could* reach her breathing conch and slipped it on. She dropped to the floor with a squelch in the coloured fog. If the k'nid spawning cycle remained true to form, she had plenty of time to do what she needed, but still felt a distinct sense of unease now that she was in their midst. Thankfully, she would not need to stay for long, intending only to retrieve the prism and leave the k'nid to the ministrations of the Final Faith.

It was then that she noticed something that had been blocked from her and Slowhand's view from above earlier. A ring of spheres encircling the edge of the birthing pool area. They were not unlike that which held Tharnak, though smaller, and they appeared to have objects *crammed* within. She frowned and began to make her way slowly across the organic floor. The birthing pools bubbled and popped, as sluggish as pits of lava, the occasional overzealous discharge spattering the bottom of her dark silk bodysuit and boots. The pools discharges were not hot, however – the processes occurring in the soup beneath here were things of biology and chemistry, not heat. It did not stop her hopping away from them *as if* she had been burnt, however, almost falling once or twice as the floor ruptured slightly beneath her.

Kali reached the spheres and rubbed the surface of one, then leapt back. Curled within, like a foetus in a womb, was a seven headed beast. The beast would never be born, however, as the sphere had long since leaked the life-giving liquids it had contained and the poor creature was mummified, having, from the look of it, died in some considerable pain.

Kali turned away, feeling sick, and examined the other spheres. Some were empty, torn apart, as if their occupants had escaped, but most were occupied by the long dead remains of other beasts she did not recognise, confirming her suspicions. She was looking at a menagerie of creatures that must have been produced in the Crucible's program of intermixing and artificial breeding. Creatures whose reason for existing had been but a means to an end and that could not – *should not* – exist in the normal scheme of things.

Again, she felt sick. *This* was what they had to do to save the world? *This* was the price for their salvation?

Kali froze suddenly, slapping a hand over her mouth and, for a second, almost *was* sick. Because right in front of her, in an adjacent sphere, was Horse. Or at least *a* Horse. Because the huge, slumped, armoured, horned corpse couldn't be anything but a relative of her own steed. *Now* she knew why Horse had been found in the Drakengrats, and now she knew why the so-called bamfcat was unique, because he had to be descended from creatures who had escaped this strange laboratory, creatures which must have bred the weakness inherent in all the Crucible's creations out of them before they died.

The discovery of Horse's origin should have been a welcome revelation but it only made Kali feel worse. How many versions of Horse had there been, she wondered? That they had probably been in pain as a result of their mutation made her think of what might have happened to *her* Horse had he been alive at the time. That such a fate could have befallen the intelligent, loyal animal she knew made her succumb to a sudden, uncontrollable fury. Without thinking, Kali raised her crackstaff and then raked its energy across the sphere, staggering back as it exploded towards her in a rain of membranous casing. Despite that, she did not dull the beam, holding the crackstaff with steadfast determination and, roaring, moving it from the bamfcat's sphere to the others, reducing their occupants to the dust they should, long ago, have been. Finally, she stopped, breathing hard.

All Kali wanted now was to find the prism and get the hells out of the Crucible. But as she made her way to the tri-arch, she suddenly found herself thrown off her feet as *Twilight* shook with one of its most violent tremors yet. And when she stood, she saw that the birthing pools had started to bubble rapidly.

What the hells? There should be hours yet!

Clearly, though, the last tremor had disturbed the processes, and the spawning cycle had begun early.

Things were rising from the floor.

Things was the only way to describe them because they were not k'nid. Not yet. Whatever processes occurred in that unnatural soup, they had clearly been interrupted part way through because what emerged before her eyes were more than monstrosities, they were true horrors. Demented things that thrashed and bashed themselves against the sides of the pools and up onto the floor like landed fish, all the while screaming in the manner of things possessed. Some of the part-formed k'nid headed directly for a wrent in the side of the Crucible but a good number began throwing themselves around the chamber in a lethal hail that threatened to tear her to pieces.

Kali didn't hesitate, running straight for the tri-arch and throwing herself onto it, scrambling up its length towards the suspended prism. The deformed k'nid leapt for her as she climbed, but thankfully, in their current state, seemed to lack the agility of their fully formed counterparts. Kali, her legs wrapped around the arch, thumped the prism repeatedly to loosen it, finally freeing it as the beleaguered structure quaked violently beneath her. She had just managed to secure the prism in her equipment belt when the whole tri-arch collapsed. Kali was already in the air, though. Launching herself towards the rope on which she'd entered and grabbing onto it with a grunt. The last thing she saw of the Crucible were the screeching k'nid being crushed beneath the tri-arch as it smashed into the birthing pools.

Kali's problems were only just beginning, however, because now that she had returned to the sphere proper, the extent of the damage from the last, dramatic tremor was clear. The whole of the sphere was skewed and groaning loudly, in danger of collapse. Worse, fires had broken out, fires that were triggering explosions in some of the laboratories – and each of those explosions were triggering others in turn. As the sphere shook once more about her, Kali realised that this was the end for *Twilight*, and she had to get back to *Kerberos* fast.

There was one thing, though, that she *had* to do first. And that was find out what Tharnak had meant when he had said she had been awaited. Because if the dwelf could answer that, maybe he could answer other questions too. Namely, why was she *different* and what, if any, connection was there between herself and the yassan?

Her hopes were dashed as soon as she entered Tharnak's chamber, however. His sphere was collapsed and leaking and the dwelf was sprawled half out of it, dying. It was a tragic and inappropriate end for such a creature and Kali knelt by him, trying to offer some comfort as she listened to his last, almost incoherent words. Then the dwelf slumped in her arms, and she realised there was nothing more she could do.

Twilight continuing to detonate around her, Kali raced for the bridge between spheres, hoping to the Gods that Dolorosa and the others had managed to free the holding mechanisms on the ship. As explosions followed her out of the doomed sphere, blowing the bridge apart yard by yard right on her heels, she burst into *Kerberos* and yelled: "*Get her up! Don't wait for me! Do it now!*"

Below, Slowhand and the others looked up quizzically. A sudden explosion that blew Kali yelling and flailing off the ledge, and into the air between them, quickly spurred them on. Within seconds Aldrededor leapt to the controls and the ship sat began to shudder upwards. Kali, meanwhile, slammed onto one of the sphere's walkways with a loud *oof* and, after a moment's disorientation, realised that the explosion had blown her within running distance of the cradle. As it rose a yard above the sphere's base, she was starting to think she might actually make it when a series of explosions from beneath the walkways blew flooring plates into her path and made a direct route to the ship impossible. Instead, she began to weave around the explosions, trying her best to estimate where the next might occur. But while she got a number of them right it *was* guesswork and, inevitably, she also got some wrong. It was during one such mistake, as she found herself being blown left, right and centre, surviving the blasts only through a series of dextrous somersaults, that she noticed Slowhand throwing the levers that had raised the cradle back to their original positions and the ship juddered to a halt.

"We're not leaving without you!"

"Like hells you're not! Slowhand, you have to get that thing out of here!"

"We'll *do* it, Hooper, but not without you!"

A detonation blew Kali forward and she cursed. "Go!"

Dolorosa joined the archer at the rail. "We cannot, because the sheep it has notta been named. Eet is very bad luck to launch a sheep withouta the name."

"It isn't launching yet, you stupid woman!"

"Eeta still musta be named!"

Kali knew full well that this was just Dolorosa using a delaying tactic, and she loved her for it, but time was fast running out.

"All right, all right!" she cried as she picked herself up and ran. "I name this ship –"

"That issa no good, Kali Hooper."

"*What?*"

"Eet is traditional to shatter the bottle of feezzy wine against the hull."

"Where am I going to get a bottle of *feezzy wine*, you daft old bat!" Kali shouted in exasperation, but it was already becoming clear that she was not going to win this exchange.

Even Aldrededor got in on the act, crowding in between them at the rail. "The alcohol is necessary, Kali Hooper. The... er... *feezziness*, it drives away the evil spirit."

"Oh, and what evil spirit would that be, Aldrededor? Your wife?"

"Hoh!" Dolorosa cried. "She thinka she issa the funny woman again!"

"Put the knife away, my angel. We are trying to save the boss, not kill her."

"Yes, yes, that ees right. I willa keel you later ..."

"Is the message clear yet, Hooper? We're *not* going without you."

"Dammit!" Kali shouted as she continued to dodge, digging into her equipment belt as she did. "Fine, you want booze, here's booze!" She plucked a bottle of thwack from the belt and hurled it towards the ship. "Now bugger off!"

"That was notta feezzy wine."

"No, but it *was* my last bottle. *That do?*"

There was a collective intake of breath.

"Her..."

"... last..."

"... bottle?"

Slowhand worked the levers, winking broadly at Kali as he did so. "Then I guess it's time to go."

Damn the three of you, Kali thought, still moving. Because even though the cradle was rising again – her friends knew what was at stake, after all – they had delayed its rise just long enough.

"Aaargh!" Kali yelled with determination, and began to pound forward, forcing everything she had into the attempt.

But the explosions beneath the sphere's floor were almost constant now, making it buck and chop like a stormy sea. Kali found herself leaping from walkway to machine and back again as if the world itself were coming apart beneath her. The situation worked somewhat to her advantage, though, as the more plates that blew, the more she could see the fiery, roiling mass below, and she was able to time and locate the next explosion with greater accuracy than she had before. With Slowhand and the others urging her on, Kali began to use the plates as stepping stones. Dancing, sometimes nimbly and sometimes not so, between them as they rose, fell or flipped across the hangar. Finally, she reached an almost leapable distance to the rising cradle and, in a last ditch attempt to reach it, she quickly calculated where the next explosion was going to come from. Slowhand, Aldrededor and Dolorosa all realised her intent at the same time, and there was a simultaneous and rapid shaking of heads. But Kali knew that really, she had little choice. She leapt forwards just as a further heavy boom from beneath the floor sent a panel shooting upwards and, calculating her trajectory perfectly, landed on its just as the force of the detonation flipped it over in mid air. Kali, however, didn't wait for the flip to complete, instead letting it throw her into the air, into a position where she was able – just – to make a grab for the cradle with one hand. This she did, and then another hand slapped onto her own. A strong hand. Slowhand's.

"Welcome aboard," he said, heaving her up.

"It isn't over yet," Kali said. "Hold on!"

Her advice was well timed because, at that very moment, what remained of the sphere floor exploded upwards, rocking the cradle as a fist of fire and debris punched it from beneath with such force that the conflagration mushroomed momentarily about its edges, bathing them in searing heat. Thankfully, though, the launchpad had moved high enough to avoid serious damage. It wasn't just moving higher any longer, either, whatever dwelven mechanisms had come into play to raise it seemingly only the first stage in an orchestrated series of manoeuvres. As they drew closer to the top of the sphere, the cradle began to revolve slowly and, amidst much groaning of metal, the two halves of the upper part of the sphere began to open. At first Kali thought that they were not going to make it, the hemispheres so rusted that they would fail to part far enough before the ship was crushed against them. But then, with some sheering of ancient and massive bolts, they juddered free and began to open. The sky was visible now, at first as an ellipse and then a much broader swathe, and then in all its azure glory as the inside of the sphere and its massive workings became fully exposed to the evening sky. Kali and the others were no longer *inside* the sphere, however, but watching, staggered, as the sky panned before them, the cradle having begun to swing out on a massive arm the moment the hemispheres had become low enough to permit it to do so, and Kali's attention moved from what they were leaving behind to what they were heading towards. Now she knew the purpose of the walkway from which she and Slowhand had gained access to *Kerberos*. Because as the giant arm continued to move it also turned slowly, the cradle rotating to fit neatly into position next to it, embraced within its stretched horseshoe shape. As the cradle docked at last inside the walkway with a vibrating *thunk*, Kali could barely hold back a giggle of admiration. She had thought the Clockwork King of Orl was a staggering achievement of Old Race engineering but *this*, this was a true marvel.

But it wasn't over yet.

"Hooper, look." Slowhand said, equally awed.

Kali watched as one of the other spheres – the one she had nicknamed *Sunsphere* – began to move on a giant arm through the trees, swinging towards them – *under* them – while at the same time opening to reveal what could only have been the power source that kept the Crucible's creations intact. This was the fire painted on the cave walls of the yassan – the fire they could not leave. Glowing bright against the azure night sky, like some vast brazier, she was looking at the biggest concentration of amberglow she had yet seen.

It came to a stop beneath the cradle and crackling fingers of energy began to dance between it and the underside of the ship. Kali stared at the hull and saw that the runes over its surface had begun to glow.

"The ship feeds," Aldrededor said from the controls. He drew a deep breath as though he himself were being vitalised. "All we can do now is wait."

"Good job, Aldrededor. Good job, everyo –" Kali began, but then stopped as a sudden massive explosion from *Kerberos* blew its interior and half of the sphere into the sky, the arm on which the cradle rested buckling partly as a result. She and the others clung onto whatever they could as the cradle dropped and skewed, coming to rest, creaking and groaning, at a thirty degree angle above the amberglow. All waited a few seconds, listening to the protesting metal beneath them, and then exhaled in relief when nothing else happened. It had been close, but they were safe.

"I guess that saves Jenna a job," Slowhand said, staring at the burning shells of the spheres.

"I guess it does," Kali replied, trying not to think of Tharnak. "So now we wait for them to come through."

"Family reunion," Slowhand said, biting his lip.

"Do you suppose that when Jenna sees what we've rescued, she might have second thoughts about blowing us out of the sky?"

Slowhand stared ahead, shook his head.

"Jenna's Final Faith now, Hooper. The Faith haven't seen this ship and they won't know what it is, but they won't care. If they *did* know, they wouldn't care. Think about it, Hooper. This thing can reach the *heavens*, and do you think they'd allow that? Gods forbid anyone knew the *truth* about what is up there, whatever it is. Because one thing's for sure – it won't be what *they* say it is."

Kali nodded. She turned away, staring beyond the platform over the valley, towards the Dragonfire. They were safe for now, but only for a matter of hours. There was no going back to the sphere now, and nowhere else to hide. They were alone out here. Alone on a precarious arm of metal, in a long lost valley, somewhere at the top of the world.

Outlined by the glow of the fires – natural and magical – she couldn't help but feel like a target.

CHAPTER SIXTEEN

The Final Faith breached the Dragonfire at dawn, just as the dwelf had predicted. Four airships as black as Long Night nosed into the lost, each of them emblazoned with the crossed circle of the church Kali knew all too well. But much as she hated everything that symbol stood for, she could not fault the machines behind it. Because while their airships differed from those of elven design – being uglier, ribbed things with more primitive gondolas and with rotors turned by steam rather than amberglow – they were nonetheless similarly and equally functional to the Old Race vessels that had inspired them.

The lead ship was larger and more ornate than its companions – the *Kesar*, *Voivode* and *Rhodon* respectively – and sported a huge gondola lifted by a double gasbag with two huge, thrumming rotors driving it from behind. This was obviously the flagship and its status was reflected in the name Kali could make out on its side: *Makennon*.

It wasn't the ship that drew her attention, though, but the figure she could just make out standing at its prow before a contingent of shadowmages. Even at this distance, a familiar blonde mane of hair could clearly be seen billowing behind the figure as it stared ahead.

"It's your sister," Kali said. "Back to mop up the mess she started."

"Then it's time we were on the move," the archer said. "You got a name for this thing yet?"

"Thought we might call it the *Tharnak*."

"Nice.

Kali followed Slowhand onto the *Tharnak* and, with a nod to everyone, decoupled the clamps securing it to the gantry.

"Aldrededor?"

"I am ready, Kali Hooper. All we need is a destination."

Actually, there are two, Kali thought.

The first had been obvious – Andon because she had to get the prism to the League – but the second had proven difficult. In fairness, it wasn't every day she had to work out where on the peninsula she could hide a *spaceship*. The problem lay in the fact that their civilisation was growing all the time, and there was no guarantee that any choice made today might not be encroached upon in a month's time, six months or a year, as both Vos and Pontaine continued to vie for dominance across their limited land. But at last she had decided. There was one place where they were unlikely to ever go. An inhospitable and downright pitsing dangerous place that defied any attempt at settlement and with which she'd had passing acquaintance. And there, in its vast sprawl, one specific location. An Old Race site that had once had a deadlier purpose but, since its destruction, would provide them with an underground harbour that should keep the ship safe for as long as needed.

"Andon and then east. We're taking this thing into the Sardenne – to the Spiral of Kos."

Aldrededor nodded in approval. Then his eyes closed. A second later, the *Tharnak* stirred, the thin traceries of hull visible between its thread funnels glowing brightly with their restored amberglow charge. There was a barely perceptible vibration in the ship and then the thread funnels themselves began to slowly move until the hull rippled like the reptilian hide it resembled. Dolorosa gasped as the *Tharnak*'s wings shifted slightly and Kali could hardly blame her – because the ship seemed *alive* beneath them.

"Take her up, Captain." Kali ordered.

Aldrededor concentrated and the *Tharnak* rose unsteadily from its cradle, tipping left and right as the ex-pirate became used to the feel of it. The sensation of leaving the ground – becoming airborne – was, Kali had to admit, a little unnerving. Even Slowhand, who had already flown, clung to the deck rails, his knuckles white. Though that, Kali suspected, might have had more to do with the fact that he and Jenna were about to become mortal enemies in a confrontation only one of them might survive.

Aldrededor steadied the ship, the ex-pirate growing more confident in its handling, before turning it towards the approaching airships. It was a manoeuvre that shifted perspective in a way that Kali had never experienced before and that first she found discomforting and dizzying, but then exhilarating.

Watching the walkway skew away beneath the ship, and then the horizon tip diagonally, Kali felt an overwhelming sense of how impossible her current situation seemed. She'd come across many artefacts that were beyond her ken but she couldn't help but wonder how the people of the peninsula might react if they knew that a battle for their future was about to be fought between airships and a flying machine here at the top of the world.

The Final Faith airships were clear now and, sure enough, their decks swarmed with figures, all gathering at their rails to stare at the Crucible's remains. The fact that she and the k'nid had done their job for them would not, Kali suspected, garner a grateful slap on the back and, equally sure enough, once the situation sank in, all eyes – including the coldly narrowing ones of Jenna – turned in the direction of the *Tharnak*. Kali wondered what she made of the strangely shaped craft, and whether, for a moment, she might reconsider her intent and call a truce to examine this remarkable find.

As the ships began to move towards them Kali stared at the *Tharnak's* controls. "I wonder if any of these farking things are weapons?"

Aldrededor spoke from the piloting panel. "Have no fear, Kali Hooper – we have other means to defend ourselves.

"We do?"

"We have the ship itself. Or rather, how it flies."

"You mean use the threads?"

"Indeed. The *Tharnak* stimulates them, and if we can fly close enough to the enemy ships we should be able to disrupt their stability, bring them down."

"Sounds good. But you've only just learned how to pilot this thing. Are you sure you –?"

Kali and the others wrapped themselves around rails as the *Tharnak* executed a perfect roll, three hundred and sixty degrees, leaving a reddened Dolorosa clutching her skirt about her knees when it righted itself.

"Convincing," Kali said, swallowing. "Do it."

Aldrededor winked and concentrated once more. The gap between the *Tharnak* and the airships closed rapidly. On the decks of the airships crewmen and shadowmages yelled in shock and surprise and, for a fleeting second as they hove in on the *Makennon*, Kali caught sight of Jenna frowning before racing along the deck, barking orders to her people.

All hells broke loose.

As the *Tharnak* drew level with the flotilla, the shadowmages aboard the *Makennon* and its sister ships began to weave their powerful magic. Suddenly the sky was filled with bolts of lightning, fire and ice. It was a devastating barrage and had Aldrededor not deftly manoeuvred their ship out of the way, the battle would have been over before it had begun. Having avoided the first barrage, the Sarcrean quickly brought the ship in close to the *Rhodon*, before veering suddenly away to starboard. The resultant play of the threads rippled along the sides of the *Rhodon*'s gasbag like a squall wind and the moorings of the cloth tore away in places, leaving flapping wrents in the envelope. The *Rhodon* lurched suddenly, narrowly avoided collision with the *Voivode*.

Aldrededor wasted no time. As the *Voivode* pulled up to avoid its sister ship, the Sarcrean brought the *Tharnak* about, climbed, and then headed bow to bow with the second craft, intending to climb once more at the last second, generating a thread *wave* to slap the enemy ship down. The *Voivode* was more prepared than her sister ship, however, and even as the *Tharnak* headed towards her, the shadowmages had already discharged a volley of defensive magic, expanding circles of fire that would have been difficult to avoid even without the fireballs that accompanied them. Rather than take their impact on the most vulnerable area of the ship, the prow, Aldrededor did the only thing he could and swung the *Tharnak* around hard, flinging Kali and the others against the rails. The sky steadied itself after a second and Kali realised that while they had been forced to turn and run, they had still managed to inflict damage on the *Voivode*, which was bucking violently in their thread wake. She had no doubt that the same thought had already occurred to the Sarcrean, but she voiced it anyway.

"Aldrededor. Accelerate, *now*."

The air behind them rippled with distortions as their slipstream kicked into overdrive. The *Voivode* flew into the disturbance and was instantly kicked back, spiralling out of control towards the valley walls. Kali had to give its pilot their due, because they managed to regain some control before the ship impacted. Even so, the *Voivode* found itself colliding with, and badly snarling on, some of the sharper, projecting rocks.

It was their second victory but any element of surprise their manoeuvrability had granted them was gone, now, and even before Dolorosa had finished yelling and punching the air, the *Kesar* was heading in on their bow, moving hull to hull and tight against them on an opposed heading. It was a manoeuvre clearly meant to give the shadowmages already clustering at its rails chance to rake their energies along the *Tharnak*'s side and Kali knew there was no way they would be able to avoid damage.

It was time to give Aldrededor a helping hand.

Unslinging the crackstaff, Kali lodged herself against the rails and let loose a burst of energy towards the nearing shadowmages. However she found she had underestimated them as, one by one, they deflected the incoming charges with hastily erected shields, ricocheting it back in her direction.

"Hooper, go for the envelope," Slowhand urged, suddenly beside her. "I'll cover you."

Kali didn't question the archer, immediately bracing the crackstaff and angling it upwards just as the *Kesar* nosed into range.

The shadowmages spotted what she was trying to do as she aimed and prepared to launch another volley at her. But before they could loose their magical assault, they fell to the deck bucking and screaming as Slowhand unleashed rapid volleys from Suresight. His arrows provided Kali with the cover she needed, and she used the time to unleash a raking assault from the crackstaff, moving it slowly and determinedly across the enemy airship and tearing a gash in its envelope Suddenly venting gas, the *Kesar* tipped violently and, amidst much scrabbling and screaming, the shadowmages tumbled from the gondola to fall through the trees to the valley floor below.

"Hah!" Dolorosa shouted after them. "Thatta is whatta you get fora working with the *Final Feelth*!"

Aldrededor banked the *Tharnak* to starboard, pulling away from the battlegroup and the *Makennon*, taking advantage of the chaos to head for the Dragonfire rather than challenge the superior ship of the Faith flotilla.

Unfortunately, the *Makennon* had not been idle while he had outmanoeuvred her smaller sisterships, bringing its heavier bulk about in a manoeuvre that was perfectly timed. Even as the *Tharnak*'s bow turned to the Dragonfire, Jenna's flagship came seemingly out of nowhere to loom massively and directly in front of them, nose to nose, blocking their way to the exit from the valley, their artillery trained on the Old Race craft.

The message was clear

You want a fight? I'll give you a fight.

Kali moved to the front of the deck and found herself in direct eye contact with Jenna. Seeing Kali, Slowhand's sister smiled coldly. Slowhand came to stand by Kali's side, but if the archer had any hope at all of his sister's resolve weakening in his presence, it was dashed as her smile failed to falter.

"I see Fitch hasn't returned with her," Kali said through clenched teeth. "You still think there's no chance we can talk her round?"

"Hooper, the *fact* Fitch hasn't returned with her answers that one. Look at her – that cadaverous bastard's job is done."

Kali swallowed. She could tell that Jenna was actually enjoying this moment.

"Back us up," Kali said to Aldrededor. "Gently."

The *Tharnak* began to slowly reverse. Slowhand looked at Kali questioningly and, on the *Makennon*, Jenna frowned. But then with a wave of her hand she ordered the *Makennon* to follow them. Keeping the ships nose to nose.

"Keep going," Kali said.

"Hooper, what the hells are you doing?"

"*Keep going.*"

The *Tharnak* continued to reverse and the *Makennon* followed her. Had they continued the game that way, they could have played all day, nudging through the valley, but then Slowhand spotted something that would soon put paid to their backward flight.

"Er, Hooper..." he said.

Kali turned and saw that, behind them, the *Rhodon*, *Voivode* and *Kesar*, scarred and damaged though they were, had taken up positions in their path, enclosing them in an arrowhead formation. And those shadowmages that had survived the first assault lined their rails ready to unleash a fresh assault.

Jenna seemed to have them exactly where she wanted them.

"Bring us to a stop." Kali said.

"So what now?" Slowhand asked. When Kali didn't answer, he added, "Hooper, she's an expert tactician. There's no shame in being outmanoeuvred."

Kali looked at the archer, but couldn't hold his gaze. Had she been facing anyone but his sister her next move would have been delivered with some degree of satisfaction but –

"I'm sorry, Liam."

"For what?"

"Finishing what you started."

"I don't understand."

"For once," Dolorosa elaborated, "the bossa lady did not make it up as she went along."

Slowhand stared at the two women as they moved to the ship's rails. He looked down. Below them, a great number of small, wavering flames were visible in the treetops, covering the canopy like stars. Slowhand knew instantly what he was seeing and snapped a look at Dolorosa and Kali – just as they raised their arms and dropped them down.

From the cover of the jungle more than a hundred burning arrows were unleashed by yassan archers and arced upward towards the three smaller airships, puncturing their envelopes and firing their rigging and gondolas A second volley came, firing those parts of the ships untouched by the first wave and doubling the damage. There was no escape and nowhere to hide from the devastating rain and, as the third volley filled the sky, it was intermingled with a renewed chorus of panicked and agonised screams. Their was nothing the shadowmages could do to prevent the surprise attack, though some of them tried, sweeping the jungle canopy with energy bolts that cut a swathe through the vegetation. But for every Yassan that was caught, three more still wielded their bows and the shadowmages themselves became targets, falling to their arrows. It took only seconds before the *Rhodon*, *Voivode* and *Kesar* were little more than flying funeral pyres and then they were only pyres, not flying at all.

Kali watched the remains of the airships spiral down into the jungle. Only the *Makennon* remained. As the flagship hung there, the yassan archers emerged fully from their cover, and once more Dolorosa and Kali raised their arms. All across the jungle canopy the Yassan waited poised. Kali and Dolorosa swallowed and turned to Slowhand, their arms stayed, awaiting the archer's word. Aldrededor, too, turned. The decision – *the word* – had to be his.

For his part, Slowhand simply moved up to stare across the gap between ships, his mane of blonde hair blowing in the wind. Across that gap, her own hair blowing and eyes defiant and unblinking, Jenna stared back.

A second – an eternity – passed.

The archer's jaw tensed.

"Fire!"

Their eyes tearing, aware of the enormity of the decision Slowhand had just made, Dolorosa and Kali dropped their arms, and the volley of arrows turned the flagship into a flying inferno within a matter of moments. While Dolorosa had not had much time to train the yassan, train them well enough she obviously had, because amidst the volley, certain arrows did not randomly target the ship itself but instead those members of the crew manning the cannon, dropping them as they prepared to return fire.

Finally, the bow of the *Makennon* began to dip.

As Dolorosa pointed out, to a chorus of curses, the flagship of the Final Faith, while indeed beginning a slow dive, did not seem to be diving fast enough. Its angle and rate of descent was sluggish and lumbering, perhaps fitting of a ship its size. This was not a problem in itself but a problem *did* lie in the fact that that same angle and rate of descent was forcing her stern upward. If it continued as it did it would soon flip completely over toward the *Tharnak*. If it hit, it would swat the ancient spaceship out of the sky.

Aldrededor was visibly struggling to pull the *Tharnak* out of its path. As the Final Faith flagship continued to nose heavily downwards, the ex-pirate finally managed to force the *Tharnak* into the beginnings of a climb. It seemed they might make it – but it was going to be close. Close enough, in fact, that they found themselves able to watch the last moments of the *Makennon* and her crew in intimate detail.

Pulling up even as the *Makennon* angled down, the *Tharnak* flew along the *Makennon*'s deck, finely manoeuvring through the metal ribcage that had supported its all but burned out envelope. As they accelerated past they could see just how much damage the yassan archers' arrows had done.

Kali watched Slowhand watching the deck of the *Makennon*, following the actions of his sister amid the chaos rapidly developing there. It was testimony to Jenna's command skills that the ordinary crewmen still followed her orders – though the contingent of shadowmages aboard had already succumbed to panic – trying to beat back the flames despite the fire's inevitable triumph. Jenna strode the deck as if she could restore the *Makennon*'s flightworthiness though, even at a distance, Kali and Slowhand could see the strain thinning and greying her face. But, in the end, Jenna had little choice other than to accept the ship's doom. The sheer amount of collapsing rigging, support struts and explosions defeating any effort that could be made to stay what had to come. And at last it happened. A combination of spreading fire and detonations that conspired to separate the ribbing and remains of the envelope from the gondola completely.

The *Makennon* began to fall to jungle below.

Jenna faced her demise with dignity, anchoring herself at the airship's wheel and standing steadfast The last thing Slowhand saw before she was obscured by the overturning hull was his sister staring directly into his eyes.

Goodbye, brother. I wish I knew what might have been.

"She's going to clip us!" Kali shouted over the roar of the dying ship as its tail swung towards the *Tharnak*. Even as Aldrededor struggled to gain more height there was a bone-shaking vibration that juddered the ancient craft right to its core, throwing Kali, Slowhand and Dolorosa to the deck.

As the Sarcrean struggled at the control panel there was a dull boom from the underside of the ship and the amberglow layer beneath the thread funnels crackled and darkened.

"We have lost the use of half of the funnels on our port side and a third on our starboard, Kali Hooper. The retro funnels are gone completely. Though we have some limited manoeuvrability remaining, I fear it is not enough to enable us to negotiate the Dragonfire."

"We're going to crash?"

"We are going to crash."

Behind her, Slowhand slammed his palms onto the rail and walked to the *Tharnak*'s stern, staring down at the smouldering remains of the three smaller airships and the *Makennon*, reflecting with a certain calm that perhaps it had indeed been fated that he and his sister should die together.

They were going down and what they needed was a miracle.

What neither he, or anyone else aboard expected, was that they got one.

From the still burning remains of the Crucible, something was rising. Something that, at first, looked like a plume of smoke but, on second glance, turned out to be something else entirely.

It moved more slowly than smoke, for one thing, and seemed to be made up of countless tiny shimmering particles. As all aboard the ship watched, the particles began to coalesce.

For Kali and Slowhand, it reminded them of the dwelf slowly taking shape within its sphere. But this was something quite different. A long, undulating worm-like was body was forming, kept aloft by majestic wings that stretched far and wide.

The red eyes of the creature regarded them. Then the dragon flew towards them.

"Oh, shit." Killiam Slowhand said.

"Great Grandma of the Gods." Aldrededor and Dolorosa breathed together.

Only Kali said nothing and smiled to herself, knowing what was actually happening. This was what the dwelf had meant when he'd said that there had been one last thing he had to do. Whatever technology and magics he had left – and she suspected this was more magic than technology – the doomed ancient one had somehow reconnected them to the dying Crucible and produced at last the one creature of peninsular legend they had never recreated. Why he was doing this now, she didn't know, and nor did she know how much of the dwelf's consciousness existed in his creation but, in the end, it didn't matter. As its people watched in awe from the jungle canopy, the Dragon God rose over them.

"It's coming right at us!" Slowhand warned.

"There is nothing I can do," Aldrededor confessed.

"I don't think it means us harm," Kali said. "It might even be coming to help..."

"Help?" Slowhand repeated.

"A-ha. Look."

Slowhand and the others did, but not for long, as they were too busy ducking. Because despite Kali's assurance, they could not help but instinctively drop as the massive creature flew directly at the ship and then swooped overhead, so close that the downdraught from its wings beat the air around them. As they watched in amazement, the claws attached themselves to the *Tharnak* and pulled the entire craft up beneath it, towards its belly, as if for protection. As soon as the ship was secure the creature proceeded to fold its vast wings about the craft, pulling it in tight.

The very last thing they saw, before the creature entirely enfolded the craft, was the Dragonfire before them.

"Hold tight!" Kali shouted. "It's taking us through!"

"What the hells do you mean, taking us through?" Slowhand screeched.

"Slowhand, sometimes you've just got to have a little faith!"

Faith and a pretty good sense of balance, Kali thought to herself. Because for the next few seconds – but what seemed like an eternity – she and the others found themselves being flung from one side of the deck to the other as the creature manoeuvred through the cave system. And then, suddenly, they were through.

The dragon's wings opened and the *Tharnak* was lowered by its claws, and they found themselves being flown high along the pass.

"My Gods!" Slowhand said.

"No," Kali corrected. "*Their* God."

The archer, like the others, looked to the rails, and saw the yassan emerging from a hundred cave mouths along the pass. As the Dragon passed over them they fell to their knees and emitted a great roar of worship that resounded deafeningly through the mountains. And as it did, the dragon's long neck waved slowly from side to side, as if in acknowledgement.

"This is the moment that they – that their ancestors – have waited countless years for," Kali said. "In a strange way, in believing what they did, they were right all along."

"I hate to spoil the moment," Slowhand pointed out, looking somewhat less elated than Kali, "but while they may have been right, something here is wrong."

"What are you talking about?"

"Well, for one thing, our friend here isn't letting go."

Kali looked up, and frowned. "I'm sure it will soon."

"No, bossa lady, it is more than that," Dolorosa said. The ex-piratess had climbed up on a rail to examine the creature more closely and she, too, frowned. "Look atta this," she added, nodding at a scabrous wound that seemed to be spreading by the second all along its underside. "Eet is injured."

"Hardly surprising," Aldrededor said. "Our passage through the Dragonfire was a rough one."

"Except only its outside hit the walls," Kali pointed out.

Slowhand bit his lip. "Hooper, are you saying –?"

Kali nodded. "Nothing except the k'nid can survive outside the valley."

"Then we are in trouble, Kali Hooper," Aldrededor piped in. "Because as my wife would say, we 'havva another problem'."

"What, Aldrededor?"

"Perhaps you and Mister Slowhand would care to take a look over the side."

"Ohhhh, fark," the archer said.

"You can say that again," Kali answered.

"*Ohhhh, fark.*"

The curse was wholly appropriate. Whilst they had all been speaking, not only had the dragon flown them out of the pass and beyond the Drakengrat Mountains but it had also, for its own reasons, climbed. Features on the landscape below were now little more than dots, the dragon having gained at least a thousand metres in height.

A thousand metres.

And it was still climbing.

CHAPTER SEVENTEEN

The dragon continued to climb, so high now that daylight began to give way to the azureness of night as the air around it and the ship thinned, and that azure glow in turn began to give way to an inky blackness that was neither night or day. Kali and the others had been unable to do anything to prevent their continued ascent and they could do nothing now except experience, in stunned silence, that which no one of their world had ever experienced before.

It was an hour after dawn.

And the stars were coming out.

"Hooper?" Slowhand said, his voice tinged with wonder.

"Oh Gods." was all Kali could say in reply, as she stared out into the void.

That either of them could speak at all was a surprise. And not only because of what lay revealed before them. All four on board the ship had suffered near unconsciousness as they had been carried further and further from the now impossibly distant and patchwork ground, breathlessness giving way to burning lungs and then an inability to breathe at all. Thankfully, though, the effects of their rising altitude had not lasted, the ship forming a membrane around the deck that sealed them in while also generating fresh air for them to breathe. This was alongside another, far more peculiar and unexpected effect which was that, a few seconds later, she and the others seemed to be able to fly!

It was as if they weighed nothing at all, victims of some mischievous sorcery wielded by an invisible hand. The expressions on her companions faces reflected the same emotions Kali felt – that it was unbelievable and strange and incredible. And liberating. *Too* liberating in one case.

Slowhand's clothes were beginning to float off.

Fortunately they didn't get chance to float all the way.

The ship dropped suddenly, Kali and the others' weightless forms thrown into turmoil within, and as Kali scrambled to see through the membrane, paddling upside down across its surface, it was clear that the dragon had begun to struggle above them. The wound on its underside that Dolorosa had noticed earlier had become livid now, and the flesh around it was falling away, first in small flakes and then larger chunks, as if the creature were infected with a virulent leprosy. Whatever had possessed the dragon to bring them here, whatever had driven it on this suicidal climb, didn't matter for the moment, because it was clear that its journey was over – and with it their own. The ship dropped once more as the dragon's grip on it became weaker, but while it didn't let go, the creature itself began to turn, as if to dive back to the surface. The turn did not look deliberate to Kali, though – as if the creature were simply too weak now to remain aloft, listing rather than manoeuvring, merely suspended momentarily in this alien space. A second later, that proved to be the case.

Both the dragon and the ship began to plummet, and Kali and the others were propelled into the membrane. As it stretched Kali began to pray that it wouldn't break. She did not have to pray for long, though, as the dragon's rate of descent was so great that the weightlessness they had experienced soon dissipated.

This resulted in all four of them being thrown about the craft like peas in a pod.

"Hooper, what in all the farking hells is going on!?" Slowhand shouted.

"Gravity, I think."

"That isn't what I mean and you know it!"

Kali stared up at the dragon and her brow furrowed. The wound on its underside had spread, encompassing now its sides and the beginnings of its wings. Cartilage and muscle and even bone were becoming visible beneath the flesh now and it was obvious to Kali what she was seeing. A reversal of the process that had formed the creature in the first place. This, then, was the fate of all those creations, bar the k'nid, who left the influence of the Crucible. The dragon was coming apart before her eyes.

And if it came apart at this height, then the ship would too.

Their dizzying fall continued and, as they dropped below a certain altitude, the membrane that had held them from the void disappeared, exposing all on the deck to the raw maelstrom of the wind. It was impossible to communicate with the others, words and even screams whipped away in the deafening roar, and it was almost as impossible to maintain their hold on the ship, winds ripping at them and making the flesh on their faces flap and ripple. Aldrededor, though, was fighting his way back to the controls, presumably in a desperate attempt to try and level them out. Even if he made it, the Sarcrean certainly had his work cut out for him, the decaying dragon having fallen now into a spiralling descent that span the world around them.

Kali willed the dragon to quite literally keep itself together for just a little longer, until they were at an altitude where Aldrededor might be able to safely regain some control. She had no doubt now that the same benign intelligence – perhaps all that was left of the dwelf – that had guided them through the Dragonfire was still at play here, because the dragon was clearly trying to raise and flex its wings and pull them out of their terminal dive. Even as great scaled and fleshy chunks of it were torn away by the tumultuous descent, the dragon, for whatever reason it had brought them here, was now trying to bring them safely home.

Kali pulled herself down the deck to Aldrededor's side, where the ex-pirate was linked to the ship once more but clearly straining to impose his will upon it. As he did, she stared at the dragon again, heart sinking as she saw its flesh had now all but been stripped away.

It was surely only a matter of minutes before there was nothing left of the creature at all. Still, as it fought, its wings, slowly, began to lift.

And as they did, the ship began to level out.

Kali looked down. Their angle of descent was still way too steep, way too fast. But it was a start. The dragon was trying, and they had to try too.

"Aldrededor, you have to pull us up!" Kali shouted. "You have to pull us up when I tell you!"

The ex-pirate's flowing moustache was plastered against his cheeks by the wind now. "I... will try... Kali Hooper."

Kali slapped him on the back. "I know you will!"

"Hooper, our friend is a goner," Slowhand shouted.

"Just a few moments more." Kali willed.

Again, she looked at the dragon and was staggered and awed as, quite deliberately, its head – actually more a cadaverous skull now – turned on its long neck and looked at her, as if acknowledging its complicitness in her plan. The creature knew what it was doing, all right, and it could *only* know if it did indeed carry the consciousness of the dwelf. Kali looked up as a beating that could be heard even above the roaring wind began and saw that at last the dragon had managed to fully flex what remained of its wings. As they slowly, majestically, swept at the air it began to pull the ship onto a more level keel.

But it would not be enough unless they did their bit.

Kali stared one last time at the dragon, swallowing as its saddened eyes began to dull, then turn grey, and then, like the rest of its form, began to discorporealise. The air around her filled with a dry, golden rain that coated her face and tasted bitter on her lips.

"Aldrededor, now," she said, a tear in her eye.

"Everybody hold on."

The Sarcrean's eyes shut, his jaw clenched and his temples throbbed with concentration. Above him, the dragon was now nothing but a skeletal afterthought and, even as he pulled back on the ship's controls, that too began to stream away into the wind.

Thank you and goodbye, Kali thought sadly, wishing she had more time to mourn the passing of the ancient creature.

As the dragon vanished on the wind, the Kerberos ship soared from its ashes, punching through its discorporealising remains into clear sky, pulling up from what had become a forty-five degree dive into a much gentler descent. Only the angle of the descent was gentle, however, the ship still hurtling through the air at previously unimaginable speed.

As Twilight rolled beneath it, Kali could not work out how high they still were because she could see no landmarks below. But then as the ship drew lower, penetrating a thin layer of cloud, she understood why – they were coming down over the sea.

Storm tossed waves roiled beneath them and lightning flashed. How far out they were, Kali didn't know, but she understood instantly why the Twilight Seas were considered so dangerous by those who sailed them. Here, beyond the Storm Wall, she could see that vast areas of the deeps were whorled by giant whirlpools. Waves clashed like opposing armies, the fallout of battle spreading for leagues and, in one place in particular, Kali saw a wall of water so high it was moving dizzying slowly, but seemingly with purpose, across the turbulent expanse. *What the hells was that?* Kali thought. It even seemed to have things riding the side of it, *something* on top of it.

Whatever it was, their passage was such that it was soon gone and at last, ahead of them, Kali began to make out the jagged edges of what looked like a large island. From its shape she recognised Allantia, and beyond that a much larger landmass that, by extension, had to be the northern coast of the peninsula. As the ship passed over Allantia, a dark mass flecked with both red and white rose ominously on the eastern horizon, bending southward for leagues after leagues – a mass that was without doubt the World's Ridge Mountains.

Kali felt a momentary stab of disappointment, that of missed opportunity, because if only they had come in the other way she might have been able to see what lay *beyond*. She shrugged the feeling aside in favour of a much more positive one, however, because Aldrededor had brought them almost exactly where they needed to be.

The ex-pirate brought the ship onto an almost level keel and Kali turned to congratulate him but, as she did, the ship shuddered violently beneath her. It sounded and felt as if it had taken far more of a battering than it could stand.

Kali looked to the east where the thick bow of the Sardenne Forest could now just be made out, wrapping the base of the World's Ridge Mountains. The problem was, she could feel the ship moving ever so slightly away from it, on a south-easterly course.

"Aldrededor, can you turn us towards the Spiral?"

The Sarcrean shook his head. "I fear not, Kali Hooper. Our manoeuvrability remains all but non-existant and many thread funnels are damaged. We are locked on this course unable to climb and, what is worse, unable to attempt a controlled descent."

"You mean we arra going to crash?" Dolorosa asked.

"Not so much crash as fly into the ground... eventually," Kali corrected. "Aldrededor, where will we come down?"

The ex-pirate closed his eyes, calculated. "With our rate of descent and crew complement we will impact several leagues outside Andon, to the east of the Anclas Territorial border."

The Anclas Territories, Kali thought. *Dammit!*

Because in other words, that meant right under the hawklike noses of the Vos military. She had never been partisan in her life, and she wasn't about to start being so now, but if that happened, even if the ship took damage, the dwelfen technology on board could unfairly tip the balance of power in Vos's favour for years to come. They *had* to get past them, bring the ship down elsewhere somehow.

But where? As Kali studied the ground flashing below, she asked herself not for the first time just where on the peninsula it would be safe from its burgeoning civilisation.

And the answer was nowhere.

Kali paused, a plan forming. A plan she was amazed she hadn't thought of before now.

"Aldrededor," she said suddenly. "You said with our 'current crew complement.' So if our crew complement were fewer, namely one, would the ship avoid coming down near the territories, even overfly Andon?"

"By a narrow margin, Kali Hooper. But I do not understand – you are thinking of hiding the ship beyond Andon?"

Kali smiled. "Something like that, Mister Pirate."

Aldrededor frowned, not understanding but willing to comply nonetheless.

"Very well, Kali Hooper. But how do my wife, Mister Slowhand and yourself plan to leave the ship exactly?"

"*I* don't. It's you lot I need to walk the plank."

The ex-pirate 's eyebrows rose. "This ship needs a pilot, Kali Hooper."

"No, Aldrededor, not any more. The ship's locked on course, right? So even if you detach yourself from the threads, it'll get me where I need to go yes?"

"Yes, but –"

"Then it's settled," Kali looked at the ground. "Get yourself ready, there isn't much time."

"Whoa, whoa, whoa," Slowhand protested. "There isn't much time for *what*? How exactly are we going to abandon ship, Hooper?"

"Once, whenna our sheep was swept into the sky by the Great Gusts of Groom," Dolorosa interjected, "Aldrededor and I escape using the sheep's flag anda feathers from its mascot. We called itta the parrot-chute!"

"You have to be kidding, right?" Slowhand sighed. "Well, unfortunately, we're all out of parrots, too."

"You havva the better idea, preety boy?"

"Pretty boy?"

"Yessa, preety boy!"

"Hey!"

"*I* have the better idea," Kali interrupted. "We use the Roaring."

"The Roaring?"

Kali nodded, picturing the giant, coolwater geyser that erupted north of Miramas and Gargas, the strange wall of water she had seen at sea having given her the idea. No one really knew what the source of the Roaring was, though some said it was an outlet for water surging underground from the other side of the World's Ridge Mountains. What she did know was that it thundered into the air for an hour each day at about this time, and the phenomenon was right in their flightpath. What was more, when the geyser crashed back to ground, its overflow became the Rainbow River which, flowing south-easterly, eventually fed Badlands Brook near which sat the *Flagons*. If Slowhand and the others gave themselves to the geyser and the current of the river they should not only be home in no time but – assuming they stayed in the moving water – relatively safe from any k'nid infestation between here and their destination.

"Let me get this straight," Slowhand said. "You want us to *jump* into the Roaring?"

"Only if it's spouting."

"What ees the matter, preety boy – afraid of a leetle water?" Dolorosa taunted. She joined Aldrededor at the ship's rails, her husband having already detached himself from the controls, trusting Kali implicitly.

"I'm not going anywhere," Slowhand said to Kali. "I'm staying with you."

"Slowhand, you *can't*. One person on board, this ship get where I need it to go. Two, it crashes and burns."

"Then you jump, too!" the archer retorted. And then, more softly: "Dammit, Hooper, I've already lost one person I love today."

Kali stared at him, momentarily speechless. The fact was, she didn't exactly relish what she planned to do as it was as potentially dangerous as Slowhand feared, but if her plan was to work she *had* to stay with the ship. "There's no choice."

"What are you going to do, Hooper, hit me again? Well, try it. You just try –"

Kali's fist landed hard. The archer staggered back and then collapsed to the deck.

Kali took a deep breath, then leaned over the rail and looked down and ahead. The Roaring was already looming, spray from it spattering her face.

"Time to go."

Both Aldrededor and Dolorosa climbed onto the rail, ready to jump, the latter hesitating slightly.

"Bossa lady? Arra you sure you know whatta you are doing?"

Kali smiled. "I thought I told you, I make this up as I go along." She looked at the prone archer. "Look after him, okay?"

"Pretty boy, he willa notta be pleased."

"I hope you survive to find out, Kali Hooper." Aldrededor said.

"Both of you," Kali said, "thank you. For everything."

The ex-pirates nodded, he with a twirl of his moustache and a twinkle of his eye, she with a smile that cracked parts of her face Kali hadn't ever seen move. And then the two of them waited until the wide geyser was beneath them and leapt.

Kali watched the two Sarcreans plunge into the seething plateau and then quickly heaved Slowhand's unconscious form onto the rail. The archer was groaning, beginning to stir, when she grabbed his legs and tipped him forward. Slowhand's semi conscious form tumbled from the ship, his clothes snagging awkwardly on some protrusion from the hull and, before Kali's disbelieving eyes, they were ripped from him, leaving him completely naked, bar his bow and quiver, to fall after the pirates.

Pits of bloody Kerberos! Just how in the hells did he do it?

Shaking her head, Kali moved to the rear of the deck and watched as Aldrededor and Dolorosa caught the spluttering archer, and then the three of them began to recede from her view as the giant geyser reached its zenith and began to drop from whence it had come.

Kali moved to the bow of the ship and stared down to study the landscape as it continued to roll beneath her. The ship was following the course of the Rainbow River. There was the Rainbow Delta and one of its various offshoots, Badlands Brook, there

Ponderfoot's Copse, there Bottomless Pit, and there – suddenly – the *Flagons* itself. The sight of home – surrounded, though thankfully still untouched, by the k'nid – tugged at her, and the desire to be down there, downing her eighth glass of thwack was almost so overwhelming that she was tempted, for a second, to leap overboard herself. The desire became all the more tempting when unexpectedly – no doubt drawn by the sound of the ship, the kind of *off key* sound that only he would recognise – Merrit Moon emerged from the doors of the tavern and stared upwards. It was odd but Kali had become somehow so used to the concept of the Kerberos ship over these last hours that she had forgotten how staggering it might be to another's eyes. She watched the old man's face gurn through a number of indefinable expressions before he mouthed the words: "My Gods."

He actually *did* stagger back when she waved to him from the deck, and for a moment she thought he might spontaneously turn into Thrutt.

Interested in Old Race artefacts, old man? Well, I got you a doozy.

She wished she could explain what was happening, have the reassuring presence of the old man with her somehow, but that task would have to be left to Aldrededor, Dolorosa and Slowhand.

The ship moved on and, after a while, Kali wondered whether she were close enough yet to put the next stage of her plan into action, studying the ground once more to sight landmarks to indicate her proximity to Andon. The effective range at which her plan might work was a complete unknown, however, and she would really lose nothing by trying to instigate it now. Decided, she steadied herself on the bow of the ship and focused all her mental energy and concentration into the formation of a single word. A name.

Sonpear.

It was a gamble, of course – a gamble that the telepathic link that the League sorcerer had established with her while she was in Domdruggle's Expanse remained effective.

Sonpear, she attempted again, trying to amplify her thoughts.

Can you hear me?

No reply.

Sonpear.

SONPEAR!

Kali's eyes squeezed shut and her brow furrowed in concentration. She was oblivious to the wind that buffeted her as the ship continued its long descent, oblivious to everything but the image of a man on whom she would never have dreamt the lives of so many would depend.

SONPEAR, YOU BASTARD, HEAR ME!

Miss Hooper? There is really no need to shout. Or, I might add, to get personal.

Kali's eyes snapped back open and, for a second, she felt the link that had just been established slip away. But she fought against it until she could once again feel the sorcerer in her grasp.

Miss Hooper, it is pleasing to hear from you. Tell me – was your mission successful?

There'll be no more k'nid from the Crucible. But the danger isn't over yet.

Indeed? And I gather that this communication is occurring because you once more need my help?

Not only yours, Sonpear. The League.

The League? Miss Hooper, I thought you already understood that the League has sealed its doors. That they are offering their help to no one.

And doing so because they know nothing works. Tell me, Sonpear – how are things in Andon?

The k'nid are ubiquitous. There is little more that can be done to prevent the city falling to them completely. Thankfully, we have managed to evacuate many of our people to the sewer network. Not the most salubrious place of refuge, as I can testify, but one that has become a necessity.

Keep them there, Sonpear. But I need you to bring a message to the League, however you can.

And that message is?

That I have the means to eradicate the k'nid. But I need you, and them, to do something for me in return.

Which is?

Open another portal to Domdruggle's Expanse.

The Expanse? But surely I alone could attempt –

I doubt it, Sonpear. This one needs to be a little bigger.

Bigger?

And in the sky

Sky?

It's a long story. Trust me.

Sonpear went silent, and whether it was the telepathic link or not, Kali could almost feel him cogitating.

Very well, Miss Hooper, I shall do as you ask. How long do we have to prepare the portal?

Ohhh... about ten minutes.

Hmph. I see.

Not yet, you don't. But you will. Later, Sonpear.

The sorcerer's voice sounded vaguely puzzled. *Very well, Miss Hooper. Later, as you say.*

Kali broke the link and returned her attention to the physical rather than the mental, staring ahead of the ship to determine its current location. Its trajectory had not wavered while she had been otherwise occupied and, while it was inevitably now slightly lower in the sky, it was also closer to Andon, whose tallest structure – the Three Towers – had now become visible. She guessed that she would know if Sonpear had been successful in his task if she saw the structure unfurl from its defensive position. For now there was nothing that she could do.

She gazed down at the passing landscape once more. Soon she would pass over the desolation surrounding Andon that was known as the Killing Ground. But, before she reached that, she was already encountering a number of smaller settlements that had established themselves between the Anclas Territories and the city. They were mining towns, mainly, what their inhabitants liked to think of as frontier towns and they provided Kali with her first chance to see the effects of the k'nid on populated areas. Having slaughtered, absorbed or driven into hiding everyone in the area, the k'nid were now the only living presence – and they were everywhere. It was as if someone had lain a grey blanket over the countryside. She realised that if the k'nid were not stopped, then the peninsula would be lost forever.

Kali looked to the horizon, filling now with the diverse shapes that made up the skyline of Andon, from besieged battlements to ramshackle merchants' houses, from the warehouses at the Skeleton Quay to Archimandrate Thomas Marek's solitary, Final Faith church; each and every structure quiet and abandoned and obscured beneath a layer of feasting k'nid. The only structure that seemed – perhaps through some magical means – to have escaped absorption was the Three Towers, but even so the headquarters of the League looked battered after enduring days of what must have been continuous assault. It did not, though, matter a jot what the Three Towers *looked* like, so long as its offences were still functional.

Dammit, Sonpear. This is cutting things fine.

But at that very moment the towers began to unfurl.

Standing at the prow of the ship, Kali watched as the three separate spires of the headquarters of the League of Prestidigitation and Prestige began to return to their normal state, shedding those k'nid that determinedly clung to the sides. It was an awesome sight but, as she watched, Kali was uncomfortably aware that she was the only spectator. The city below was deserted. But the restoration of the Three Towers to their normal state was a sight that instilled confidence, and not a little pride, in her. And her confidence was further bolstered when she began to make out a considerable number of figures exiting the spires and lining the bridges that were beginning to snap back into place.

Sonpear had done it. He had managed to persuade the mages to come out of their hidey-hole and join the final battle.

Still, what she was asking them to do was, as Sonpear himself had admitted, going to be far from easy. She wasn't exactly convinced that it was even possible – there was certainly no sign of any portal that she could see. Kali reckoned that she had approximately two or three minutes before the ship intercepted the Three Towers and she was knocked out of the sky. They all had only one chance at this, and if they failed the rune-covered crystal she carried with her would be lost, possibly for ever.

Suddenly, however, something began to happen. The mages lining the bridges turned as one to face the approaching ship and though she could not hear them, the gesticulations they made with their arms made Kali realise, that they had begun to chant. Led by Poul Sonpear – and Kali was convinced she spotted Lucius Kane in there too – every man and woman present was mouthing the same invocation over and over again, the volume growing as she neared them. And as the volume grew, so did something else.

Kali's previous experience of a magical portal had been pressured and fleeting to say the least, but there was no mistaking what was forming before her and the ship now. Smack in the middle of the triangle formed by the three towers, above the bridges, the sky was opening. The portal began to spread across the sky like a bleeding wound, as if the heavens themselves had been knifed, and through it Kali could see the shadowy netherworld that was Domdruggle's Expanse. The perfect hiding place, she thought, where the ship could remain in limbo until, if ever, it was needed. And the ship was heading straight for it. Which, of course, meant that it was time to go.

Kali had had her escape route mapped out from the moment Andon had appeared on the horizon, a sequence of buildings she intended to use as stepping stones to get her safely down to ground level, starting with the steeple of the Final Faith church. She was sure the Archimandrite in charge of the place wouldn't mind the sacrilege, after all it was his lot that had started this mess in the first place. Of course, she would have to contend with the k'nid on her way down, but she still had her crackstaff and that should keep her safe enough until she could reach the Three Towers and hand over the crystal whereupon – hopefully – *that* particular problem would become academic. All she had to do was time her drop right so that she didn't break her legs.

She was beginning to unfurl a rope from her equipment belt, intending to tie it off and lower herself part of the way, when the ship shook violently and unexpectedly beneath her. She glanced worriedly ahead, saw that the ship was veering off course slightly.

And if it continued the way it was going, it would veer away from the portal and into one of the towers themselves.

Dammit! Kali thought, dropping the rope and returning to the controls.

She had little, if any, idea of their internal workings and so did the only thing she could – thump them. *Hard.* She thumped them again but there was no response. And then, for the sake of variety, she kicked them. There was a slight response then and the course of the ship corrected slightly. But only for a second. Clearly the ship had leaked too much charge to continue without some persuasion and the implication of that couldn't have been worse.

She couldn't abandon the ship. She had to ride with it into the portal. And this time she doubted she would be coming back.

Kali looked up. The portal was directly in front of her now, fully formed, filling her world. The junction between realities seemed to slow the world around it, so that the ship edged rather than raced forward, but Kali wasn't sure whether that was a good thing or not, because it gave her more time to see what was waiting for her *inside*. Looming large, directly on the other side of the portal – *filling it* – was Domdruggle's face. That angry, wizened, no longer human face. And it was roaring at her.

"Hooper!" it shouted.

Or did it? The voice seemed to come from behind and below her, faint on the wind, and somehow not possessing the rumbling, vocal *gravitas* one might expect from an ages old, spectral wizard.

"Hooper!"

No, she thought. *It couldn't be.*

Kali raced to the rear of the deck and looked down. *Oh Gods, no, it really, really couldn't be...*

But it was.

There was a naked man on a horse following the ship.

Correction. There was a naked man on *Horse* following the ship.

Riding him across the rooftops.

Kali stared, and despite her predicament couldn't help but

smile. The fact was, Slowhand wasn't so much riding Horse as Horse was allowing him to stay mounted as he galloped in pursuit, the great beast taking the gaps between buildings with powerful leaps, flinging the archer about in the saddle. Quite how he had gotten here so quickly she could only guess at, but presumably filled with indignant anger at being unceremoniously – and literally – dumped, Slowhand had survived the Rainbow River and hot-footed it to the *Flagons* and coaxed Horse from his sickbed with warnings about how she was in mortal danger. The bamfcat's unusual abilities took care of the rest. Kali's heart lifted to see how well the beast had recovered under Merrit Moon's tender ministrations, and having him nearby made her feel less alone against what she faced. The archer, too, she supposed begrudgingly.

"Hooper, jump!" Slowhand shouted, his voice faint across the distance between them.

"I can't!" she shouted back, hoping that he not only heard but realised there was a reason for her refusal beyond the dizzying height. Fortunately, the ship juddered once more to illustrate her point.

A second passed, Slowhand sizing the situation up. As Kali corrected the ship's course once more, she heard: "Hooper, just time it!"

Time what? Kali thought.

Because despite their mutual effort, Slowhand and Horse remained too far away. But at that second the nose of the ship impacted with the portal, squelching as it entered, and the effect the portal had on seeming to slow time was magnified tenfold as it slowly began to suck the ship through the bridge between worlds. Two things became immediately apparent to Kali – one, that this would give Slowhand and Horse time to draw closer and, two, that the ship no longer needed to be steered. It was entering the portal now no matter what and that made the difference between heroism and suicide. The jump itself might be suicide but at least she could *try*.

Again, she raced to the back of the ship, saw Slowhand and Horse had drawn closer, galloping now across some of the higher rooftops surrounding the Andon Heart. But they were still some way away and one hells of a long way down. She'd never make it.

Still, Slowhand had to have some kind of plan. She knew he thought she thought he was an idiot but he was an idiot she had learned to trust. Even Slowhand wouldn't suggest she leap to her death. She *had* to trust him, whatever his plan.

As he had said, she had to time it, wait until the last possible moment before she leapt. Decided, Kali returned to the bow of the ship and stood directly before the portal, drawing a deep breath to steady herself against Domdruggle's immense, looming visage. And as the ship penetrated ever further into the portal she began to back up, keeping the threshold at a safe distance all the time. As she did, she mentally envisaged the deck shortening behind her, waiting for the *exact* moment when it had become just short *and* long enough to make her leap a viable one. And then, with a roar of determination, she turned and ran.

Kali pounded along the remaining deck, legs thumping, arms pumping, her panting drowning out every other sound as she watched the Andon skyline bob before her. And then she was in the air.

She soared from the end of the ship, legs still pumping, arms windmilling as, behind her, the ship continued to be absorbed by the portal, but she was no longer interested in what was behind her, only what was in front and below. As the air whistled about her she tried to orientate herself enough to spot Slowhand and there he was, spurring Horse up the sixty degree slope of the roof of an Inn. And then, at full gallop, he spurred Horse off it so that the great beast seemed, momentarily, to be making a jump towards the heavens.

Then the pair of them disappeared.

Suddenly they were gone. Completely.

Oh crap.

She had recognised the disturbance in the air about Horse enough to know that he had just made one of his 'leaps' but she had no idea if the leap had been made by accident or design. Maybe Horse had simply panicked at what the archer had made him do, or maybe it had been a deliberate, if mistimed, attempt to somehow reach her.

Alone now, Kali watched the rooftops grow beneath her and tried not to anticipate the impact she would soon feel. It wasn't the first time she had been in a situation such as this but it *was* different. Falling from a suicide slide above the rooftops of Scholten was one thing but here she was, having leapt from somewhere almost forty stories high, and that was something else entirely.

Suddenly Horse appeared directly in front and a little below her, a roaring Slowhand on his back. The shock was so great that Kali almost dropped right past them thinking: *Hey, that was neat.* Then her survival instincts kicked in and she grabbed for the beast – and missed. Luckily, in the second she'd made her attempt, Horse's momentum had carried him slightly further forward and, with the aid of a horn that he suddenly thrust forward, she was able to flail and grab again, flinging herself up onto his back behind Slowhand. At the exact moment she did, all three of them succumbed to gravity and they fell.

The world disappeared around her.

Reappeared.

Horse impacted with the ground so hard that his hooves shattered the stone flagging.

But they were down.

Safe.

Almost.

"Thanks, Slowhand," Kali said, and leaving a stunned and naked archer behind, began to run off along the street.

"Where the hells are you going?"

Kali produced the prism from her equipment belt, waved it in the air.

"Have to see a man about a god!"

CHAPTER EIGHTEEN

The sky above the *Here There Be Flagons* raged with a storm unlike any heard or seen before – a storm of turbulent, clashing clouds and roaring thunder, green forked lightning and a strange syrupy rain. The same storm as raged over Tarn raged over the rest of Pontaine and over the Anclas Territories and Vos too. Coast to coast as far as the Storm Wall, reaching every edge and every corner of the land to cleanse it of those who would have destroyed it. There was nowhere for these things – for the k'nid – to escape, because this was a storm visited on the land not by nature but supernature. A phenomenon born somewhere between the ancient magics and the final, doomed technological achievements of the Old Races.

The storm had raged for three days now, and would rage for three more. It was not a time to go out.

Watching the tumult at the windows of the *Flagons*, its violence muted by the thick glass and offset by the warm glow of the fire, Kali sipped from a tankard of thwack and reflected that the contrast between where she stood now and what she had seen and done in recent days couldn't have been more dramatic.

The crackling of the fire, the whinnying of horses from the stables and the simple talk around the bar – of work needed to repair the fields, of blacksmithing new tools and of the coming harvest – only served to heighten the difference between her world and that of the Old Races. There were no damned airships here, no damned mad scientist laboratories and, most importantly of all, no damned race against time. The pace was slower, gentler, and she realised how much she appreciated that right now. How much she *needed* it. That wasn't to say that she might not be off on her travels once again when the storm died down, but for the moment she needed time to think.

And, of course, to drink.

Kali downed the remainder of the thwack in one and went for another, squeezing in at the bar. She found one waiting for her, already poured by Red, who had volunteered to play host for the festivities; giving Dolorosa and Aldrededor a break from their usual duties, a break which Kali felt they had wholeheartedly earned. Red's displacement from barstool to his position behind the bar seemed to suit him, and despite the fact that the *Flagons* was jam-packed, he was doing sterling work.

Kali wandered through the crowd, nodding to those she knew and those whose acquaintance she had made in the past few days, pleased that she had invited them all here. The fact that the storm effectively stymied any normal outside activity had, to some, presented a problem. Namely, how to occupy themselves while it lasted, but the solution had seemed obvious to her.

Let's get betwattled.

At the Flagons.

On me.

Kali smiled. Her unusual tolerance for alcohol had, of course, given her the advantage in this prolonged session. Looking around now, it was clear that some of her guests were becoming somewhat the worse for wear. Sitting by the temporary stage, Jengo Pim and his lieutenants were waiting patiently for the appearance of the night's cabaret – if the slumped and, in some cases, face down on the table positions they had gradually adopted could be called waiting patiently. Still, they weren't completely out of it yet, stirring with a groan every time there was a creak on the stairs, only to collapse again despondently when the objects of their affections – Pim's, in particular – failed to appear. She could hardly blame the Hells' Bellies for taking their time in getting on stage. After all, they had been nowhere else for a week and they had only agreed to one final performance when, on his behalf, she had told them that Jengo Pim was their greatest admirer and fan. It hadn't hurt that the Grey Brigade's leader had personally agreed to treble their fee too.

Kali looked towards the crowded bar and smiled again. At first she had thought Poul Sonpear and his friends from the League were holding up – somewhat surprisingly – better than the streetwise, heavy drinking thieves, but now she saw that the mages were hardly playing fair. Sonpear himself appeared to be handling his drink naturally, standing tall amongst them, downing shot after shot, but his companions were clearly using a couple of old tricks to maintain the illusion that they were still one of the boys. Kali noticed the giveaway pink puff of smoke following a belch that denoted a sobriety spell and, further along the bar, two mages who were taller than when they had arrived, due only to the fact that they were hovering a few inches above the floor so as not to betray any unsteadiness on their feet. Kali moved past them, gave them both a nudge and they rose like balloons, crashing back to the floor when their heads hit the ceiling. She noticed as she did that Sonpear appeared to be muttering to himself between slugs. Ah, so that was it, she thought. He wasn't handling his drink naturally at all, it was the old Hollow Legs invocation.

Kali turned and crashed right into Dolorosa, who was weaving her way back from the bar with two more 'stalkers' for herself and Hetty Scrubb. The two women had been hitting the lethal cocktails – so named because they lurked before hitting you from behind – since the morning, and even the fact that both umbrellas flew out of the drinks in the collision didn't stop the Sarcrean making a narrow-eyed and dedicated beeline back to her seat, where she and Hetty continued cackling as if Kali had never been there. Kali shook her head, hoping that Aldrededor served up some food soon, not only because it might help to sober the old bat up but also slow her down so that she and the herbalist didn't bankrupt the *Flagons* with their drinking.

Kali nodded to Merrit Moon at a table further along the bar and then popped her head into the kitchen to see how Aldrededor was getting on. The Sarcrean had volunteered to cook, as everyone was heartily sick of Dolorosa's Surprise Stew after the batch she had prepared for Kali's memorial drinking session the week before.

"How goes it, Mister Pirate?"

Aldrededor looked up at her from the stove as he stirred, then bent, inhaling deeply from the cooking pot. "Ahhh, sproing, crackfish and limpods, everything the stomach of a true mariner could desire."

Kali smiled, and dipped a spoon for a sample. "At least you're willing to admit what's in it."

"Indeed. And in honour of these ingredients, I name it Seaman Stew."

Kali's smile froze, as did the spoon at her lips. "You know, Aldrededor. I might be tempted to have another think about that ..."

"Oh?"

"You know. *Think* about it."

"Why should I think about it, Kali Hooper?"

Kali stared at him as he stared at her, wondering whether he was going to crack a smile. "Well, *because*..." She shrugged when there was no response. Maybe pirates had a different sense of humour, she thought. Or maybe, more worryingly, it was just her.

"I'll get Slowhand to explain it. See you later."

She returned to the bar, noticed that Pim and his men were once more staring in expectant hope at the stairs, and looked up herself to see what had caused the creak this time. Still no Hells Bellies but, as the thieves slumped once more, she smiled, seeing the one person who had so far been missing from the festivities.

Though she had given Slowhand Jenna's bracelet in the yassan caves the night before they had left for the Crucible, the archer – perhaps so as not to be distracted from the task at hand – had decided not to activate it until now, and had spent the best part of the day watching his sister's recordings over and over. She had, every now and then, gone up to check on him, but had never made it through the door, Jenna's voice speaking so gently to Slowhand – of their childhood together – that she had felt it improper to intrude.

"Hey," she said, "fancy a drink?"

Slowhand nodded and smiled.

"Except there doesn't seem to be anywhere to sit."

"Not a problem," Kali said. She moved over to the bar and nudged two of Sonpear's hovering companions, so that they floated off across the tavern, clearing two stools. There was a belch and a pink puff from the mage next to them.

"Want to talk about?" Kali said.

Slowhand took a sip of thwack. "If you're asking if I'm all right, Hooper, yes, I am. It's funny but, despite her conditioning, Jenna remembered more of our early years than I did myself. Maybe that's the reason she was able to resist as she did, by holding those memories close."

"I wish there could have been more," Kali said softly. She hesitated. "'Liam, I'm sorry about what had to be done."

"Don't be. I'd have done the same myself. Besides, it was me who gave the order, wasn't it?" Slowhand downed more beer. "I found her too late, Hooper, but in a funny way I also found her in time. She would not have wanted to be what she had become and at least I helped her... not be."

Kali studied Slowhand. He wasn't quite as calm as he seemed to be, that she could tell, but she didn't think the reason was Jenna herself. No, there was a tension in his face that was more anger than grief, and it didn't take much to realise who that anger was directed towards. She wouldn't like to be in Querilous Fitch's shoes when her lover found him.

"Can we talk about something else?" Slowhand asked.

"Sure," Kali said, signalling for two more drinks from Red. "For one thing, I never got a chance to thank you for coming after me at Andon. That was quite a stunt with Horse."

"Don't mention it."

"There's one thing I don't get, though. Horse. How'd you manage to get him out of his sick bed – sick stable, I suppose?"

Slowhand produced a small vial from his pocket. "Essence of worgle. Swiped it from one of the laboratories in the Crucible. Here, have it."

Kali took the vial. "I'll save it for emergencies."

"Don't give him any more than a drop, though. It makes him frisky."

Kali laughed but the sound was drowned out by a sudden clamouring from Jengo Pim and his men, the thumping of hands on table. She and Slowhand looked over and saw that they were staring at the stairs and, this time, with good reason. The Hells Bellies musicians were descending the creaking risers, and where musicians came the Hells Bellies themselves could not be far behind. Jengo Pim was on his feet now, his tongue hanging out, applauding loudly as a female leg appeared at the top of the stairs. The leg was followed by its owner and then the rest of the dancing troupe. And then Jengo Pim's applause stopped and the thief collapsed back into his chair, his arms hanging limp by his side. Seeing this, Kali almost choked on her thwack, because she had never seen a man look so crestfallen.

The reason for Pim's dramatic disappointment was the equally dramatic difference in the Hells' Bellies since he had last seen them. Because each of his beloved dancers must have shed at least twenty stone, the obvious result of a week's hoofing to stay the advance of the k'nid. They were now, Kali had to admit, really quite elfin, and their new stage costumes – made, it seemed, from the pockets of their old – while not making much of an impression on Pim, had certainly got the attention of the rest of the men in the *Flagons*.

The music started, the dancers began to dance, and the tavern *didn't* shake.

"At least the k'nid caused something good to happen," Kali said to Slowhand's back.

"What?"

"I said, at least the k'nid caused something good to happen," Kali repeated, cursing as Red poured beer over her hand. "Oh pits, Slowhand are you *listening* to me?"

The archer stared at the stage as the Hells' Bellies slithered provocatively through their old garters. "Of... course... I... am."

"Well, then – all that dancing," Kali persisted. "The dancing that stopped the k'nid?"

"Actually," Slowhand said slowly, "I don't think it was the dancing."

"What are you talking about? What else could it have been?"

"Remember that eerie wailing in the Crucible? The one that sounded like an old elven instrument ...?"

It took Kali a second to register what he meant, but then she stared at the Hells' Bellies, or rather the stage behind them where the musicians were beamingly strumming and fiddling away. One on his old elven instrument.

The theralin?

Kali swallowed. "You think that I made them dance all week for *nothing*?"

"Yup."

"My Gods, they'll *kill* me."

"Ah well, never mind."

"What the hells do you mean, 'ah well, never mind'?" Kali protested. She looked towards the stage again, where the dancers were now slithering *two at a time* through their garters, a manoeuvre that evidently required them to slither rather slowly over each other as well. "Oh, fark it, you're not listening again, are you? ARE YOU?"

Kali shook her head and gave up. She grabbed her thwack and left the bar, debating whether to chance her arm in the bragging barrel while everyone else seemed occupied. But then she caught sight of Merrit Moon, the old man sitting exactly where she'd seen him last, alone at a table at the far end of the bar, and looking as if he wasn't enjoying the festivities at all.

No, she realised. It wasn't that he wasn't enjoying himself. He was concentrating on what was in his hand.

Ah. So that was it.

The fact was, the essence of worgle hadn't been the only essence that had been taken from the Crucible, she herself having removed a sample from that part of the laboratory that dealt with human specimens. And she had taken it to give to the old man. She didn't know whether it would be of any help to him, but she figured there had to be some link between the body-changing experiments at the Crucible and the Scythe Stone that had originally transformed Moon into the half-ogur he now was. The point was, she thought it might help him in his own experiments to find a full cure for himself – or thought it worth a chance anyway. But by the look of things it hadn't been.

"No good?" she asked, slipping into a seat opposite him and nodding at the vial he was rolling between his hands.

Merrit Moon looked up from it slowly.

"On the contrary, young lady. This essence is really quite potent, far more powerful in its capabilities than that responsible for my original condition. I imagine, in fact, that were I to imbibe it, it would effectively eradicate all ogur tendencies within my body."

Whatever answer Kali had been expecting, it wasn't that and she sat back, stunned.

"What? You're joking, right?"

"I wish I were. Because then I wouldn't be facing this dilemma."

"*What* dilemma? For pit's sake, it's what you've been looking for, old man. Knock it back! Hells, I'll even get you a brolly for it!"

"No. The time is not yet right."

"What the hells do you mean, not right? *Why?*"

The old man stared her straight in the eyes.

"Perhaps because there is something you're not telling me."

Kali tried her best to hold his gaze, swallowing slightly. "What's to tell? We won and the k'nid are gone or, at any rate, will be soon. Slowhand and I saw them starting to dissolve on the way here from Andon. And the *Tharnak*'s safe in the Expanse. Hells, Sonpear even told me that when the portal closed the Expanse reverted to a state of stasis, so the ship didn't even crash!" She smiled in a way she hoped would bring the conversation to an end. "Let's hope we never need it, eh, old man?"

"But we will, won't we young lady?"

"What do you mean?"

"What are you not telling me?"

Kali stood up. "Look, will you *stop* it. It's a day for celebration, so why don't we *celebrate* okay? Enough talk about the end of the farking world."

Moon raised his eyebrows. "Did I mention the end of the world?"

"No, but... oh, look, I don't want to hear any more – really I don't!" Kali shouted, much to Moon's surprise. "I mean, why me, why Kali Hooper, or whatever the hells my true name is? All I ever wanted to do was get drunk, find places and poke around in the dark. Instead, what do I find? That I'm some kind of demi-human, that you died and became some half-ogur *thing*, that Horse isn't a horse, that Slowhand's sister died, and now – now..."

Moon's surprise at the unexpected outburst turned into a look of concern. "Kali what is it?

"Steaming pits of Kerberos, old man, I'm twenty-three years old. *Twenty farking three!* I don't want the weight of the whole world on my shoulders!"

"Young lady ..."

"It just isn't fair!"

"Kali ..."

"*It isn't farking fair!*"

"Hey, hey, hey, what's going on?" Killiam Slowhand said, suddenly behind Kali and taking her by the shoulders. He turned her towards him, surprised to see the tears in her eyes. "Hooper?"

Kali thumped him on the chest, repeatedly, as he drew her close. "Godsdammit, Slowhand, this never ends!"

"Hey, whoa, whoa, whoa, what's the matter, what do you mean. We won didn't we? Didn't we?"

The old man nodded, but his face remained troubled. "This is about something else."

"What?" Slowhand asked Kali, softly. "What is it?"

Kali tensed in his arms but said nothing. And then, after a second, she broke away, grabbed some bottles from the bar and, without a word to he or Moon, headed outside, slamming the door behind her. Slowhand started to follow but Moon stopped him, spinning him around with a hand on his shoulder which, being half ogur, Slowhand could hardly resist.

"Leave her be," he said and then, after a few more moments, led him over to the bar, signalling drinks from Red. "So, young man. Why don't you tell me *exactly* what your intentions towards my protégé are..."

Outside, Kali leaned for a few seconds with her back against the door, catching her breath. The fact was, her reaction had surprised her as much it had the old man and Slowhand, but she guessed that a bellyful of thwack and the fact that what was on her mind had to out somehow was pretty much responsible for her uncharacteristic display. But what could she tell her friends? She knew full well that she couldn't have done what she'd done over the last few days without their help. So how could she tell them that it might all have been for nothing?

That's right, she thought, *nothing*.

Gods, she had to talk to someone about this, didn't she? Or she would likely go insane.

Kali drew a deep breath and made her way to the top of the hill beyond the tavern, ignoring the syrupy rain. There, she pushed her way through a gap in the bushes into a small glade, wherein a solitary grave was illuminated by a flash of green lightning. The grave's headstone was carved with one simple word – Horse – and Kali touched it and smiled. It had become her habit to escape up here on the occasional night to tell Horse of the adventures she'd had since he'd been taken. And these chats were usually relaxed, meandering affairs, but the events of these last few days had left her hardly knowing where to start.

Kali slumped with her back to the headstone, cracked a bottle of flummox and began. She told him how the world – *her* world – had changed so much this past week that he would barely recognise it, and then she told him that what troubled her the most was that she had seen what the Old Races had ultimately been capable of, but that for all their greatness and the levels of technology, they had still been unable to stop whatever it had been that had wiped them out. And if *they* had been unable to prevent their extinction, then what hope did she and the others have of preventing theirs? Because the threat was as real to them as it had been to the Old Races, she knew that now. She knew that because she had finally realised why the dragon had taken them to the edge of the heavens – it had wanted to show them something. And that something had been a smudge on the side of the sun. With that realisation she had also worked out the purpose of the strange black sphere at the Crucible, the one that had once moved slowly forward on its straight tracks. It had done so because it wasn't a sphere, it was a *countdown.* A countdown the dwelf had obliquely referred to in the fading moments of his life.

She never had found out why she had been *awaited.* And she never had found out why she was like she was. And, now, she knew, there was a possibility that she never would.

Kali took a slug of her thwack as she remembered the dwelf's last words once more.

"This world is called Twilight for a reason," he had told her. "Once in an age, to every civilisation, a great darkness comes."

THE END

Mike Wild is much older than he has a right to be, considering the kebabs, the booze and the fags. Maybe it's because he still thinks he's 15. Apart from dabbling occasionally in publishing and editing, he's been a freelance writer for ever, clawing his way up to his current dizzy heights by way of work as diverse as *Doctor Who*, *Masters of the Universe*, *Starblazer*, *'Allo 'Allo!* and – erm – *My Little Pony*. Counting one *Teen Romance*, one *ABC Warriors* and two *Caballistics Inc*, *The Crucible of The Dragon God* is his sixth novel. However, only his beloved wife and tuna-scoffing cat give him the recognition he deserves.

TWILIGHT of KERBEROS

coming
soon

Now read the first chapter of the next exciting novel in
the *Twilight of Kerberos* series...

WWW.ABADDONBOOKS.COM

TWILIGHT of KERBEROS

The CALL of KERBEROS

Jonathan Oliver

ISBN: 978-1-906735-28-9

£6.99/$7.99

UK RELEASE DATE: OCTOBER 2009
US RELEASE DATE: JANUARY 2010

WWW.ABADDONBOOKS.COM

CHAPTER ONE

Stealing a ship from the harbour at Turnitia would have been an audacious enough task in itself, but stealing a vessel belonging to the Final Faith – the dominant religion of the peninsula – was another matter entirely. When Dunsany had first suggested it to Kelos he had stared blankly at him for a moment and then said: "Have you seen what they do to heretics? Have you seen the rather fetching collection of dried flayed skins Makennon keeps as mementos?"

Katherine Makennon was the flame-haired, hot-tempered, Annointed Lord, the leader of the Final Faith. A religious tyrant who kept a firm hand on her church and made sure that its message was heard by all. Whether they wanted to listen or not.

"I may have no love for the Faith, Dunsany, but I rather value my fingernails."

"But we're in a perfect position to do this. We have my contacts on Sarcre and a hiding place that's virtually impossible to find.

Besides, who's in a better position to pull this off than the Chief Engineer and the Head Mage on the project?"

The designs for the ship had been found almost a year before in an Elvish ruin near Freiport by an adventurer called Kali Hooper. Hooper had been 'persuaded' to part with her find once Makennon's people had got wind of the importance of the artefact. Ancient texts had spoken of the elve's mastery of the rough seas of Twilight and of how they had ventured far beyond the Storm Wall and the Sarcre Islands but, until now, no reference had been found as to the design of their ships.

And just as Kali Hooper had been persuaded to part with her find, so Dunsany and Kelos had been persuaded to work for Katherine Makennon and the Final Faith.

Dunsany had been working as a shipping engineer in Turnitia for the last ten years, before that he had been the Captain of a merchant vessel plying its trade between Sarcre and Allantia. He was a master of the rough seas that surrounded the peninsula and the ships he sailed, and later designed, were considered to be some of the finest in existence. When the Anclas Territories fell to Vos and the Final Faith tightened its grip on the city, Dunsany was the first person corralled into working for the church's naval division.

The second was Kelos.

With the subjugation of Turnitia, Kelos had considered fleeing across the border to nearby Andon, but before he could act on his decision booted feet had kicked down his door and he had been dragged into the night.

Makennon had heard rumours of the powerful mage who worked his magic at the Turnitia docks; of how his wards protected the ships against the ravages of the Twilight seas and how his mastery of the elements had guided many a battered vessel back to safety. It was true that Kelos's magic was no match for the angry waters beyond the Storm Wall but, even so, it was reckoned that his power was one of the main reasons Turnitia thrived as a harbour town.

When Dunsany had looked up from his diagrams one night to see Kelos standing over him, he had grinned and said: "What took you so long?"

So the two men applied themselves to whatever martitime problem Makennon had thrown their way; Dunsany maintaining the fleet and mapping routes, while Kelos empowered the ships with his charms and wards. The crossed circle of the Final Faith soon became a familiar sight at the docks, as it was painted onto the ships preparing to bring indoctrination to the coastal towns of Twilight.

As the Faith's power had grown, so Kelos and Dunsany's resentment had increased. It was true that they were spiritual men, to a certain degree, but they resented being forced along one path of belief. "All paths lead to Kerberos," Kelos's mother had once said. But if either Dunsany or Kelos dared mention the old ways, the penalty would be severe indeed and they'd soon be joining their ancestors.

And so they strengthened their comradeship in the hatred they held for the church, while maintaining their masks of diligent civility.

With the discovery of the designs for the elf ship, that hatred soon found purpose.

In the Elven tongue it was called the *Llothriall* and it was a song ship. As Dunsany and Kelos had been presented with the ancient scrolls, containing the designs for the craft, their awe had been palpable to Makennon. Both men had heard of the song ships but neither had ever imagined they'd see the plans for such a vessel. Dunsany had never thought that a ship could be so beautiful, or so difficult to build. As he and Kelos had worked through the list of materials required they realised that the construction of the vessel would be the least part of the project.

The hull was to be composed primarily of iron wood, found only in the Drakengrat mountains. Even with their enchanted armour and cadre of mages, the detachment sent there suffered massive losses when a pride of bamfcats smelt the human meat entering their territory. The pitch required to coat the hull had also been somewhat difficult to source, having to come – as it did – from the veins of the many-spiked, semi-sentient and highly poisonous Spiritine tree. Twenty-five men were sent into the Sardenne and only five made it out. The fate that they suffered, however, was as nothing compared to the torment experienced by the young men and women sent to steal the silk for the sails from the X'lcotl. All forty sent on that mission to the World's Ridge mountains returned, but their minds did not. Their consciousnesses remained with the X'lcotl – now a part of their web – and as those strange creatures traversed the strands, the vibrations echoed out, inducing visions and delirium in the souls captured there. The shells of humans who sat and muttered in the padded cells of the Final Faith would die in time and their bodies would return to the earth, but their souls would always be caught in that terrible web.

The heart of the *Llothriall* – the great gem whose magic powered the ship – was thankfully already in the possession of the Faith. The iridescent mineral had sat in Katherine Makennon's private quarters and had been used variously over the years, as a footstool, a table and a support for a bookshelf. It was only after the discovery of the designs for the song ship that Makennon realised the worth of the artefact. Originally a General had found it in a field during the war between Vos and Pontaine, and it had been presented to Makennon as a tribute. When Kelos told her what she had, Makennon's estimation of the General was greatly raised. If he had still been alive she may even have made him an Eminence.

The power within the gem, however, required a key to unlock it, and that was where Emuel had come into the picture.

Elf magic was based on song and no human could achieve the pitch required to unlock the stone. No normal human, at least. Emuel had been the priest of a small parish in the Drakengrats. He was devoted to the church and, even through the soft, lilting tones of his voice, he managed to communicate that passion to his congregation. His parishioners had often speculated as to whether elf blood ran in Emuel's veins, for he was unnaturally tall, unusually pale and unquestionably feminine. So it was that his was one of the first names put forward for the role of ship's eunuch; a role that he accepted demurely and gratefully. Once the surgeon's knives had raised the pitch of Emuel's musical tone and the elven runes and songlines were needled into his flesh, Kelos wondered whether that gratitude remained.

The *Llothriall's* construction was brought through suffering and loss and there was no limit to the number of men and women Katherine Makennon was willing to spend in building the Faith's flagship vessel. Unfortunately, there also seemed to be no limit to the amount of the faithful who were willing to give their lives for the cause. Dunsany and Kelos wouldn't have given their time so freely had it not been for the threat of certain heresies and indiscretions suddenly being 'remembered' by Makennon. Even through their resentment, however, both men couldn't deny the majesty of what was taking shape at the Turnitia docks.

And it was partly because of that, and because of their hatred of the Final Faith and all it stood for, that they planned to steal the *Llothriall.*

"Makennon can't be allowed to keep it," Dunsany said one evening when they were away from the ears of the faithful. "It's bad enough that they use the regular ships to enforce their beliefs on the coastal towns, but the *Llothriall* can go further than them. Make no mistake, Makennon isn't planning some altruistic voyage of discovery. She's on a mission of religious conquest."

Kelos stared into the depths of his ale, behind him two sailors were beating a sea shanty into a broken piano. "No one's been beyond the Sarcre Islands before, no ship could survive those seas."

"The *Llothriall* can and just imagine what it may find."

"New lands."

"New people."

"New races with new ideologies. What do you think will happen, Dunsany, when those ideologies come up against the Final Faith?"

"What do you think?" Dunsany sighed and ran his fingers through his beard. "Gods, whatever happened to discovery for discovery's sake? Why does every pitsing artefact, every pitsing scroll and spell that's unearthed instantly become a weapon in somebody's war?"

"We could always run away to Allantia. Start up a small fishing concern. I could do cantrips for the locals."

Dunsany shook his head and smiled. "Or we could take Makennon's weapon away from her."

This time, when Kelos looked at him, Dunsany could see something like resolve in his eyes. "Discovery for discovery's sake?"

"Discovery for discovery's sake," Dunsany confirmed, raising his tankard. "Cheers."

"Get down!"

Dunsany shoved them behind a crate as the guard rounded the hull of the vast ship and headed their way.

Besides them Emuel whimpered softly, the strange runes and illustrations inked on his body glowing with a blue-black sheen in the Kerberos-lit dusk.

"Was it really necessary to bind him like that?" Kelos whispered, looking over at the shivering tattooed eunuch.

"If he gets away we're buggered, you know that. No one else can sing to that gem and unlock the magic but him. Unless, that is, you'd like me to perform an impromptu operation on you right here?" Dunsany slowly unsheathed his dagger, a disturbing smile playing across his lips.

"No, no that's fine. *Really.*"

It didn't look like Emuel was going to make a break for it though. He'd been close to a state of catatonic shock ever since they had sprung him from the deep cells at Scholten cathedral. All they had to do now was board the ship, make him sing and they were away.

"God's Dunsany, are you sure that this is a good idea? I count three men with crossbows on the foremast and I wouldn't put it past Makennon to have a shadowmage tucked in there somewhere."

"Well then, old friend," Dunsany said, putting an arm around Kelos' shoulder. "You'll just have to weave your magic won't you? Now, keep Emuel quiet while I take care of this guard."

The guard was coming towards them again, having completed a circuit of the ship. Dunsany knelt down and loaded a quarrel into his crossbow. Slowly, he edged around the crate, carefully drawing a bead on the guard while keeping to the shadows. The weapon was custom made, expertly crafted, and the quarrel made almost no noise as it exited the crossbow and entered the throat of the man in the robes of the Final Faith. Dunsany briefly left cover and grabbed the corpse, pulling it out of sight of the ship.

Emuel looked down at the pool of blood edging towards him from the body and, before Kelos had time to clamp his hand over his mouth, emitted a piercing shriek. Instantly there was movement on the foremast. Dunsany glared at Emuel and briefly considered cracking him round the head with the stock of his crossbow, but without the eunuch they weren't going anywhere.

"Kelos, remember that magic I mentioned? Well, now's the time."

Kelos closed his eyes, summoning the threads of elemental power. A coolness coursed through him as the pounding of waves thundered in his head. Beside him, Emuel and Dunsany backed away as they tasted the tang of ozone that told them something big was about to happen.

Kelos stepped around the crate and raised his hands.

The ships in this part of the docks were already swaying drunkenly, the fierce power of the sea only slightly dissipated by the massive breakwaters, but the *Llothriall* now began to lurch even more than its neighbours. The guards in the foremast were having great difficulty in keeping their aim on the man who emerged from the shadows below them. One let loose with his bow just as the boat lurched hard to starboard and the arrow sailed high into the night. A few almost found their target but Kelos didn't even flinch as the arrows thudded into the wood of the crate behind him. Instead, he concentrated on the great wheel of energy that spun through his mind. The sea surrounding the ship began to churn more furiously now and Kelos spat out the syllables that he had memorised five years before from a rare and mildewed book. For each guttural exclamation a thick rope of water erupted from the waves surrounding the *Llothriall*.

As the tentacles of sea rocketed high above the Tunritia docks, Emuel's keening stopped as he stared in awe at the lashing elemental tendrils. His panic returned in force, however, as the arms of sea whipped around the ship and found the men there.

One of them dropped his weapon as a tentacle of water snaked around his neck. Hearing the snap of vertebrae his comrade started to scramble down the rigging, but before he could reach the deck he was thrown clear of the ship, crashing into the side of a warehouse. The last man was picked from the foremast, where he had been standing frozen in shock. His bow dropped from his numb fingers as a tentacle of sea encircled his waist. He looked down as the ship receded below him and then, suddenly, he was the wrong way up and the sea was rushing towards him.

Kelos lowered his hands and edged towards the dock wall but the guard didn't resurface. The tendrils of water fell, lifeless, and Dunsany and a shaken Emuel emerged from hiding.

"I think that you found a new way to clear the decks. Don't suppose there's anything you can do for laughing boy here is there?" Kelos cast a silence spell on the eunuch. Emuel looked offended for a moment and opened his mouth, but his protest failed to emerge. "Thank the Gods for that. I didn't fancy boarding the *Llothriall* while he continued to scream the place down. Now, when we want you to sing, you'll sing okay? Kelos, lead the way."

On the *Llothriall* the three men stopped in front of a door at the bottom of the steps leading below deck. Dunsany cocked his crossbow and put his ear to the wood. He was raising his arm to signal that it was safe for them to proceed when twelve inches of steel erupted from the door just by his nose. The sword was quickly withdrawn and the door burst open. Kelos flung his palms out and a fireball thudded into the chest of the man who emerged, launching him backwards down the corridor behind him.

"Well that seemed pretty straight forward." Dunsany stepped over the felled guard, trying not to look at the smoking cavity in his chest.

"I'm warning you now that I can't keep this up for too much longer," Kelos panted.

"Relax, we're almost there."

Two more short flights of steps and a long corridor led them to the heart of the ship. They stopped in front of a reinforced door, elvish script covering its surface. Kelos traced the design with his fingers, muttering something to himself. Eventually he stepped back and nodded to his friend. "That's the advantage of designing the wards, I know how to counteract them. On three?" He drew a short sword from its scabbard on his belt.

"On three." Dunsany agreed, drawing his own blade.

As they charged into the room Kelos was flung against the ceiling. For a moment he thought that the boat had taken a massive hit but then he saw the man in the corner, smiling as he weaved threads of magic, muttering strange syllables. Kelos's windpipe started to flex and constrict as the shadowmage increased his hold on the threads. Below him, Dunsany was squaring off against the guards who stood in front of the magical gem that was the engine of the vessel. The stone, sitting in its housing of metal and wood, seemed to whisper to Kelos as he gasped for breath.

He watched as Dunsany swung at one of the guards and Emuel cowered by the door. Kelos saw the man tumble to the side to avoid the blow. Dunsany took the opportunity to fire a quarrel at his comrade, piercing his shoulder.

The man grunted and took a step back. Kelos could see that the injury hadn't slowed him, however, as – tearing the bolt from his flesh – he roared and shoulder charged Dunsany into the wall. The guard pushed his blade against Dunsany's throat and Kelos realised that it may all be over for his friend. But Dunsany gritted his teeth, reversed his grip on his sword and rammed the pommel into the base of the guard's neck. The man dropped and Kelos cried out a warning as the remaining guard stepped in to fill the gap. Dunsany failed to dodge the blow and the blade sliced into his cheek, flicking blood into his eyes. He staggered and almost tripped over Emuel, who was on the floor behind him, rocking back and forth. The guard took advantage of the stumble and swung again, this time nicking Dunsany's wrist and making him drop his sword. Dunsany raised his crossbow and fired. Kelos saw the mage in the corner blink and the quarrel turned to powder millimetres from the guard's face.

"I knew Makennon should never have trusted scum like you." The guard brushed the remains of the quarrel from his robe. "If you ask me we didn't do enough in converting this shit hole you people call home. Unbelievers should have been put to the sword a long time ago."

Kelos continued to gasp for breath, barely conscious now. The stone was practically screaming into his head and, with a jolt of realisation that briefly cleared his vision, he realised what had to be done. He gestured with his right hand and cancelled the silence spell he had placed on Emuel.

"Sing Emuel! Sing or we'll all die!"

Emuel looked up at Kelos and, for a terrible moment, he thought that the eunuch was going to defy him. But then, he stopped shivering and stood up.

"That's it retard, sing a lament for the death of your friends." The guard raised his sword. The sound that emerged from Emuel, however, stayed his hand.

The room shivered as Emuel's song reached out to the gem. The magical energy traced veins of midnight-blue fire in the stone and all in the room felt the ship shudder as it responded to the song. On Emuel's body the designs flowed as the song possessed him. The shadowmage stepped into the centre of the room and Kelos could see a dark warning in his eyes. He could almost taste the magic flowing from the stone now and, concentrating, Kelos called forth a thread of that energy. The mage below him realised what was happening too late. He tried to finish Kelos with a word but, before he could utter the syllable, the sorcerer had concentrated the thread of energy from the stone and blasted it into the shadowmage. The room filled with a searing light as his body burned. Kelos dropped to the floor and lashed out with his sword. The stunned guard didn't even feel the blade enter his belly. All he felt was the song and its ethereal cadences as it followed him into darkness.

Kelos put a hand on Emuel's shoulder. "You can stop now. It's over."

As the Turnitia docks fell away behind them, Dunsany nervously scanned the shoreline.

"Don't worry," Kelos said. "They can't see us. I've cloaked the ship."

Dunsany turned to look at his friend. Wisps of arcane energy surrounded him in a dark amber corona.

"Shouldn't one of us be piloting this vessel Kelos?"

"Actually, I am. And have you noticed something *really* strange?"

"Apart from your new hair-do and ruddy orange glow you mean?"

Dunsany looked around him and had to admit that *everything* was really strange. The sails billowed with the wind but were utterly silent, the rainbow sheen of the X'lcotl silk moving across the material like oil on water as it reflected back the soft light of Kerberos. Around them the ship thrummed with magical energy, veins of which ran through every part of the *Llothriall*. The vessel cut through the sea with a sureness and ease that Dunsany had never before witnessed in a ship.

"We're so still." he said.

"Indeed, the ship should be furiously pitching beneath our feet and we should be staggering around like two drunks at the end of a wedding party. Instead, we have this unnatural serenity. Deceptive really, as the power of the *Llothriall* is so vast that it should *feel* like something is happening. And it is, look back at Turnitia."

Dunsany turned. The coast was dwindling rapidly behind them, almost imperceptible through the spray and the mist. In any other ship it would have taken them most of the day to leave sight of the peninsula and, even then, they wouldn't have been able to venture too far from land due to the vicious and unpredictable currents that surrounded Twilight. But the *Llothriall* was not at all effected by the pitch of the waves. Instead, it seemed to skim across the surface.

"I'm glad that we took this away from the Faith," Kelos said. "I just hope that this hiding place you have in mind is as good as you say."

"Oh yes. And, once we reach Sarcre itself I can introduce you to our crew."

"And do they know that they are going to be shipmates on this mighty vessel?"

"Well, not quite. But once they see the *Llothriall* they're not going to take much persuading. Talking of ship mates, where's Emuel?"

"All sung out. Sleeping soundly below. You think that boy's going to be a problem?"

"Nah. He's terrified of everything. He's too timid to be a threat. Anyway, there's no way for him to get back to Makennon now."

The sound of Katherine Makennon's rage was so great that the Eternal Choir almost stopped singing. The congregation who sat with bowed heads looked up from their prayers for a moment as they sensed the anger that flowed through the many halls, chambers and chapels of Scholten cathedral from Makennon's quarters. At his pulpit the Eminence's hand was momentarily stayed from making the sign of benediction.

In her private chamber Makennon stood over the priest who had delivered the news of the *Llothriall's* theft and, for the briefest of moments, considered having him excommunicated. But decisions driven by emotion were not becoming of a leader of Twilight's true faith. Seating herself once more Makennon resumed an air of authoritative calm.

"Why is it that Old Race secrets and artefacts have a habit of slipping out of our grasp? Don't these people realise that we are merely trying to use the knowledge of our ancestors to unite the peninsula and spread our message beyond civilisation?"

Around the room, the members of the faithful looked at one another, wondering if an answer were required of any of them. One cleared his throat and seemed about to speak, but Makennon dismissed his words before he could form them with a wave of a hand.

"It was a rhetorical question Rudolph. I do not require your observations. However... do you know whether our guest has regained consciousness?"

"Our guest Anointed Lord?"

"Yes, the marine creature we recently acquired."

"Ah yes, I shall enquire right away."

"Thank you Rudolph."

Rudolph edged slowly from the room, making sure not to present his back to the Anointed Lord. Once beyond the chamber he descended through the many levels of Scholten until he was far below the foundations of the cathedral. In a corridor lined with cells he stopped at a particular door and slid back the viewing hatch. The stench that poured from the room beyond made him take a step back. For a moment he thought the creature within had died but then there was the sound of it moving from its water trough and it approached the door.

"Prepare yourself to meet the Anointed Lord," Rudolph piously informed the prisoner.

He couldn't be sure but the sound that came from the creature in response sounded almost like a laugh.

TWILIGHT of KERBEROS

For information on this and other titles, visit
www.abaddonbooks.com

Abaddon
Books

TWILIGHT *of* KERBEROS

SHADOW MAGE

MATTHEW SPRANGE

Price: **£6.99** ★ **$7.99**

ISBN 13: **978-1-905437-54-2**

TWILIGHT of KERBEROS

THE CLOCKWORK KING OF ORL

MIKE WILD

Price: **£6.99 ★ $7.99**

ISBN 13: **978-1-905437-75-7**

TWILIGHT *of* KERBEROS

THE LIGHT OF HEAVEN

DAVID A. MCINTEE

Price: **£6.99** ★ **$7.99**

ISBN 13: **978-1-905437-87-0**

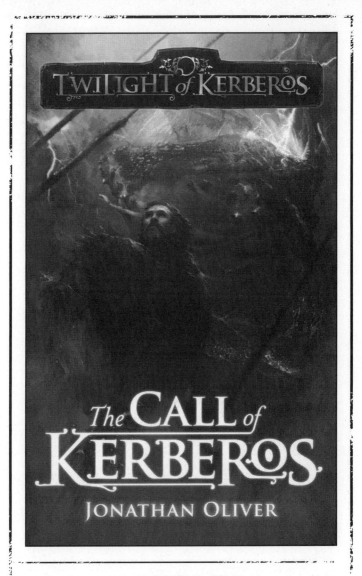

Price: **£6.99 ★ $7.99**

ISBN 13: **978-1-906735-28-9**

Coming Soon!

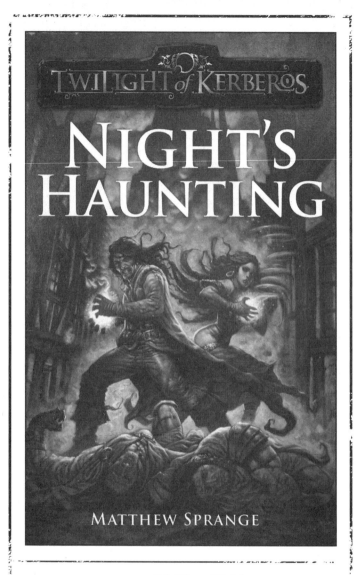

TWILIGHT of KERBEROS

NIGHT'S HAUNTING

MATTHEW SPRANGE

Price: **£6.99** ★ **$7.99**

ISBN 13: **978-1-906735-25-8**

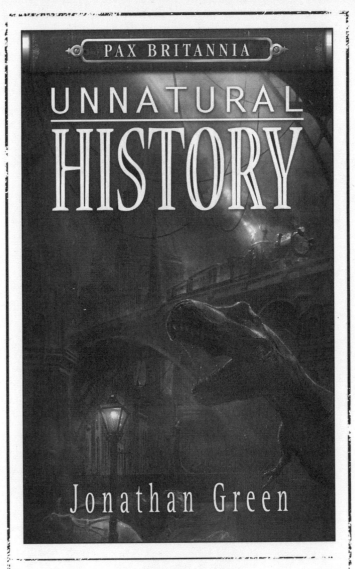

PAX BRITANNIA

UNNATURAL
HISTORY

Jonathan Green

ISBN 13: **978-1-905437-10-8**

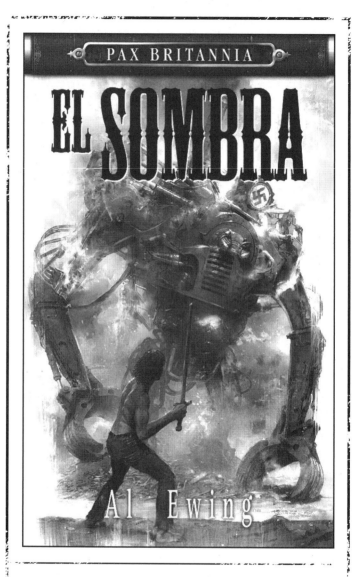

PAX BRITANNIA

EL SOMBRA

Al Ewing

Price: **£6.99 ★ $7.99**

ISBN 13: **978-1-905437-34-4**

PAX BRITANNIA

LEVIATHAN RISING

JONATHAN GREEN

Price: **£6.99** ★ **$7.99**

ISBN 13: **978-1-905437-60-3**

Price: **£6.99 ★ $7.99**

ISBN 13: **978-1-905437-86-3**

Price: **£6.99** ★ **$7.99**

ISBN 13: **978-1-906735-05-0**

THE AFTERBLIGHT CHRONICLES

The CULLED

Simon Spurrier

Price: **£6.99 ★ $7.99**

ISBN 13: **978-1-905437-01-6**

THE AFTERBLIGHT CHRONICLES

KILL OR CURE

Rebecca Levene

Price: **£6.99 ★ $7.99**

ISBN 13: **978-1-905437-32-0**

THE AFTERBLIGHT CHRONICLES

OPERATION MOTHERLAND

SCOTT ANDREWS

Price: **£6.99 ★ $7.99**

ISBN 13: **978-1-906735-04-3**